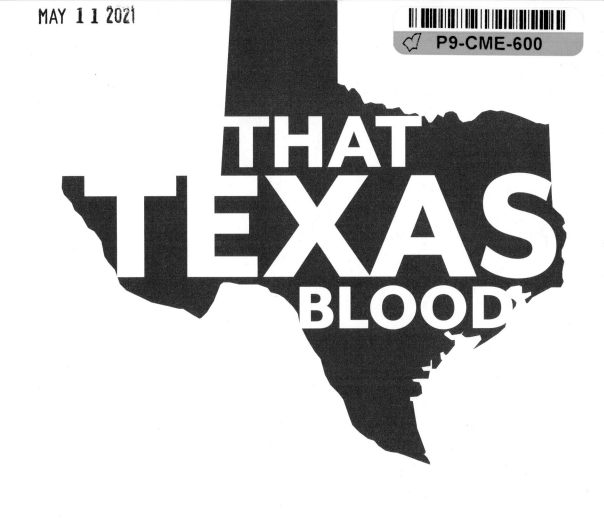

THAT TEXAS BLOOD

IMAGE COMICS, INC.
Todd McFarlane – President
Jim Valentino – Vice President
Marc Silvestri – Chief Executive Officer
Erik Larsen – Chief Financial Officer
Robert Kirkman – Chief Operating Officer

Eric Stephenson – Publisher / Chief Creative Officer
Shanna Matuszak – Editorial Coordinator
Marla Eizik – Talent Liaison

Nicole Lapalme – Controller
Leanna Caunter – Accounting Analyst
Sue Korpela – Accounting & HR Manager

Jeff Boison – Director of Sales & Publishing Planning
Dirk Wood – Director of International Sales & Licensing
Alex Cox – Director of Direct Market & Speciality Sales
Chloe Ramos-Peterson – Book Market & Library Sales Manager
Emilio Bautista – Digital Sales Coordinator

Kat Salazar – Director of PR & Marketing
Drew Fitzgerald – Marketing Content Associate

Heather Doornink – Production Director
Drew Gill – Art Director
Hilary DiLoreto – Print Manager
Tricia Ramos – Traffic Manager
Erika Schnatz – Senior Production Artist
Ryan Brewer – Production Artist
Deanna Phelps – Production Artist
IMAGECOMICS.COM

Ⓢ Publication design by Sean Phillips

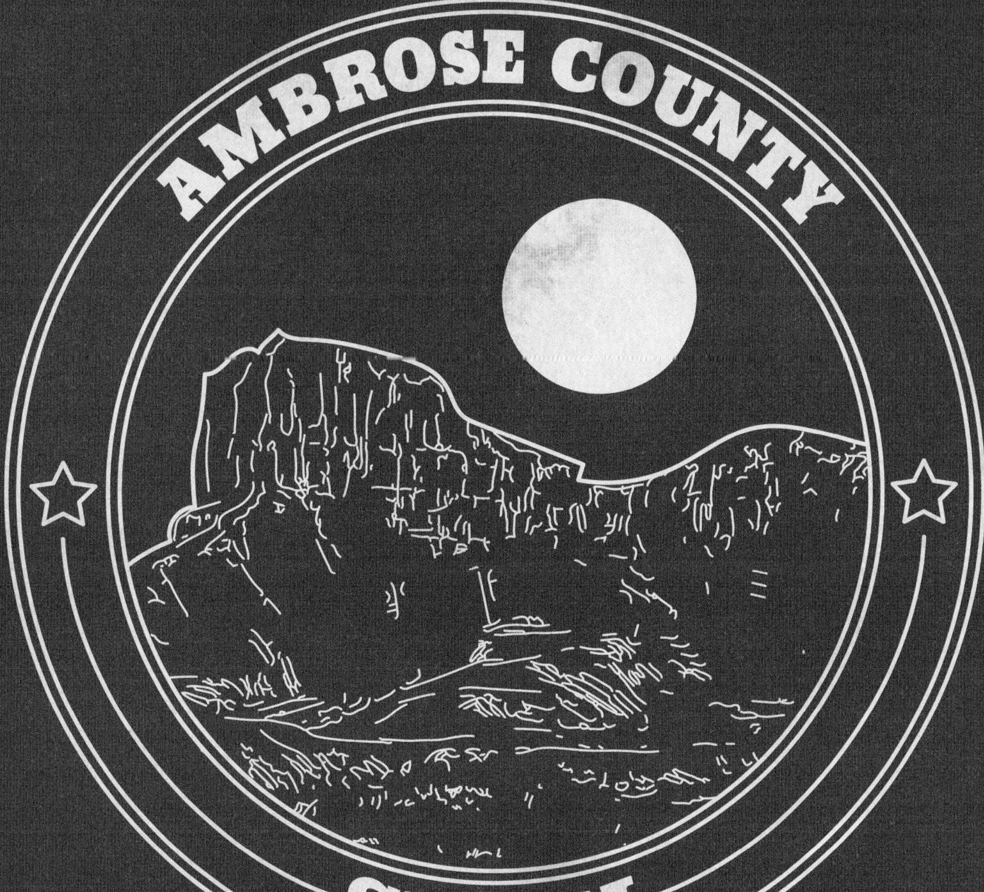
AMBROSE COUNTY
TEXAS

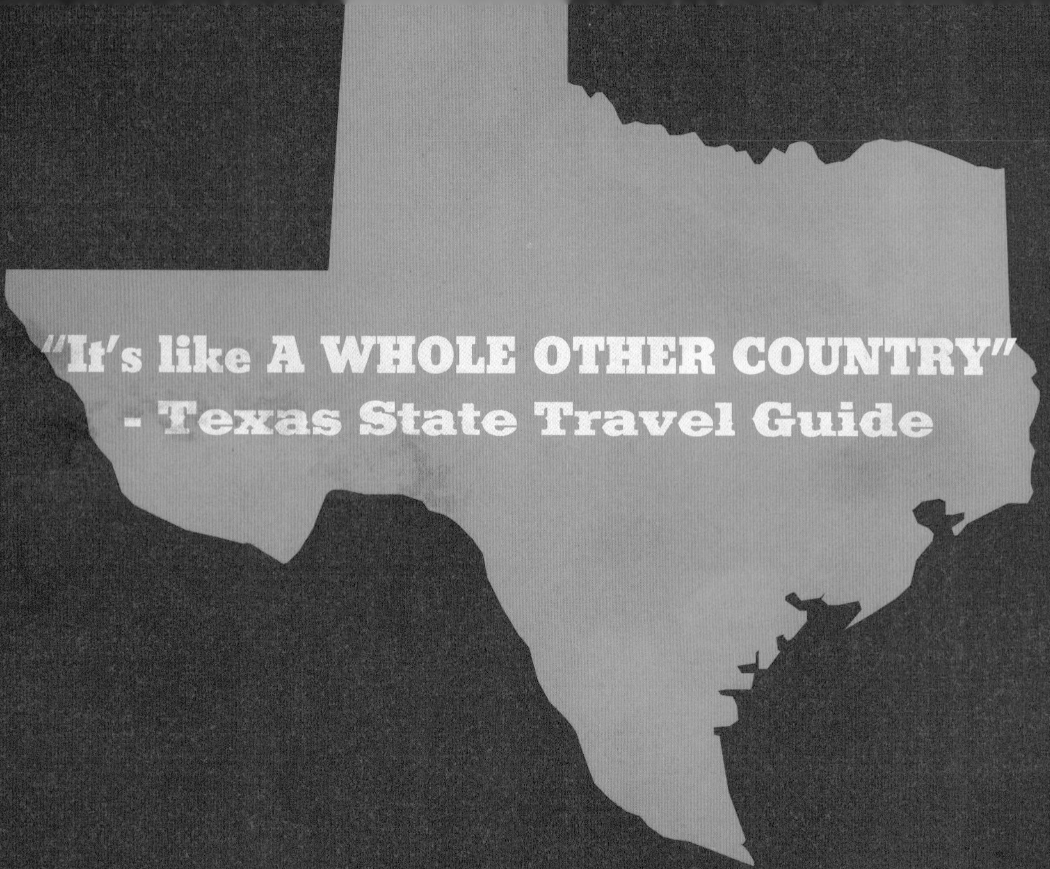
"It's like A WHOLE OTHER COUNTRY"
- Texas State Travel Guide

The Casserole Dish

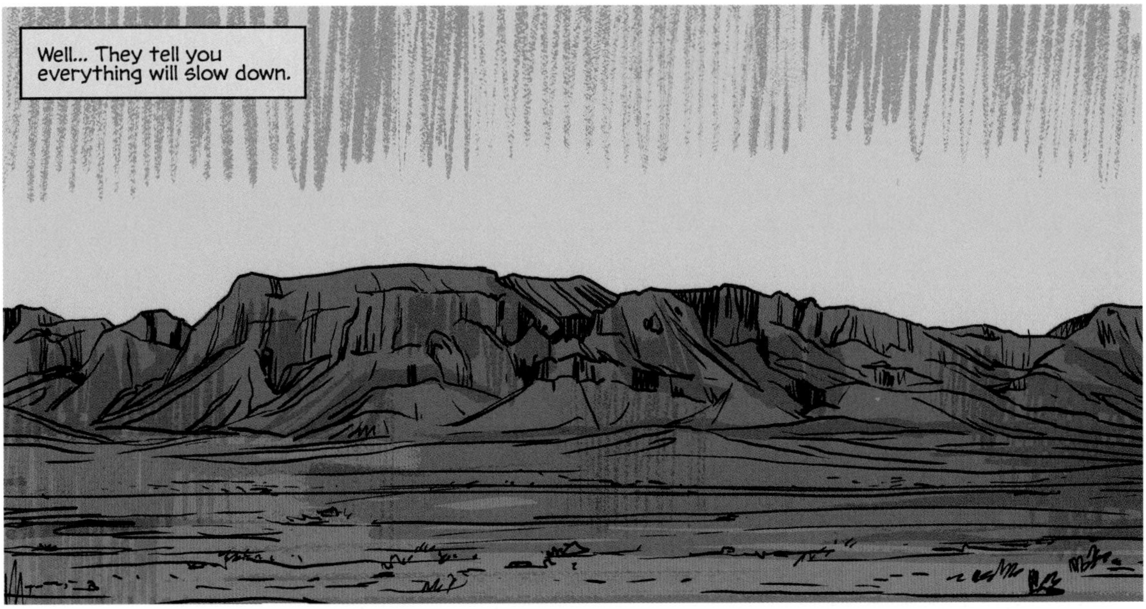
Well... They tell you everything will slow down.

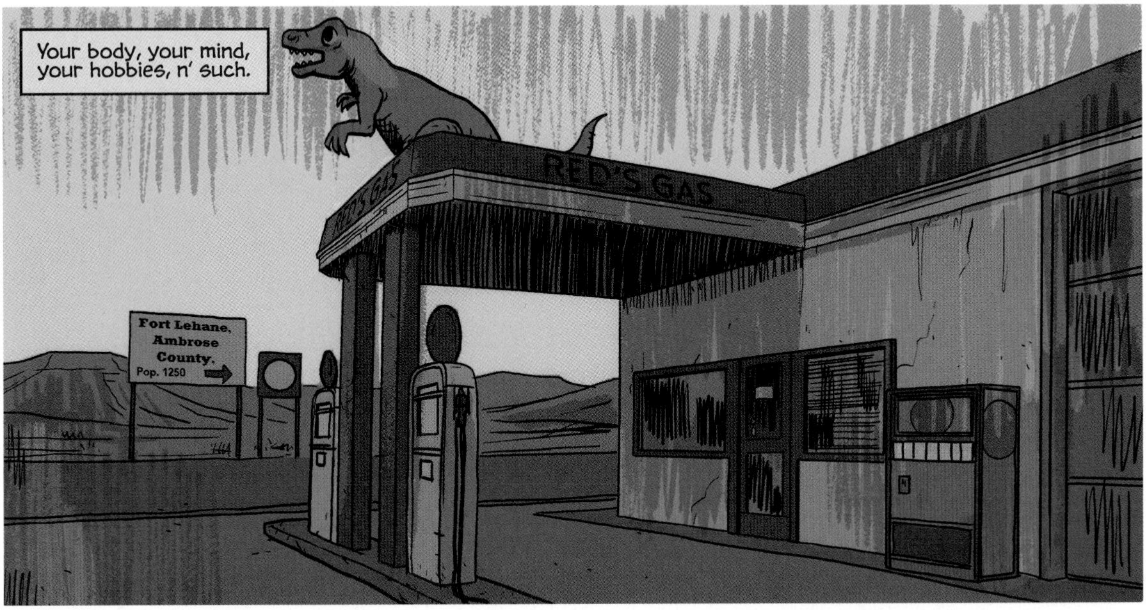
Your body, your mind, your hobbies, n' such.
RED'S GAS
Fort Lehane, Ambrose County, Pop. 1250

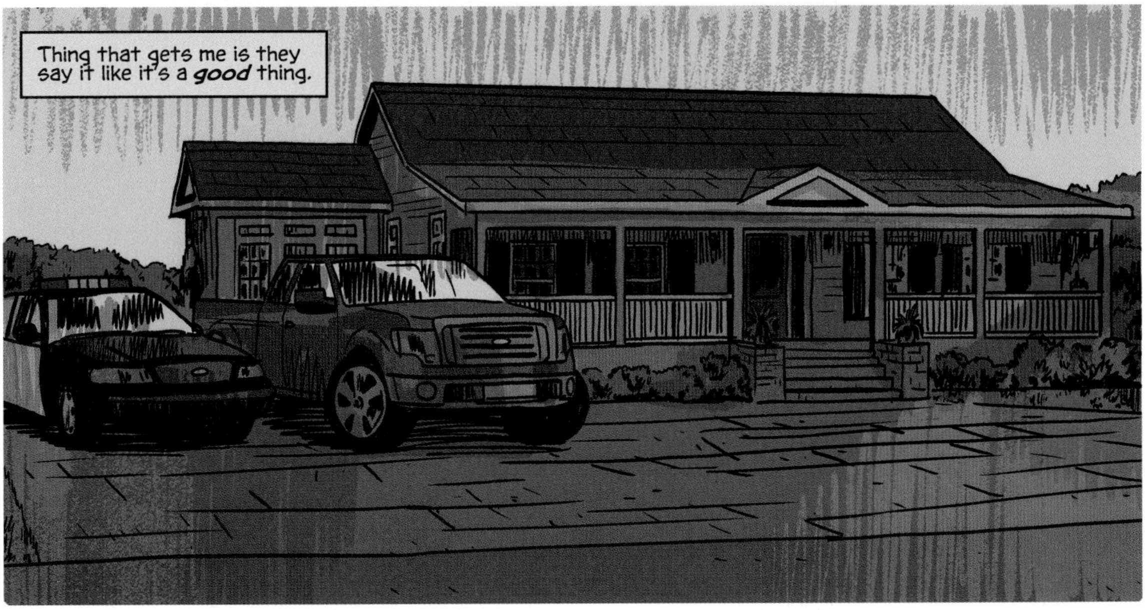
Thing that gets me is they say it like it's a *good* thing.

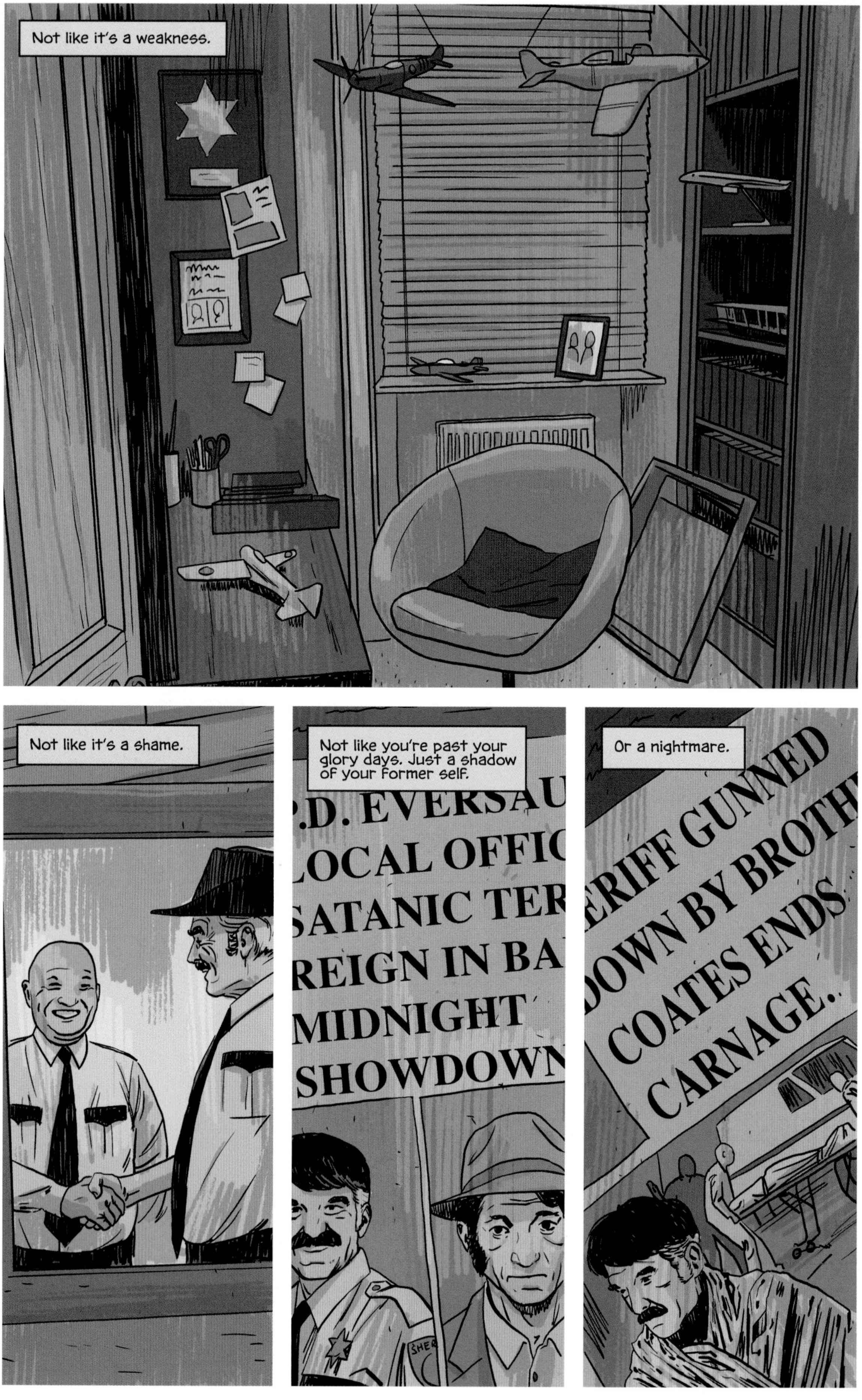
Not like it's a weakness.
Not like it's a shame.
Not like you're past your glory days. Just a shadow of your former self.
.D. EVERSAU
LOCAL OFFIC
SATANIC TER
REIGN IN BA
MIDNIGHT
SHOWDOWN
Or a nightmare.
ERIFF GUNNED
DOWN BY BROTH
COATES ENDS
CARNAGE..

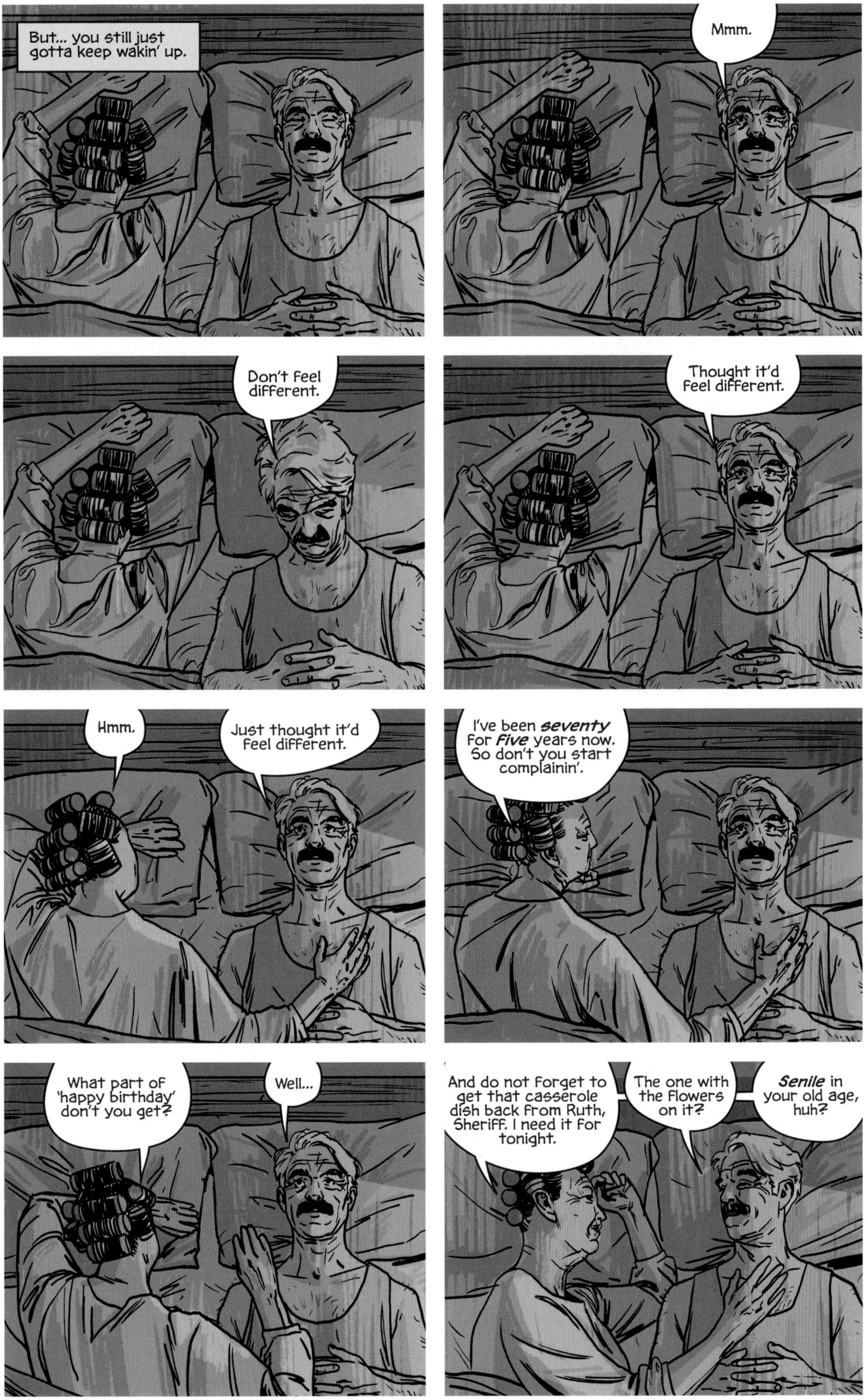

But... you still just gotta keep wakin' up.
Mmm.
Don't feel different.
Thought it'd feel different.
Hmm.
Just thought it'd feel different.
I've been **seventy** for **five** years now. So don't you start complainin'.
What part of 'happy birthday' don't you get?
Well...
And do not forget to get that casserole dish back from Ruth, Sheriff. I need it for tonight.
The one with the flowers on it?
Senile in your old age, huh?

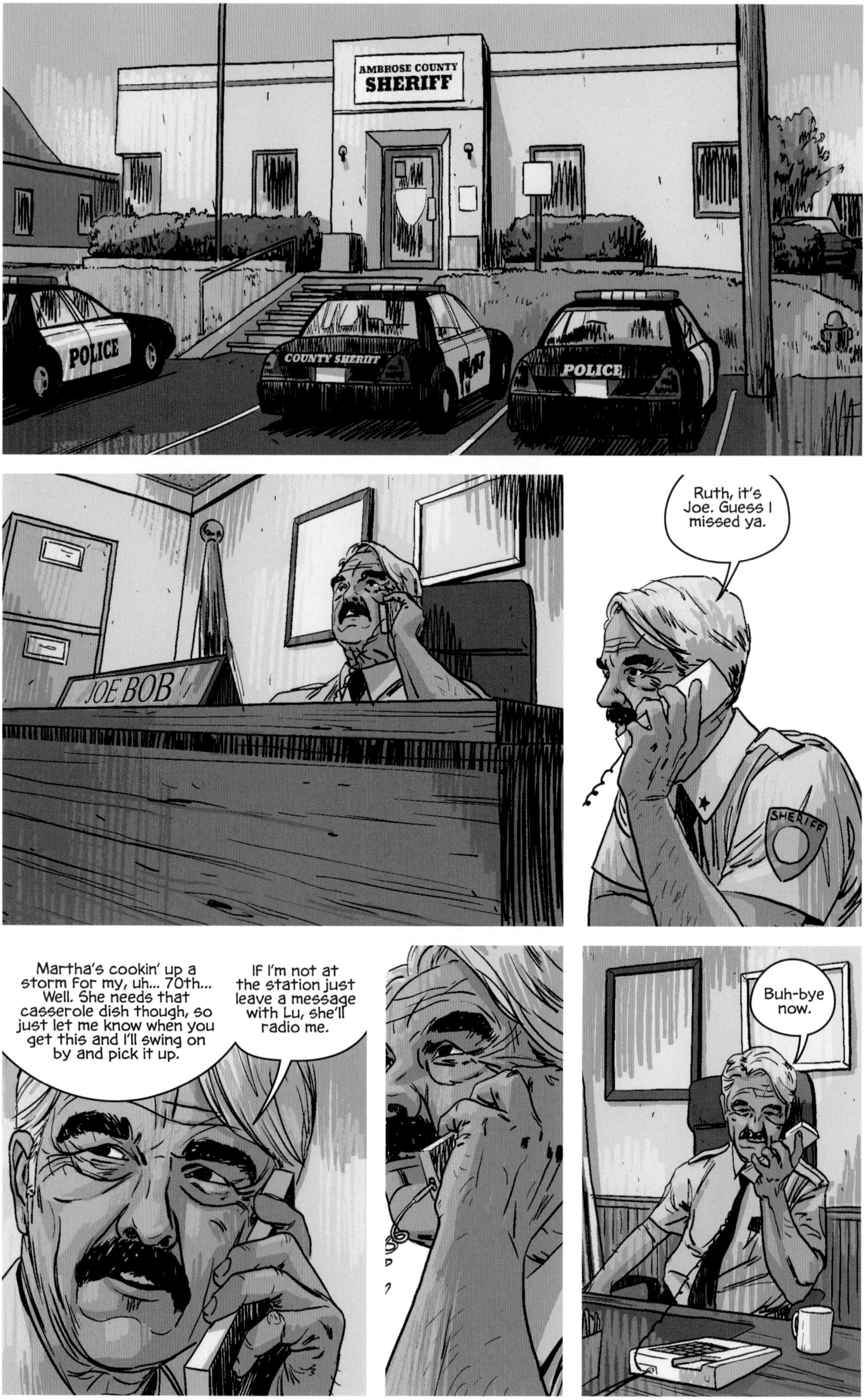
AMBROSE COUNTY SHERIFF
POLICE
COUNTY SHERIFF
POLICE
JOE BOB
Ruth, it's Joe. Guess I missed ya.
Martha's cookin' up a storm for my, uh... 70th... Well. She needs that casserole dish though, so just let me know when you get this and I'll swing on by and pick it up.
If I'm not at the station just leave a message with Lu, she'll radio me.
Buh-bye now.

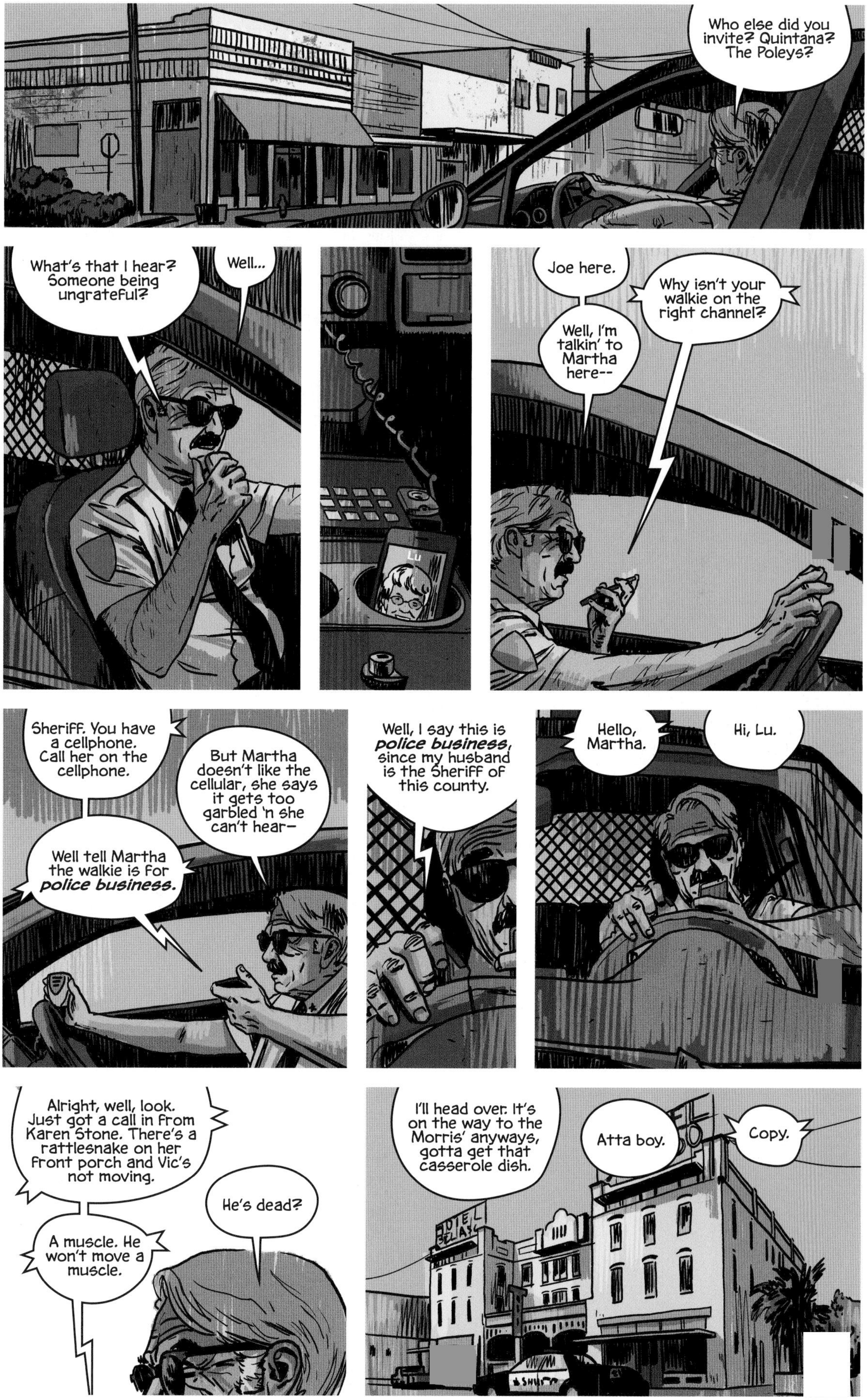
Who else did you invite? Quintana? The Poleys?
What's that I hear? Someone being ungrateful?
Well...
Lu
Joe here.
Why isn't your walkie on the right channel?
Well, I'm talkin' to Martha here--
Sheriff. You have a cellphone. Call her on the cellphone.
But Martha doesn't like the cellular, she says it gets too garbled 'n she can't hear–
Well tell Martha the walkie is for *police business.*
Well, I say this is *police business*, since my husband is the Sheriff of this county.
Hello, Martha.
Hi, Lu.
Alright, well, look. Just got a call in from Karen Stone. There's a rattlesnake on her front porch and Vic's not moving.
He's dead?
A muscle. He won't move a muscle.
I'll head over. It's on the way to the Morris' anyways, gotta get that casserole dish.
Atta boy.
Copy.

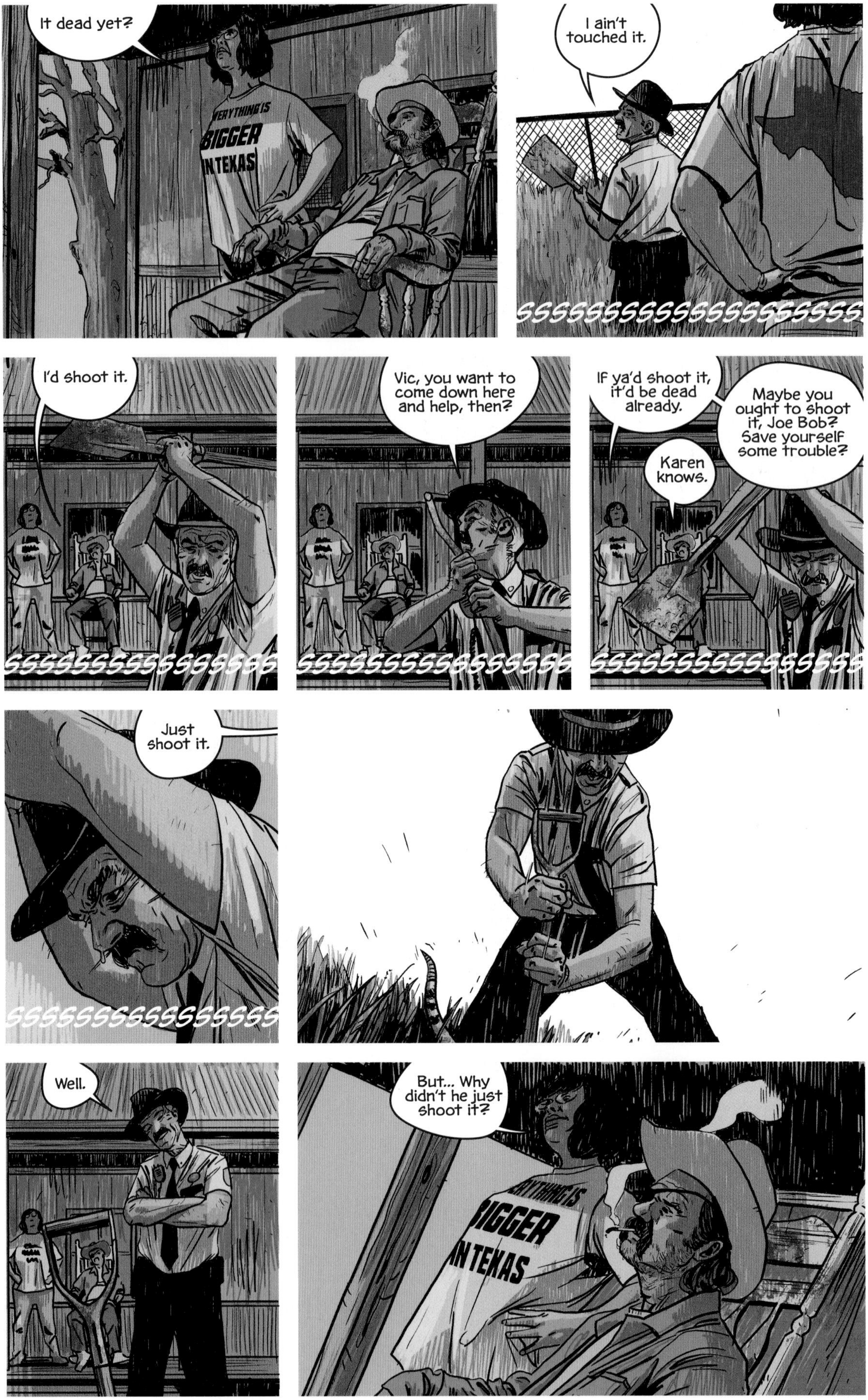
It dead yet?
EVERYTHING IS BIGGER IN TEXAS
I ain't touched it.
SSSSSSSSSSSSSSSSSSSSSS
I'd shoot it.
SSSSSSSSSSSSSSSSSSS
Vic, you want to come down here and help, then?
SSSSSSSSSSSSSSSSSSS
If ya'd shoot it, it'd be dead already.
Karen knows.
Maybe you ought to shoot it, Joe Bob? Save yourself some trouble?
SSSSSSSSSSSSSSSSSSS
Just shoot it.
SSSSSSSSSSSSSSSSSS
Well.
But... Why didn't he just shoot it?
EVERYTHING IS BIGGER IN TEXAS

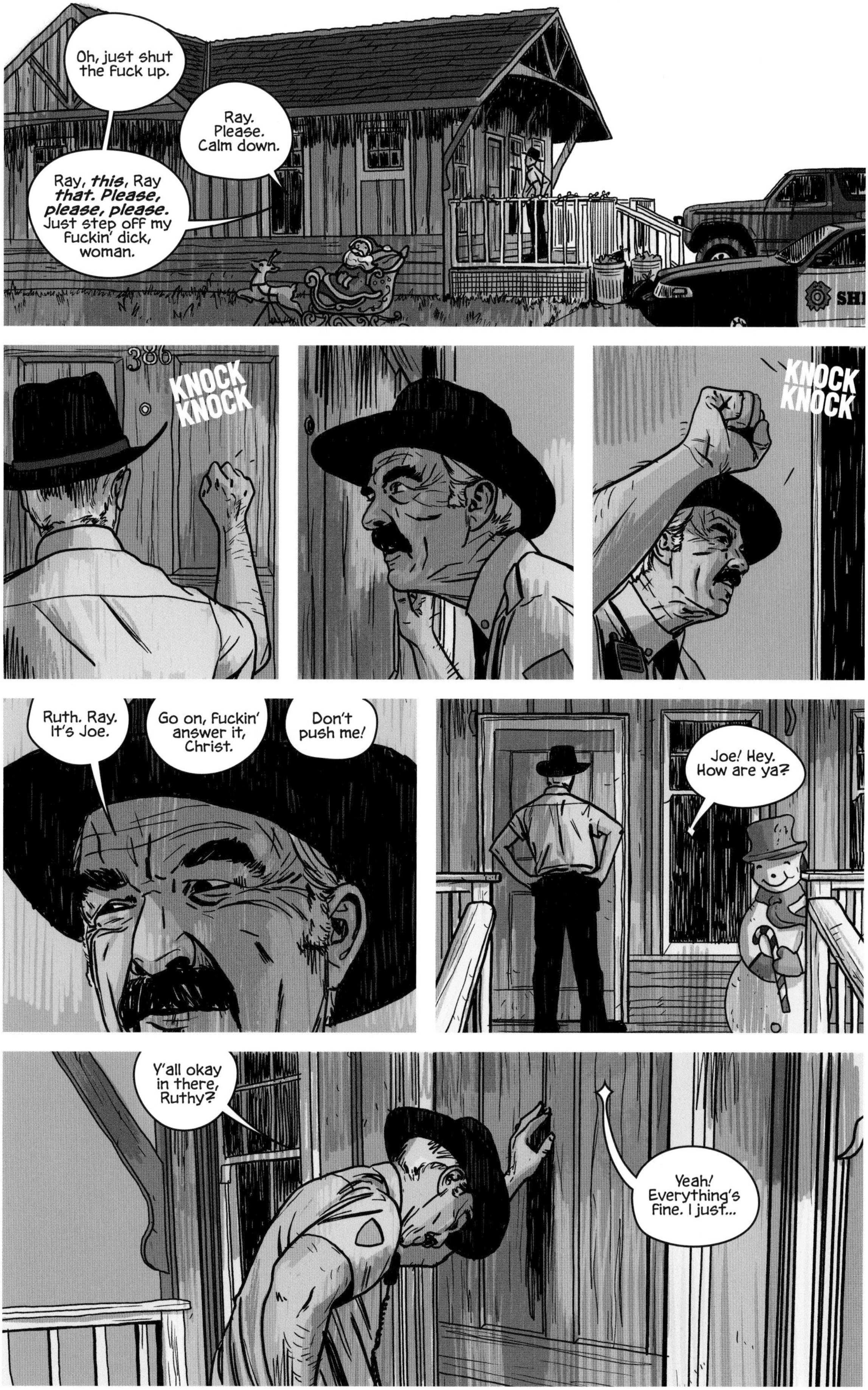
Oh, just shut the fuck up.
Ray, this, Ray that. Please, please, please. Just step off my fuckin' dick, woman.
Ray. Please. Calm down.
386
KNOCK KNOCK
KNOCK KNOCK
Ruth. Ray. It's Joe.
Go on, fuckin' answer it, Christ.
Don't push me!
Joe! Hey. How are ya?
Y'all okay in there, Ruthy?
Yeah! Everything's fine. I just...

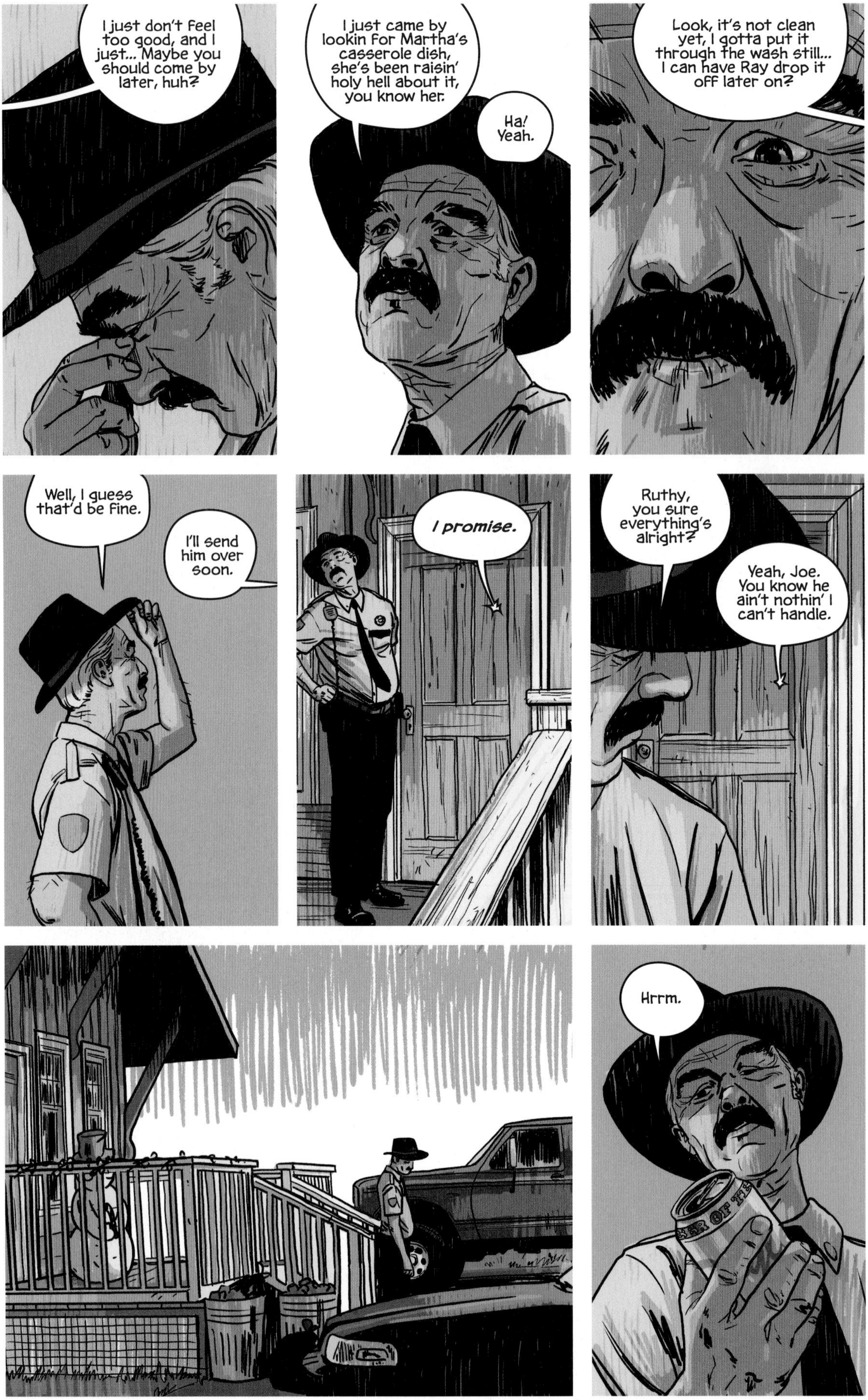

I just don't feel too good, and I just... Maybe you should come by later, huh?
I just came by lookin for Martha's casserole dish, she's been raisin' holy hell about it, you know her.
Ha! Yeah.
Look, it's not clean yet, I gotta put it through the wash still... I can have Ray drop it off later on?
Well, I guess that'd be fine.
I'll send him over soon.
I promise.
Ruthy, you sure everything's alright?
Yeah, Joe. You know he ain't nothin' I can't handle.
Hrrm.

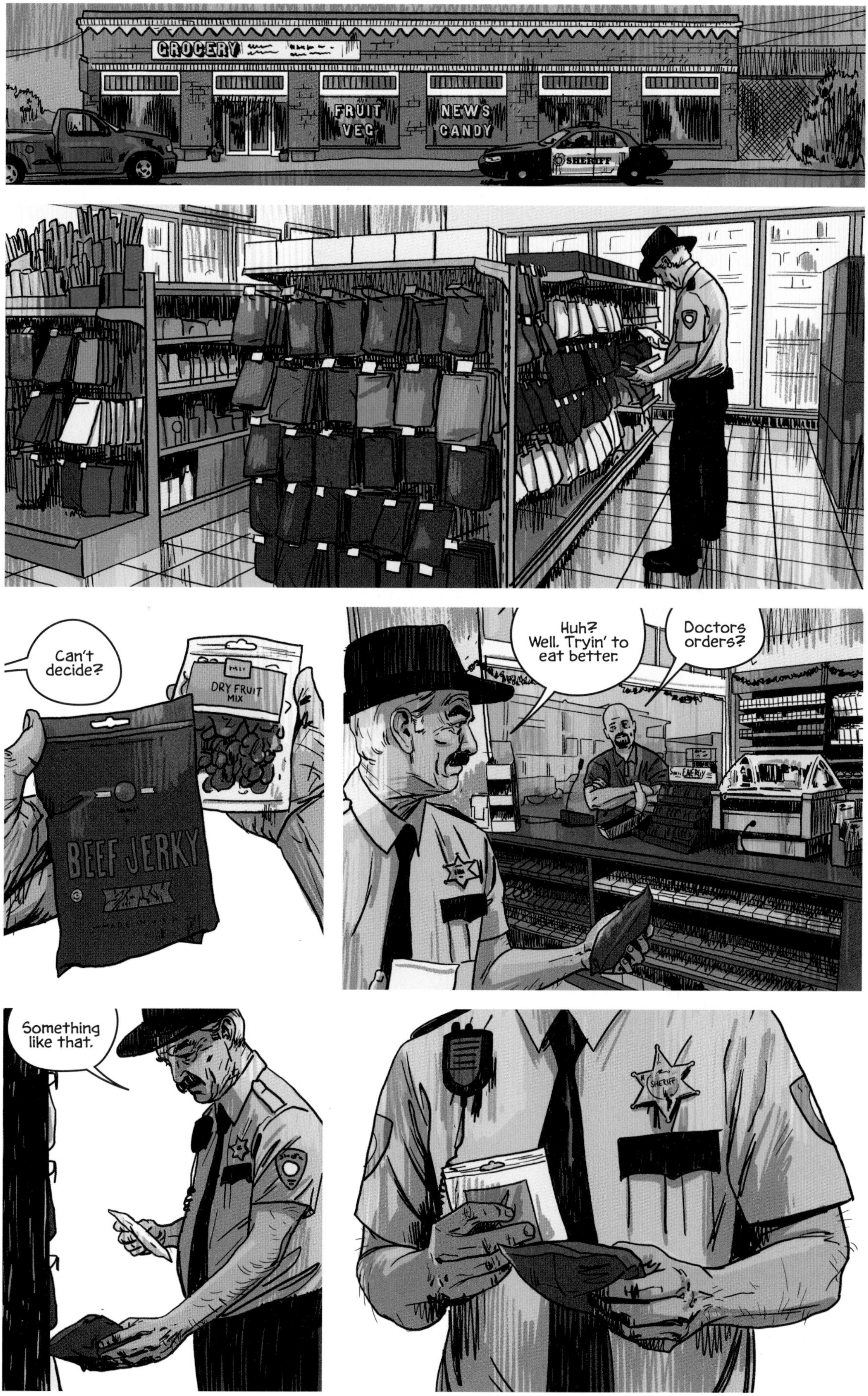
GROCERY
FRUIT VEG
NEWS CANDY
SHERIFF
Can't decide?
DRY FRUIT MIX
BEEF JERKY
MADE IN U.S.A.
Huh? Well. Tryin' to eat better.
Doctors orders?
Something like that.
SHERIFF

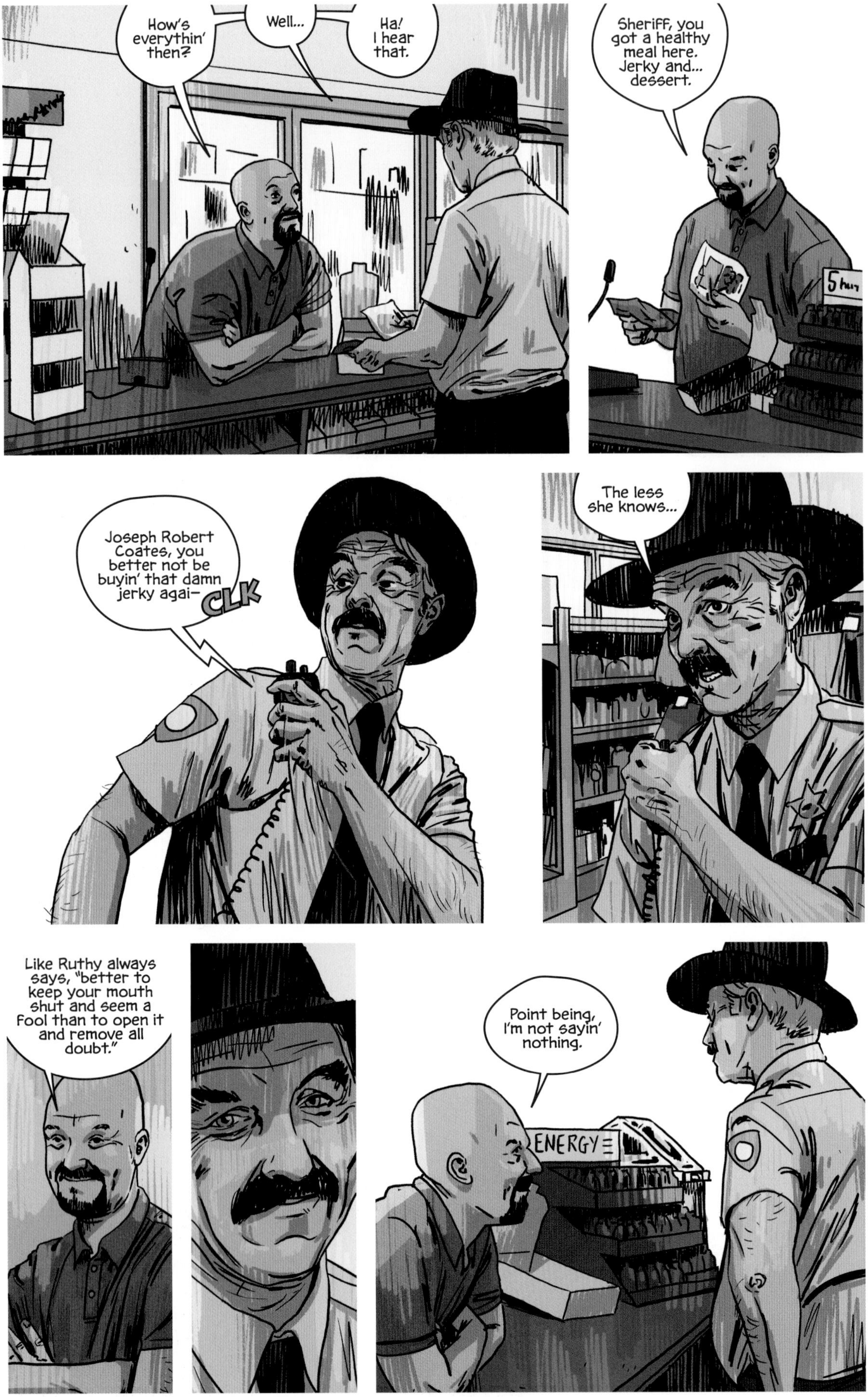
How's everythin' then?
Well...
Ha! I hear that.
Sheriff, you got a healthy meal here. Jerky and... dessert.
Joseph Robert Coates, you better not be buyin' that damn jerky agai—
CLK
The less she knows...
Like Ruthy always says, "better to keep your mouth shut and seem a fool than to open it and remove all doubt."
Point being, I'm not sayin' nothing.
ENERGY

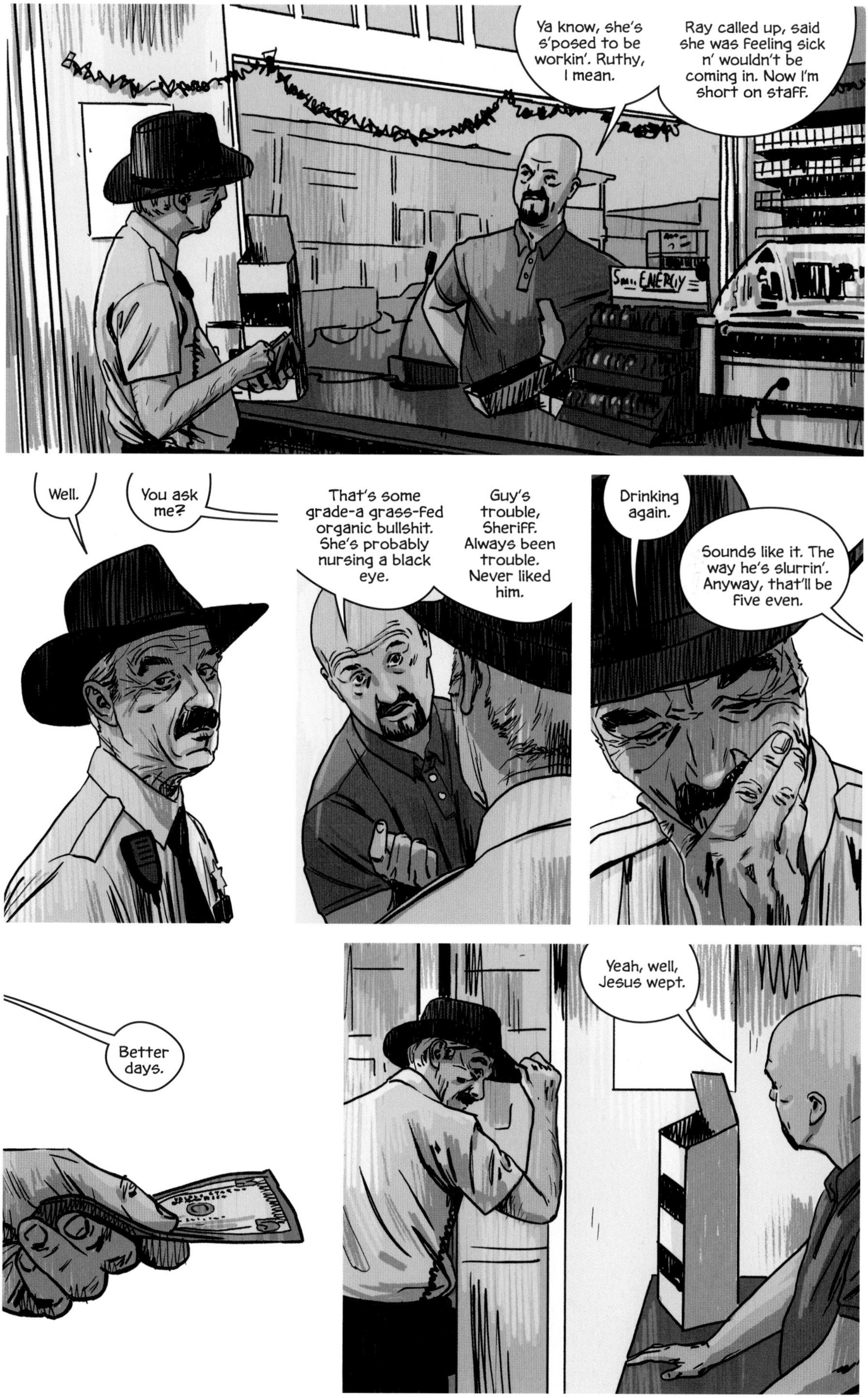
Ya know, she's s'posed to be workin'. Ruthy, I mean.
Ray called up, said she was feeling sick n' wouldn't be coming in. Now I'm short on staff.
ENERGY
Well.
You ask me?
That's some grade-a grass-fed organic bullshit. She's probably nursing a black eye.
Guy's trouble, Sheriff. Always been trouble. Never liked him.
Drinking again.
Sounds like it. The way he's slurrin'. Anyway, that'll be five even.
Better days.
Yeah, well, Jesus wept.

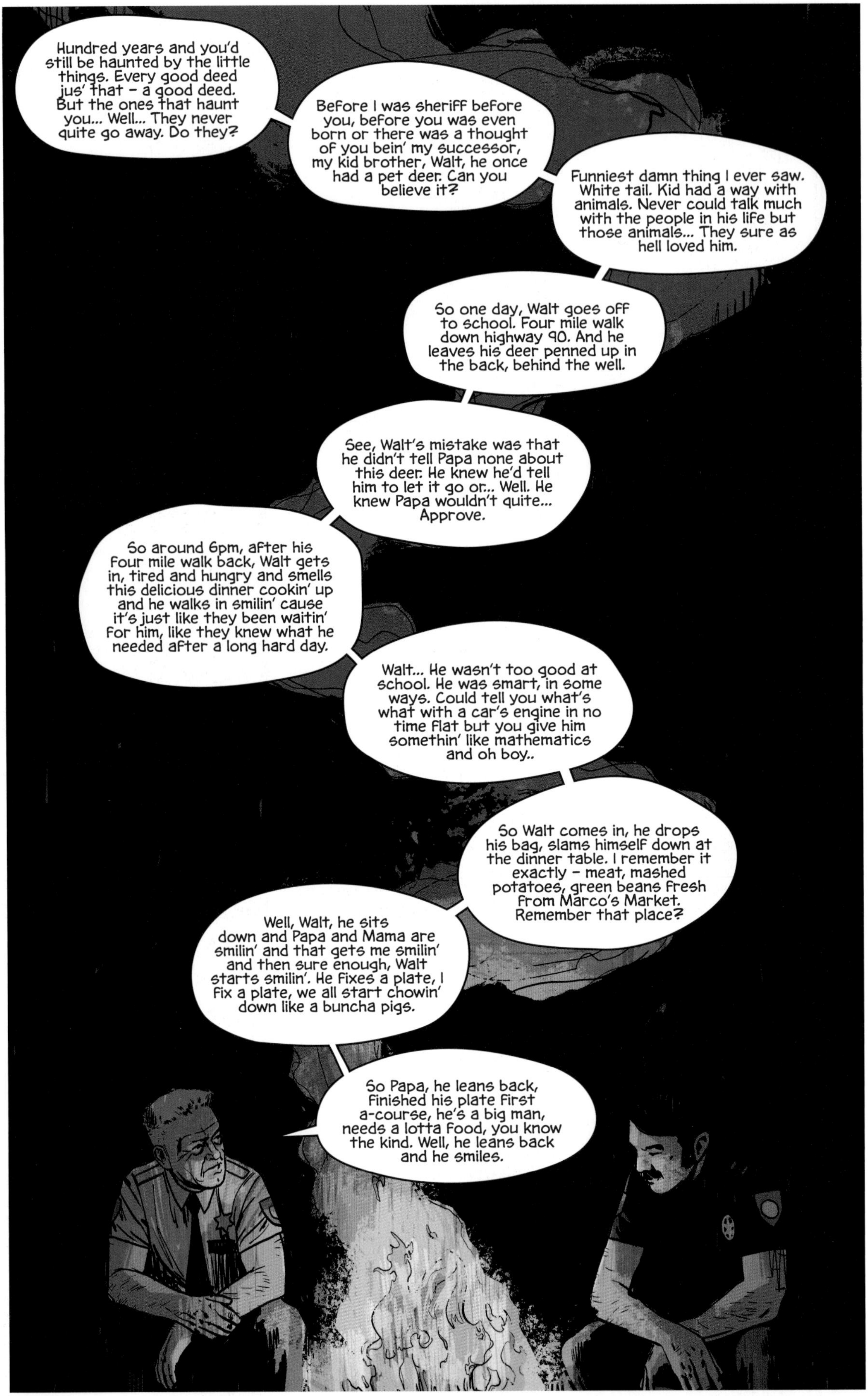
Hundred years and you'd still be haunted by the little things. Every good deed jus' that - a good deed. But the ones that haunt you... Well... They never quite go away. Do they?
Before I was sheriff before you, before you was even born or there was a thought of you bein' my successor, my kid brother, Walt, he once had a pet deer. Can you believe it?
Funniest damn thing I ever saw. White tail. Kid had a way with animals. Never could talk much with the people in his life but those animals... They sure as hell loved him.
So one day, Walt goes off to school. Four mile walk down highway 90. And he leaves his deer penned up in the back, behind the well.
See, Walt's mistake was that he didn't tell Papa none about this deer. He knew he'd tell him to let it go or... Well. He knew Papa wouldn't quite... Approve.
So around 6pm, after his four mile walk back, Walt gets in, tired and hungry and smells this delicious dinner cookin' up and he walks in smilin' cause it's just like they been waitin' for him, like they knew what he needed after a long hard day.
Walt... He wasn't too good at school. He was smart, in some ways. Could tell you what's what with a car's engine in no time flat but you give him somethin' like mathematics and oh boy..
So Walt comes in, he drops his bag, slams himself down at the dinner table. I remember it exactly - meat, mashed potatoes, green beans fresh from Marco's Market. Remember that place?
Well, Walt, he sits down and Papa and Mama are smilin' and that gets me smilin' and then sure enough, Walt starts smilin'. He fixes a plate, I fix a plate, we all start chowin' down like a buncha pigs.
So Papa, he leans back, finished his plate first a-course, he's a big man, needs a lotta food, you know the kind. Well, he leans back and he smiles.

Walt starts playin' 'round with the food. 'Cause it don't quite taste like beef, he's wonderin' what the hell is wrong with it if it *is* beef. He looks up at Papa and Mama and he asks what it is exactly.

Papa smiles and lifts the napkin from his collar and he just smiles and smiles and then he says there was a deer playin' out back just settin' there, like God almighty had just plopped 'im down and said, "My children, here is your dinner for the rest of the week."

Walt's mouth drops. A-course, he knows it wasn't God what plopped down the deer in the back, *it was him.*

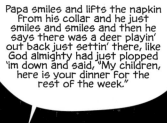

Walt ran out back and he runs to the spot and there is the string he tied him up with just lyin' there cut and there's blood on the ground. He turns and hangin' up out back is the body, just hangin' down, torn, ripped open and shredded.

Walt just start's screamin'. Not words, just screamin', Fuckin' bloody Goddamn murder, you know.

And he never was the same after that. I mean, you know that. You're the one what shot him after he blown a hole in my chest.

My point bein'... Sometimes you can't help but walk into a dirty deed...

Sometimes... Sometimes the world, well...

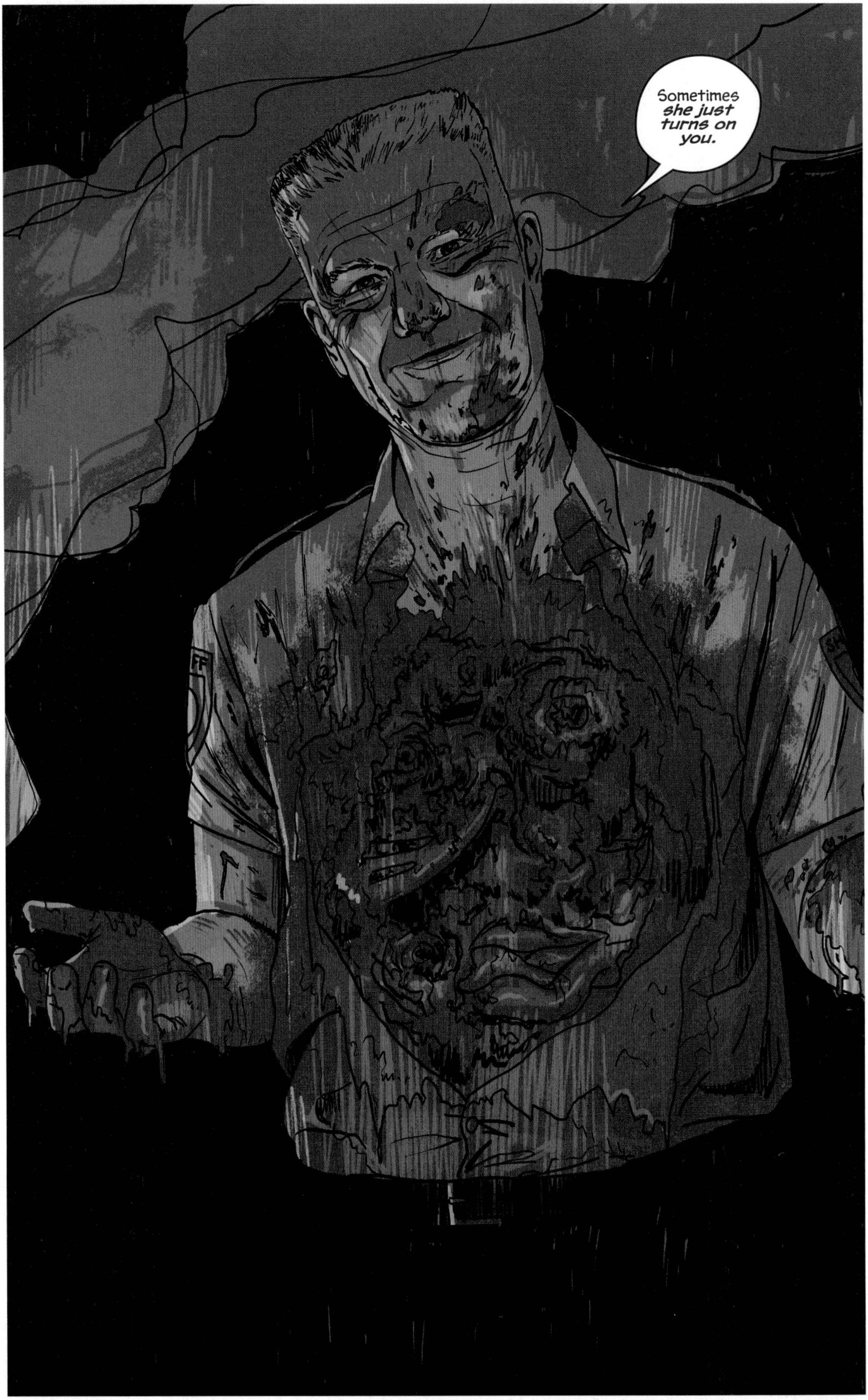
Sometimes *she just turns on you.*

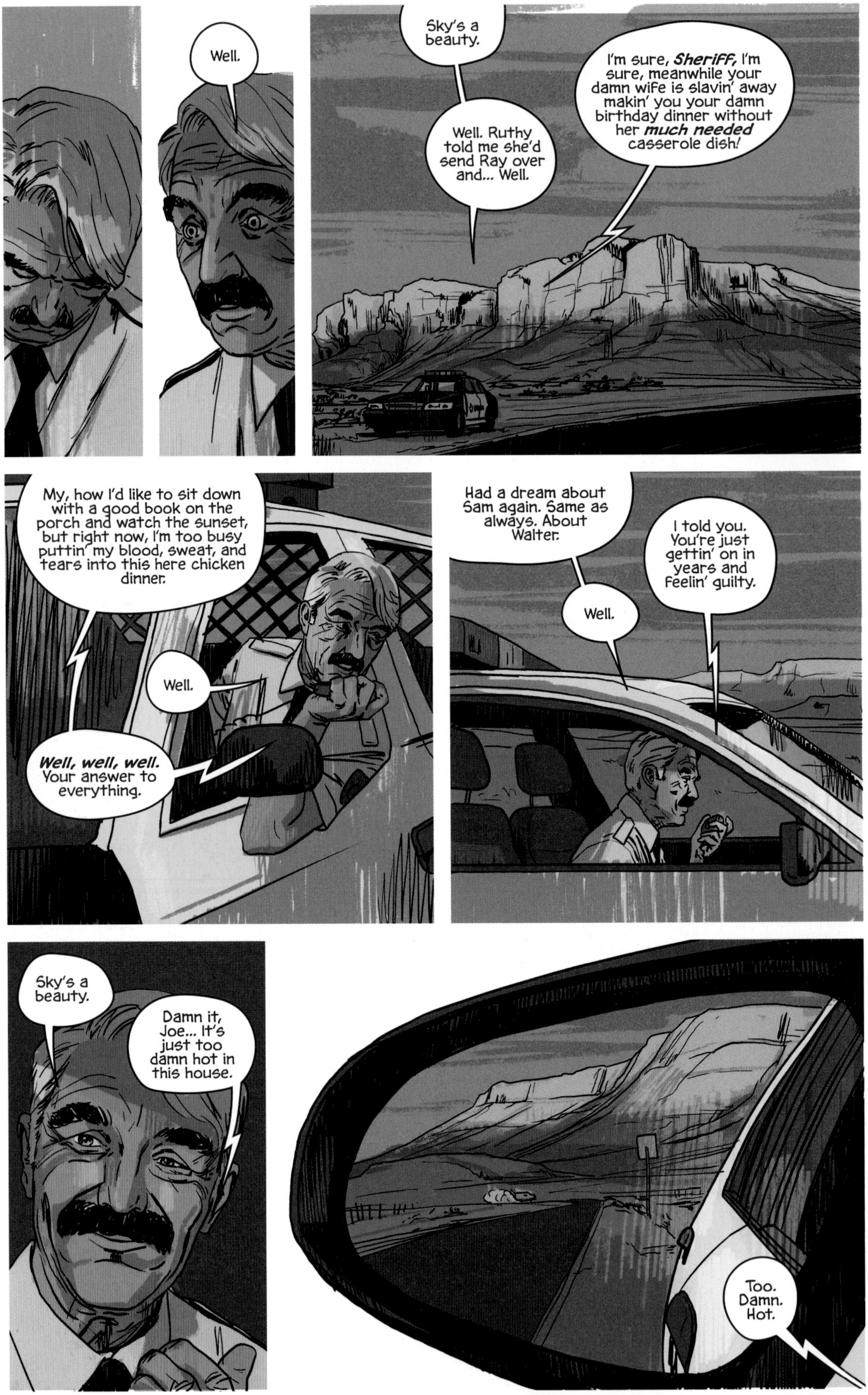
Well.
Sky's a beauty.
Well. Ruthy told me she'd send Ray over and... Well.
I'm sure, *Sheriff,* I'm sure, meanwhile your damn wife is slavin' away makin' you your damn birthday dinner without her *much needed* casserole dish!
My, how I'd like to sit down with a good book on the porch and watch the sunset, but right now, I'm too busy puttin' my blood, sweat, and tears into this here chicken dinner.
Well.
Well, well, well. Your answer to everything.
Had a dream about Sam again. Same as always. About Walter.
Well.
I told you. You're just gettin' on in years and feelin' guilty.
Sky's a beauty.
Damn it, Joe... It's just too damn hot in this house.
Too. Damn. Hot.

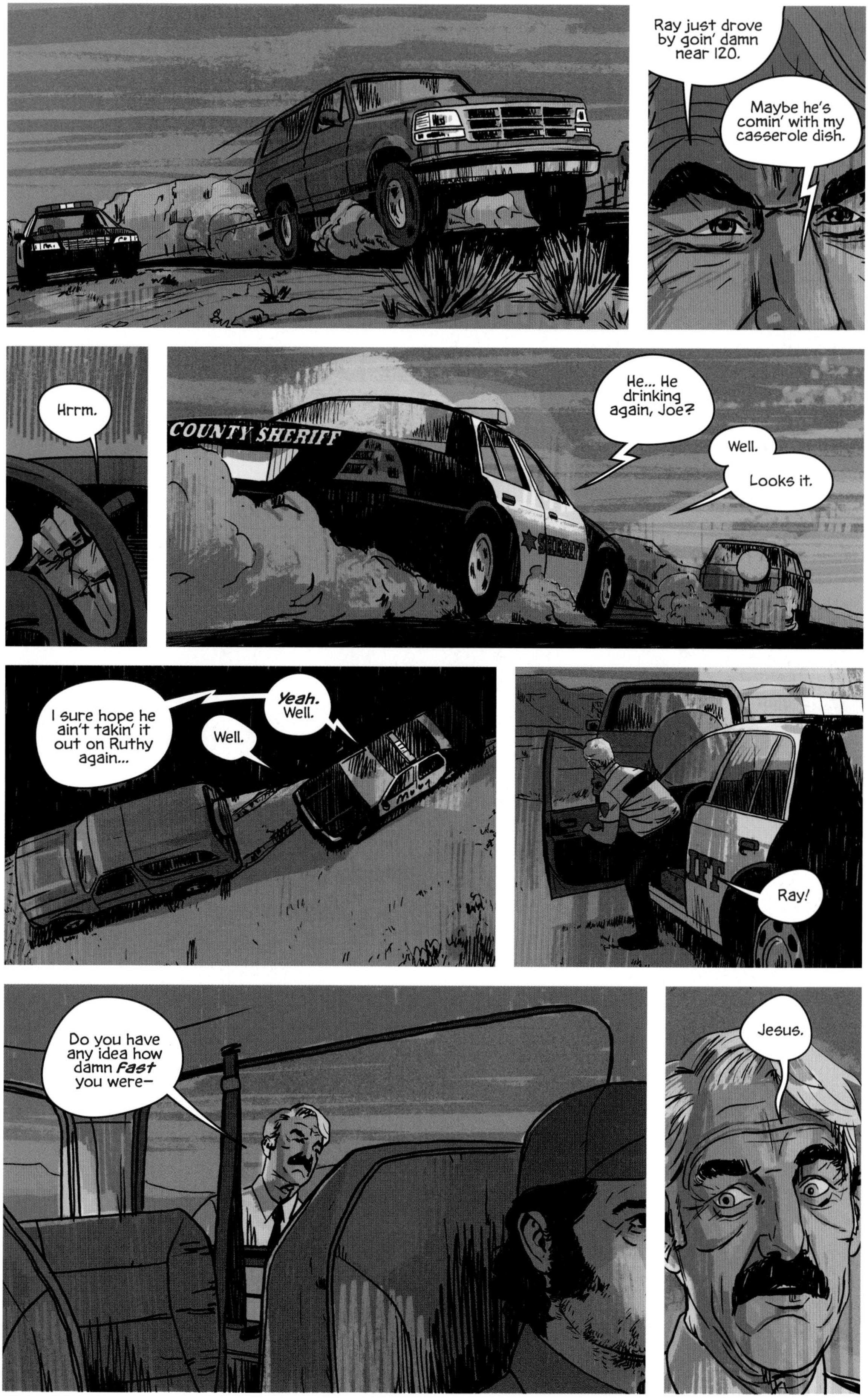

Ray just drove by goin' damn near 120.
Maybe he's comin' with my casserole dish.
Hrrm.
COUNTY SHERIFF
He... He drinking again, Joe?
Well.
Looks it.
I sure hope he ain't takin' it out on Ruthy again...
Yeah. Well.
Well.
Ray!
Do you have any idea how damn *Fast* you were—
Jesus.

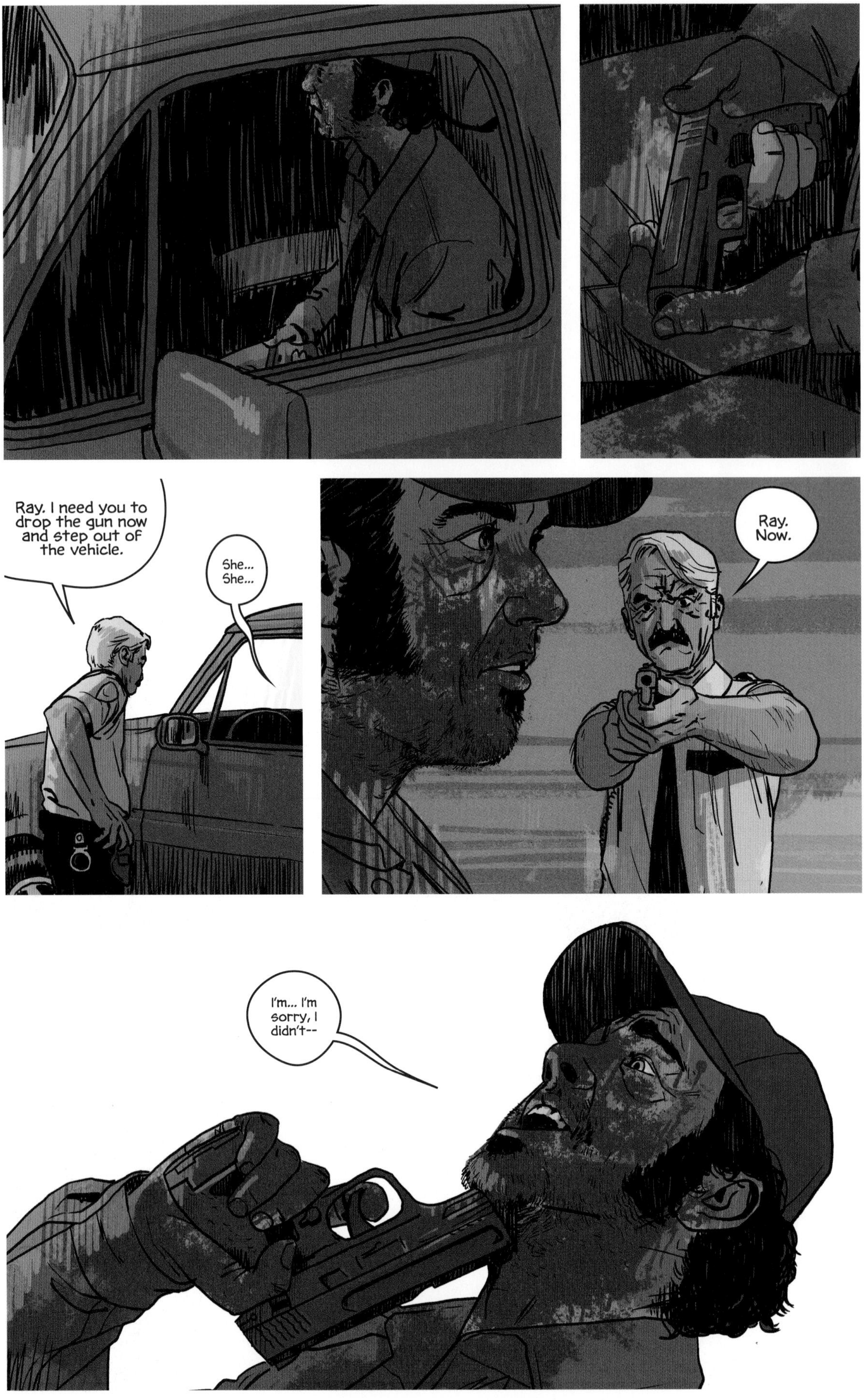
Ray. I need you to drop the gun now and step out of the vehicle.
She... She...
Ray. Now.
I'm... I'm sorry, I didn't--

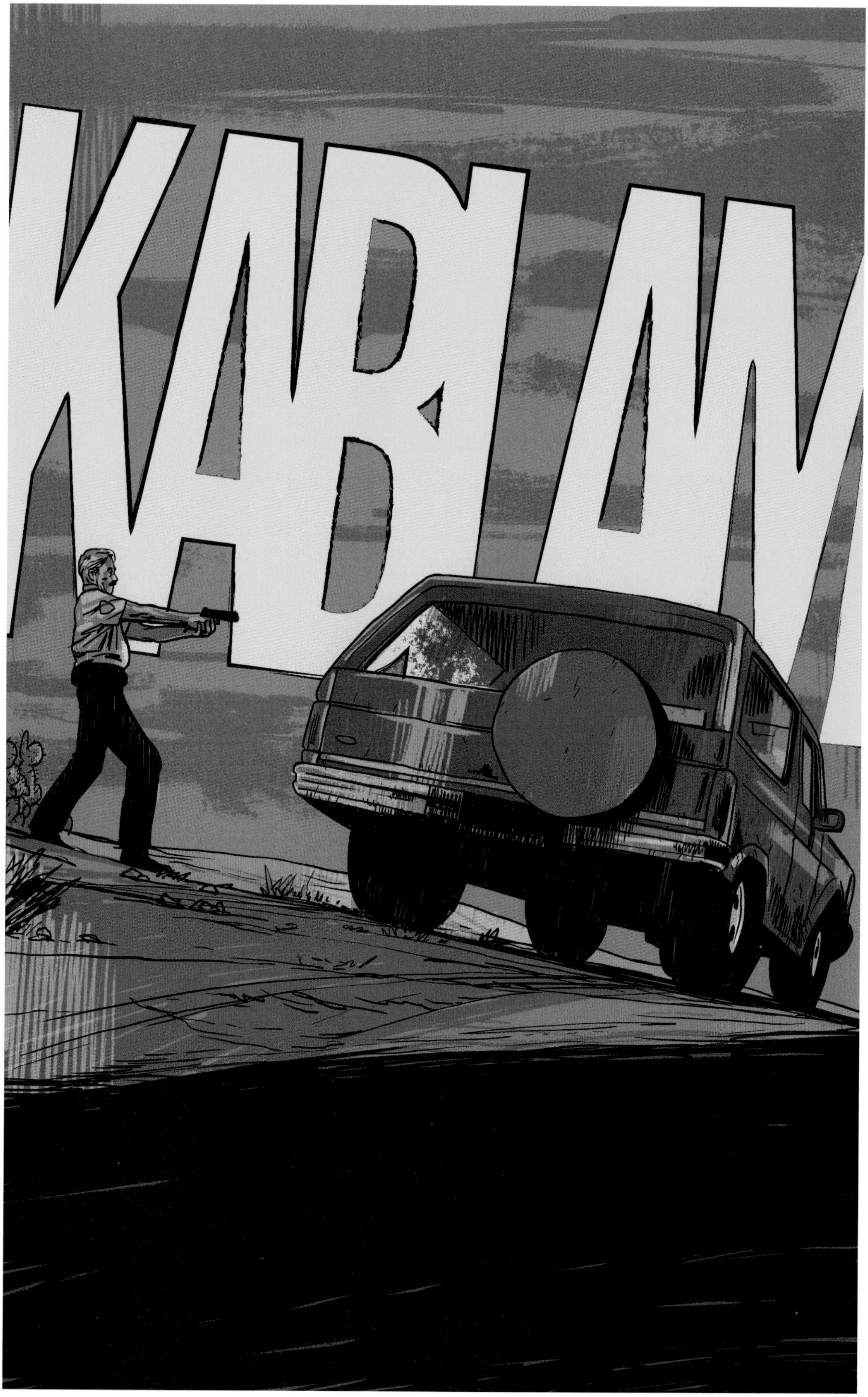
KABLAM

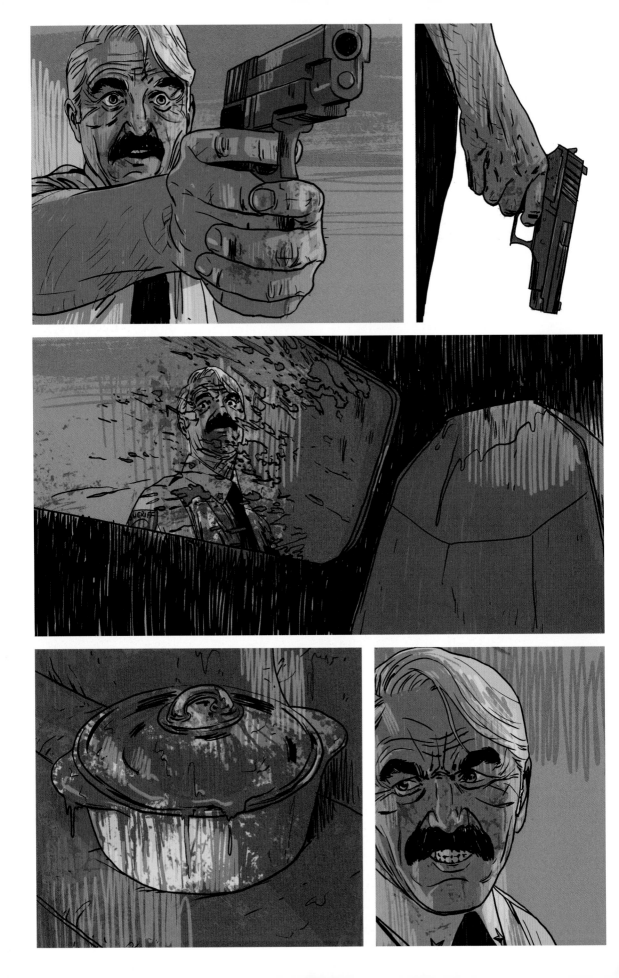

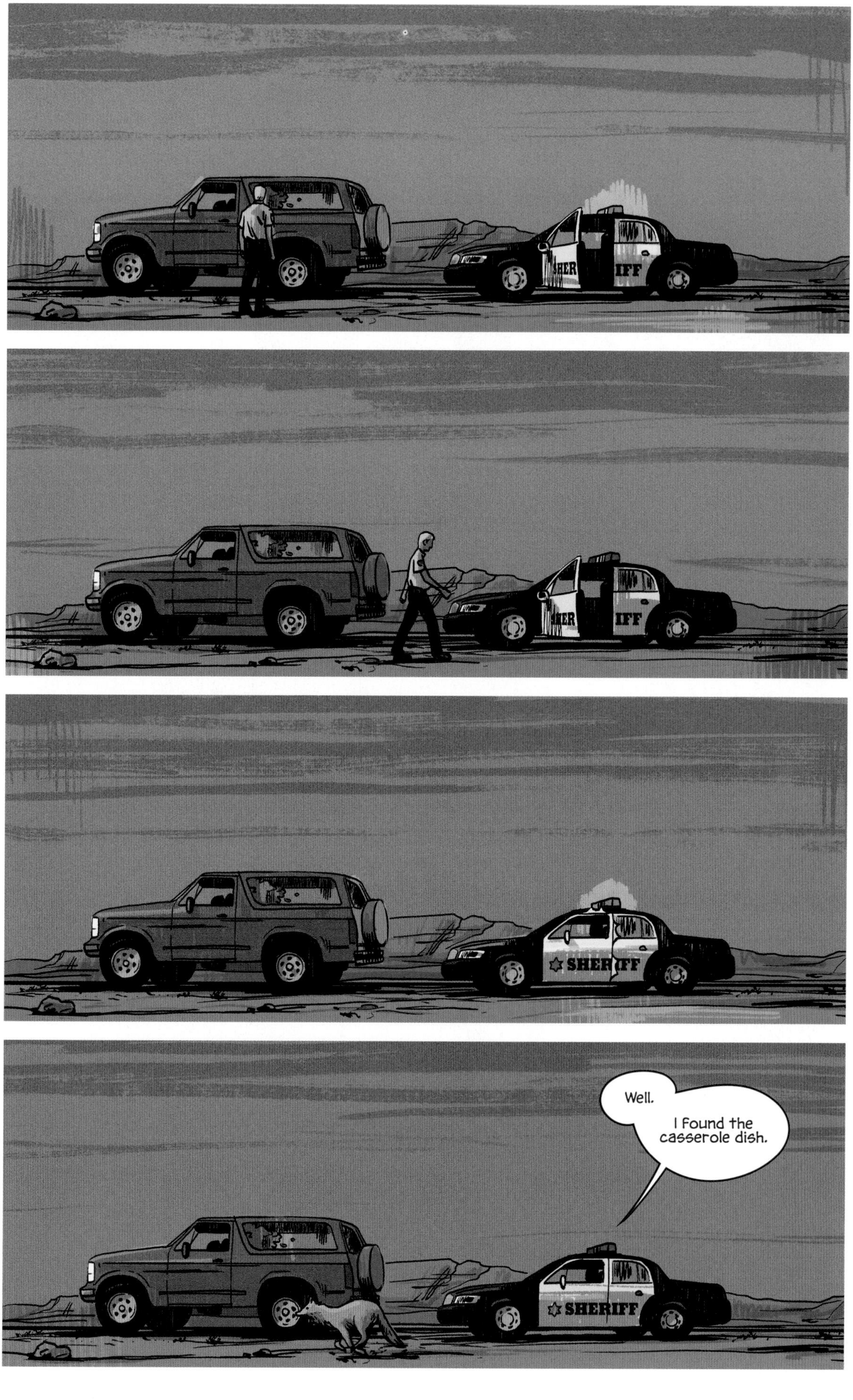
SHERIFF
SHERIFF
SHERIFF
Well.
I found the casserole dish.
SHERIFF

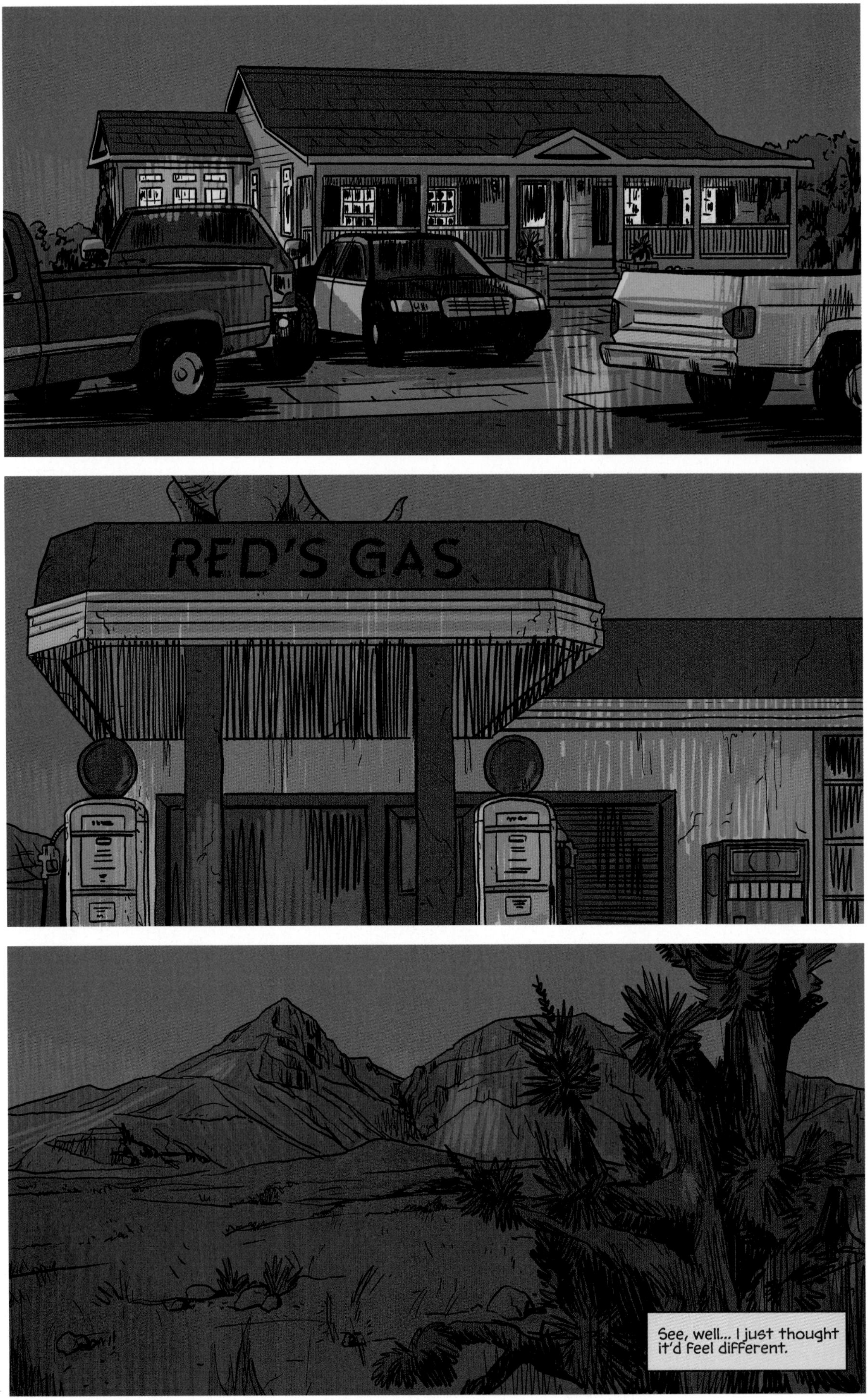
RED'S GAS
See, well... I just thought it'd feel different.

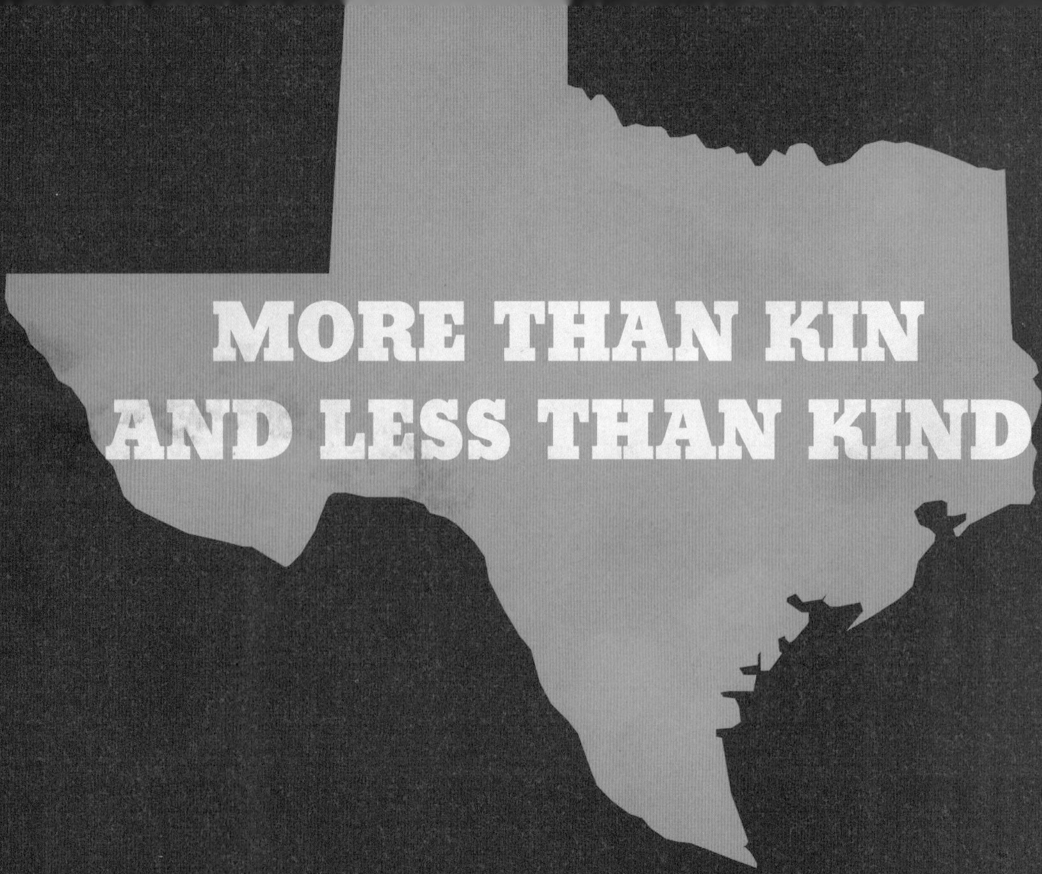
MORE THAN KIN
AND LESS THAN KIND

A Brother's Conscience

Part One

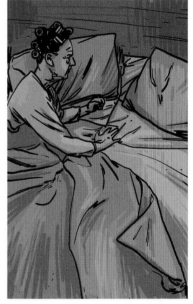

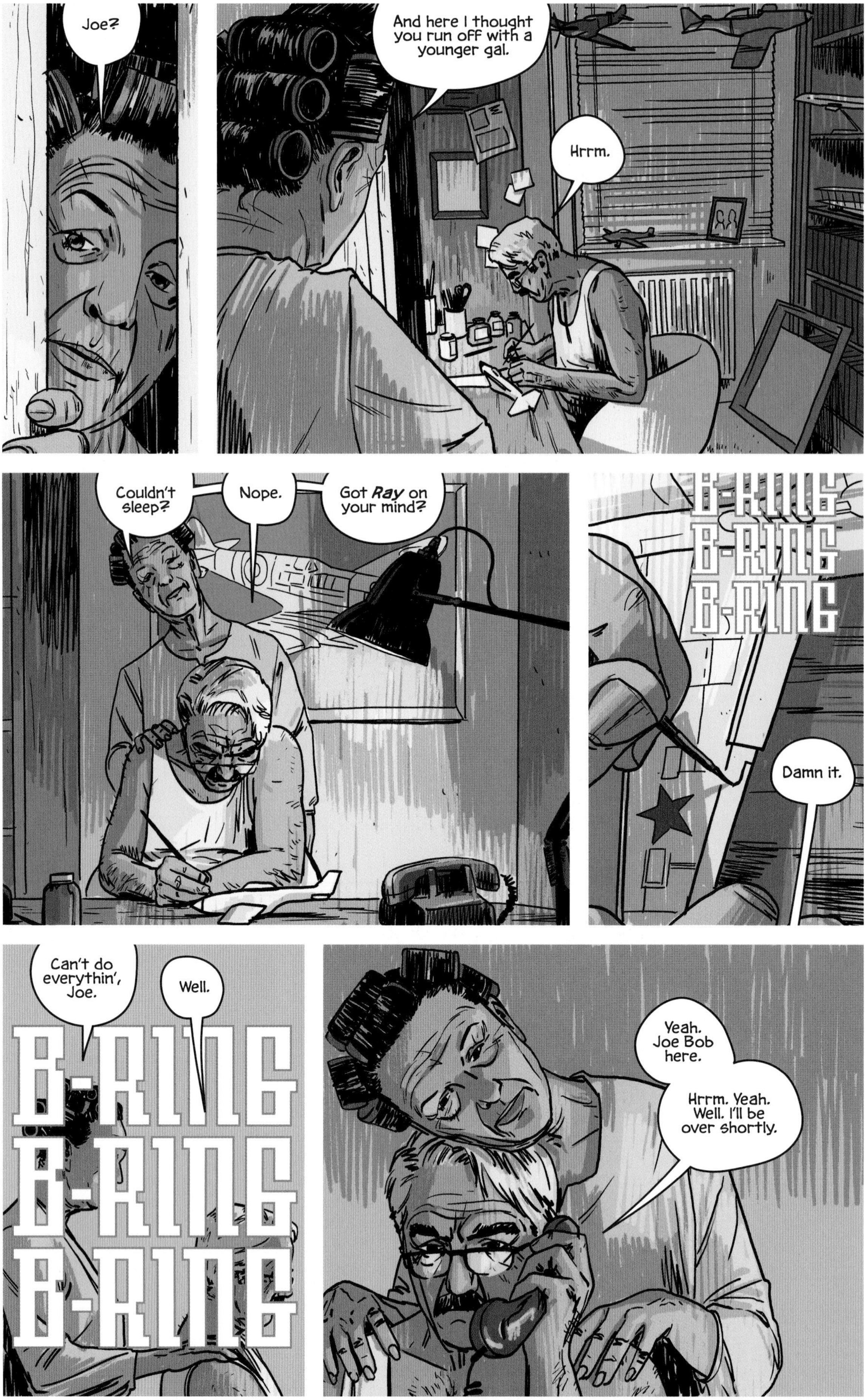
Joe?
And here I thought you run off with a younger gal.
Hrrm.
Couldn't sleep?
Nope.
Got *Ray* on your mind?
B-RING
B-RING
B-RING
Damn it.
Can't do everythin', Joe.
Well.
B-RING
B-RING
B-RING
Yeah. Joe Bob here.
Hrrm. Yeah. Well. I'll be over shortly.

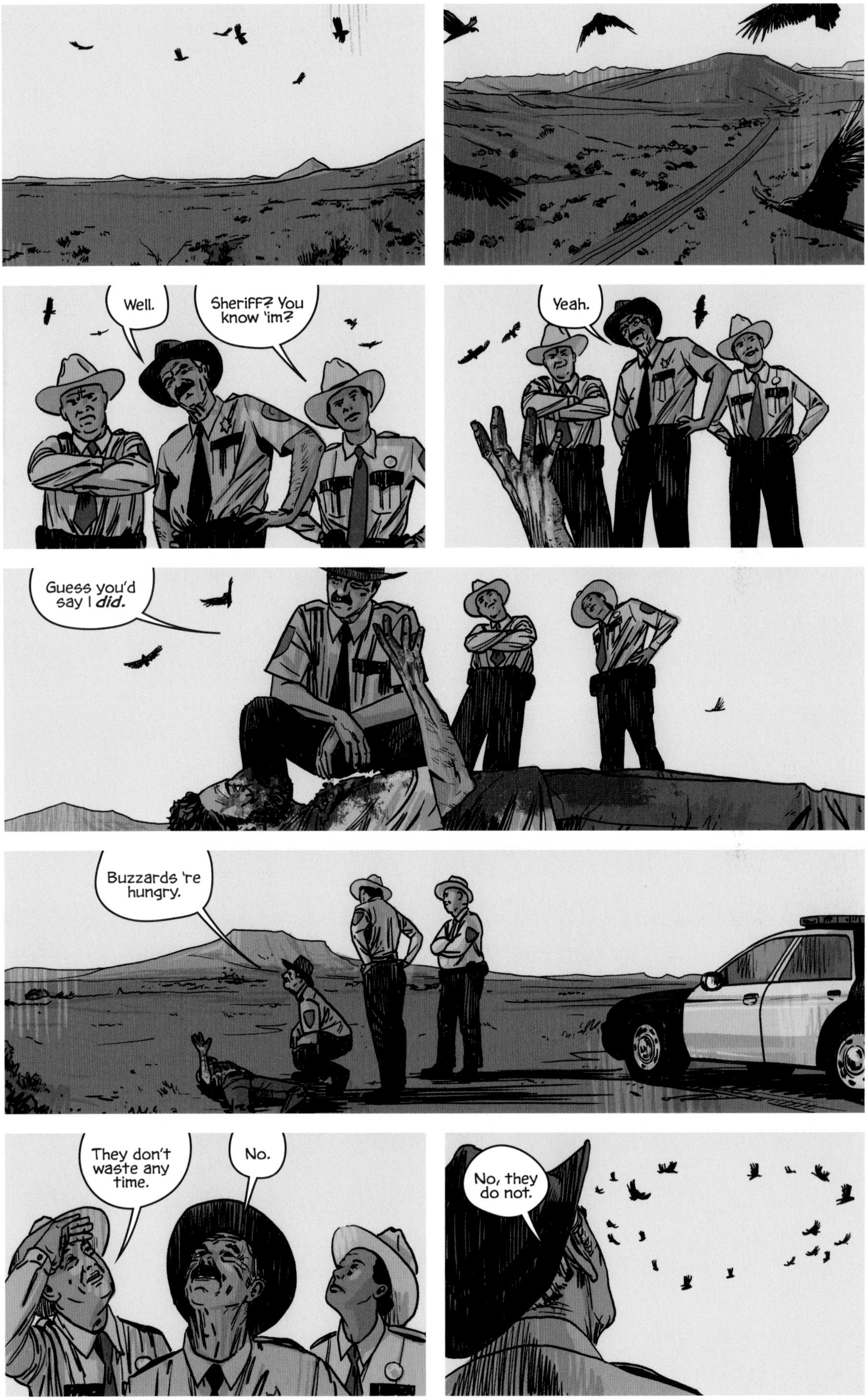
Well.
Sheriff? You know 'im?
Yeah.
Guess you'd say I *did.*
Buzzards 're hungry.
They don't waste any time.
No.
No, they do not.

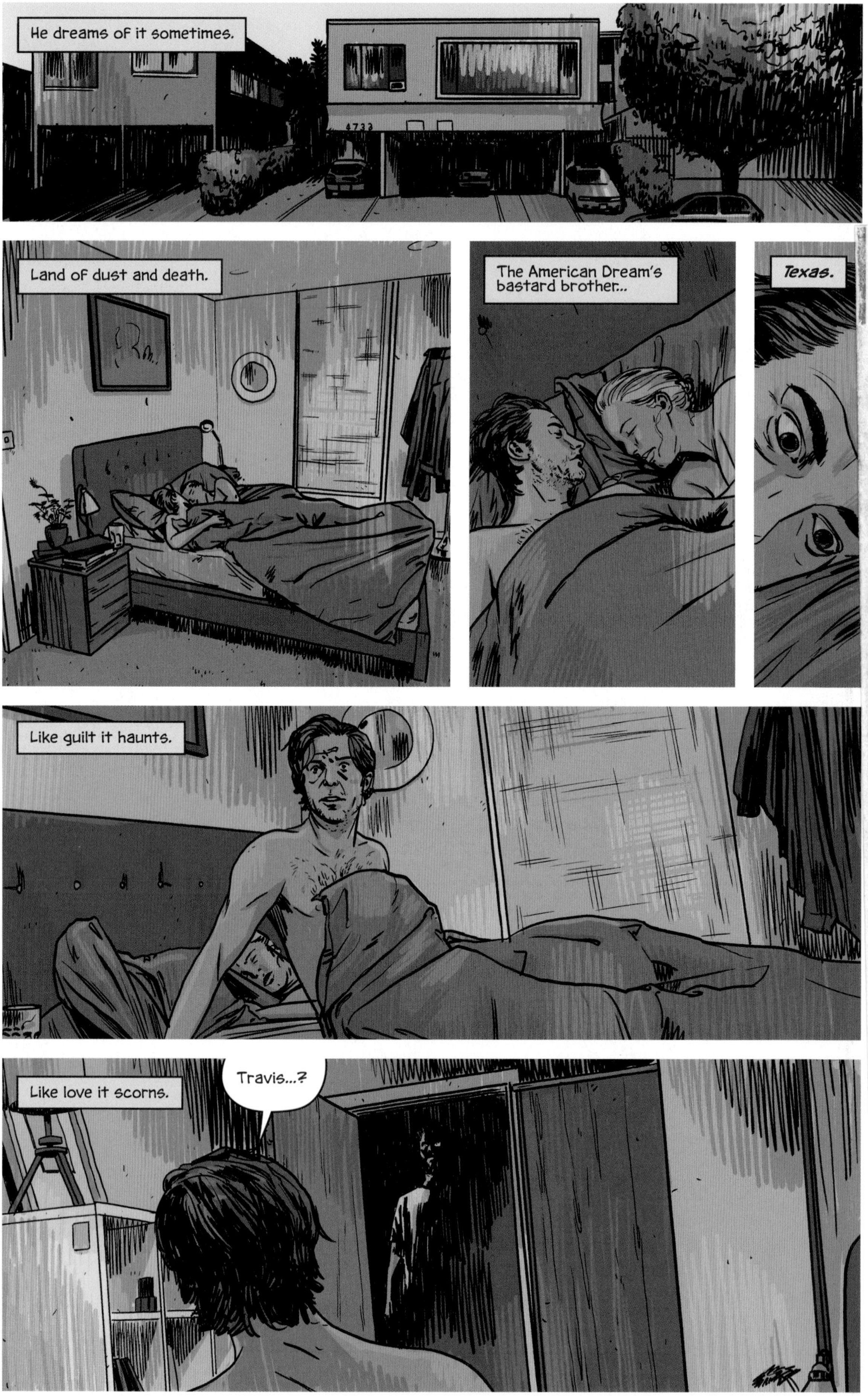
He dreams of it sometimes.
Land of dust and death.
The American Dream's bastard brother...
Texas.
Like guilt it haunts.
Like love it scorns.
Travis...?

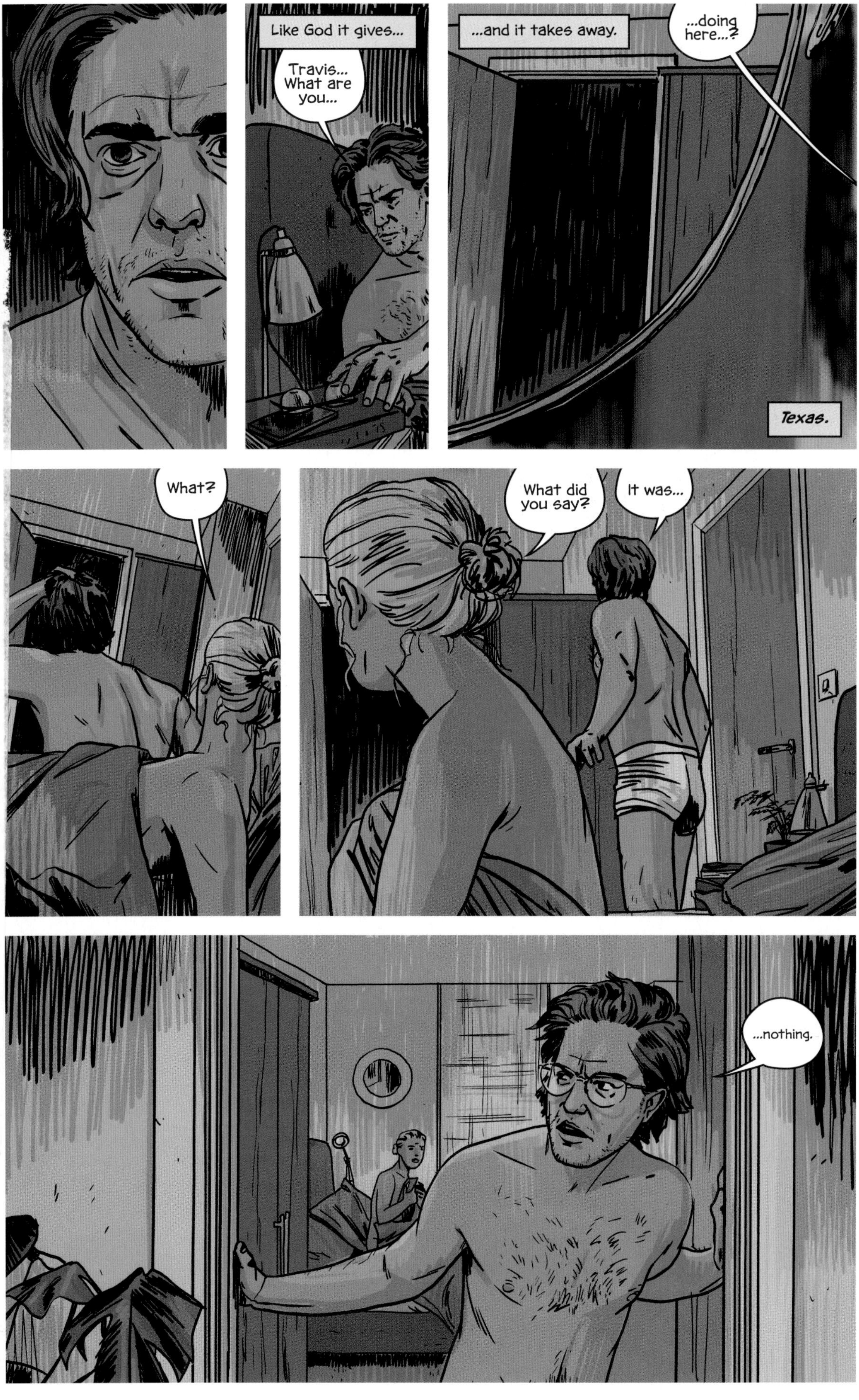
Like God it gives...
Travis... What are you...
...and it takes away.
...doing here...?
Texas.
What?
What did you say?
It was...
...nothing.

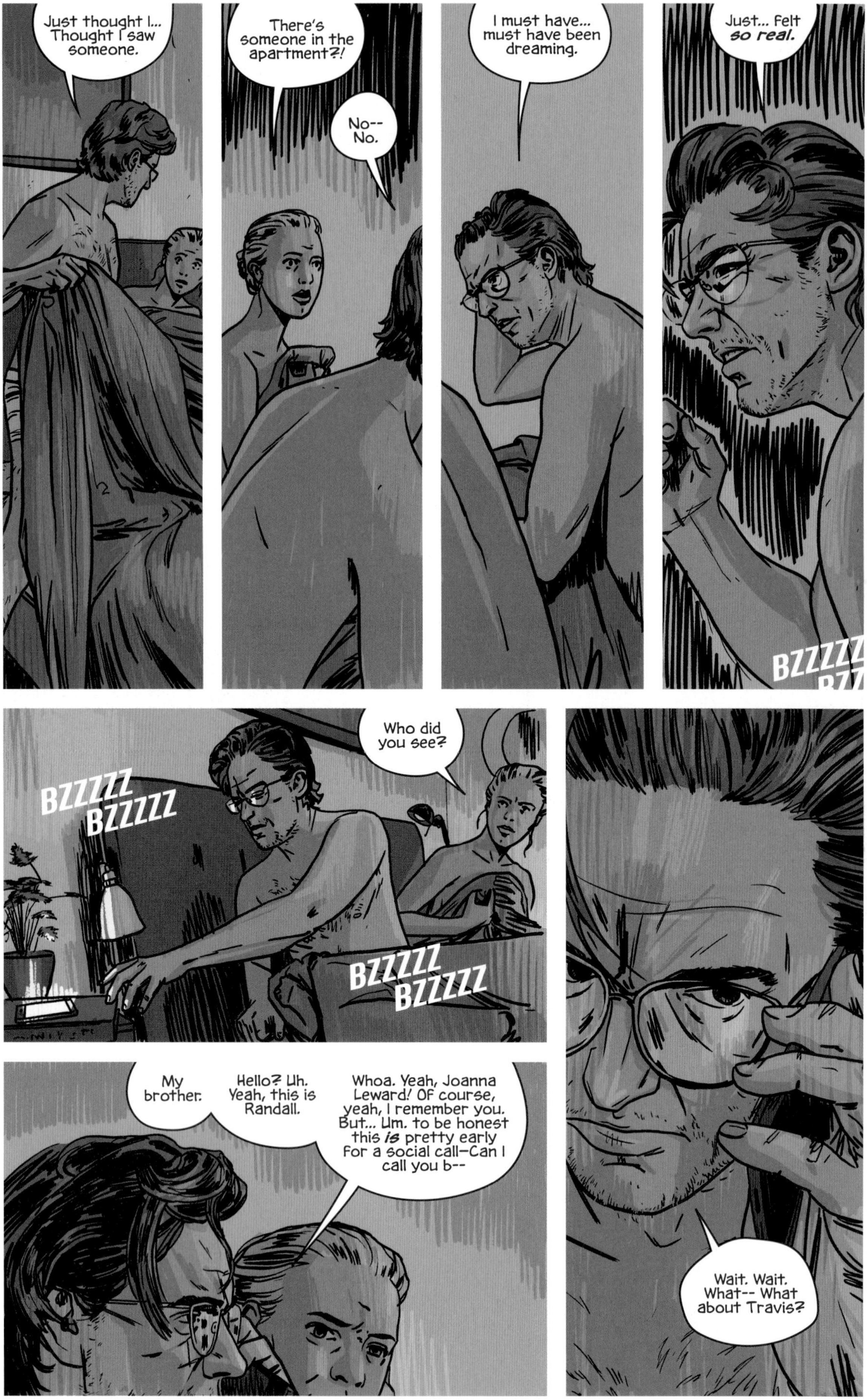

Just thought I... Thought I saw someone.
There's someone in the apartment?!
No-- No.
I must have... must have been dreaming.
Just... felt *so real.*
BZZZZZ
BZZZZZ BZZZZZ
Who did you see?
BZZZZZ BZZZZZ
My brother.
Hello? Uh. Yeah, this is Randall.
Whoa. Yeah, Joanna Leward! Of course, yeah, I remember you. But... Um. to be honest this *is* pretty early for a social call—Can I call you b--
Wait. Wait. What-- What about Travis?

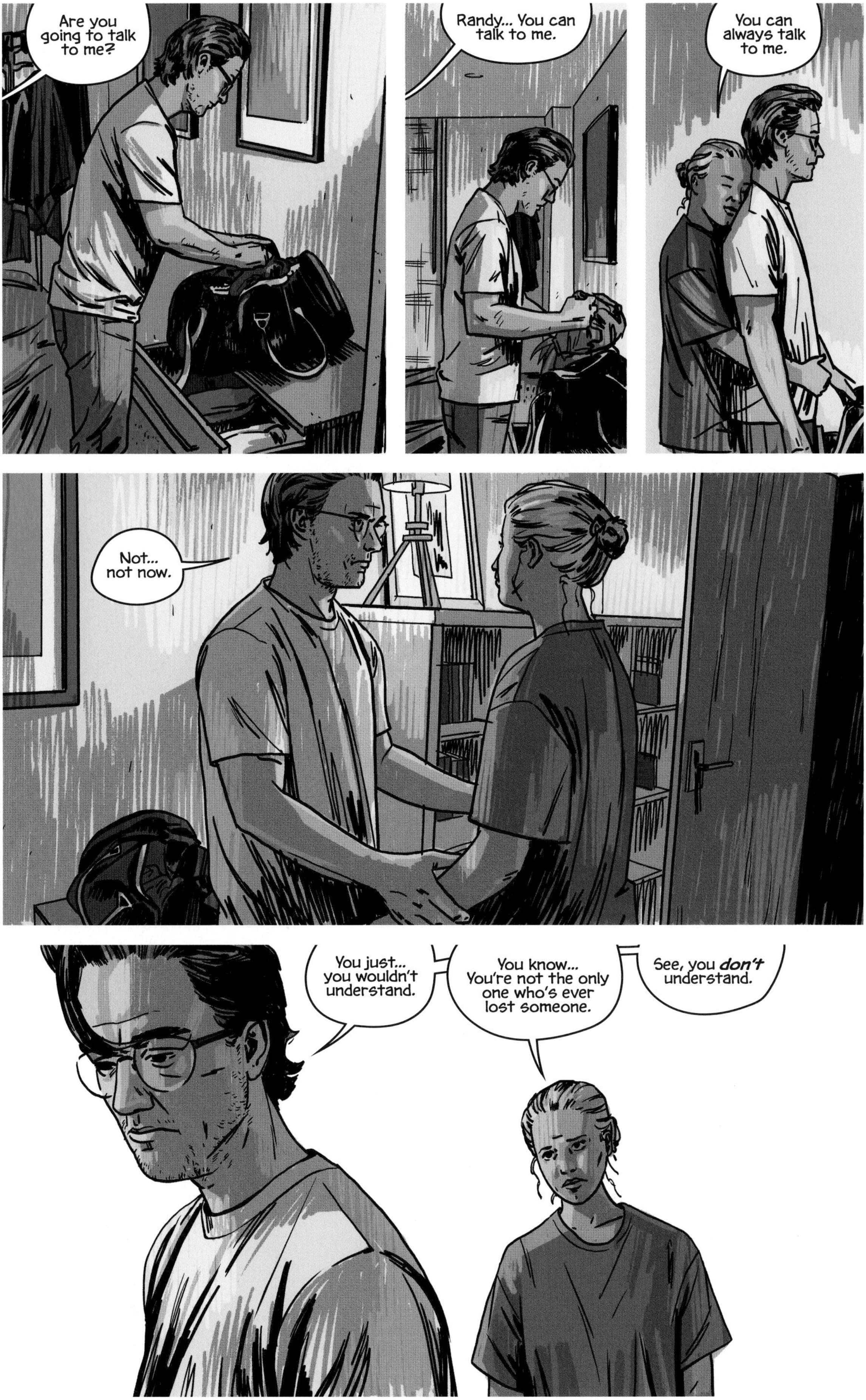
Are you going to talk to me?
Randy... You can talk to me.
You can always talk to me.
Not... not now.
You just... you wouldn't understand.
You know... You're not the only one who's ever lost someone.
See, you *don't* understand.

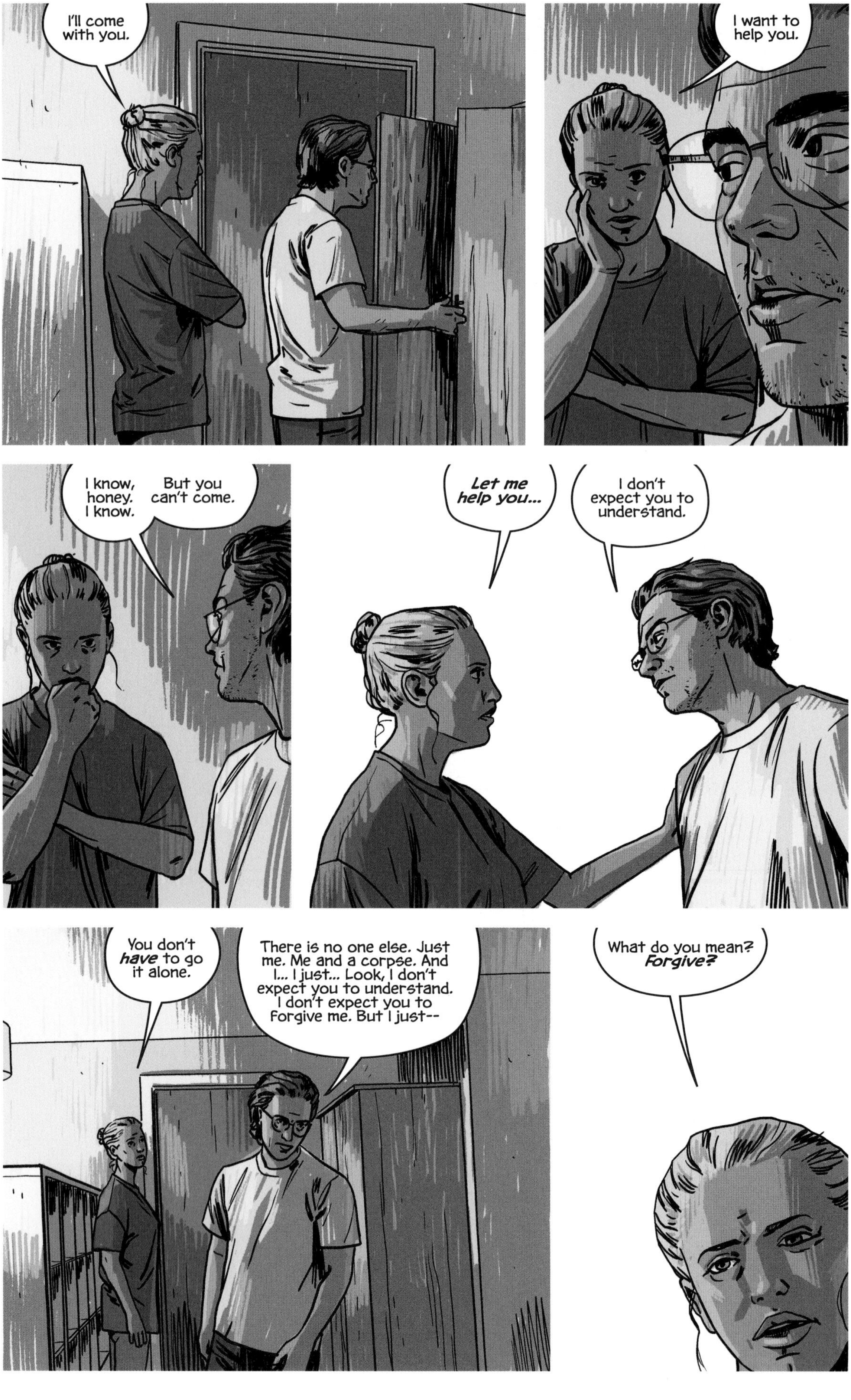
I'll come with you.
I want to help you.
I know, honey. I know.
But you can't come.
Let me help you...
I don't expect you to understand.
You don't have to go it alone.
There is no one else. Just me. Me and a corpse. And I... I just... Look, I don't expect you to understand. I don't expect you to forgive me. But I just--
What do you mean? Forgive?

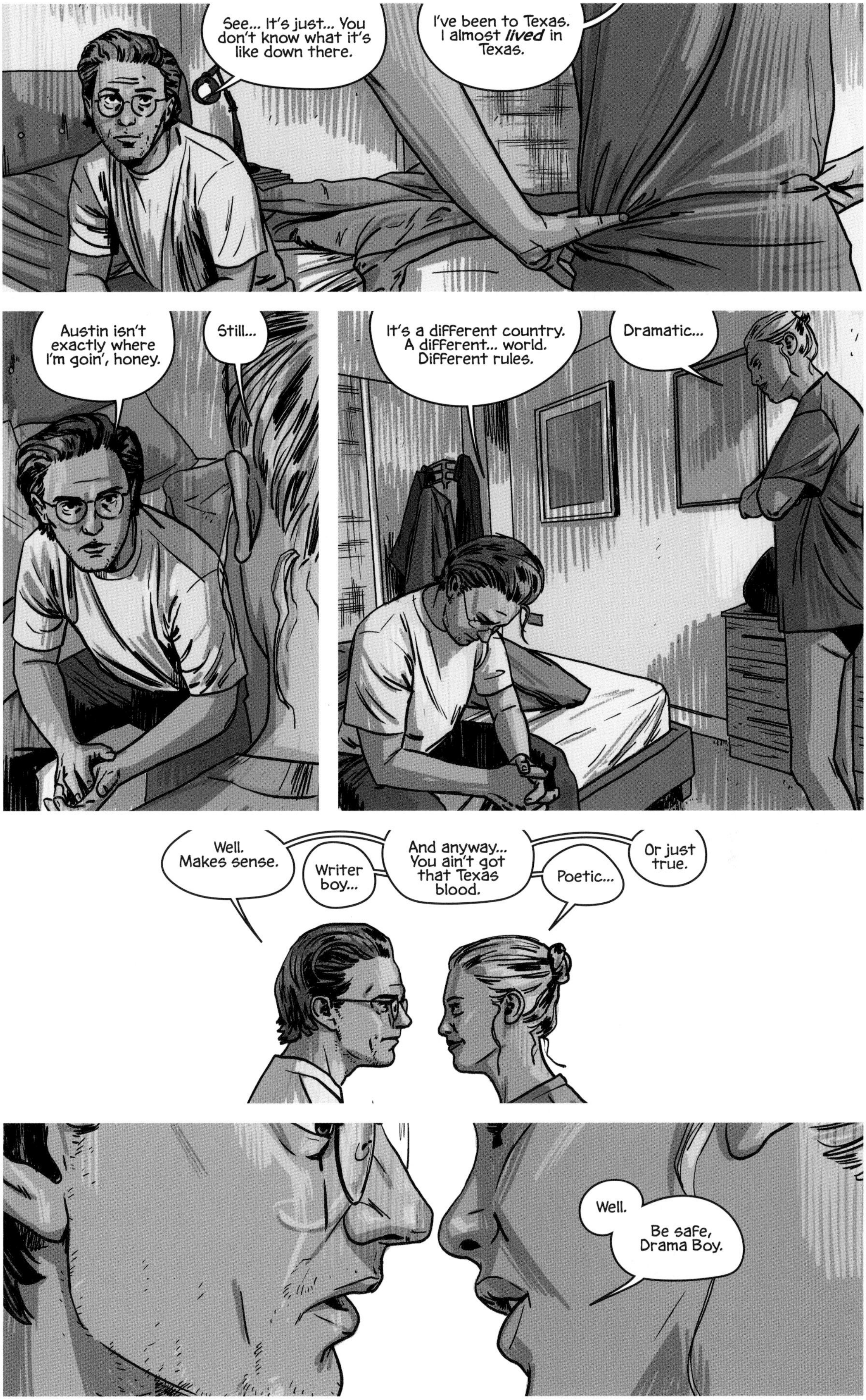
See... It's just... You don't know what it's like down there.
I've been to Texas. I almost *lived* in Texas.
Austin isn't exactly where I'm goin', honey.
Still...
It's a different country. A different... world. Different rules.
Dramatic...
Well. Makes sense.
Writer boy...
And anyway... You ain't got that Texas blood.
Poetic...
Or just true.
Well.
Be safe, Drama Boy.

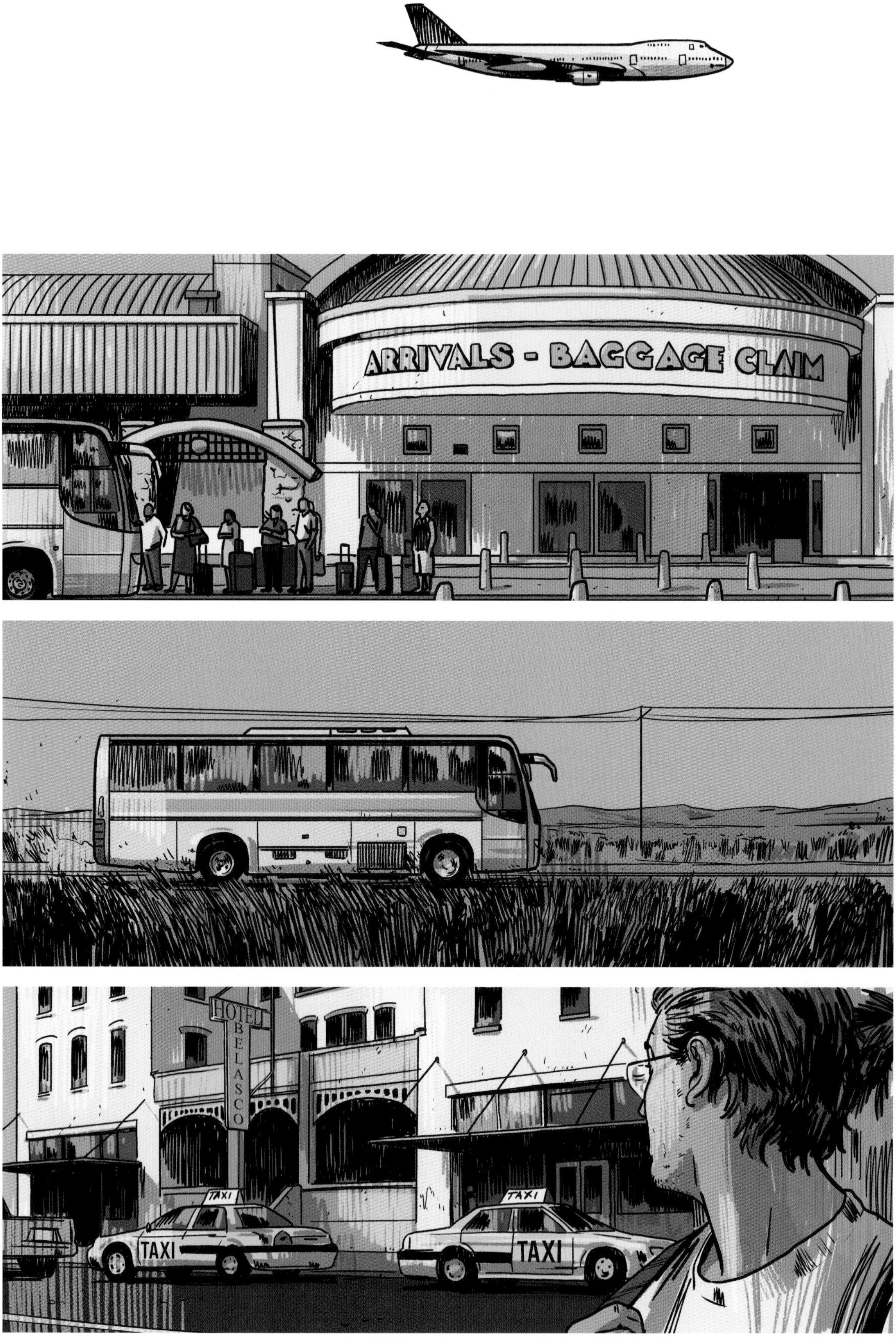
ARRIVALS - BAGGAGE CLAIM
HOTEL
BELASCO
TAXI
TAXI
TAXI
TAXI

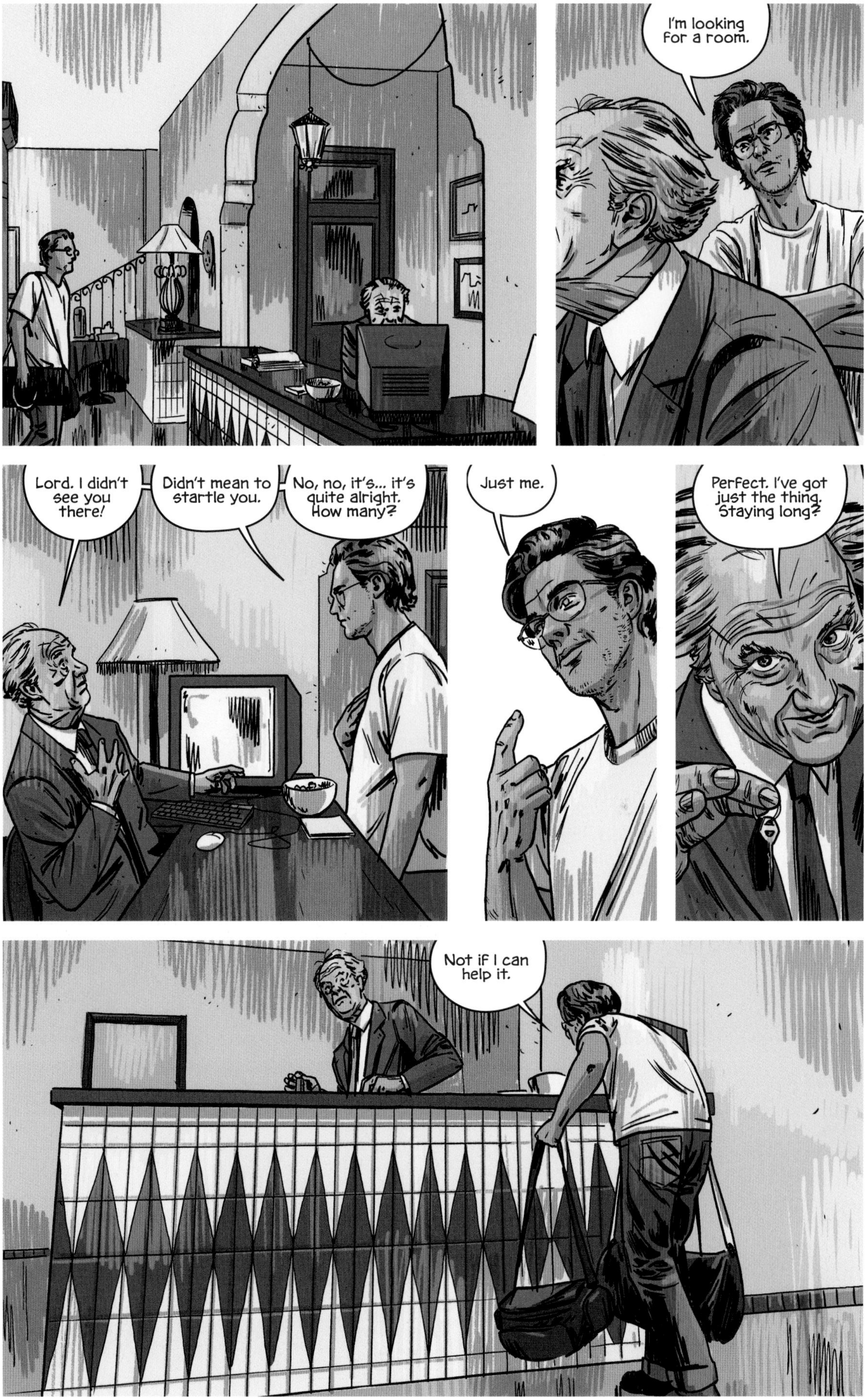

I'm looking for a room.
Lord. I didn't see you there!
Didn't mean to startle you.
No, no, it's... it's quite alright. How many?
Just me.
Perfect. I've got just the thing. Staying long?
Not if I can help it.

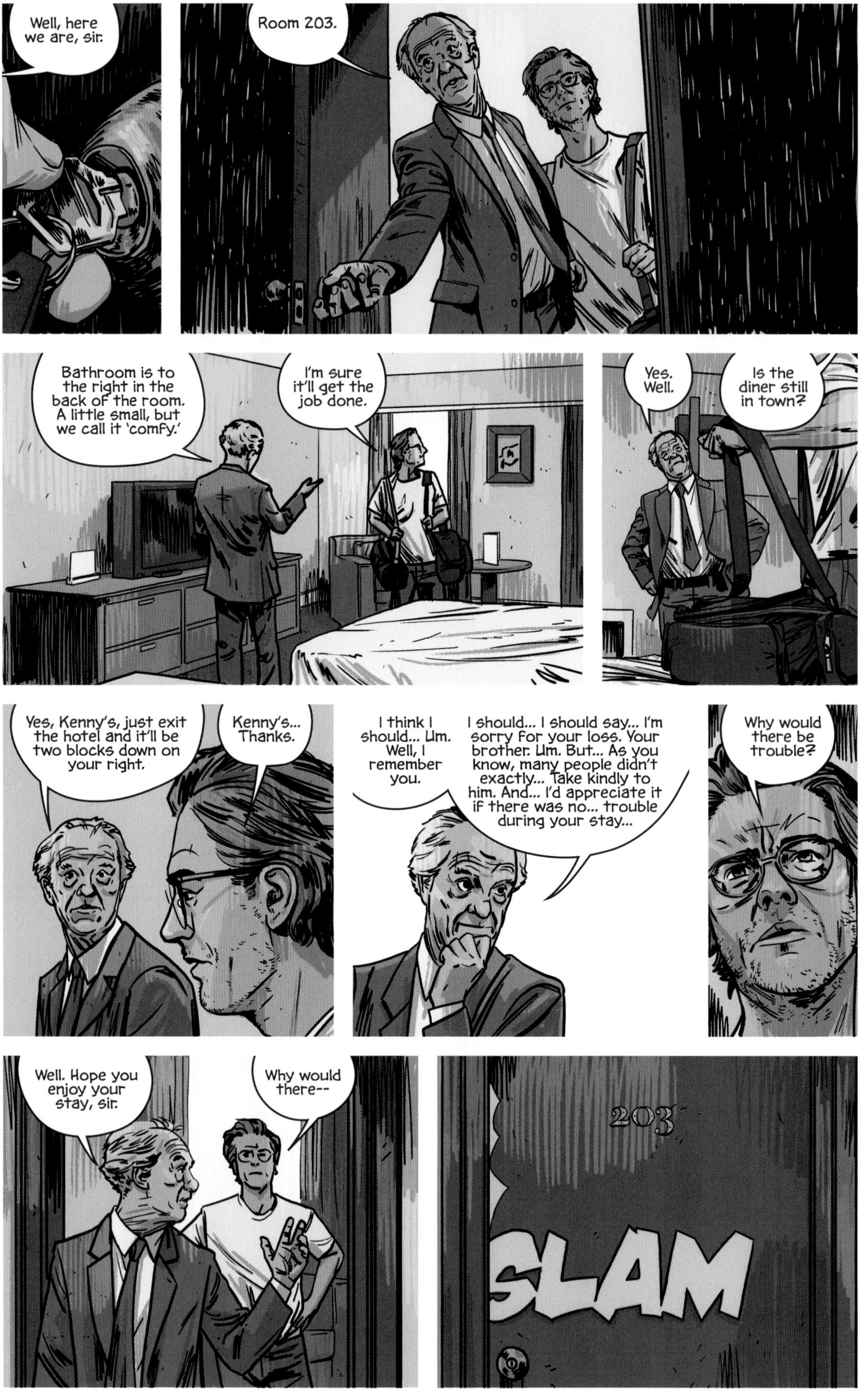

Well, here we are, sir.
Room 203.
Bathroom is to the right in the back of the room. A little small, but we call it 'comfy.'
I'm sure it'll get the job done.
Yes. Well.
Is the diner still in town?
Yes, Kenny's, just exit the hotel and it'll be two blocks down on your right.
Kenny's... Thanks.
I think I should... Um. Well, I remember you.
I should... I should say... I'm sorry for your loss. Your brother. Um. But... As you know, many people didn't exactly... Take kindly to him. And... I'd appreciate it if there was no... trouble during your stay...
Why would there be trouble?
Well. Hope you enjoy your stay, sir.
Why would there--
203
SLAM

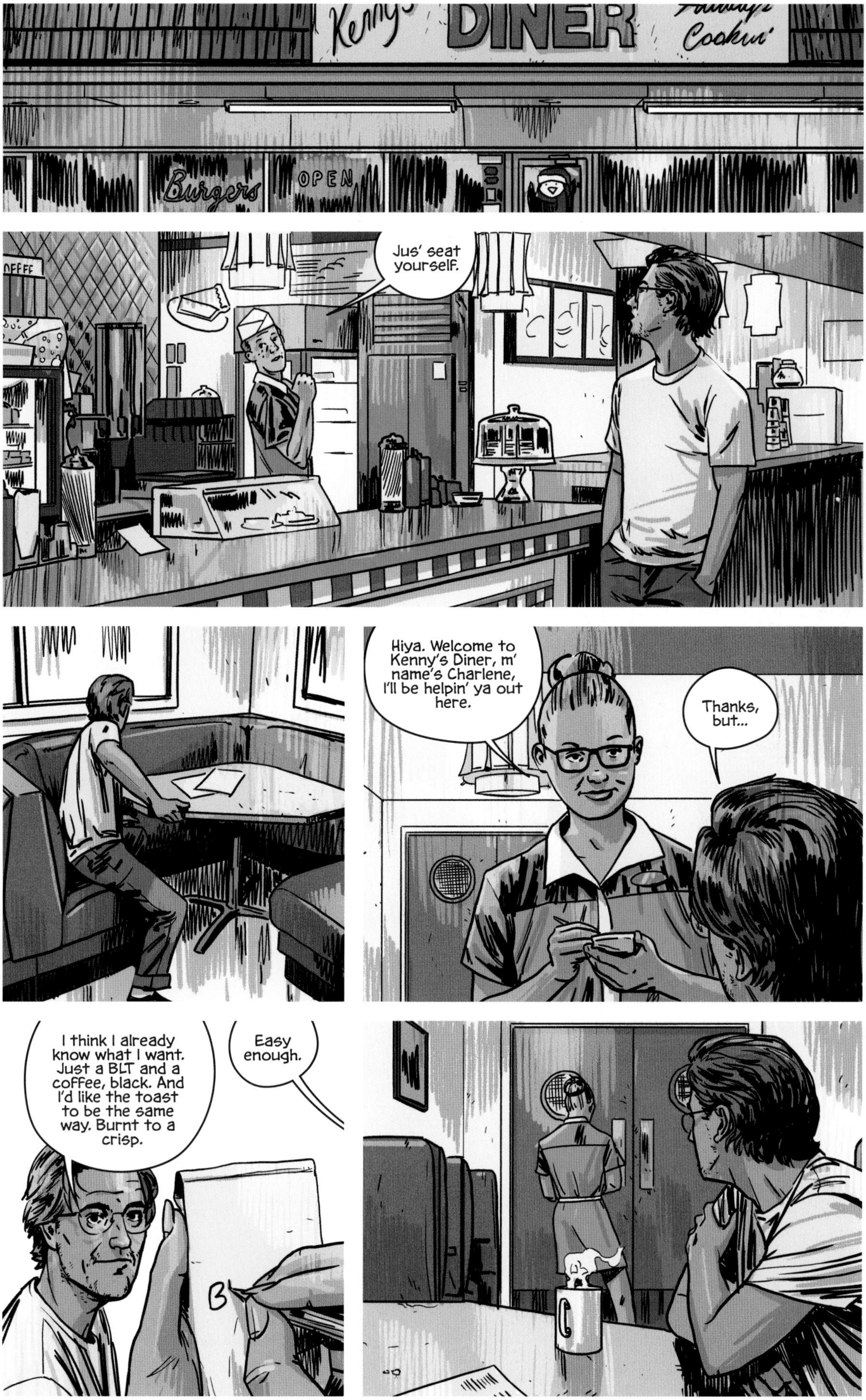
Kenny's DINER Always Cookin'
Burgers
OPEN
Jus' seat yourself.
Hiya. Welcome to Kenny's Diner, m' name's Charlene, I'll be helpin' ya out here.
Thanks, but...
I think I already know what I want. Just a BLT and a coffee, black. And I'd like the toast to be the same way. Burnt to a crisp.
Easy enough.

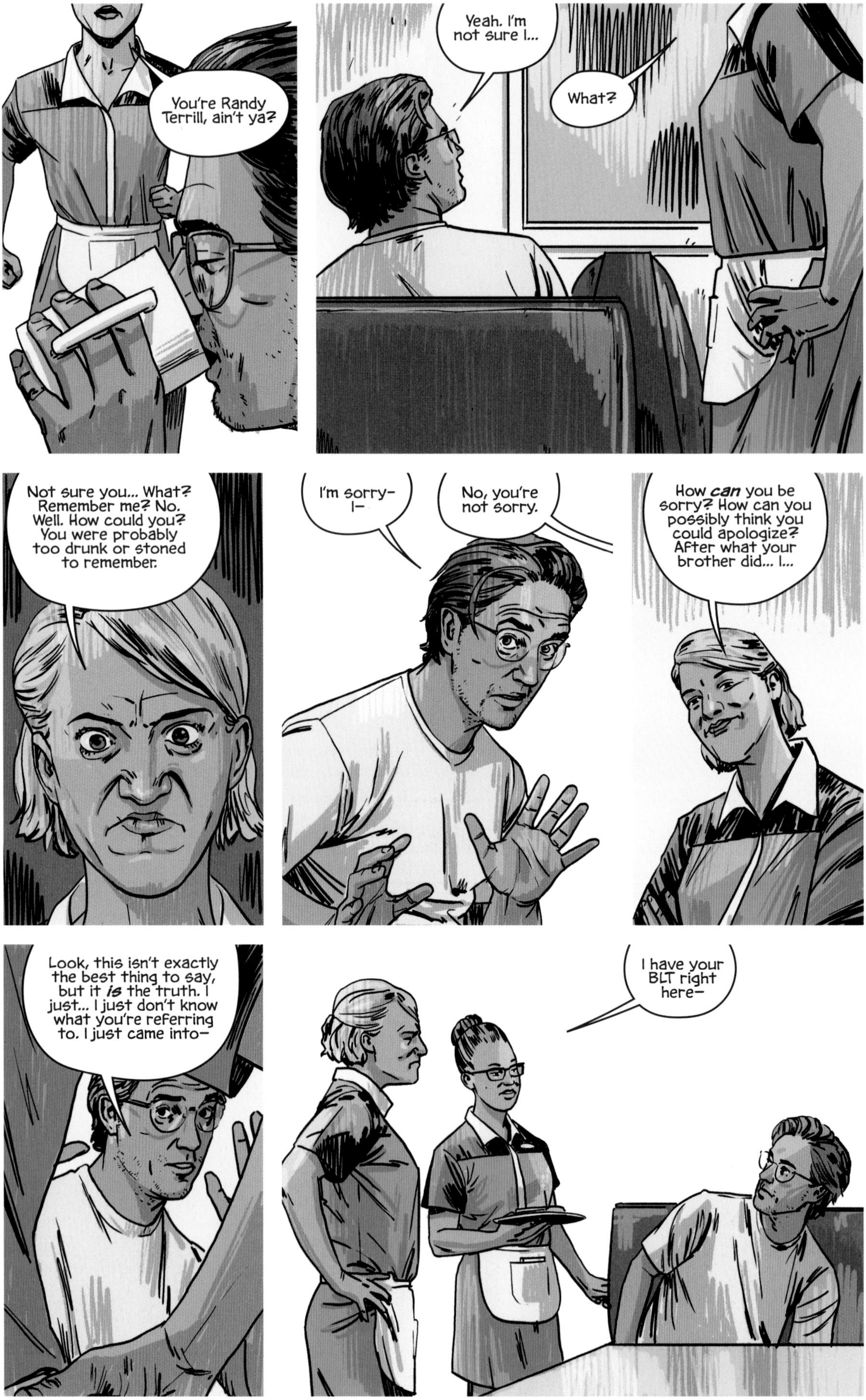
You're Randy Terrill, ain't ya?
Yeah. I'm not sure I...
What?
Not sure you... What? Remember me? No. Well. How could you? You were probably too drunk or stoned to remember.
I'm sorry- I-
No, you're not sorry.
How *can* you be sorry? How can you possibly think you could apologize? After what your brother did... I...
Look, this isn't exactly the best thing to say, but it *is* the truth. I just... I just don't know what you're referring to. I just came into-
I have your BLT right here-

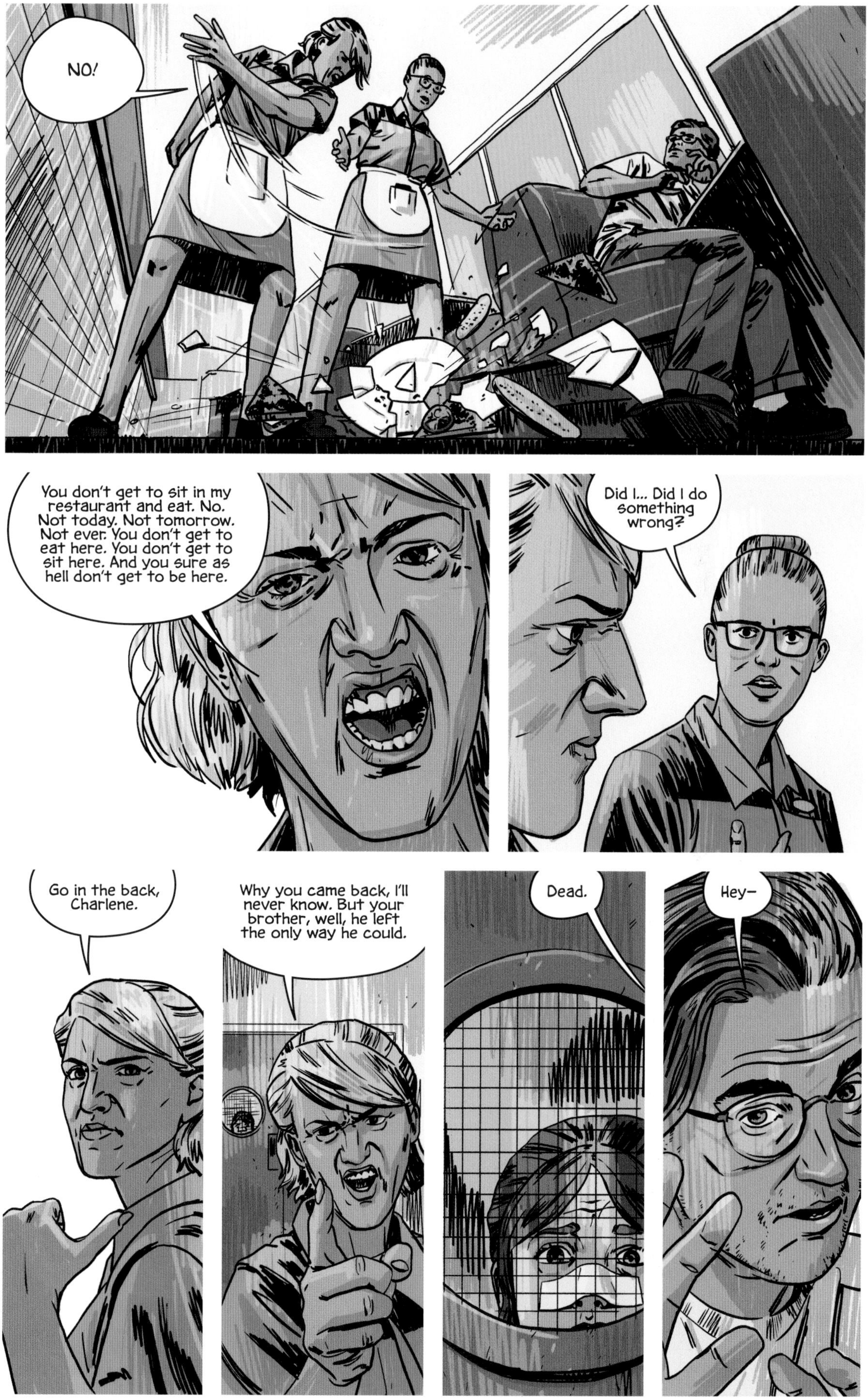
NO!
You don't get to sit in my restaurant and eat. No. Not today. Not tomorrow. Not ever. You don't get to eat here. You don't get to sit here. And you sure as hell don't get to be here.
Did I... Did I do something wrong?
Go in the back, Charlene.
Why you came back, I'll never know. But your brother, well, he left the only way he could.
Dead.
Hey—

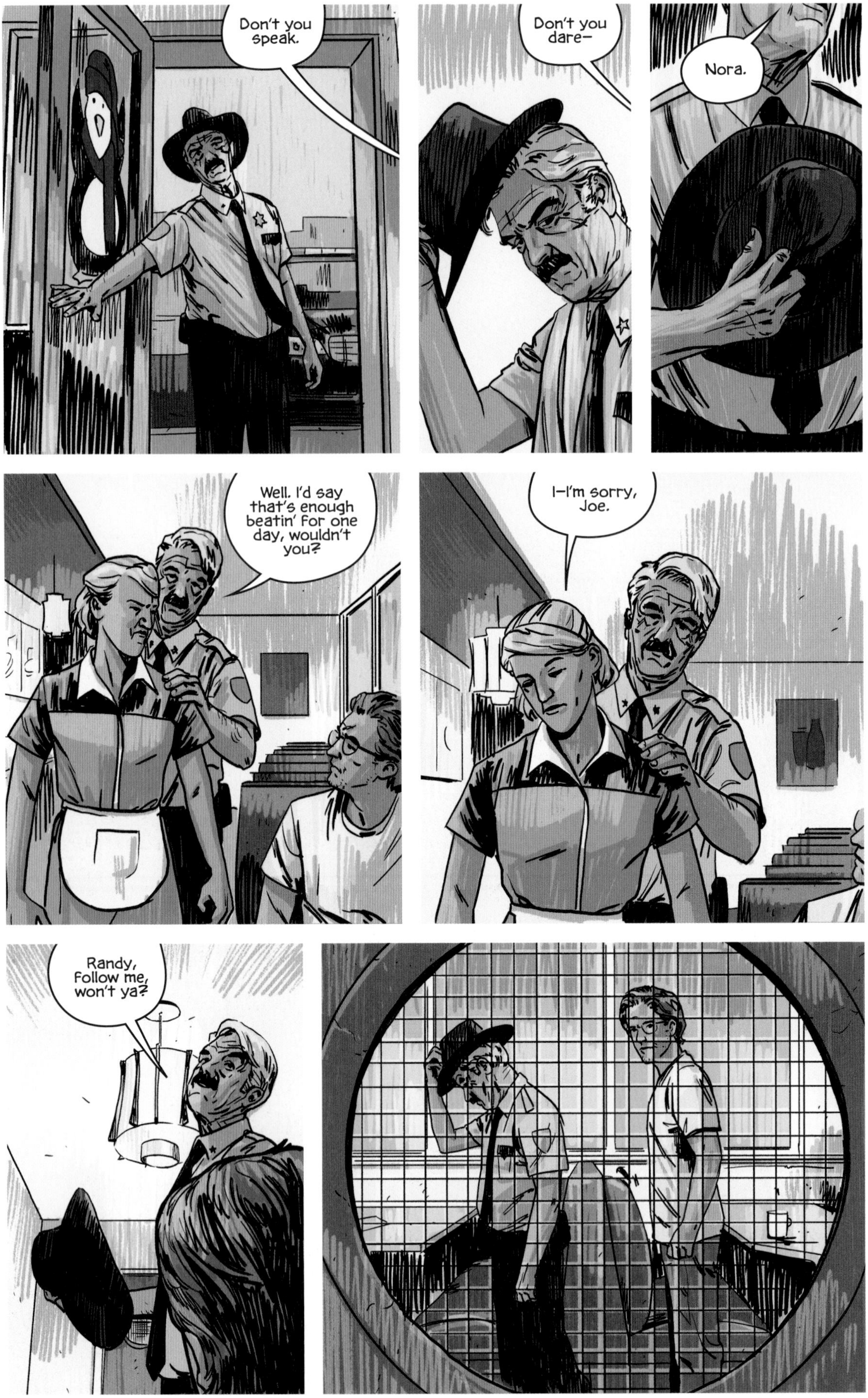
Don't you speak.
Don't you dare–
Nora.
Well. I'd say that's enough beatin' for one day, wouldn't you?
I–I'm sorry, Joe.
Randy, follow me, won't ya?

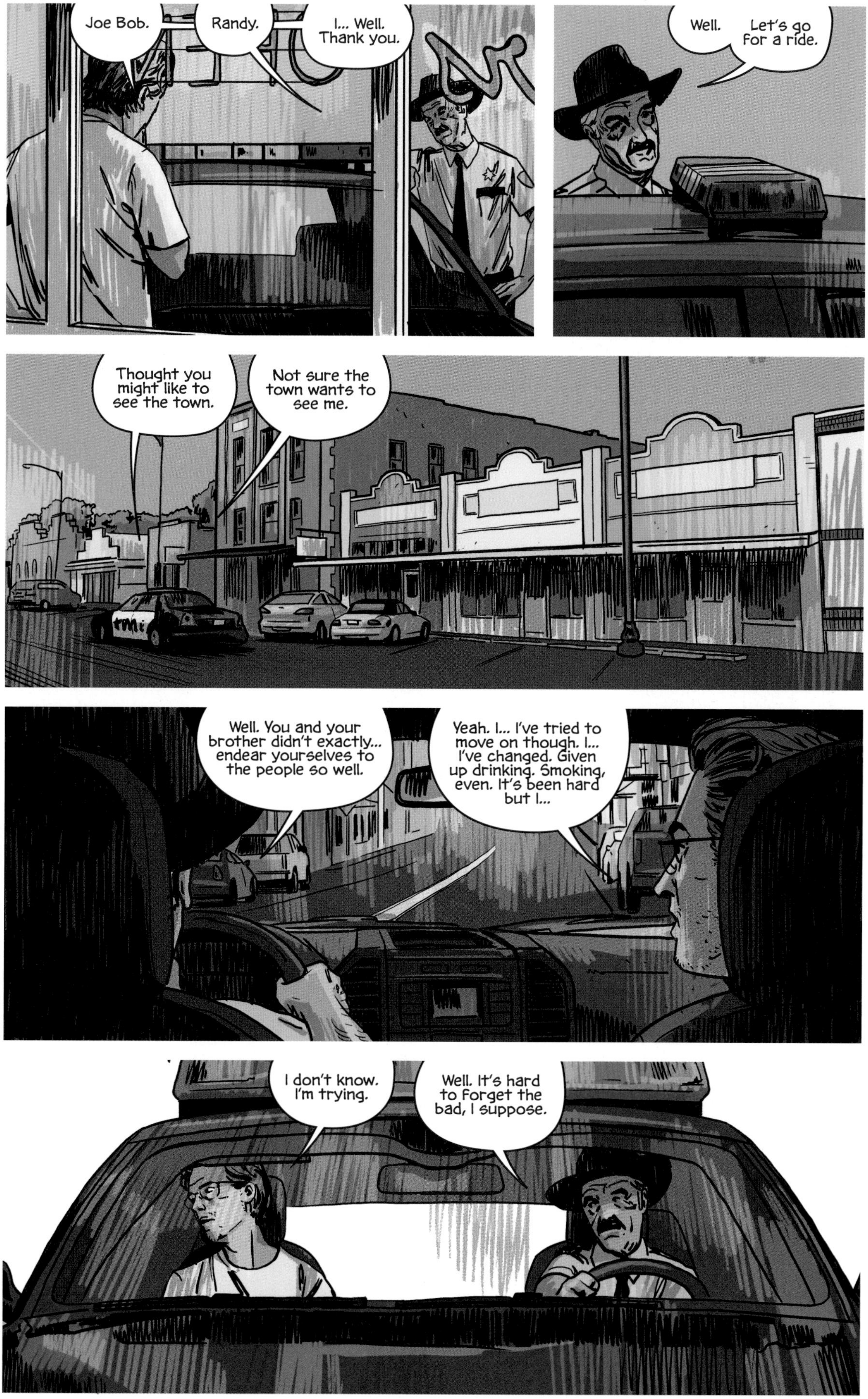

Joe Bob.
Randy.
I... Well. Thank you.
Well.
Let's go for a ride.
Thought you might like to see the town.
Not sure the town wants to see me.
Well. You and your brother didn't exactly... endear yourselves to the people so well.
Yeah. I... I've tried to move on though. I... I've changed. Given up drinking. Smoking, even. It's been hard but I...
I don't know. I'm trying.
Well. It's hard to forget the bad, I suppose.

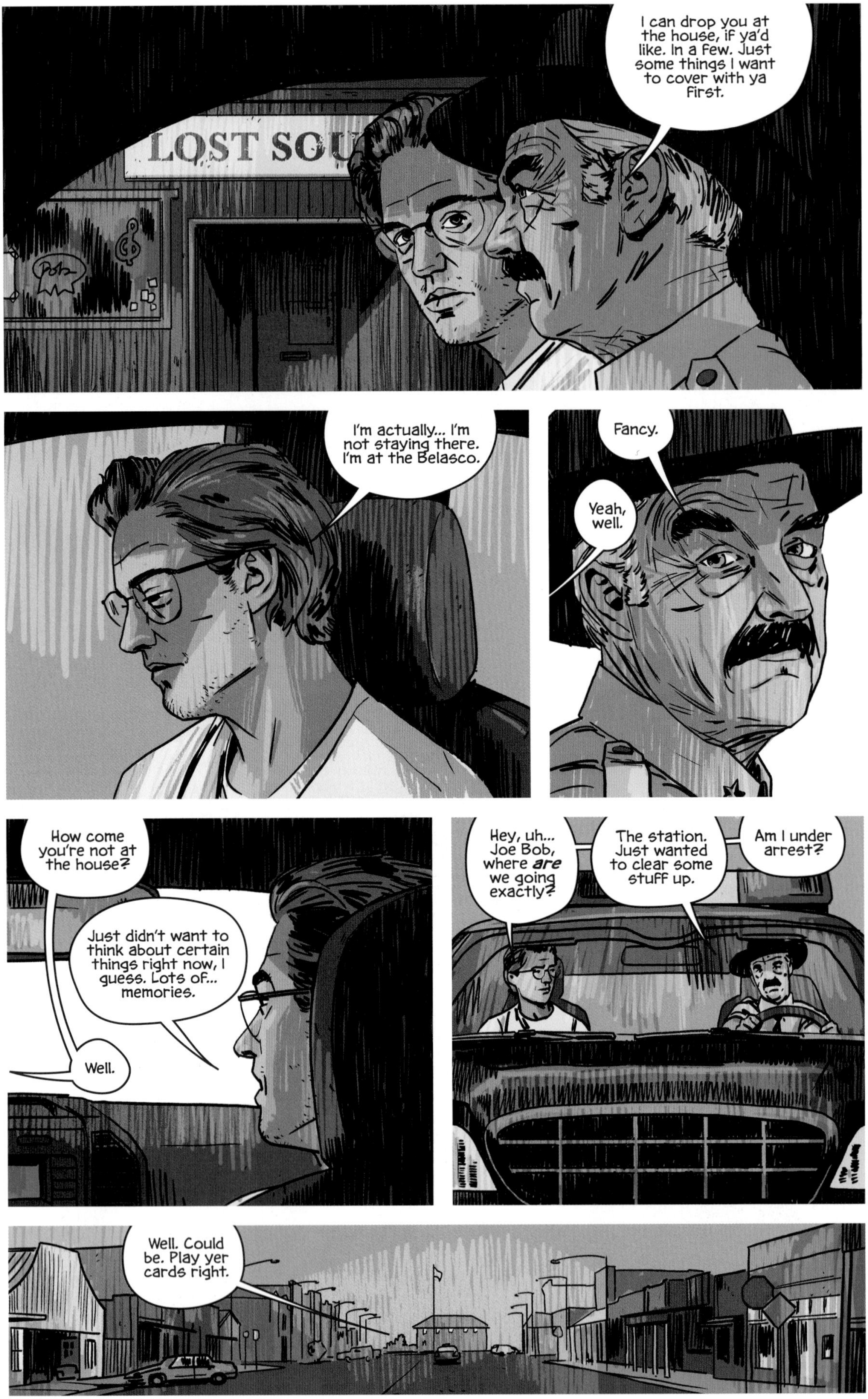
I can drop you at the house, if ya'd like. In a few. Just some things I want to cover with ya first.
LOST SOU
I'm actually... I'm not staying there. I'm at the Belasco.
Fancy.
Yeah, well.
How come you're not at the house?
Just didn't want to think about certain things right now, I guess. Lots of... memories.
Well.
Hey, uh... Joe Bob, where *are* we going exactly?
The station. Just wanted to clear some stuff up.
Am I under arrest?
Well. Could be. Play yer cards right.

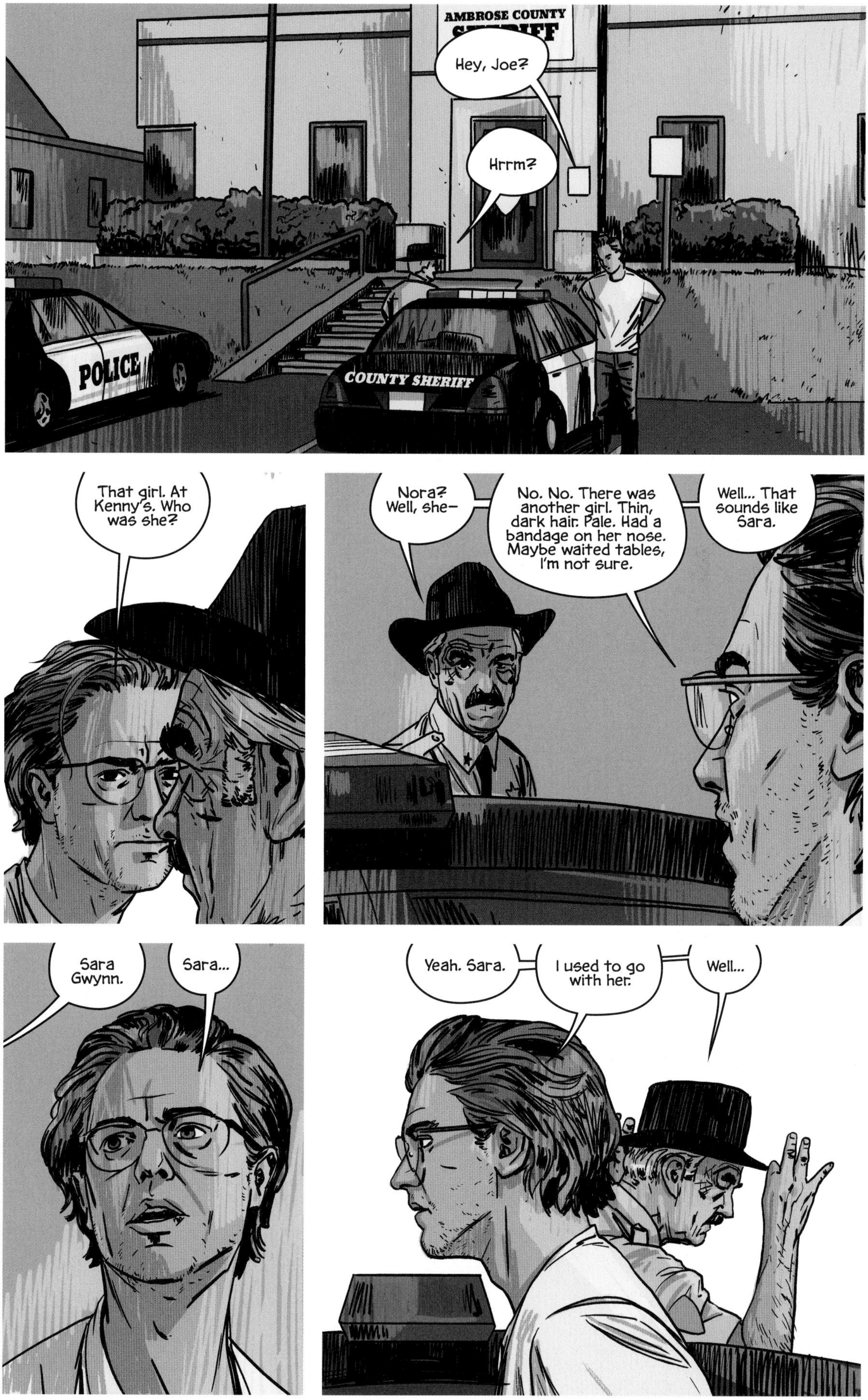
AMBROSE COUNTY SHERIFF
Hey, Joe?
Hrrm?
POLICE
COUNTY SHERIFF
That girl. At Kenny's. Who was she?
Nora? Well, she–
No. No. There was another girl. Thin, dark hair. Pale. Had a bandage on her nose. Maybe waited tables, I'm not sure.
Well... That sounds like Sara.
Sara Gwynn.
Sara...
Yeah. Sara.
I used to go with her.
Well...

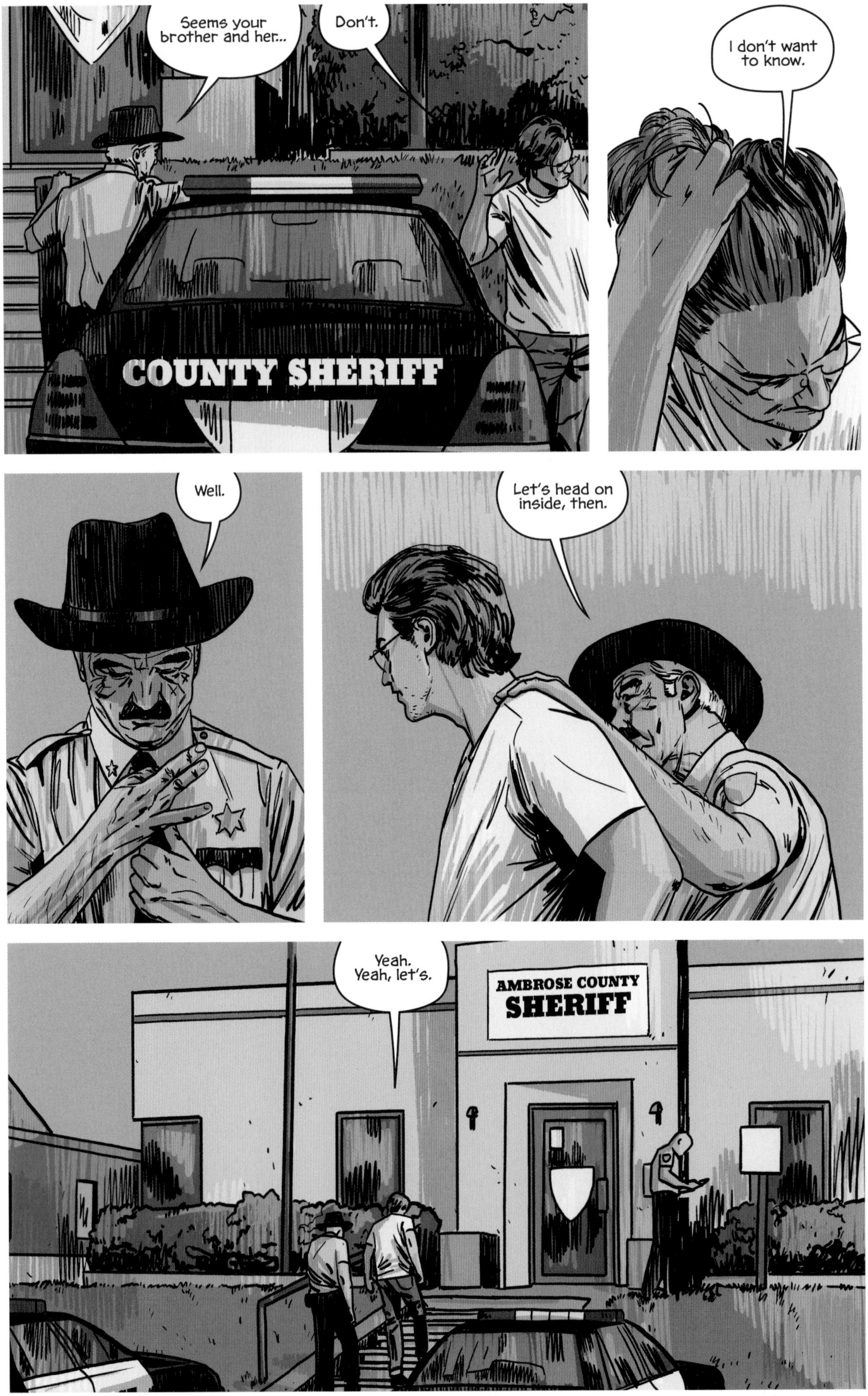
Seems your brother and her...
Don't.
COUNTY SHERIFF
I don't want to know.
Well.
Let's head on inside, then.
Yeah. Yeah, let's.
AMBROSE COUNTY SHERIFF

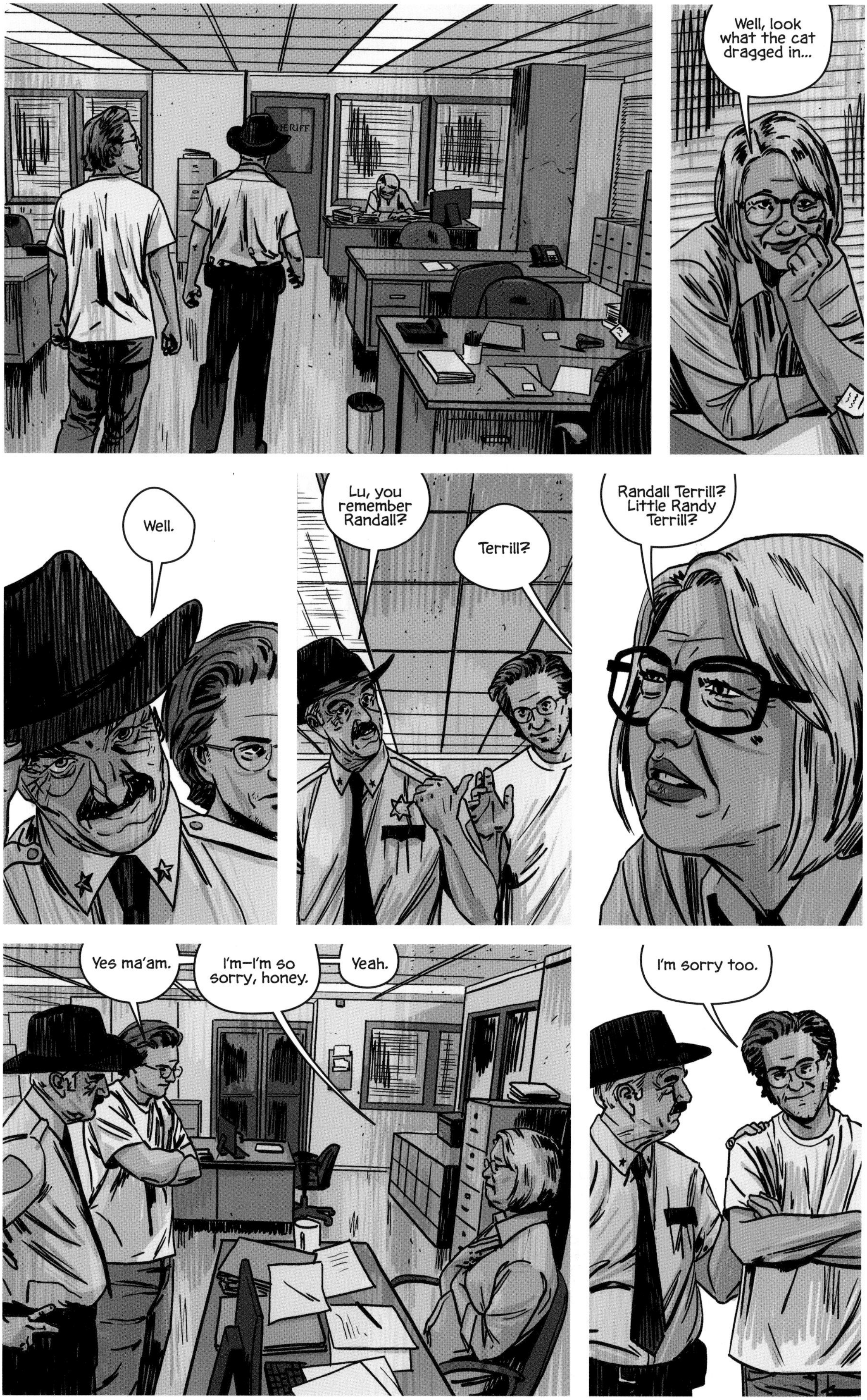
SHERIFF
Well, look what the cat dragged in...
Well.
Lu, you remember Randall?
Terrill?
Randall Terrill? Little Randy Terrill?
Yes ma'am.
I'm—I'm so sorry, honey.
Yeah.
I'm sorry too.

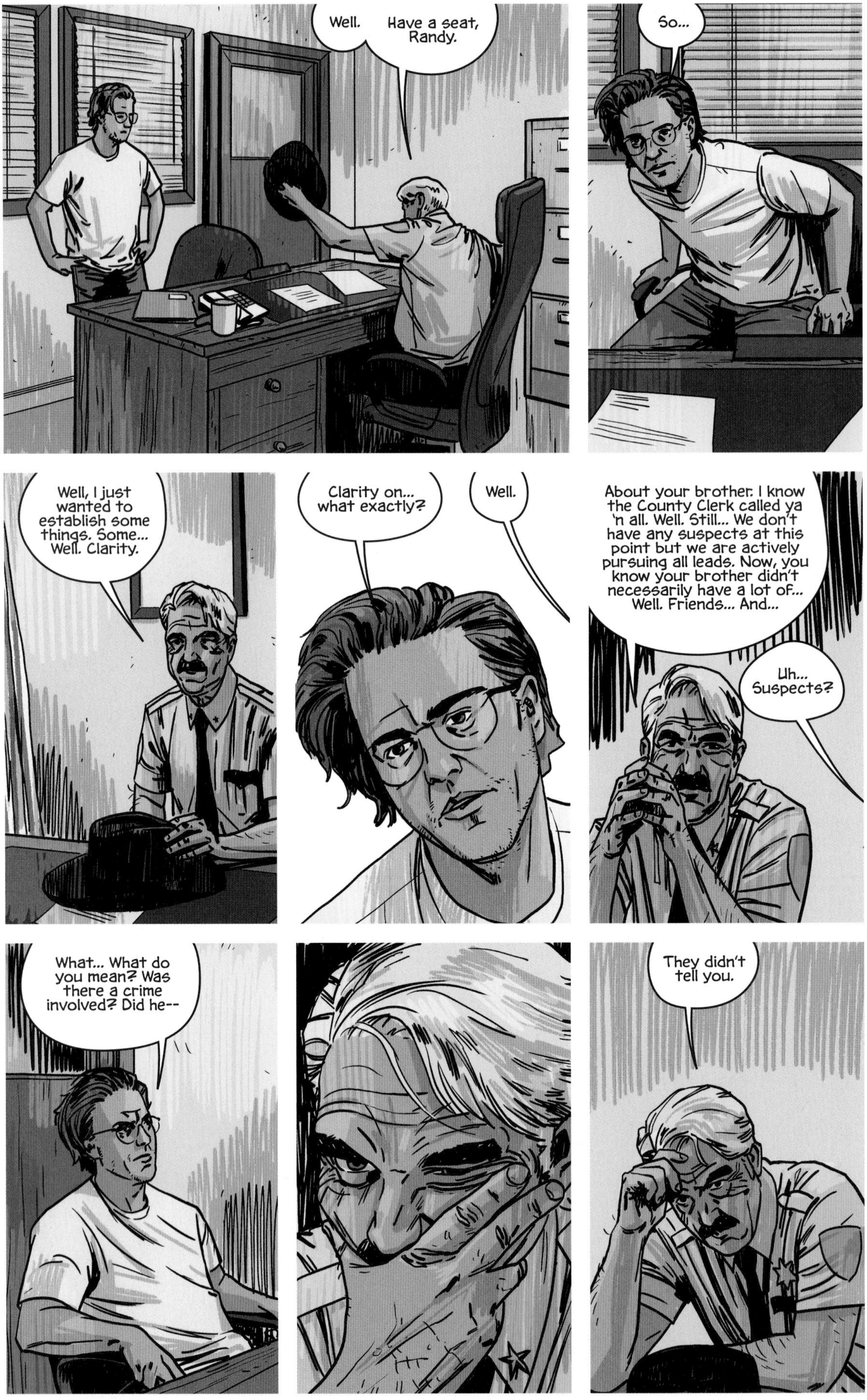
Well.
Have a seat, Randy.
So...
Well, I just wanted to establish some things. Some... Well. Clarity.
Clarity on... what exactly?
Well.
About your brother. I know the County Clerk called ya 'n all. Well. Still... We don't have any suspects at this point but we are actively pursuing all leads. Now, you know your brother didn't necessarily have a lot of... Well. Friends... And...
Uh... Suspects?
What... What do you mean? Was there a crime involved? Did he--
They didn't tell you.

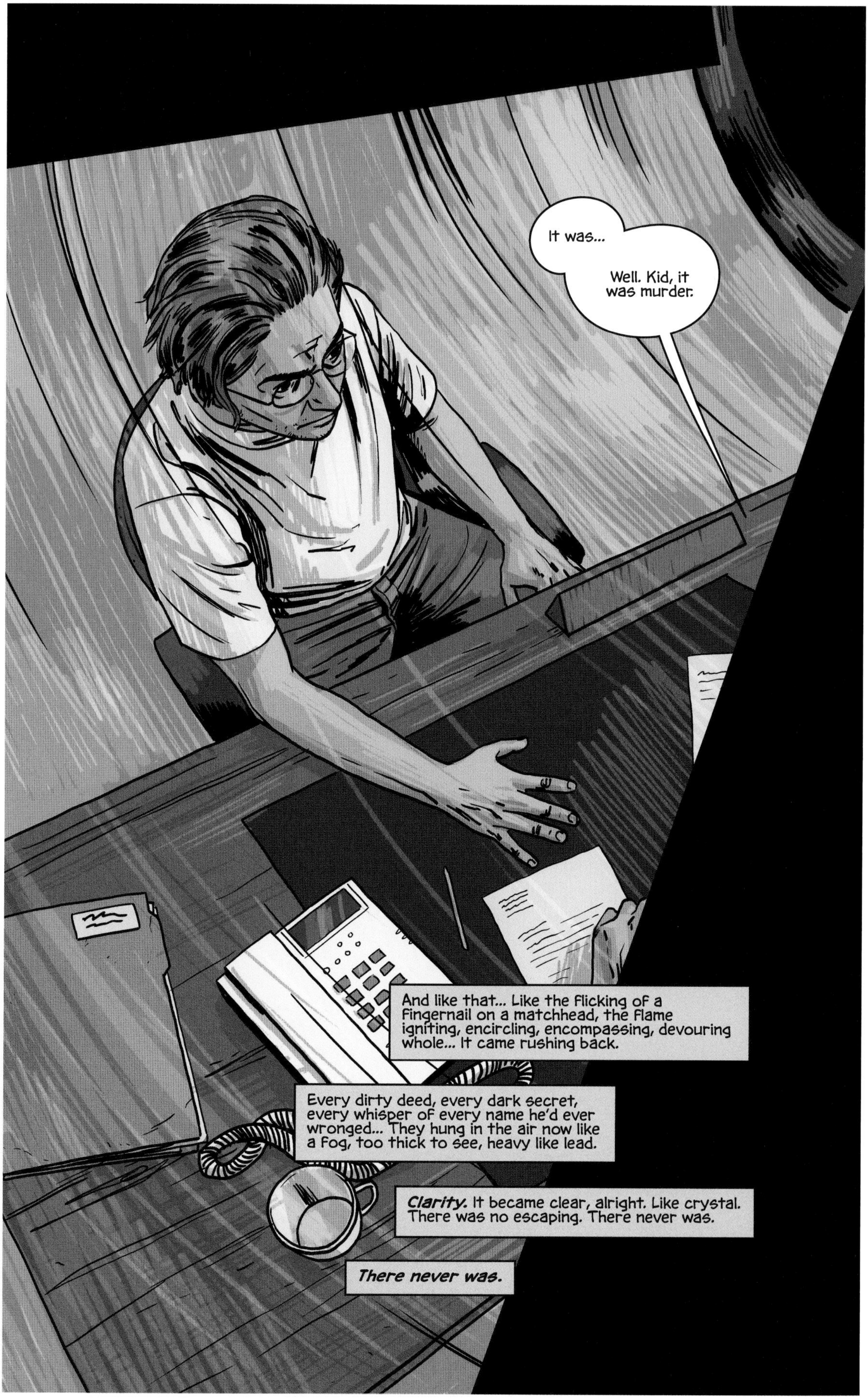
It was...
Well. Kid, it was murder.
And like that... Like the flicking of a fingernail on a matchhead, the flame igniting, encircling, encompassing, devouring whole... It came rushing back.
Every dirty deed, every dark secret, every whisper of every name he'd ever wronged... They hung in the air now like a fog, too thick to see, heavy like lead.
Clarity. It became clear, alright. Like crystal. There was no escaping. There never was.
There never was.

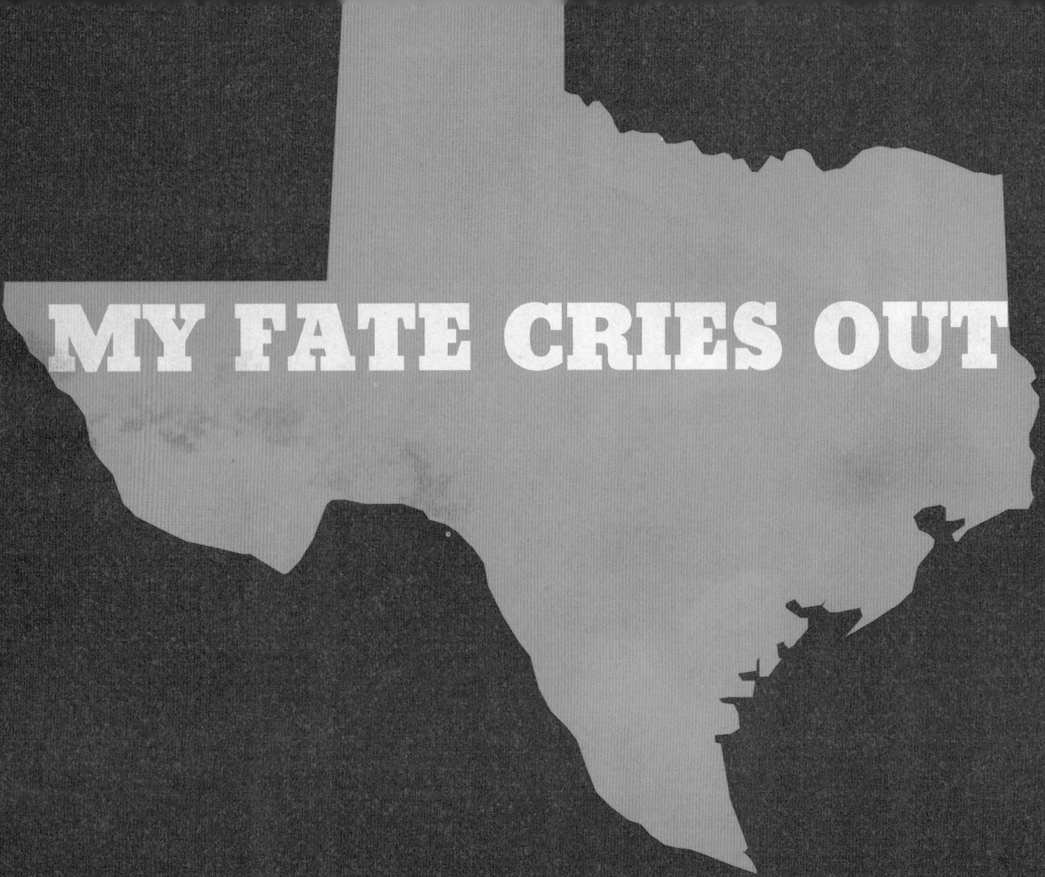
MY FATE CRIES OUT

A Brother's Conscience

Part Two

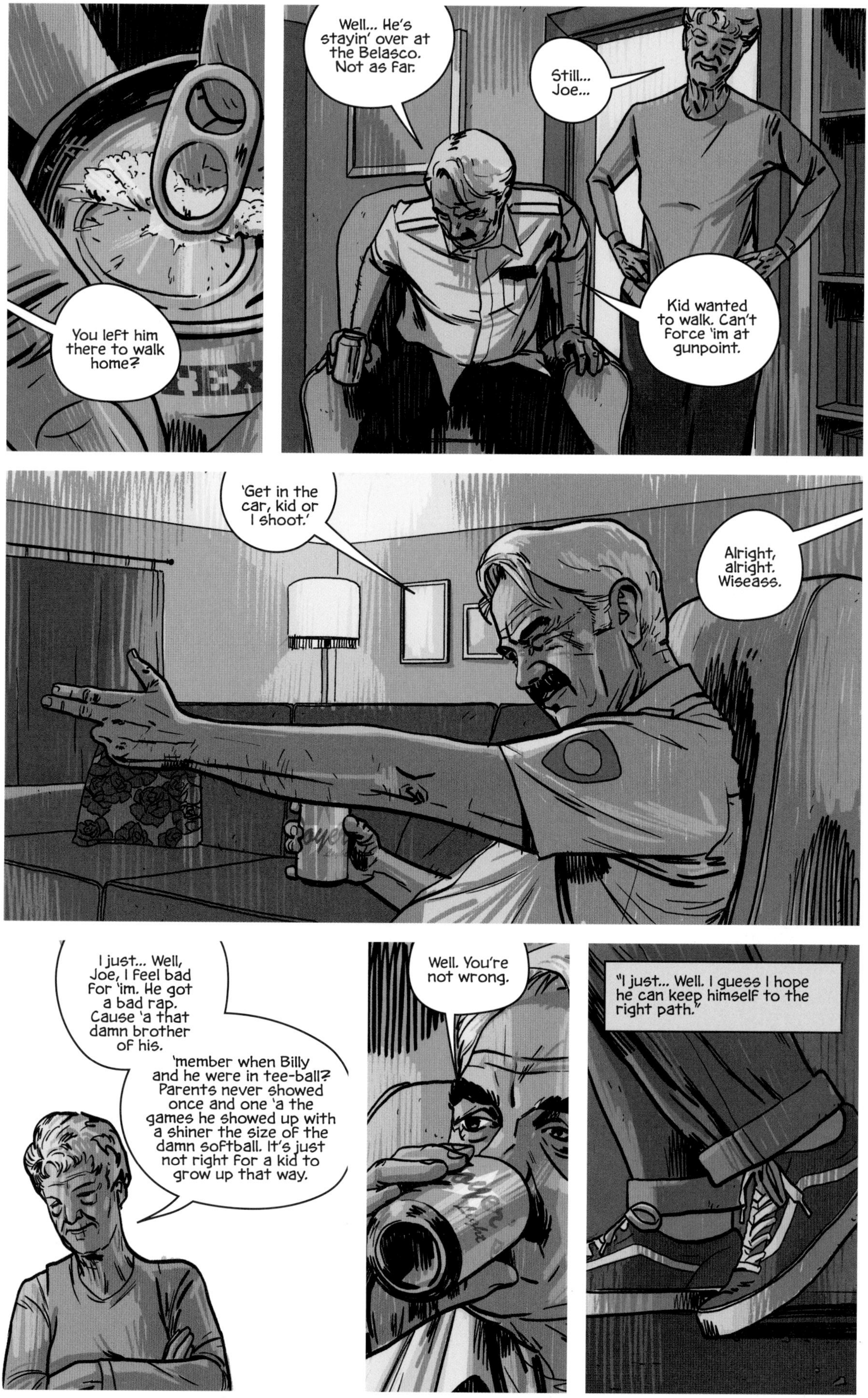
You left him there to walk home?
Well... He's stayin' over at the Belasco. Not as far.
Still... Joe...
Kid wanted to walk. Can't force 'im at gunpoint.
'Get in the car, kid or I shoot.'
Alright, alright. Wiseass.
I just... Well, Joe, I feel bad for 'im. He got a bad rap. Cause 'a that damn brother of his.
'member when Billy and he were in tee-ball? Parents never showed once and one 'a the games he showed up with a shiner the size of the damn softball. It's just not right for a kid to grow up that way.
Well. You're not wrong.
"I just... Well. I guess I hope he can keep himself to the right path."

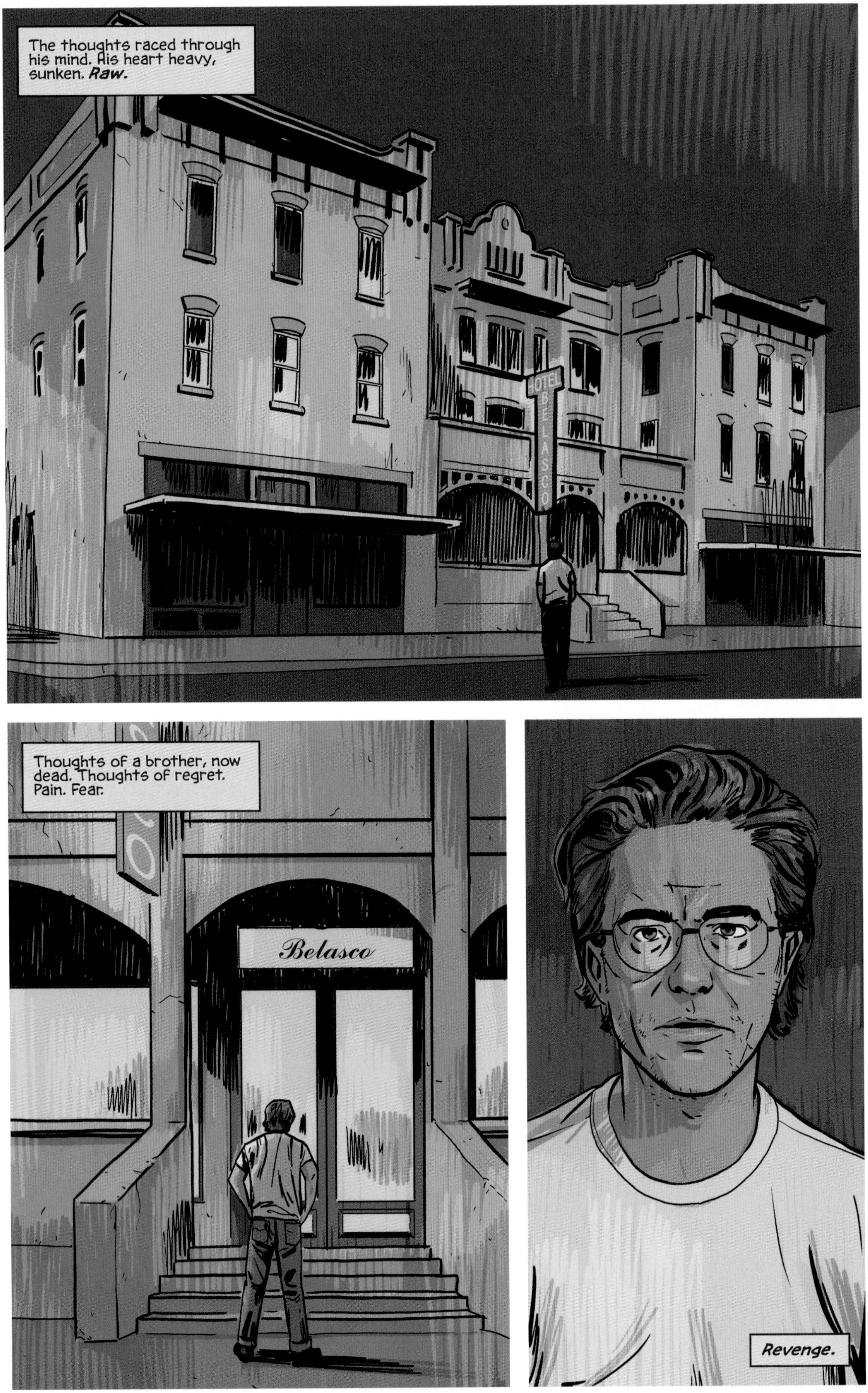
The thoughts raced through his mind. His heart heavy, sunken. ***Raw.***
HOTEL BELASCO
Thoughts of a brother, now dead. Thoughts of regret. Pain. Fear.
Belasco
Revenge.

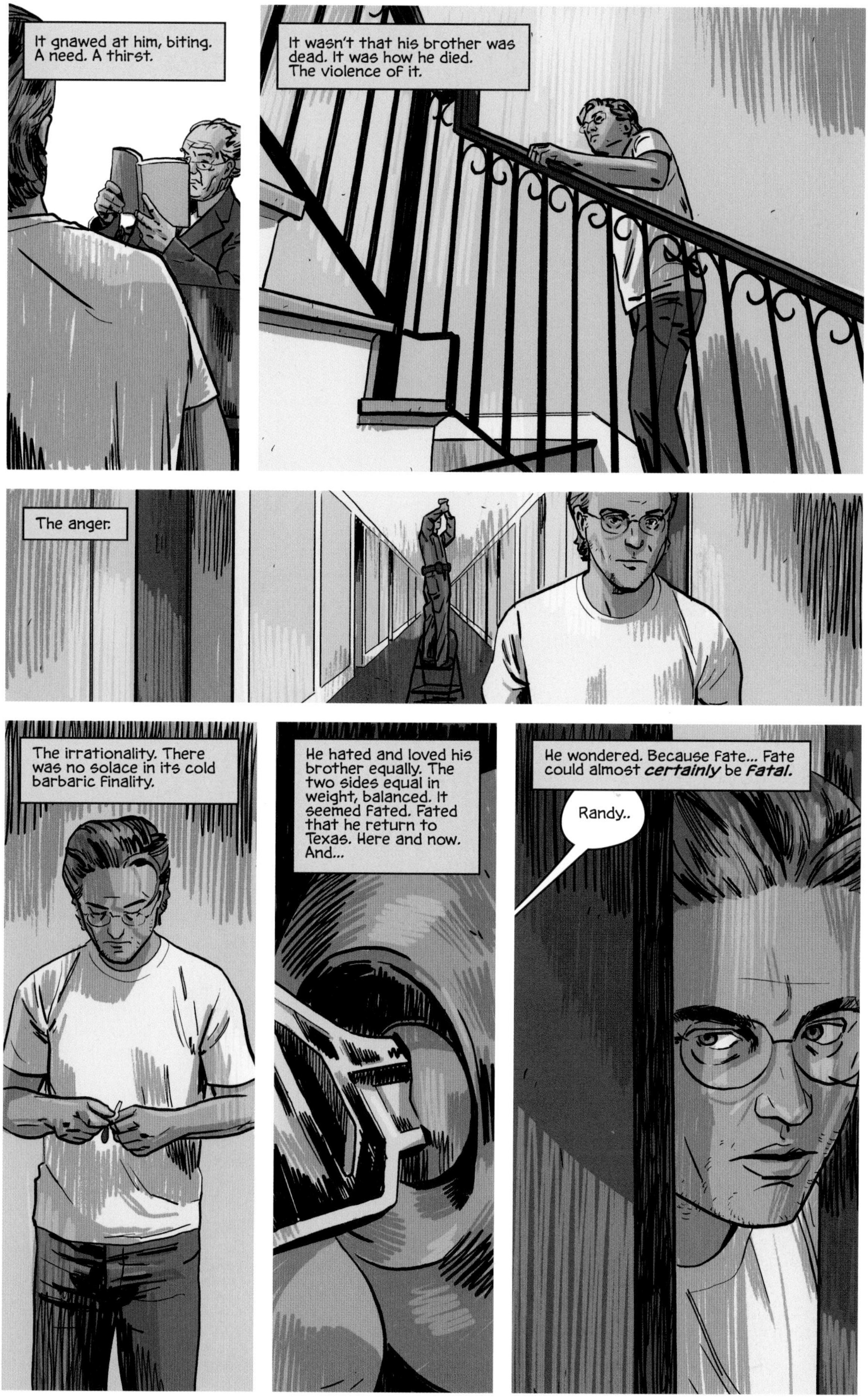
It gnawed at him, biting. A need. A thirst.
It wasn't that his brother was dead. It was how he died. The violence of it.
The anger.
The irrationality. There was no solace in its cold barbaric finality.
He hated and loved his brother equally. The two sides equal in weight, balanced. It seemed fated. Fated that he return to Texas. Here and now. And...
He wondered. Because fate... Fate could almost *certainly* be *fatal.*
Randy..

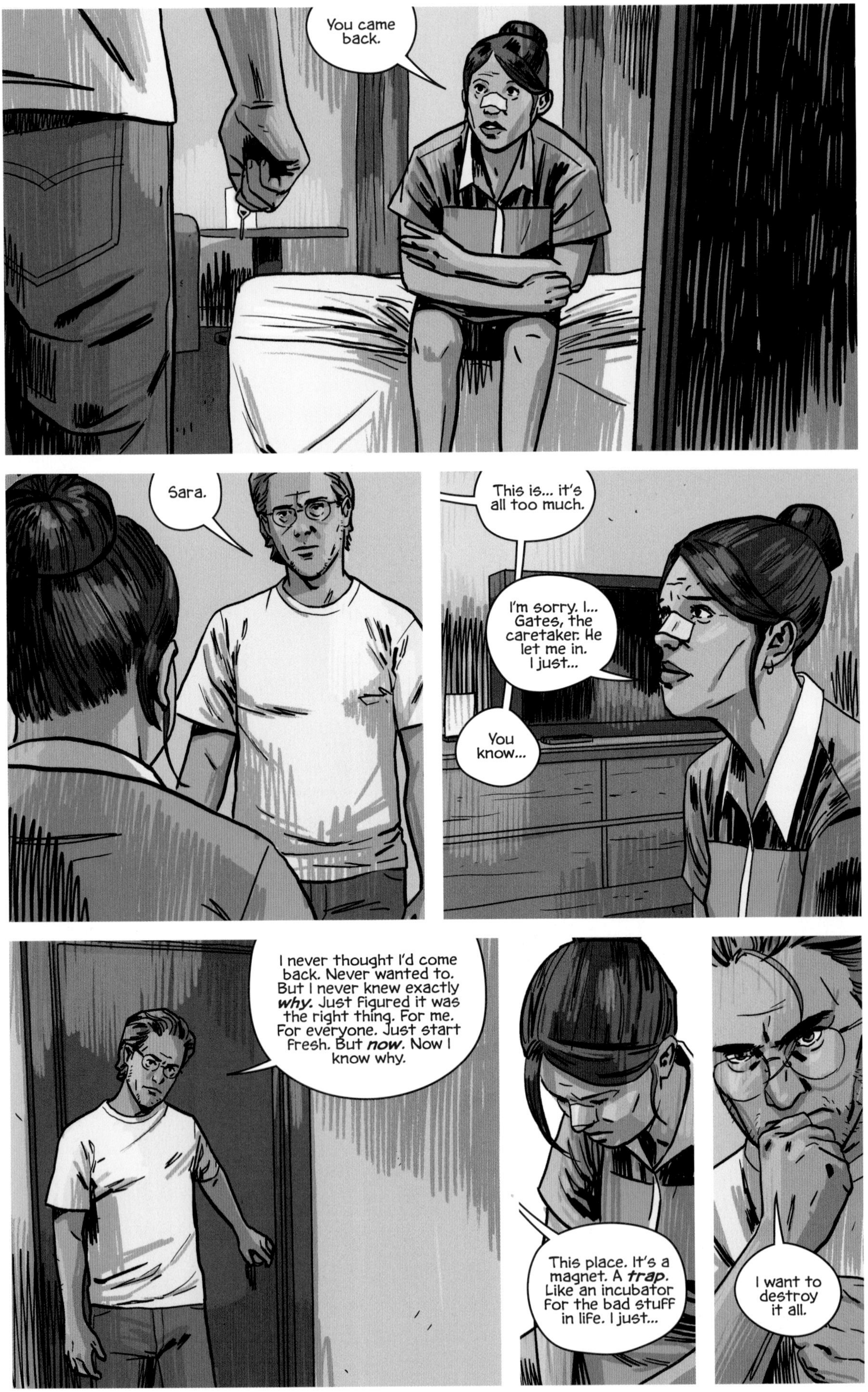
You came back.
Sara.
This is... it's all too much.
I'm sorry. I... Gates, the caretaker. He let me in. I just...
You know...
I never thought I'd come back. Never wanted to. But I never knew exactly *why*. Just figured it was the right thing. For me. For everyone. Just start fresh. But *now*. Now I know why.
This place. It's a magnet. A *trap*. Like an incubator for the bad stuff in life. I just...
I want to destroy it all.

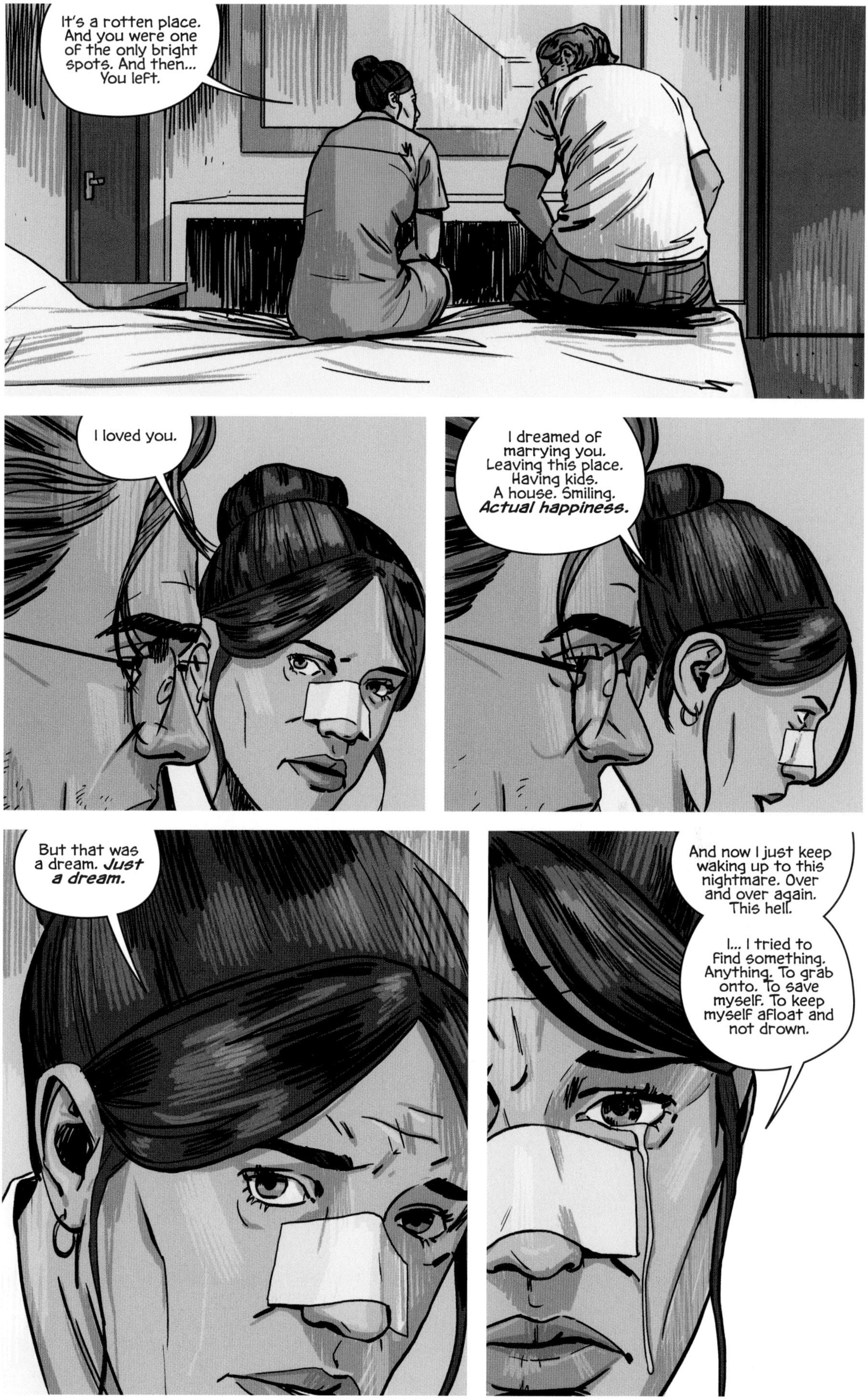
It's a rotten place. And you were one of the only bright spots. And then... You left.
I loved you.
I dreamed of marrying you. Leaving this place. Having kids. A house. Smiling. *Actual happiness.*
But that was a dream. *Just a dream.*
And now I just keep waking up to this nightmare. Over and over again. This hell.
I... I tried to find something. Anything. To grab onto. To save myself. To keep myself afloat and not drown.

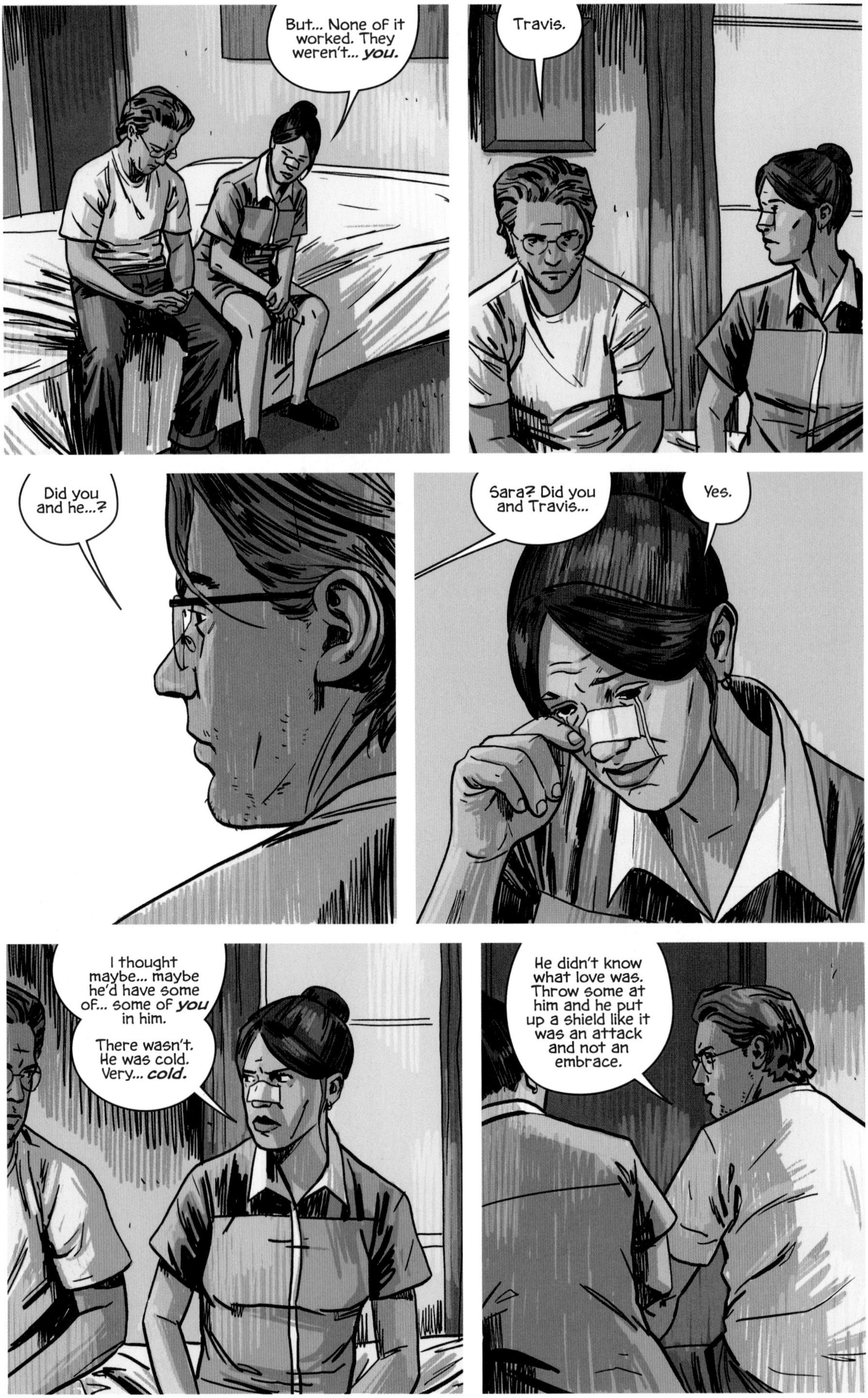
But... None of it worked. They weren't... *you.*
Travis.
Did you and he...?
Sara? Did you and Travis...
Yes.
I thought maybe... maybe he'd have some of... some of *you* in him.
There wasn't. He was cold. Very... *cold.*
He didn't know what love was. Throw some at him and he put up a shield like it was an attack and not an embrace.

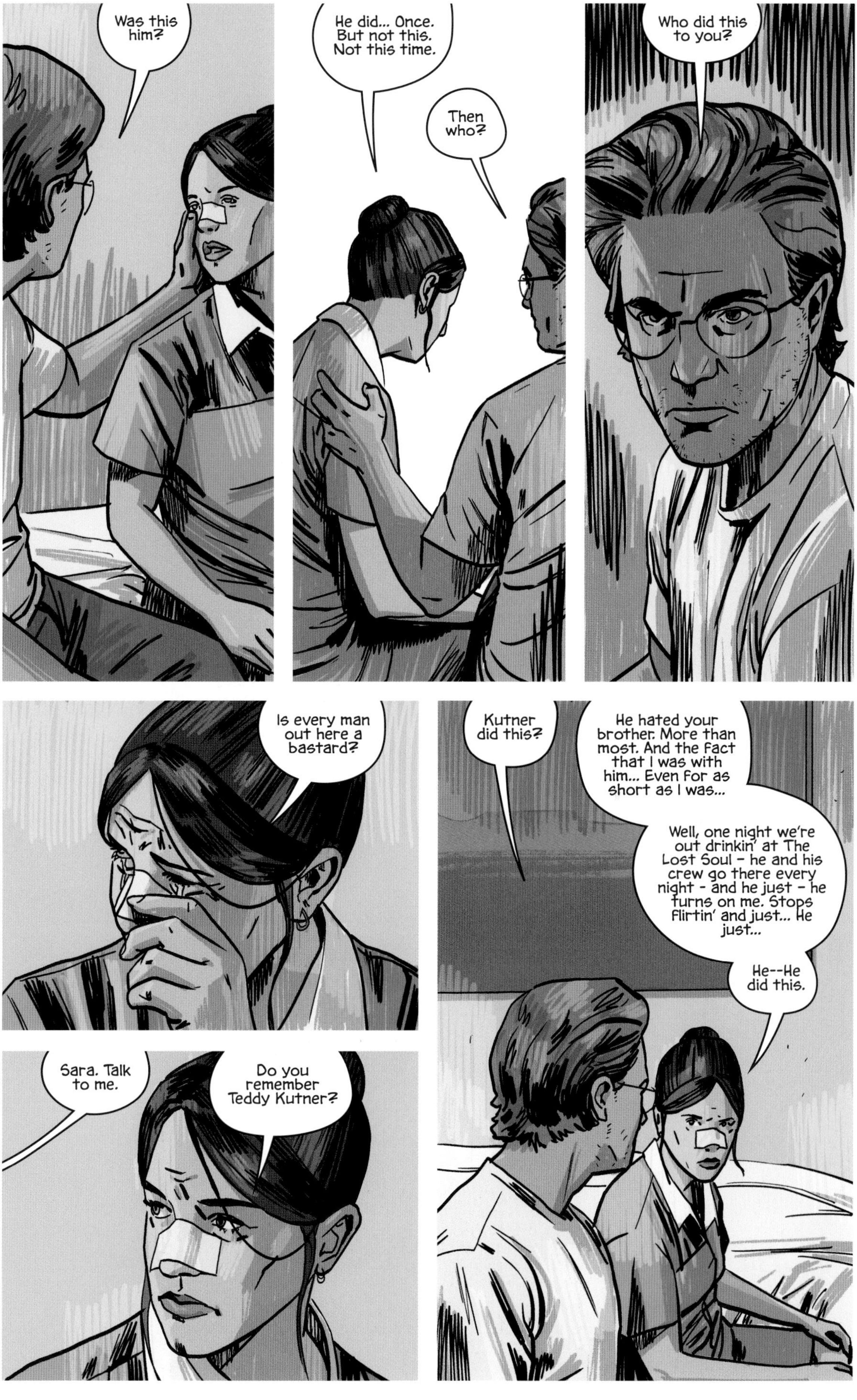
Was this him?
He did... Once. But not this. Not this time.
Then who?
Who did this to you?
Is every man out here a bastard?
Sara. Talk to me.
Do you remember Teddy Kutner?
Kutner did this?
He hated your brother. More than most. And the fact that I was with him... Even for as short as I was...
Well, one night we're out drinkin' at The Lost Soul - he and his crew go there every night - and he just - he turns on me. Stops flirtin' and just... He just...
He--He did this.

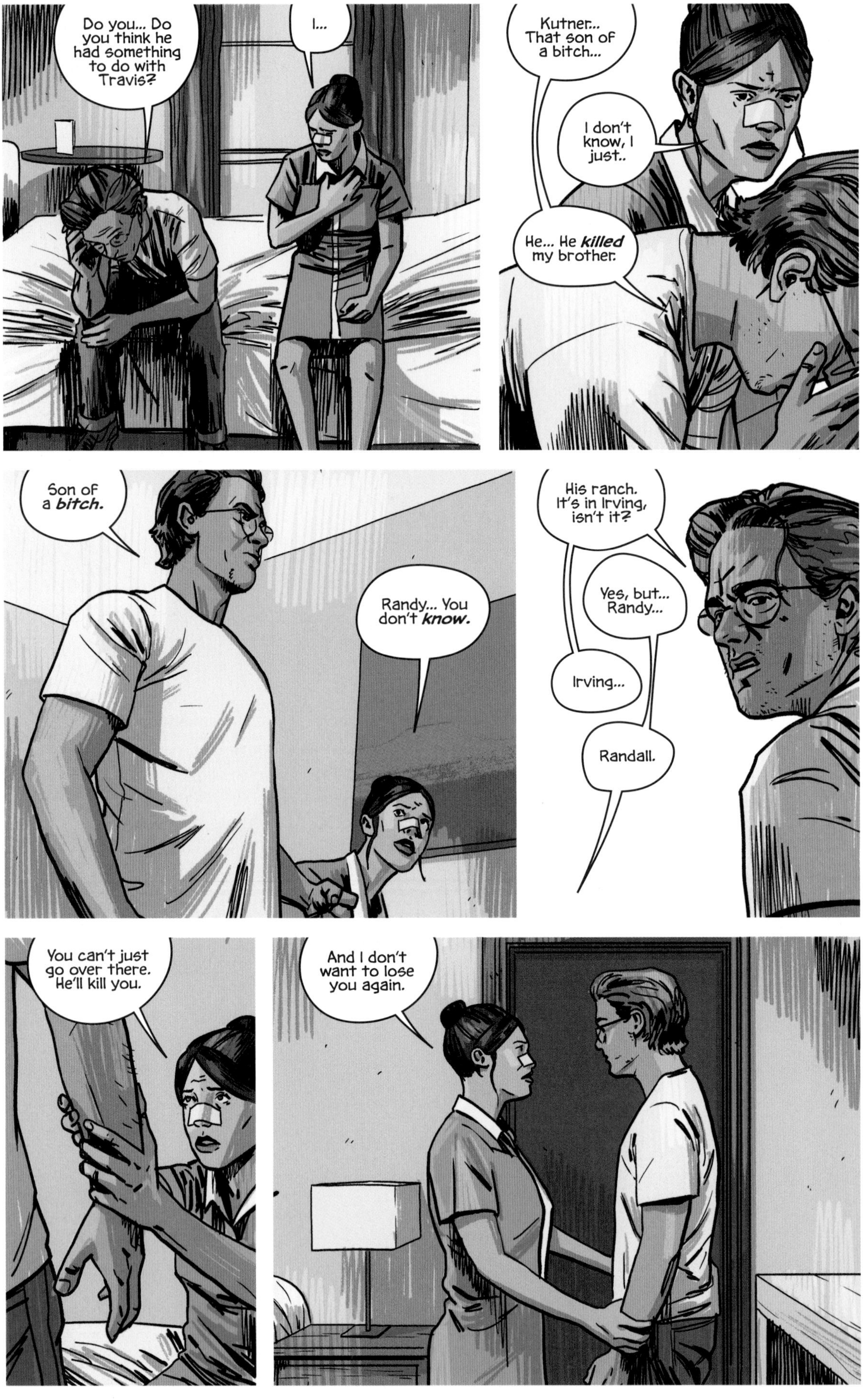
Do you... Do you think he had something to do with Travis?
I...
Kutner.. That son of a bitch...
I don't know, I just..
He... He *killed* my brother.
Son of a *bitch*.
Randy... You don't *know*.
His ranch. It's in Irving, isn't it?
Yes, but... Randy...
Irving...
Randall.
You can't just go over there. He'll kill you.
And I don't want to lose you again.

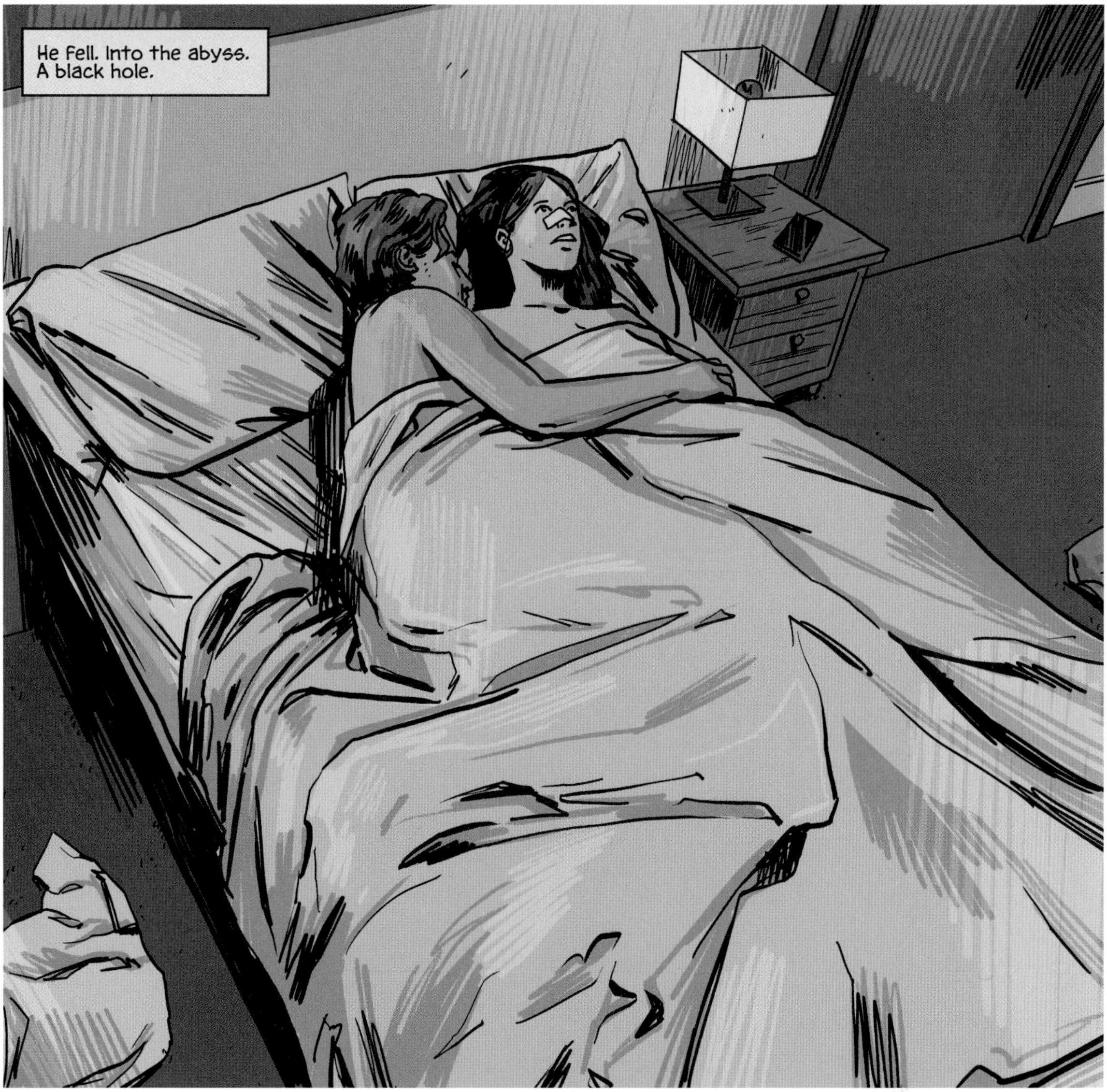
He fell. Into the abyss.
A black hole.

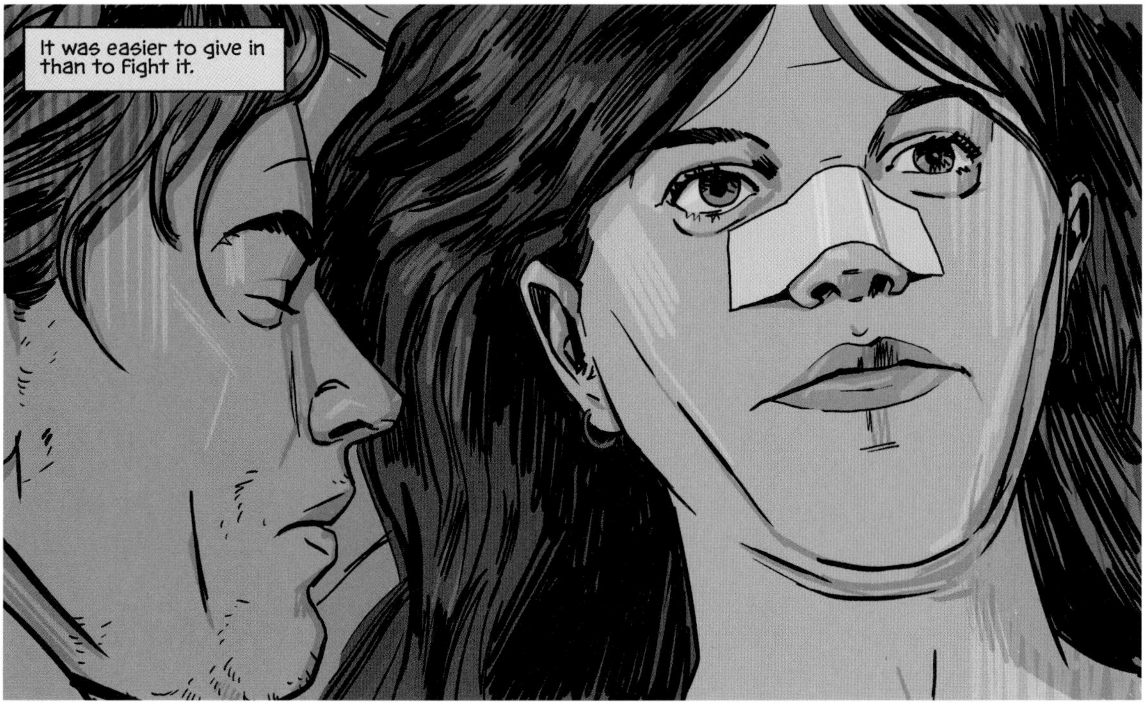
It was easier to give in
than to fight it.

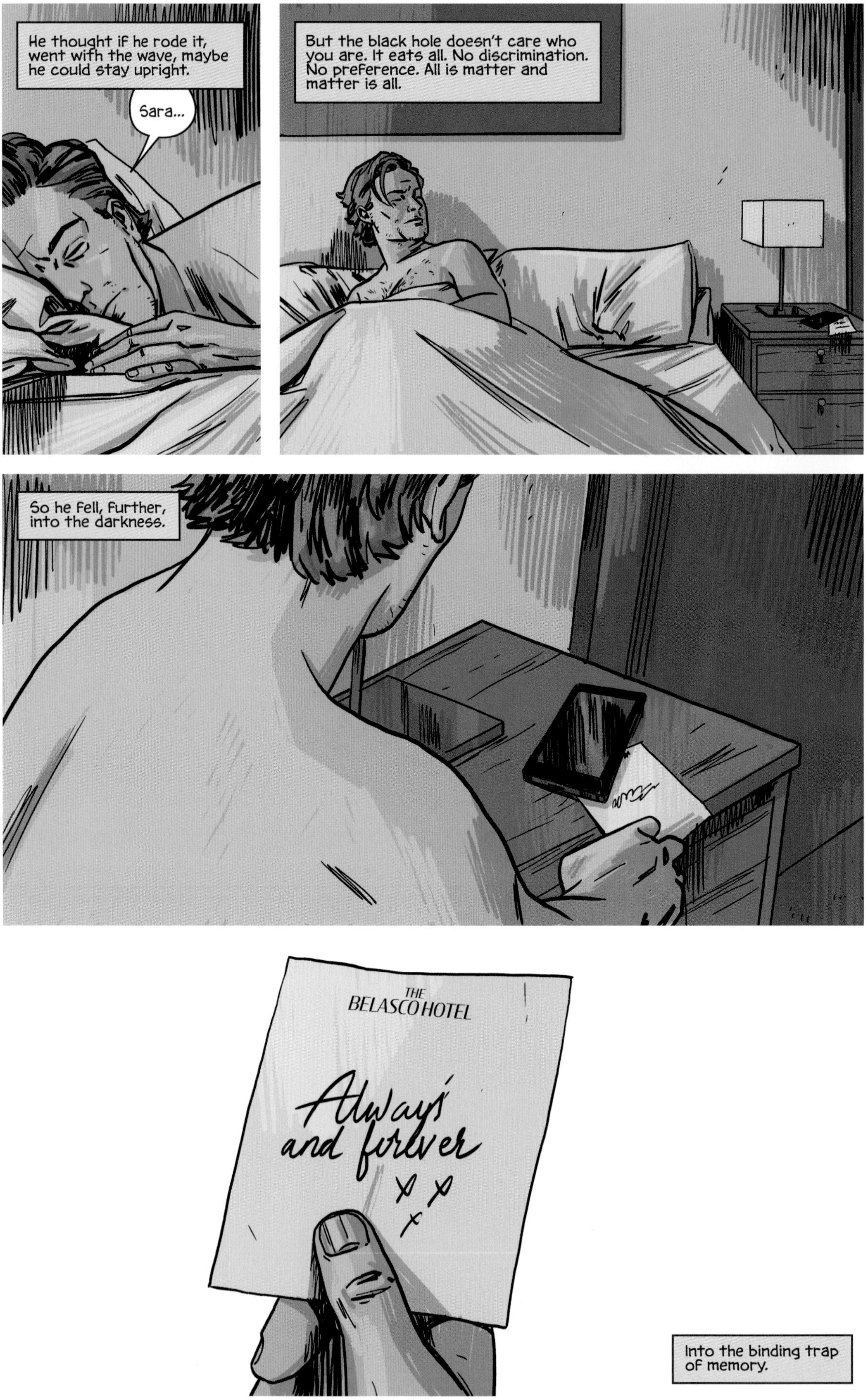
He thought if he rode it, went with the wave, maybe he could stay upright.
Sara...
But the black hole doesn't care who you are. It eats all. No discrimination. No preference. All is matter and matter is all.
So he fell, further, into the darkness.
THE BELASCO HOTEL
Always and forever
Into the binding trap of memory.

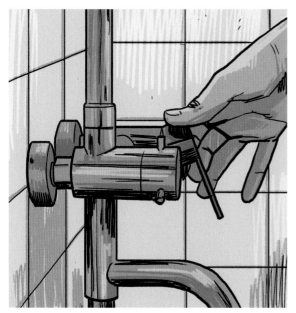

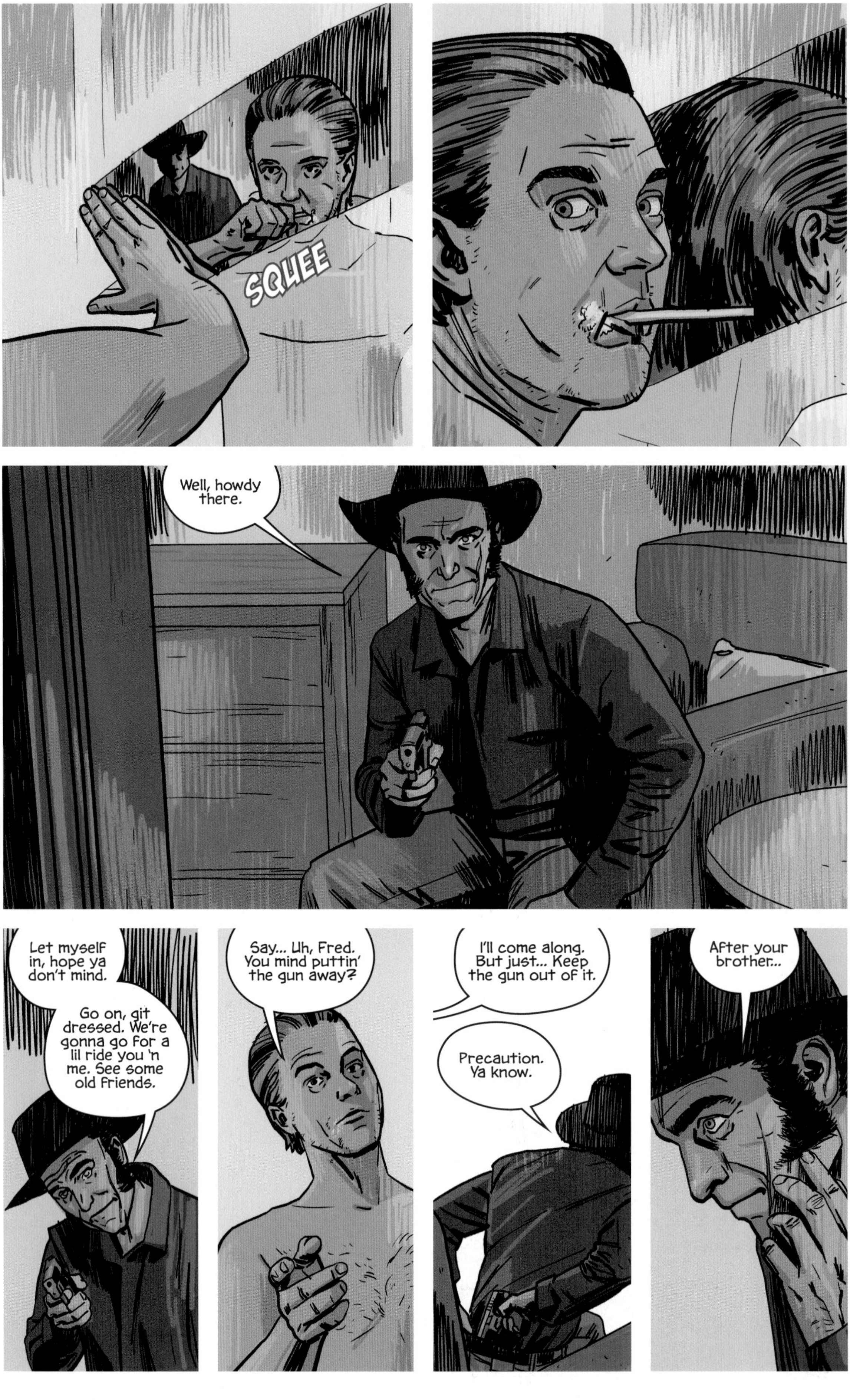
SQUEE
Well, howdy there.
Let myself in, hope ya don't mind.
Go on, git dressed. We're gonna go for a lil ride you 'n me. See some old friends.
Say... Uh, Fred. You mind puttin' the gun away?
I'll come along. But just... Keep the gun out of it.
Precaution. Ya know.
After your brother...

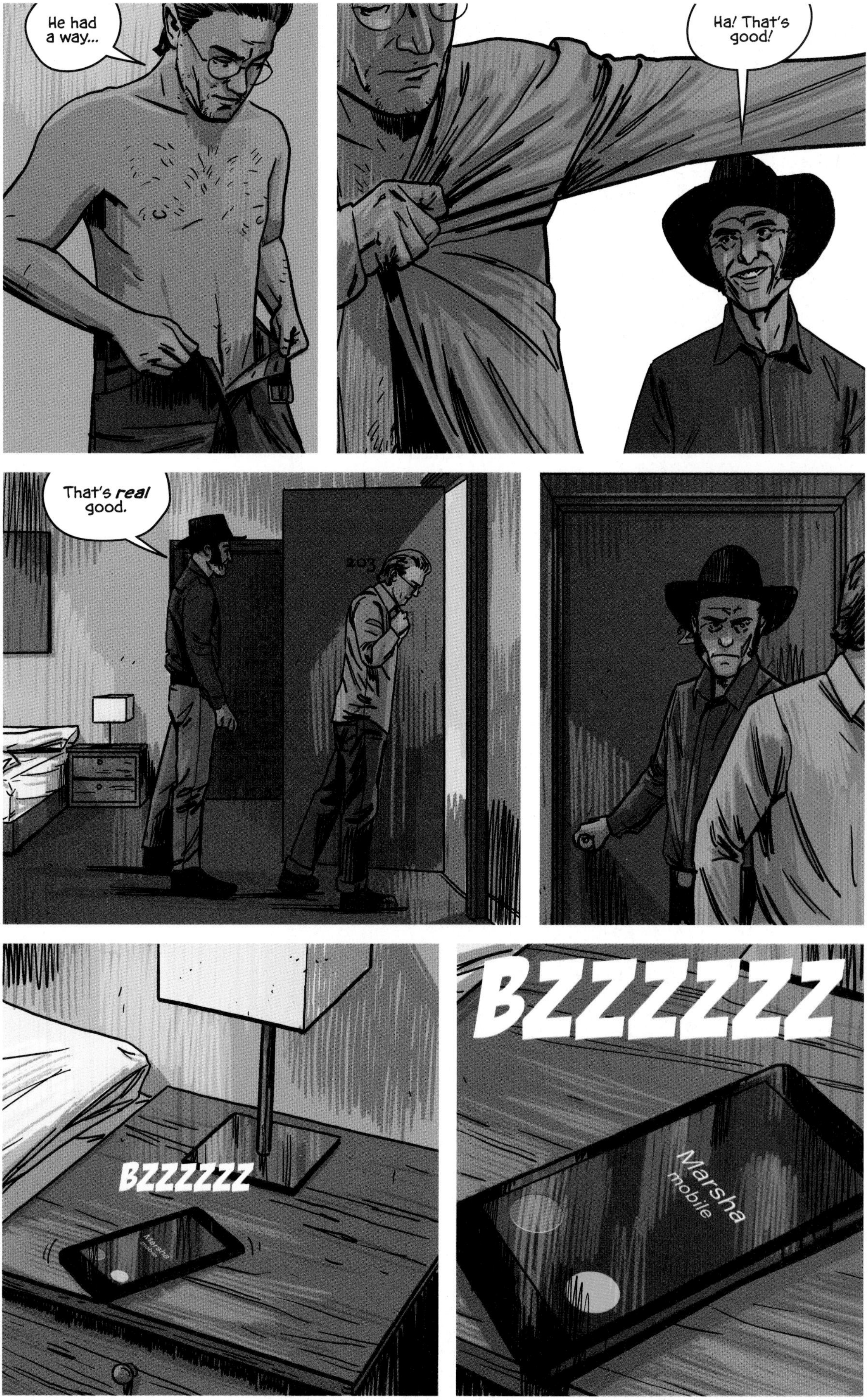
He had a way...
Ha! That's good!
That's *real* good.
203
BZZZZZZ
Marsha
mobile
BZZZZZZZ
Marsha
mobile

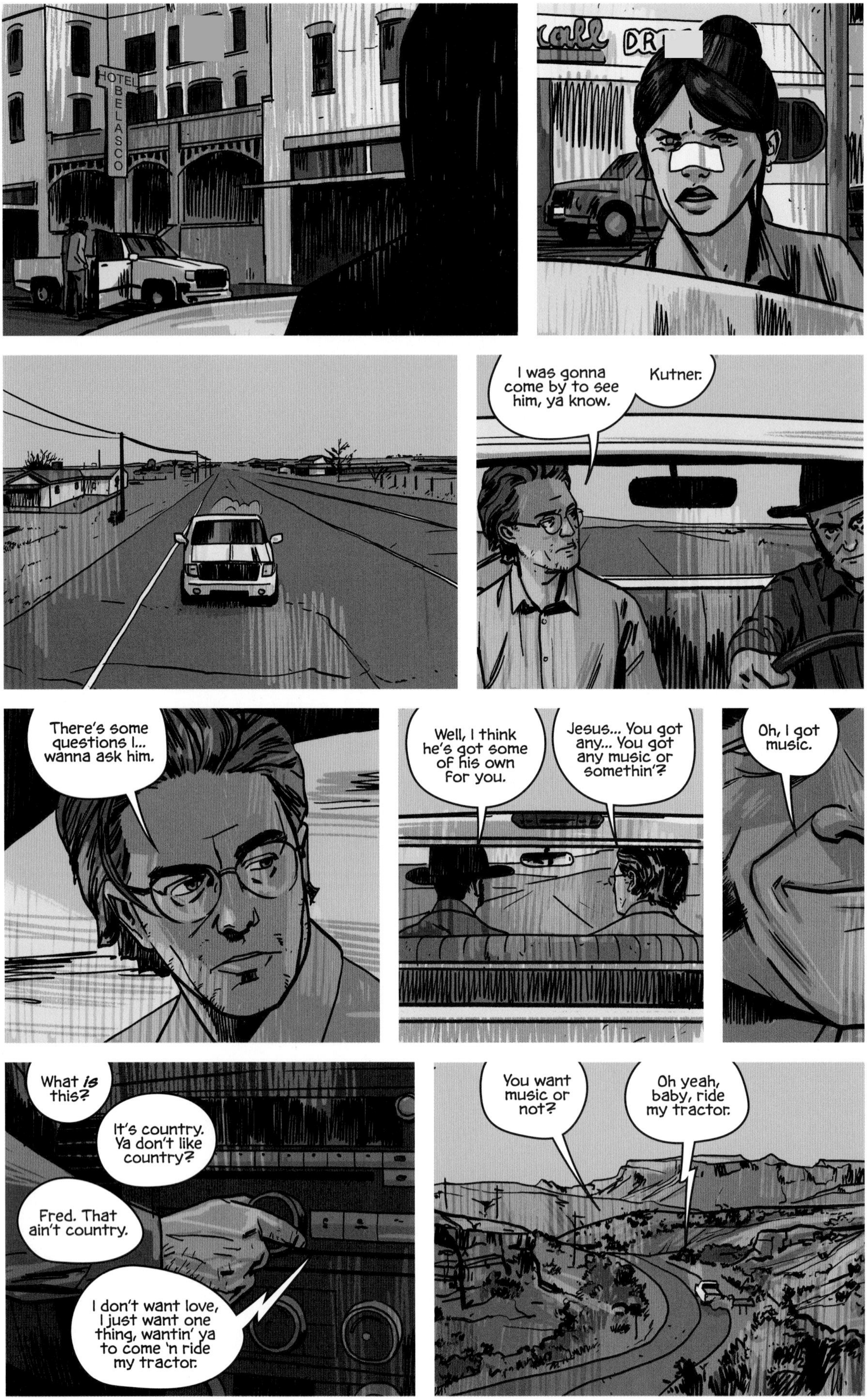
HOTEL BELASCO
Kutner.
I was gonna come by to see him, ya know.
There's some questions I... wanna ask him.
Well, I think he's got some of his own for you.
Jesus... You got any... You got any music or somethin'?
Oh, I got music.
What *is* this?
It's country. Ya don't like country?
Fred. That ain't country.
I don't want love, I just want one thing, wantin' ya to come 'n ride my tractor.
You want music or not?
Oh yeah, baby, ride my tractor.

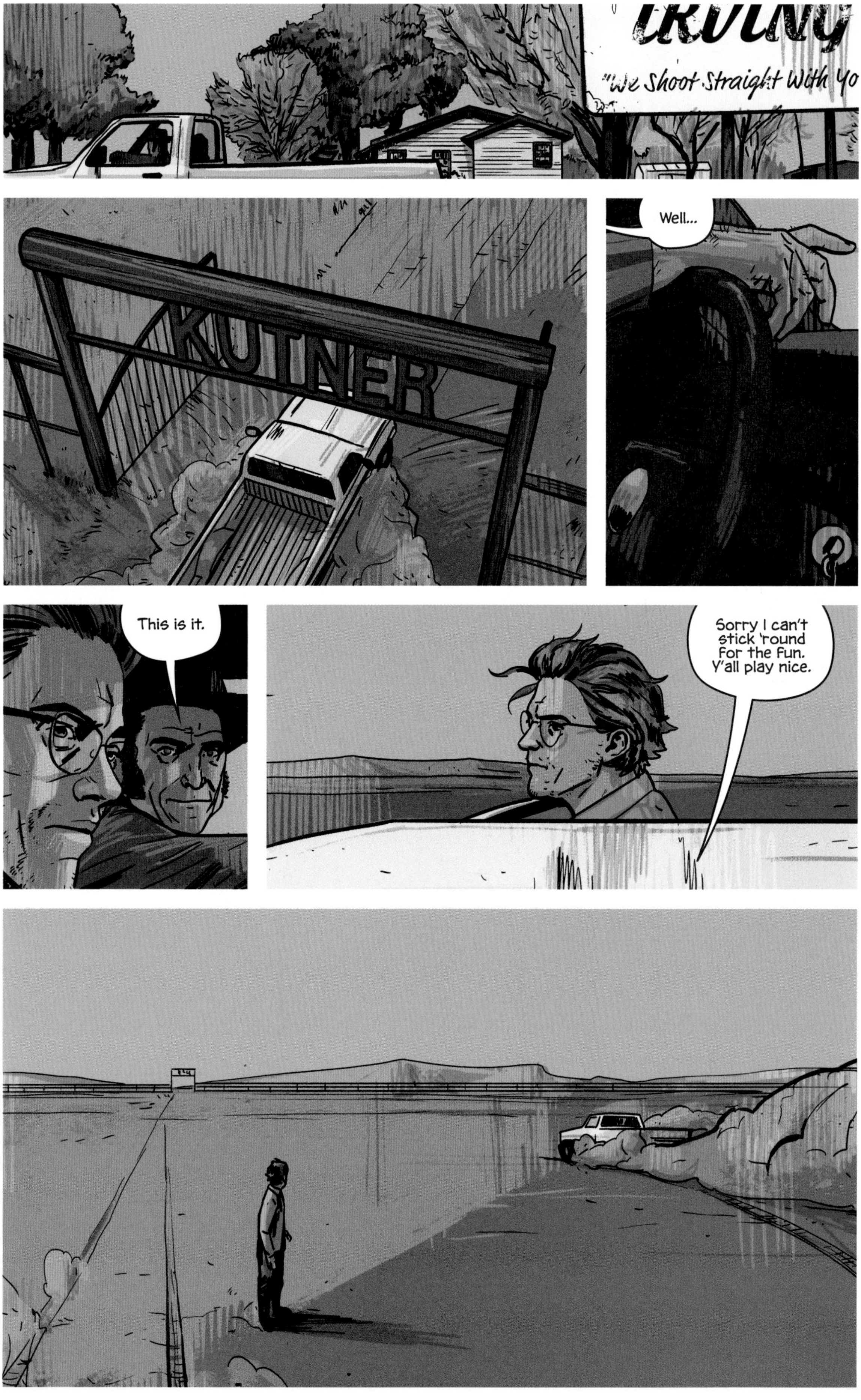
"We Shoot Straight With Yo
KUTNER
Well...
This is it.
Sorry I can't stick 'round for the fun. Y'all play nice.

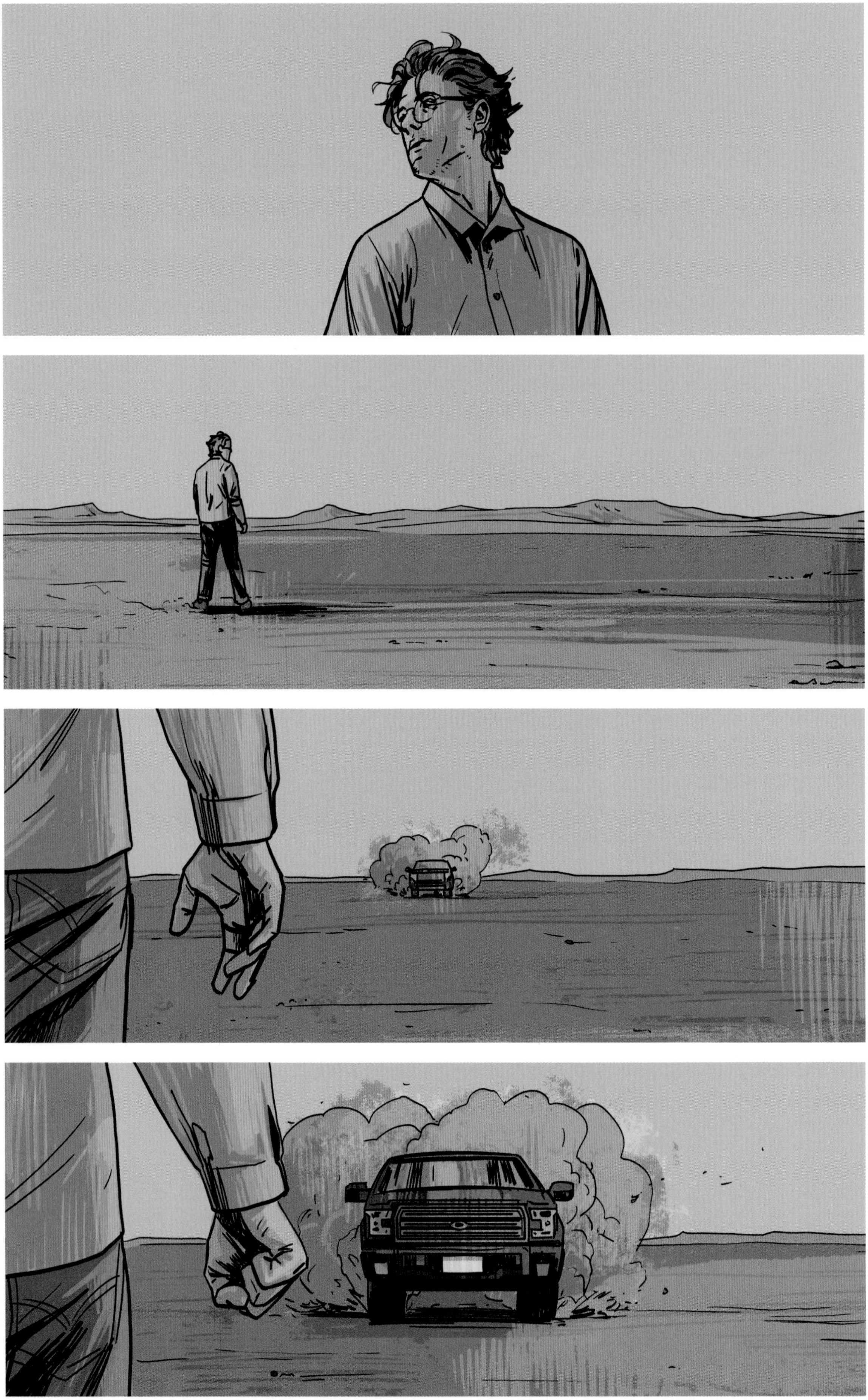

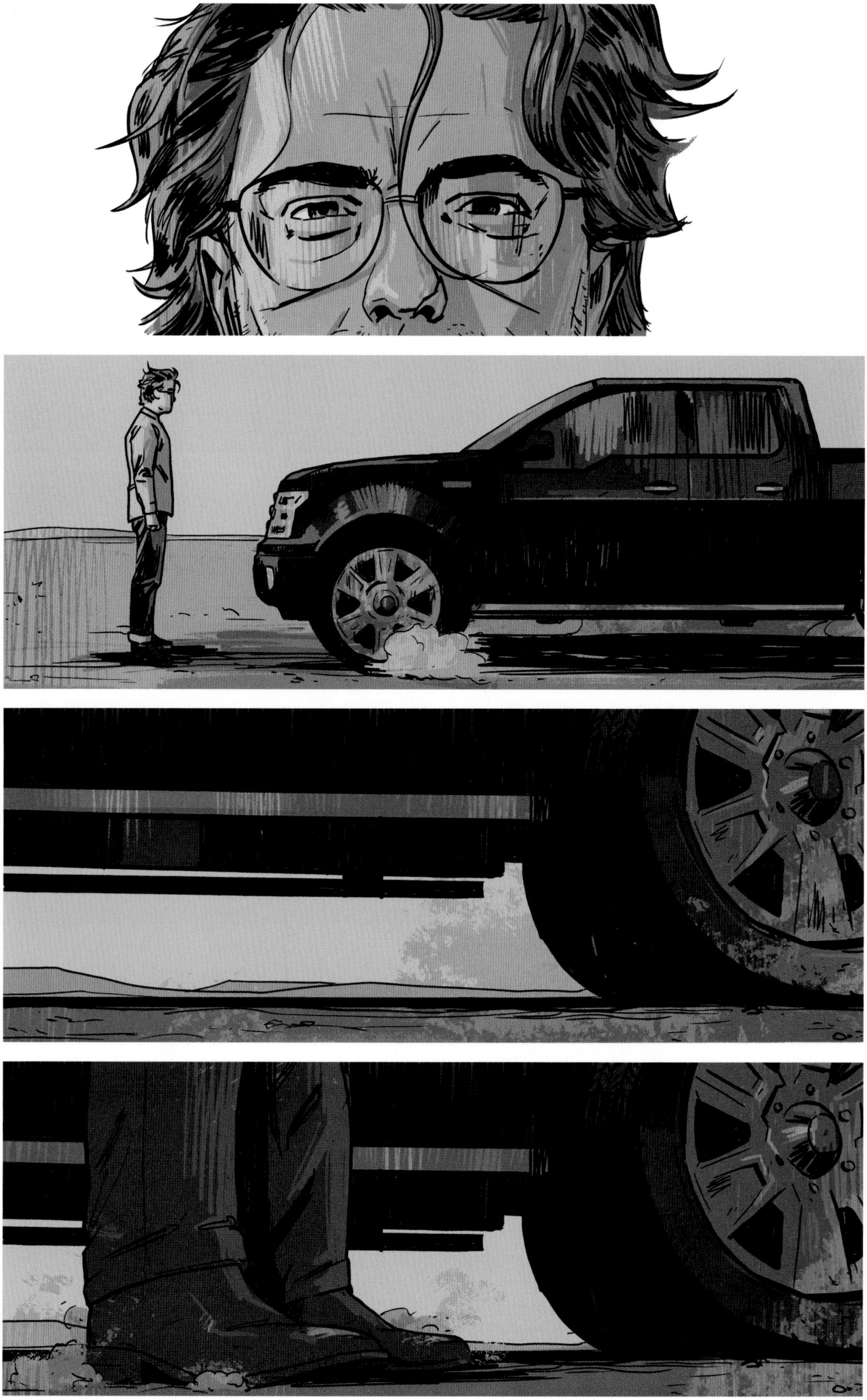

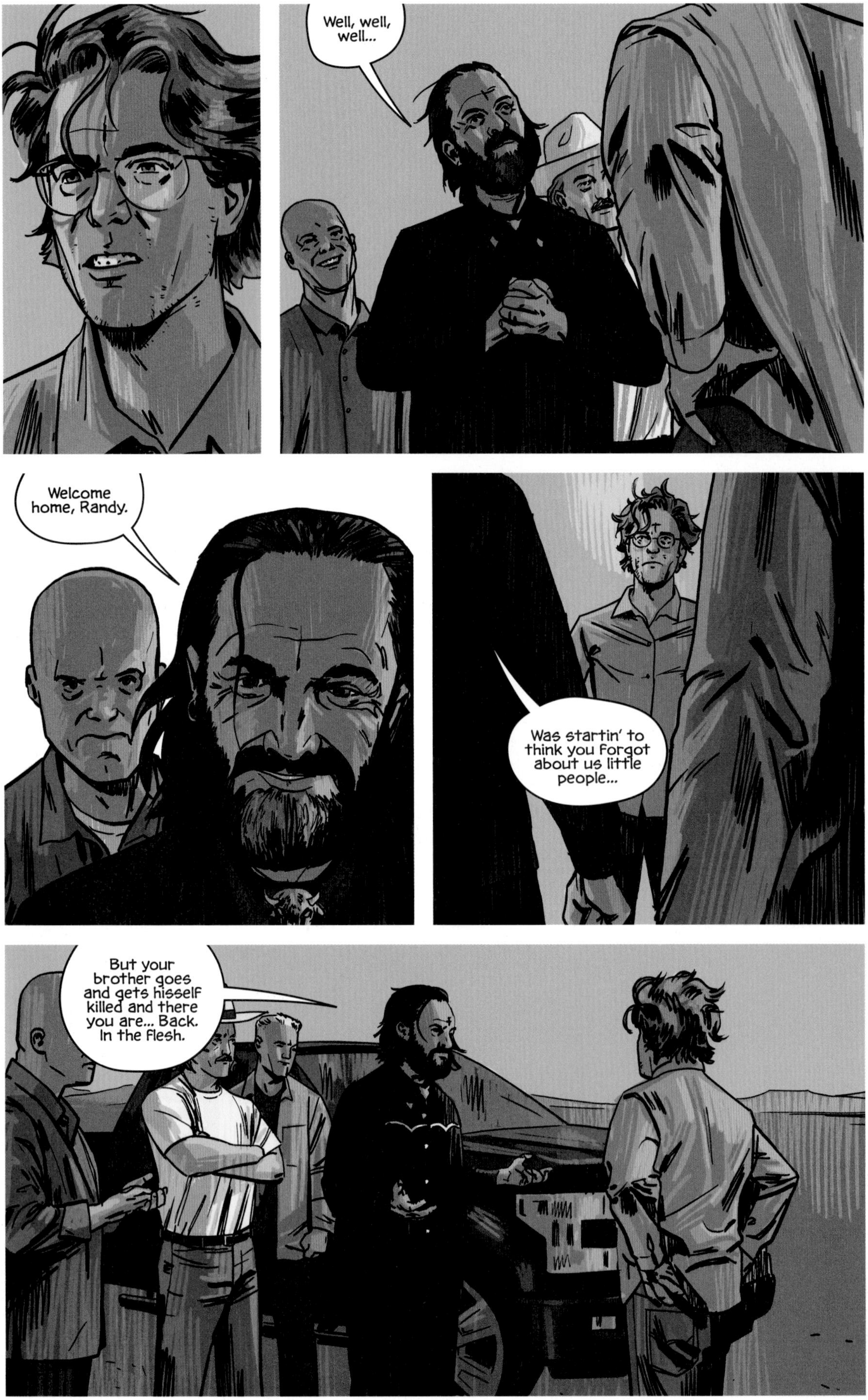
Well, well, well...
Welcome home, Randy.
Was startin' to think you forgot about us little people...
But your brother goes and gets hisself killed and there you are... Back. In the flesh.

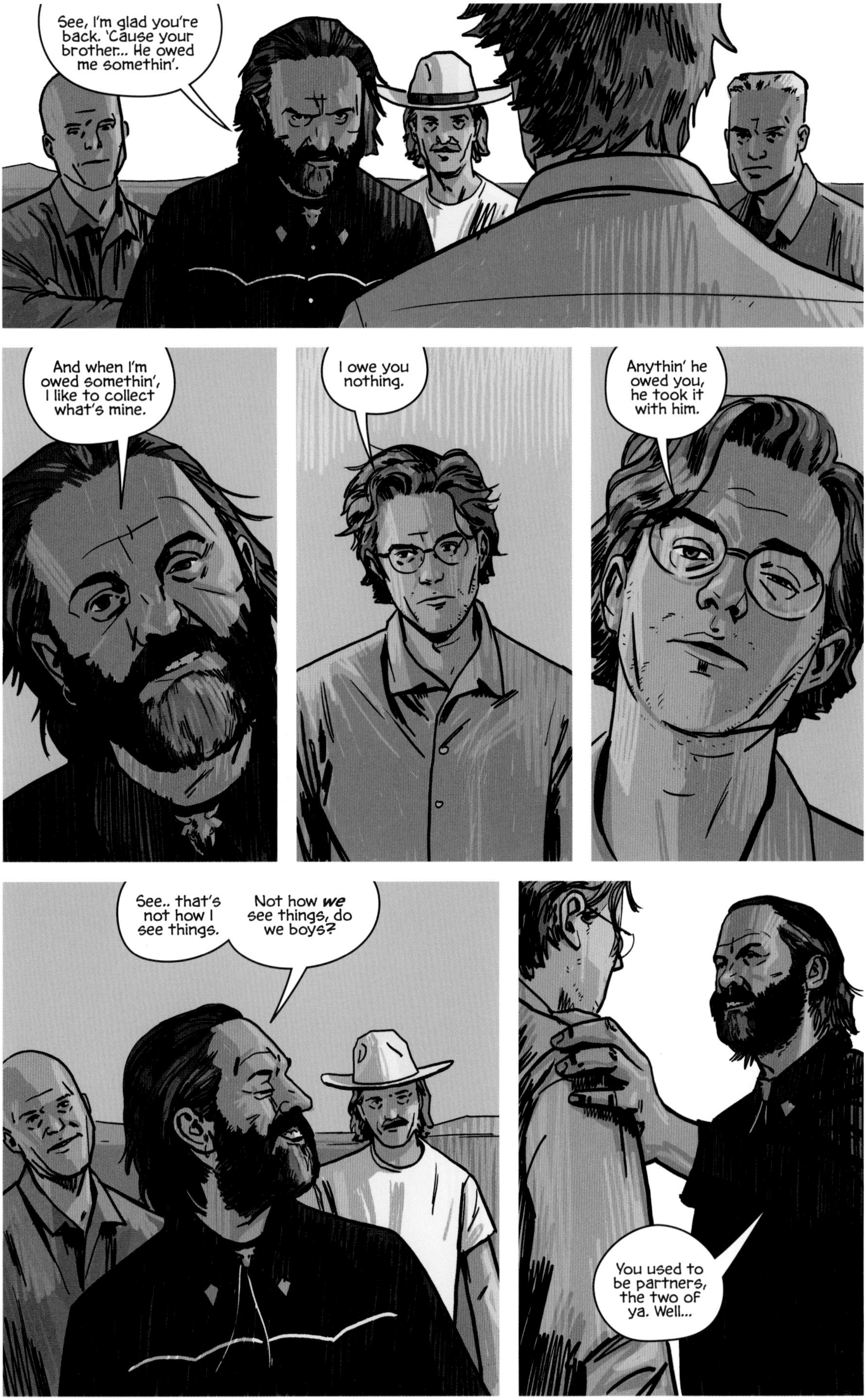
See, I'm glad you're back. 'Cause your brother... He owed me somethin'.
And when I'm owed somethin', I like to collect what's mine.
I owe you nothing.
Anythin' he owed you, he took it with him.
See.. that's not how I see things.
Not how *we* see things, do we boys?
You used to be partners, the two of ya. Well...

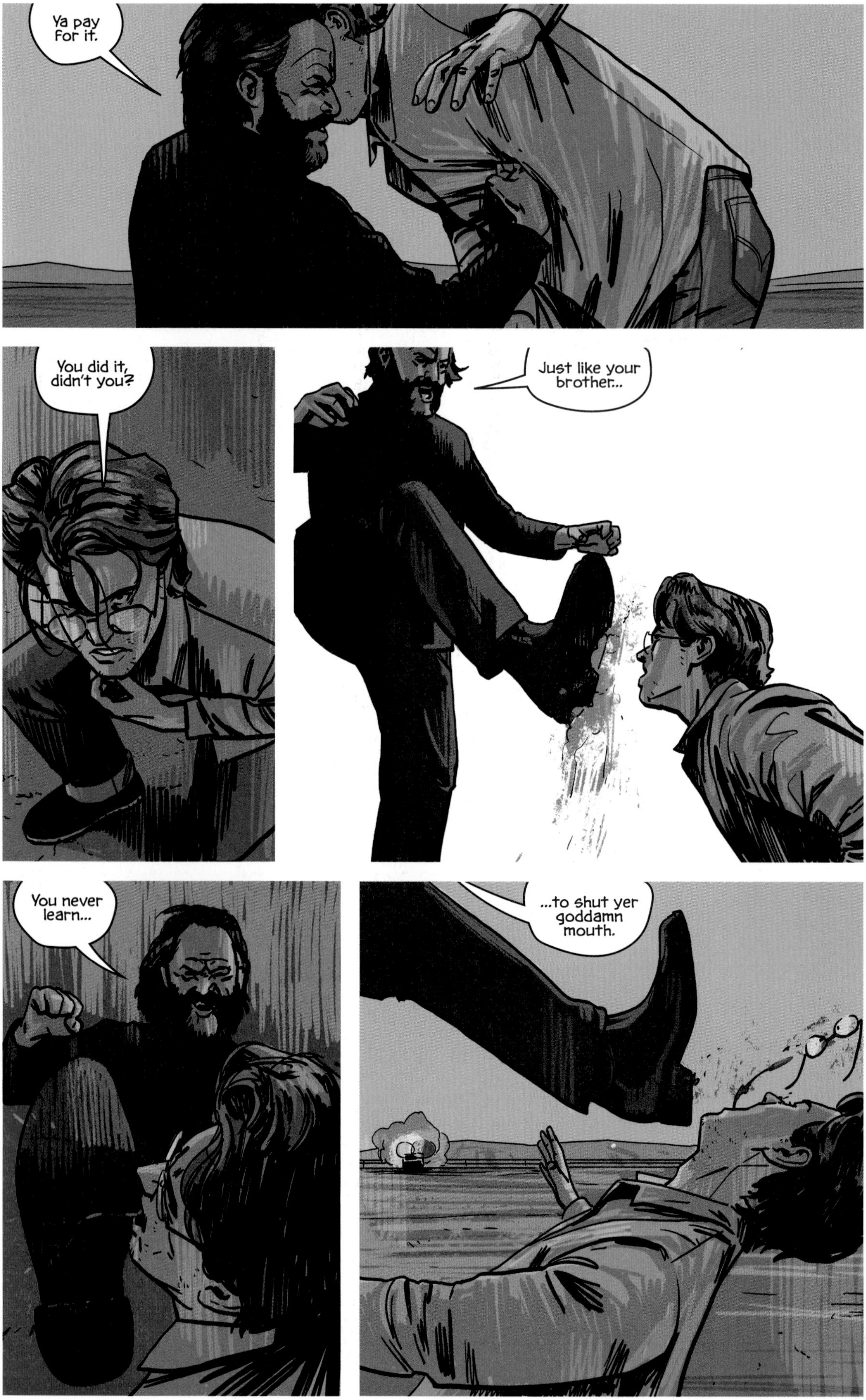
Ya pay for it.
You did it, didn't you?
Just like your brother...
You never learn...
...to shut yer goddamn mouth.

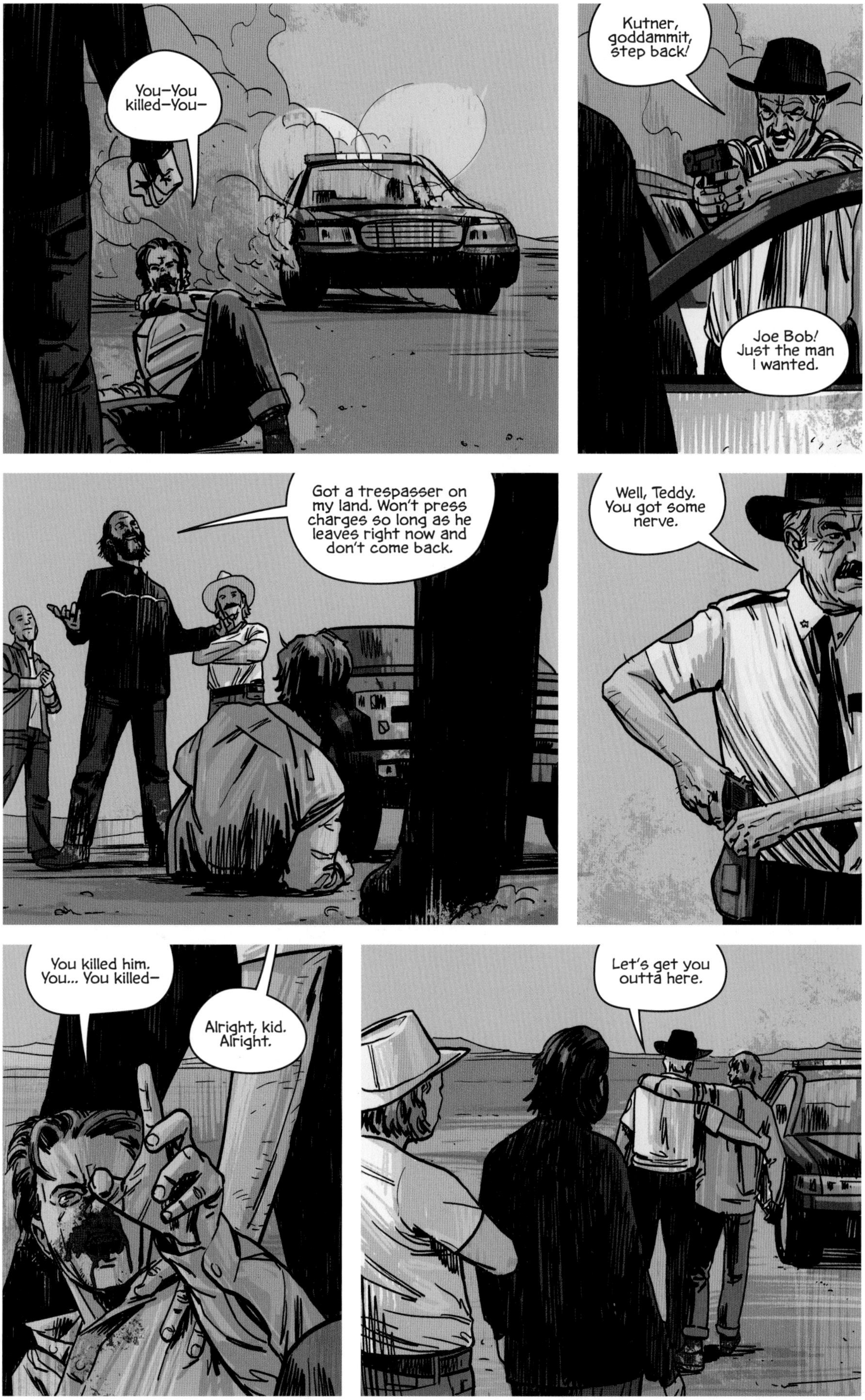
You—You killed—You—
Kutner, goddammit, step back!
Joe Bob! Just the man I wanted.
Got a trespasser on my land. Won't press charges so long as he leaves right now and don't come back.
Well, Teddy. You got some nerve.
You killed him. You... You killed—
Alright, kid. Alright.
Let's get you outta here.

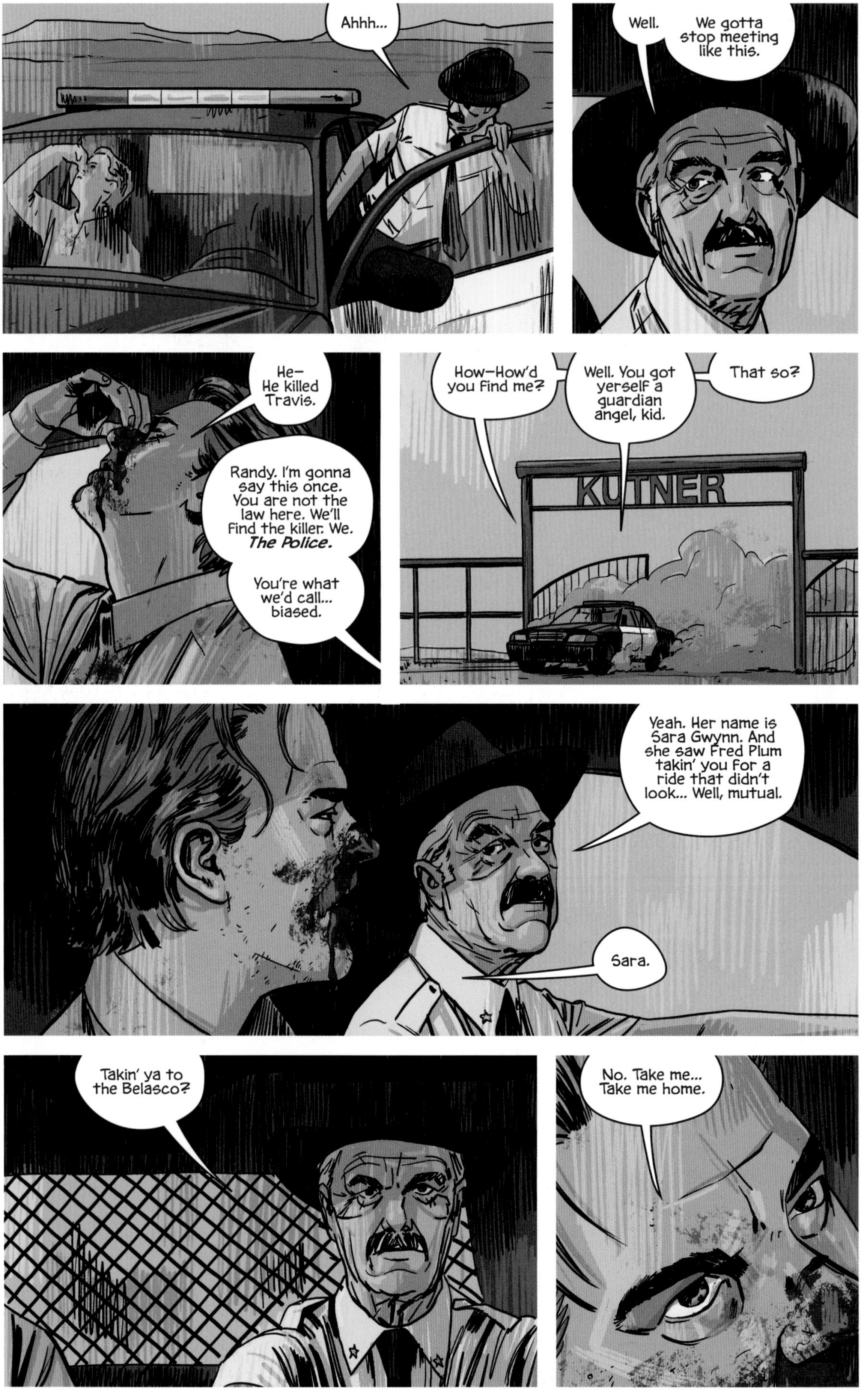
Ahhh...
Well.
We gotta stop meeting like this.
He— He killed Travis.
Randy. I'm gonna say this once. You are not the law here. We'll find the killer. We. *The Police.*
You're what we'd call... biased.
How—How'd you find me?
Well. You got yerself a guardian angel, kid.
That so?
KUTNER
Yeah. Her name is Sara Gwynn. And she saw Fred Plum takin' you for a ride that didn't look... Well, mutual.
Sara.
Takin' ya to the Belasco?
No. Take me... Take me home.

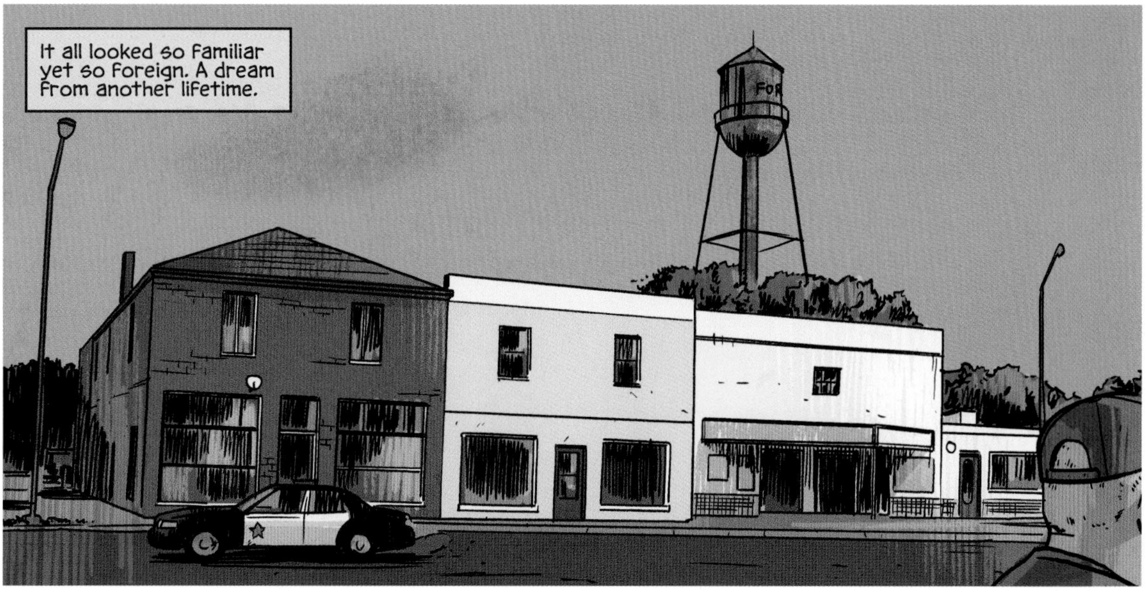
It all looked so familiar yet so foreign. A dream from another lifetime.
FOR

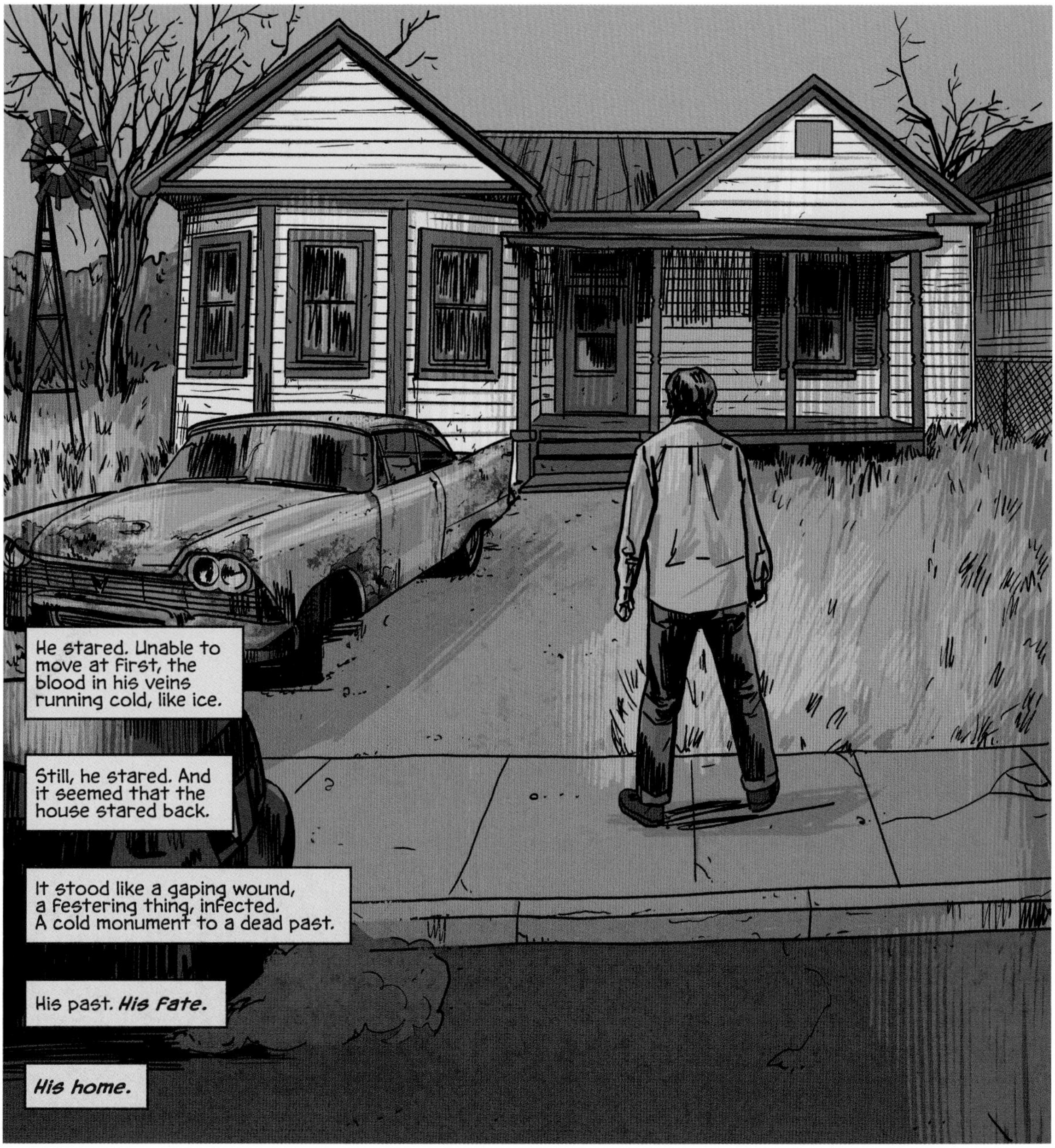
He stared. Unable to move at first, the blood in his veins running cold, like ice.
Still, he stared. And it seemed that the house stared back.
It stood like a gaping wound, a festering thing, infected. A cold monument to a dead past.
His past. *His fate.*
His home.

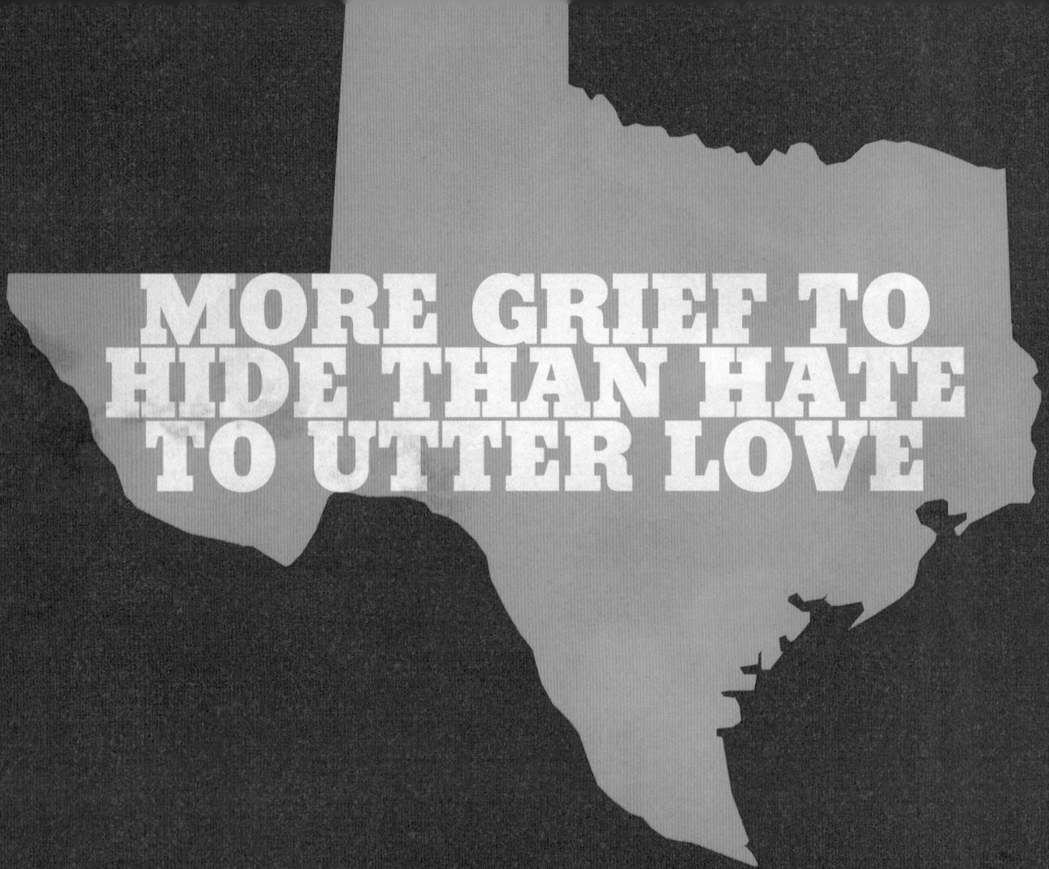
MORE GRIEF TO
HIDE THAN HATE
TO UTTER LOVE

A Brother's Conscience

Part Three

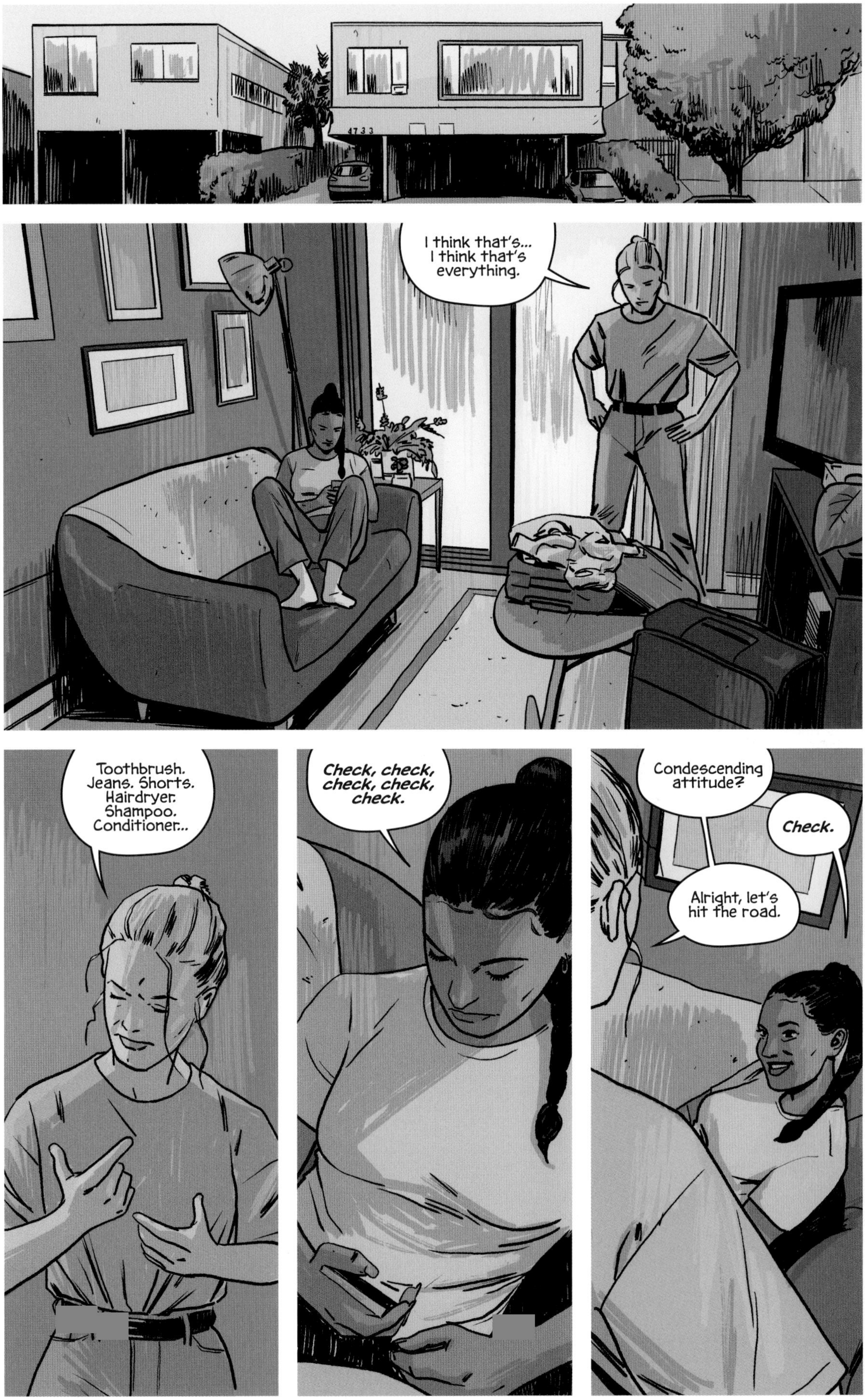
I think that's... I think that's everything.
Toothbrush. Jeans. Shorts. Hairdryer. Shampoo. Conditioner...
Check, check, check, check, check.
Condescending attitude?
Check.
Alright, let's hit the road.

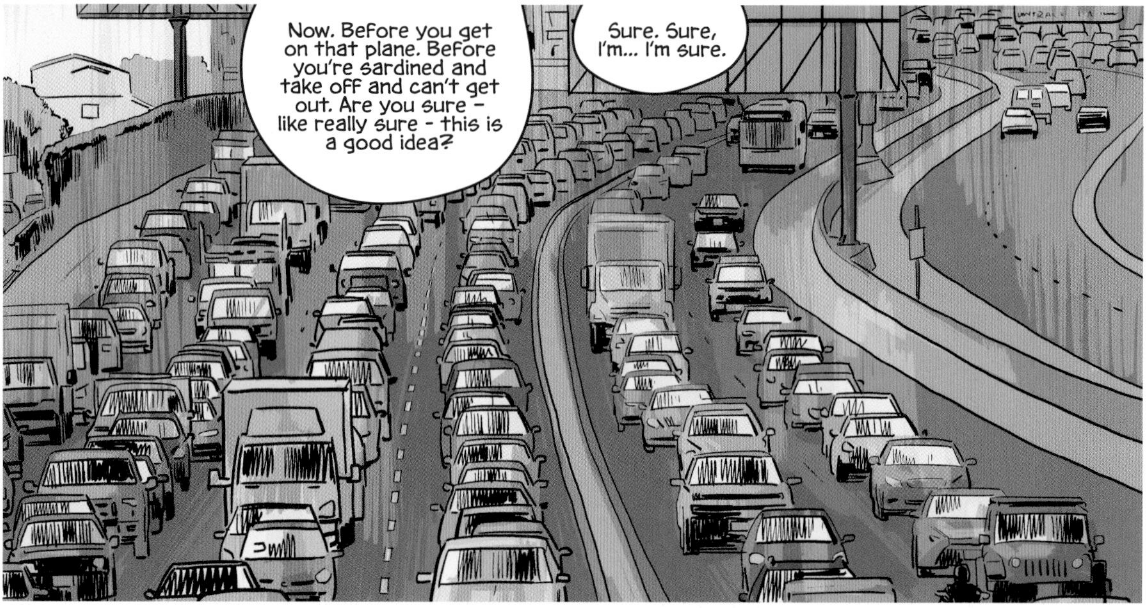
Now. Before you get on that plane. Before you're sardined and take off and can't get out. Are you sure - like really sure - this is a good idea?
Sure. Sure, I'm... I'm sure.

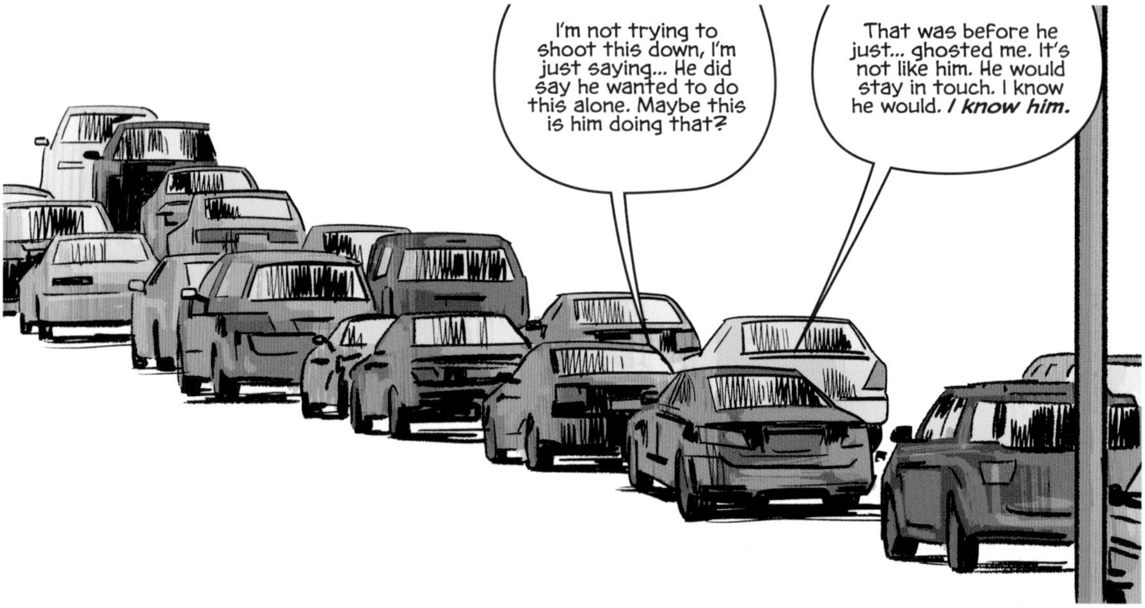
I'm not trying to shoot this down, I'm just saying... He did say he wanted to do this alone. Maybe this is him doing that?
That was before he just... ghosted me. It's not like him. He would stay in touch. I know he would. *I know him.*

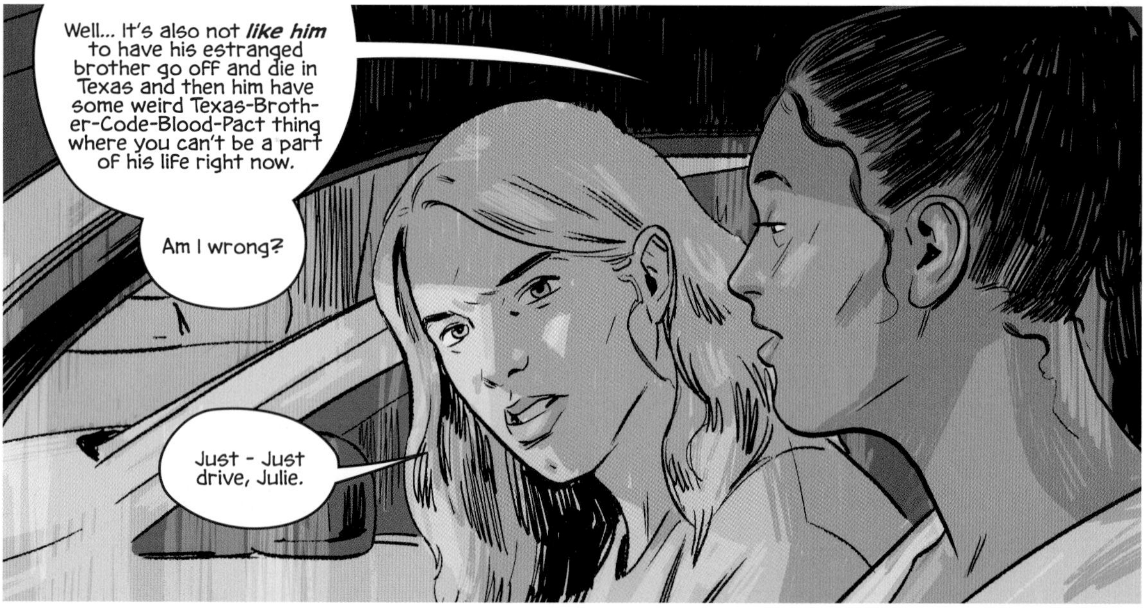
Well... It's also not *like him* to have his estranged brother go off and die in Texas and then him have some weird Texas-Brother-Code-Blood-Pact thing where you can't be a part of his life right now.
Am I wrong?
Just - Just drive, Julie.

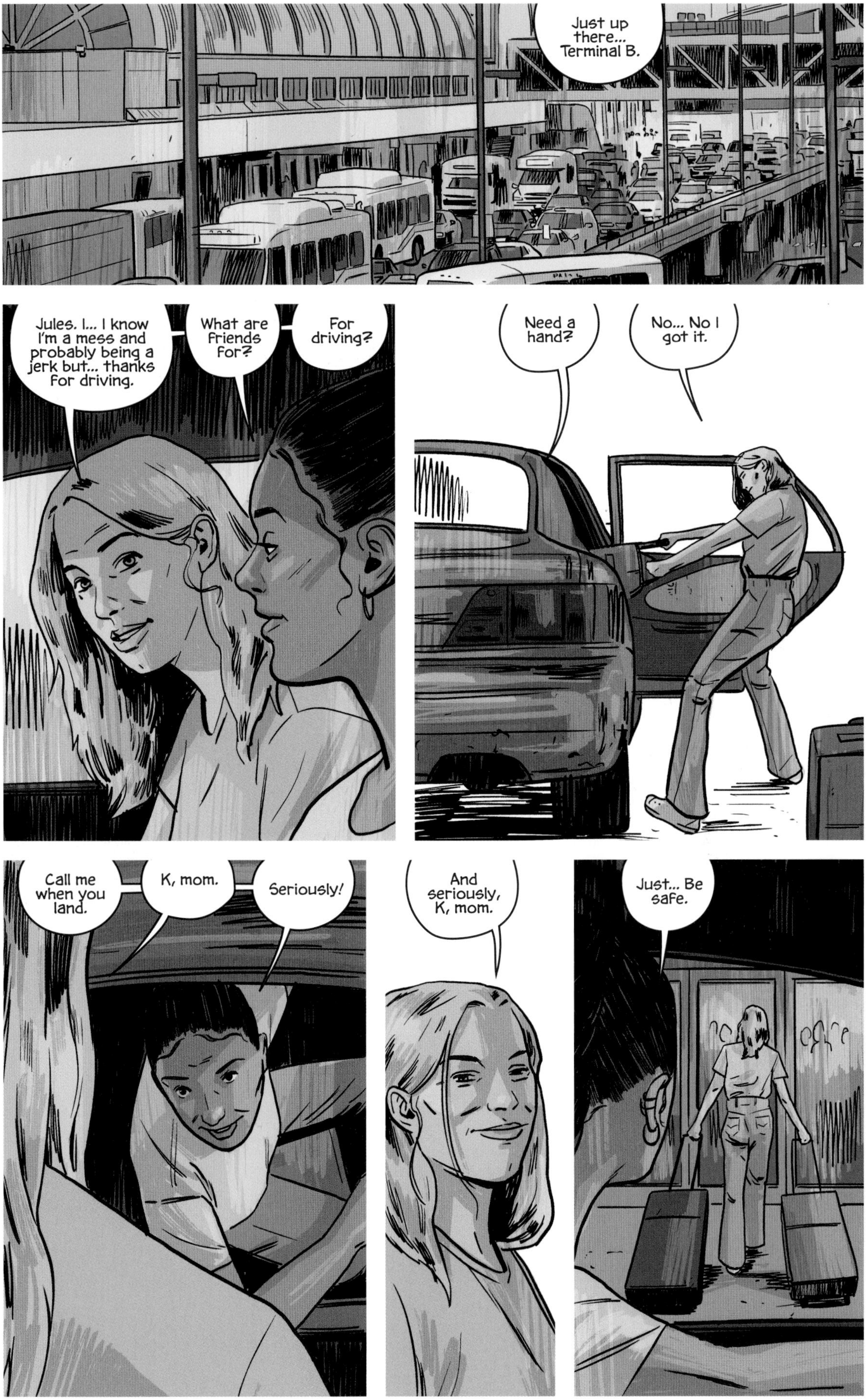
Just up there... Terminal B.
Jules. I... I know I'm a mess and probably being a jerk but... thanks for driving.
What are friends for?
For driving?
Need a hand?
No... No I got it.
Call me when you land.
K, mom.
Seriously!
And seriously, K, mom.
Just... Be safe.

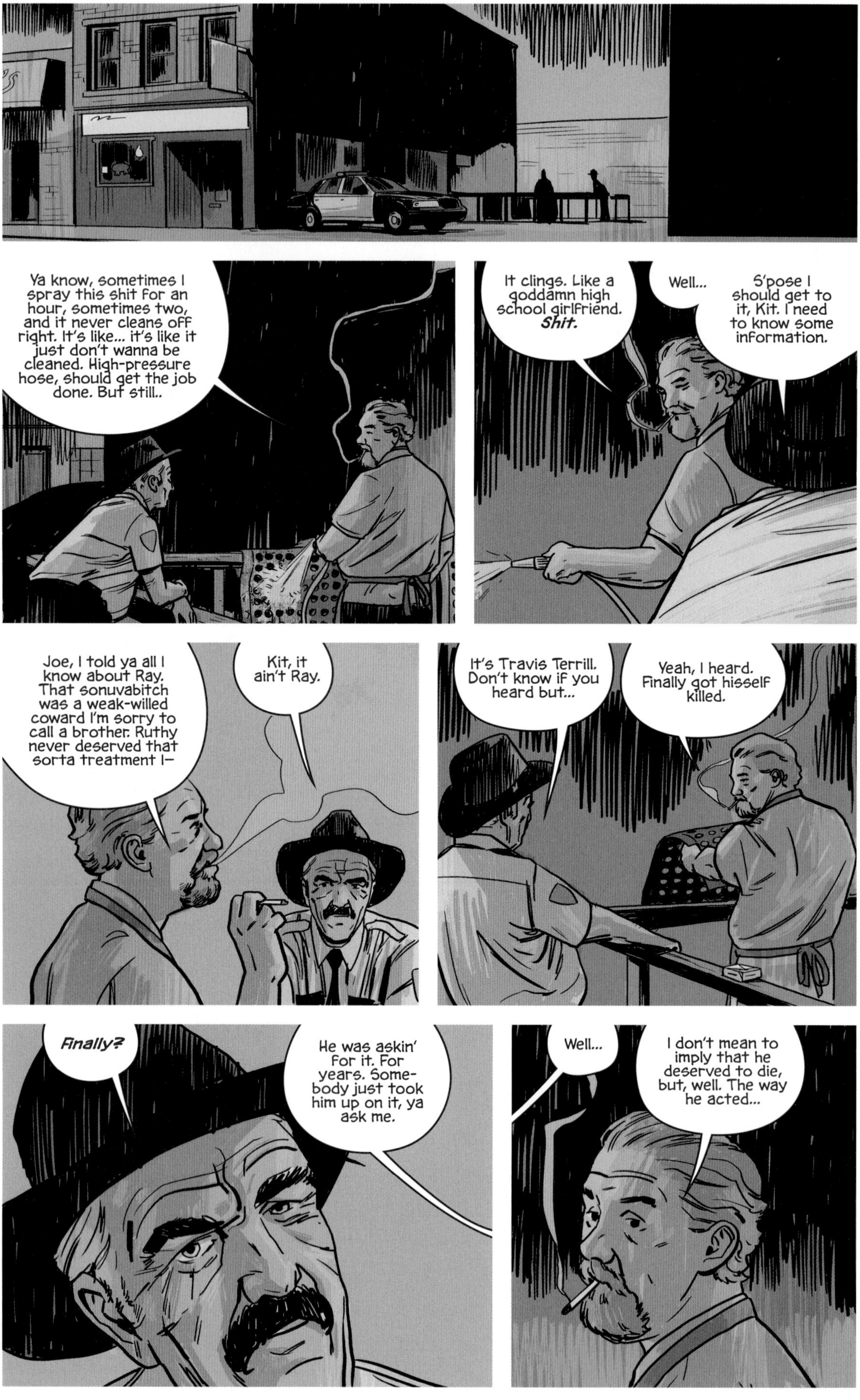

Ya know, sometimes I spray this shit for an hour, sometimes two, and it never cleans off right. It's like... it's like it just don't wanna be cleaned. High-pressure hose, should get the job done. But still..
It clings. Like a goddamn high school girlfriend. *Shit.*
Well...
S'pose I should get to it, Kit. I need to know some information.
Joe, I told ya all I know about Ray. That sonuvabitch was a weak-willed coward I'm sorry to call a brother. Ruthy never deserved that sorta treatment I—
Kit, it ain't Ray.
It's Travis Terrill. Don't know if you heard but...
Yeah, I heard. Finally got hisself killed.
Finally?
He was askin' for it. For years. Somebody just took him up on it, ya ask me.
Well...
I don't mean to imply that he deserved to die, but, well. The way he acted...

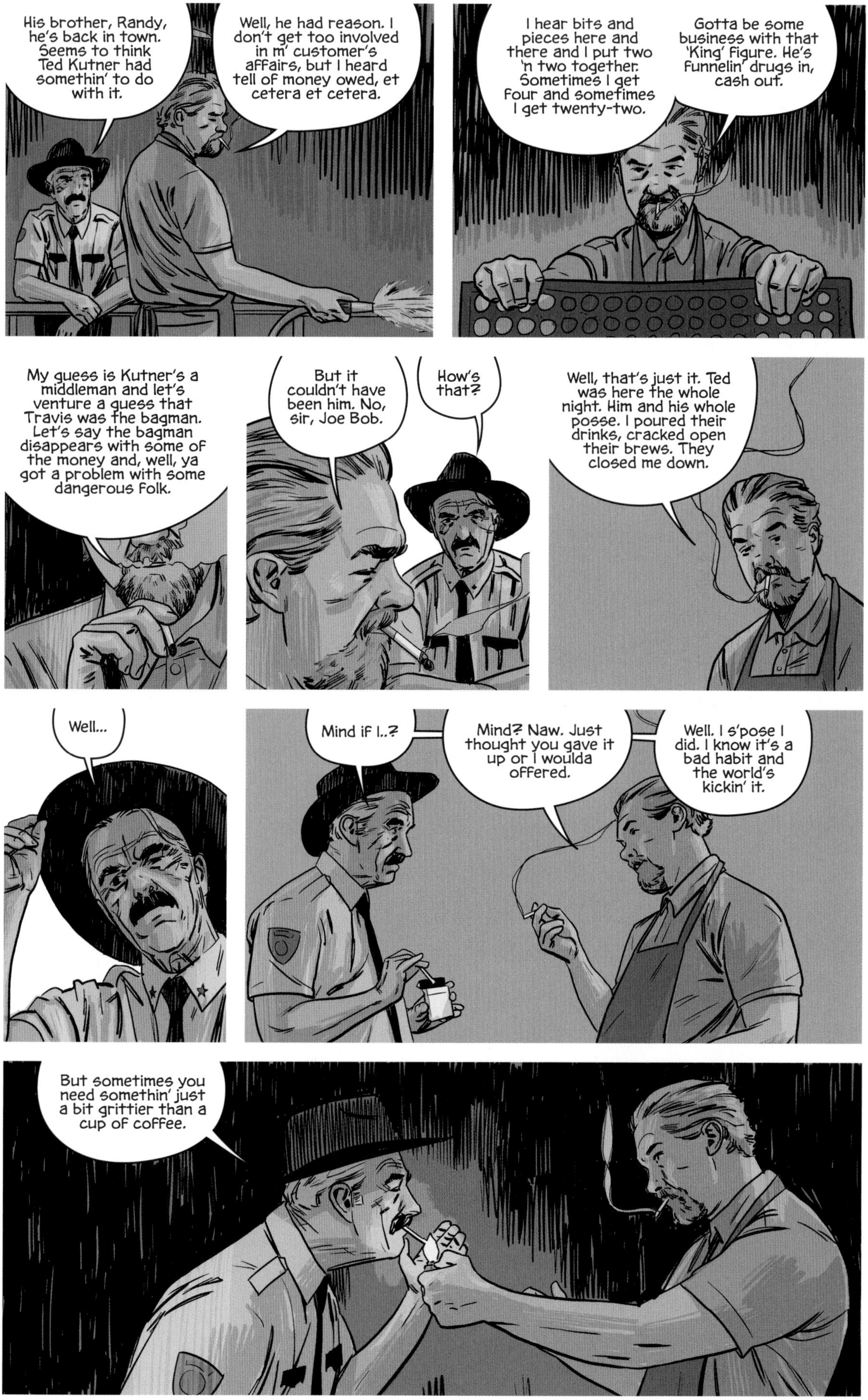

His brother, Randy, he's back in town. Seems to think Ted Kutner had somethin' to do with it.
Well, he had reason. I don't get too involved in m' customer's affairs, but I heard tell of money owed, et cetera et cetera.
I hear bits and pieces here and there and I put two 'n two together. Sometimes I get four and sometimes I get twenty-two.
Gotta be some business with that 'King' figure. He's funnelin' drugs in, cash out.
My guess is Kutner's a middleman and let's venture a guess that Travis was the bagman. Let's say the bagman disappears with some of the money and, well, ya got a problem with some dangerous folk.
But it couldn't have been him. No, sir, Joe Bob.
How's that?
Well, that's just it. Ted was here the whole night. Him and his whole posse. I poured their drinks, cracked open their brews. They closed me down.
Well...
Mind if I..?
Mind? Naw. Just thought you gave it up or I woulda offered.
Well. I s'pose I did. I know it's a bad habit and the world's kickin' it.
But sometimes you need somethin' just a bit grittier than a cup of coffee.

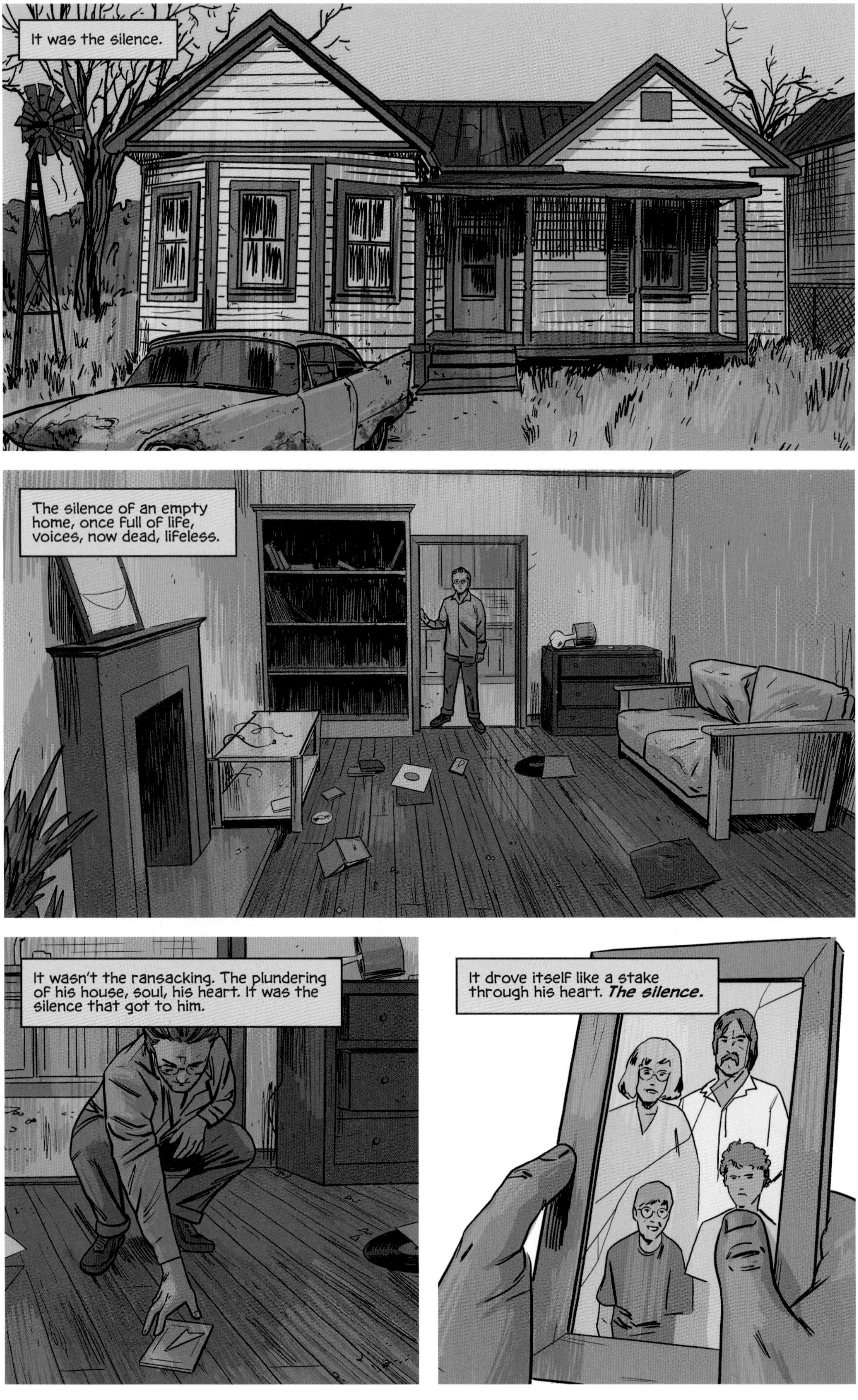
It was the silence.
The silence of an empty home, once full of life, voices, now dead, lifeless.
It wasn't the ransacking. The plundering of his house, soul, his heart. It was the silence that got to him.
It drove itself like a stake through his heart. *The silence.*

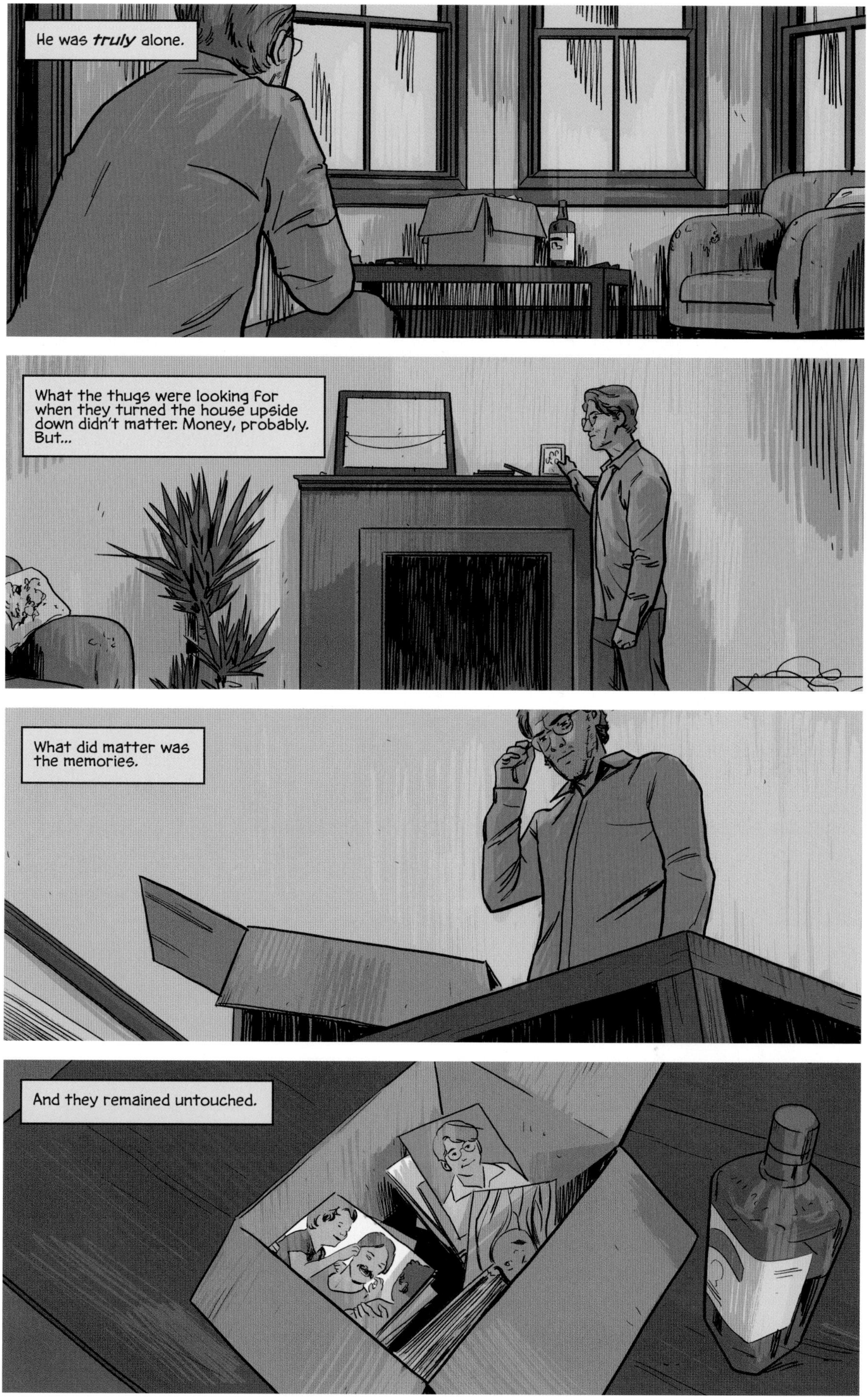
He was *truly* alone.
What the thugs were looking for when they turned the house upside down didn't matter. Money, probably. But...
What did matter was the memories.
And they remained untouched.

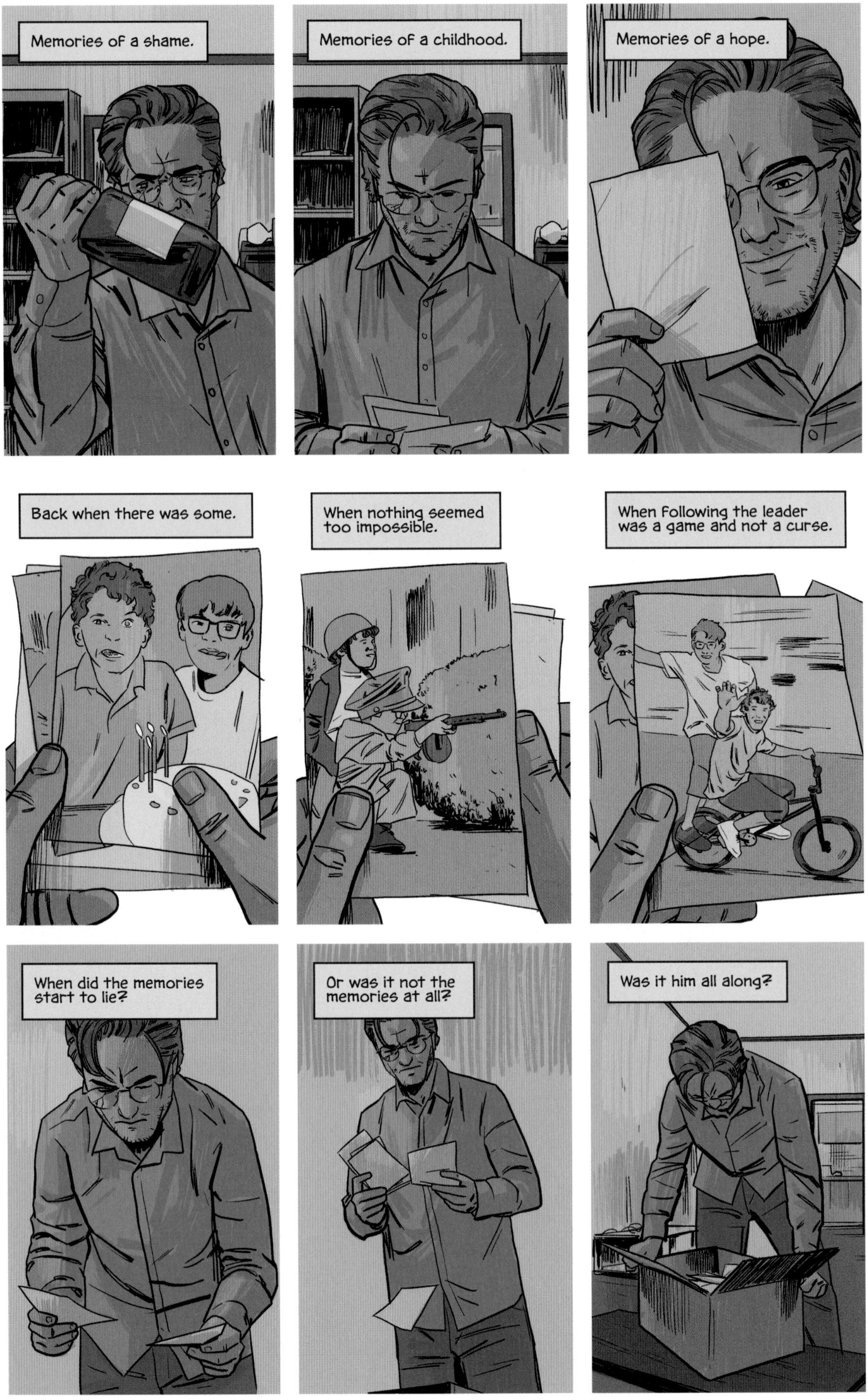
Memories of a shame.
Memories of a childhood.
Memories of a hope.
Back when there was some.
When nothing seemed too impossible.
When following the leader was a game and not a curse.
When did the memories start to lie?
Or was it not the memories at all?
Was it him all along?

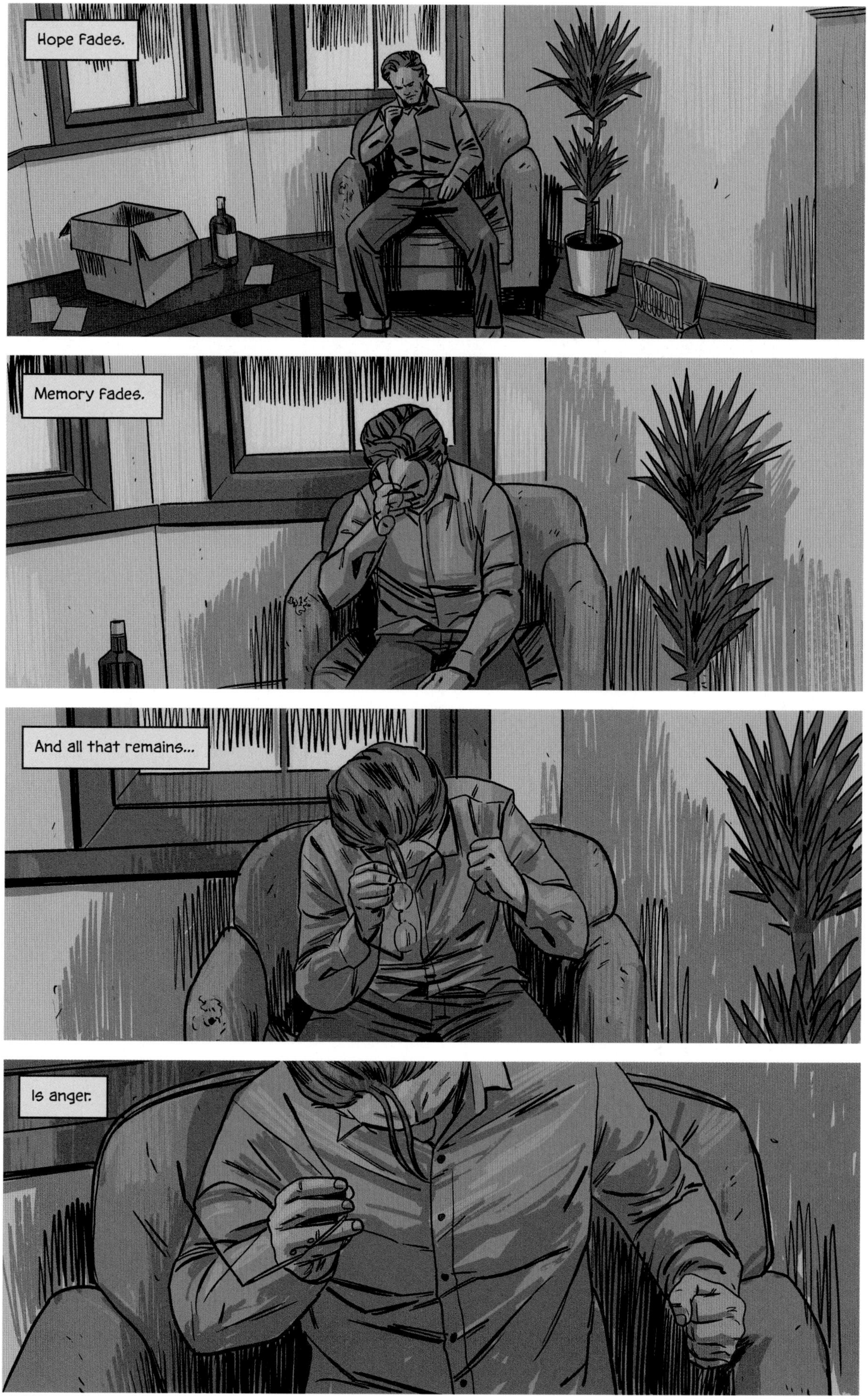
Hope fades.
Memory fades.
And all that remains...
Is anger.

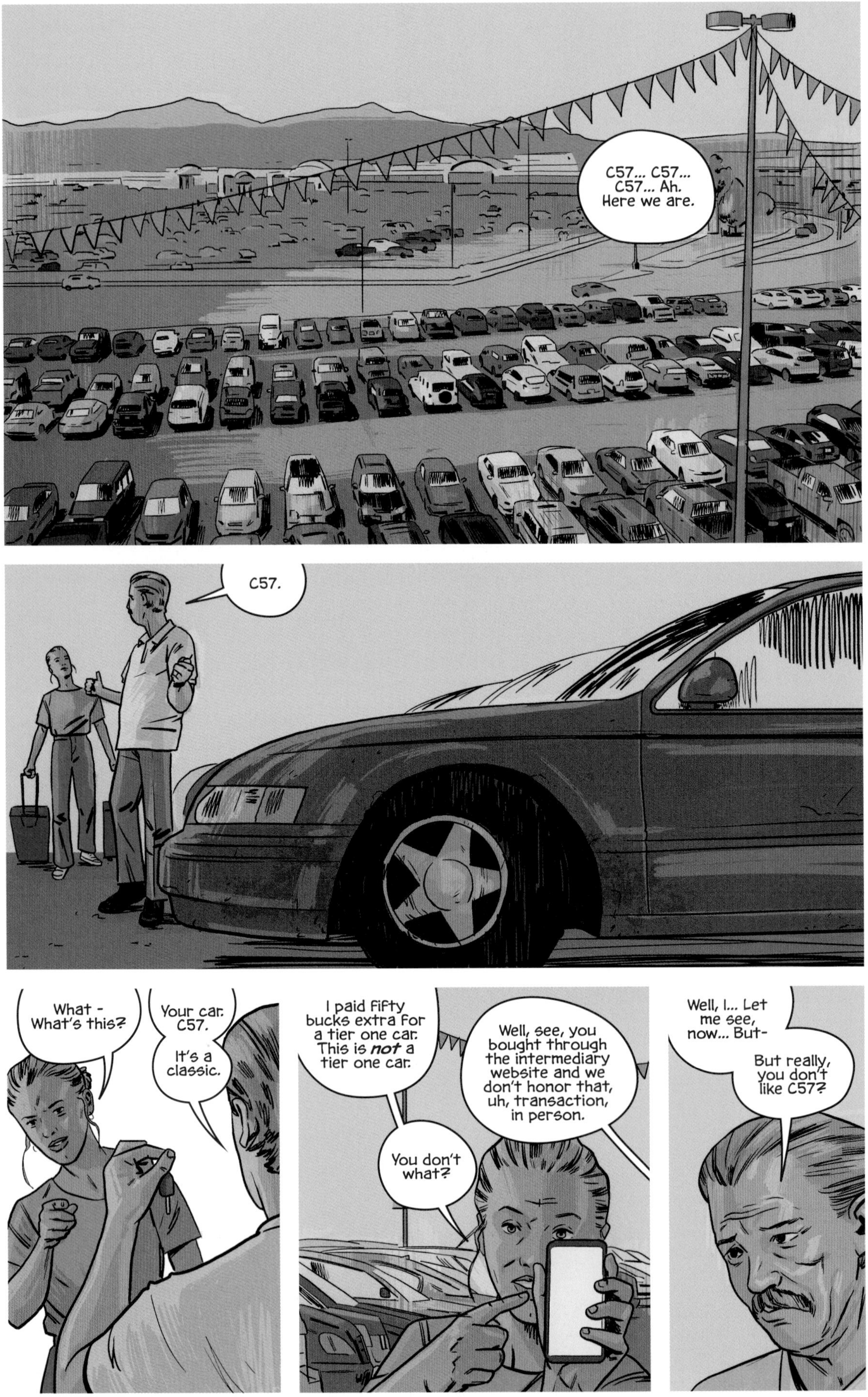
C57... C57... C57... Ah. Here we are.
C57.
What - What's this?
Your car. C57.
It's a classic.
I paid fifty bucks extra for a tier one car. This is *not* a tier one car.
Well, see, you bought through the intermediary website and we don't honor that, uh, transaction, in person.
You don't what?
Well, I... Let me see, now... But-
But really, you don't like C57?

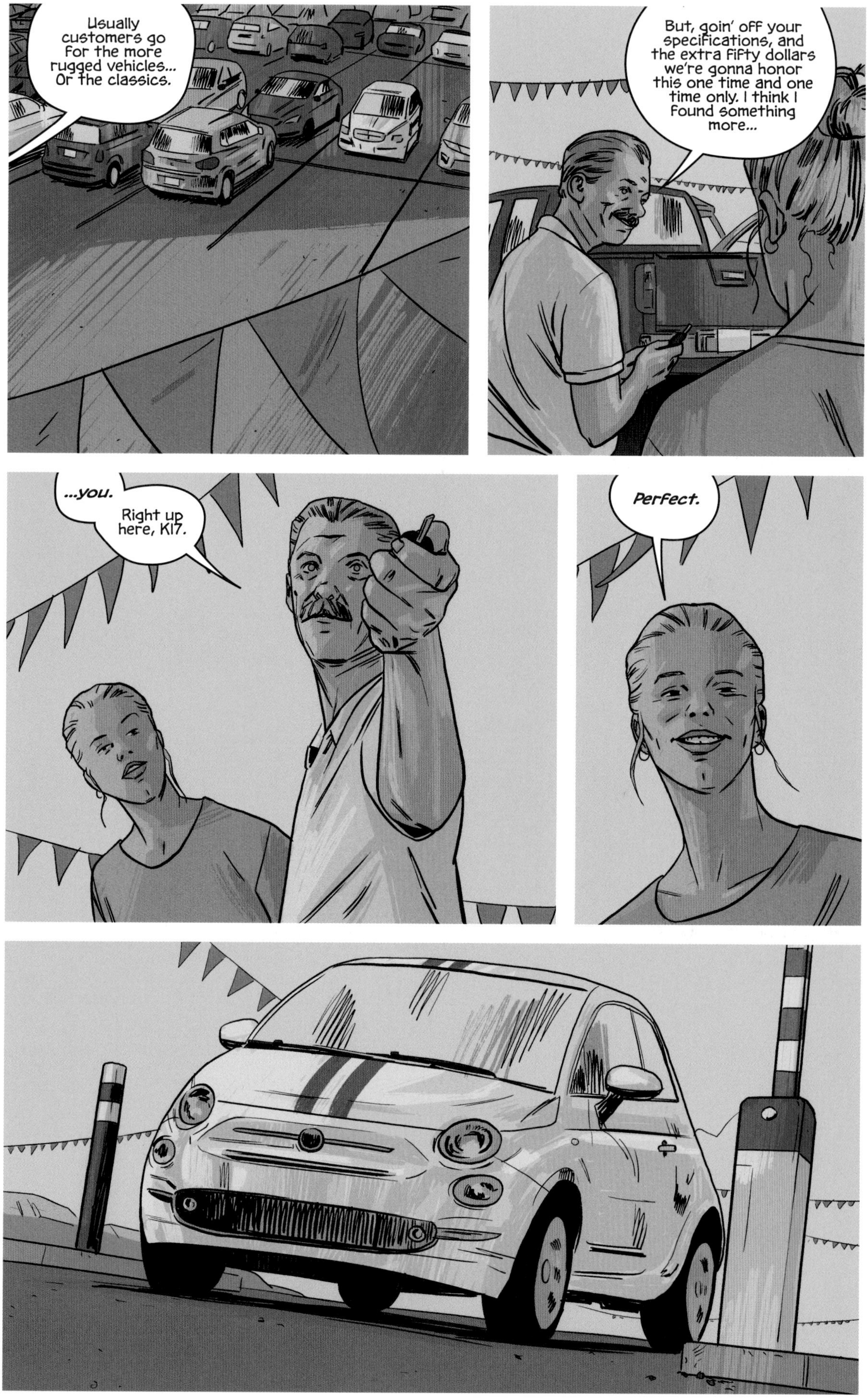
Usually customers go for the more rugged vehicles... Or the classics.
But, goin' off your specifications, and the extra fifty dollars we're gonna honor this one time and one time only. I think I found something more...
...you.
Right up here, KI7.
Perfect.

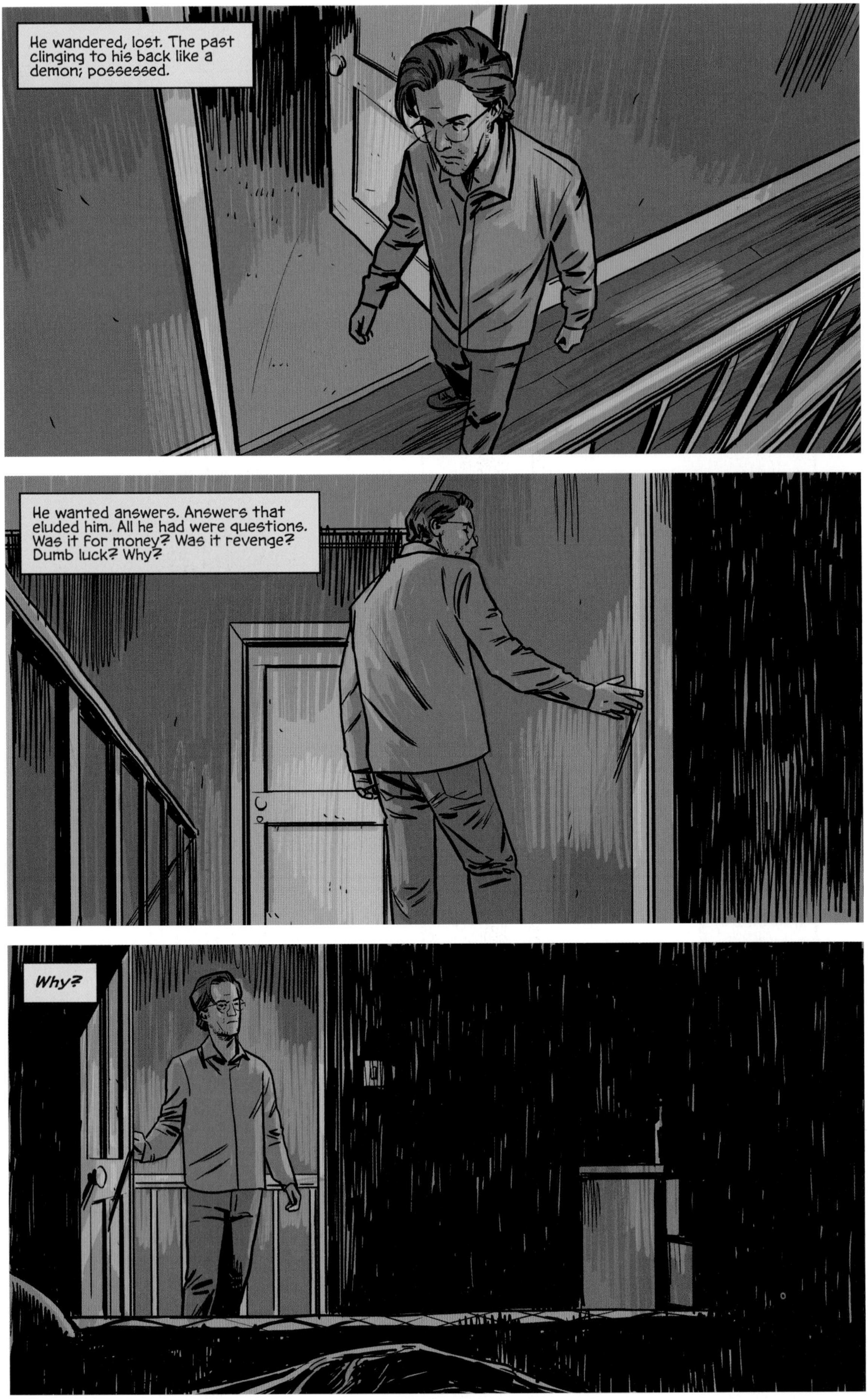
He wandered, lost. The past clinging to his back like a demon; possessed.
He wanted answers. Answers that eluded him. All he had were questions. Was it for money? Was it revenge? Dumb luck? Why?
Why?

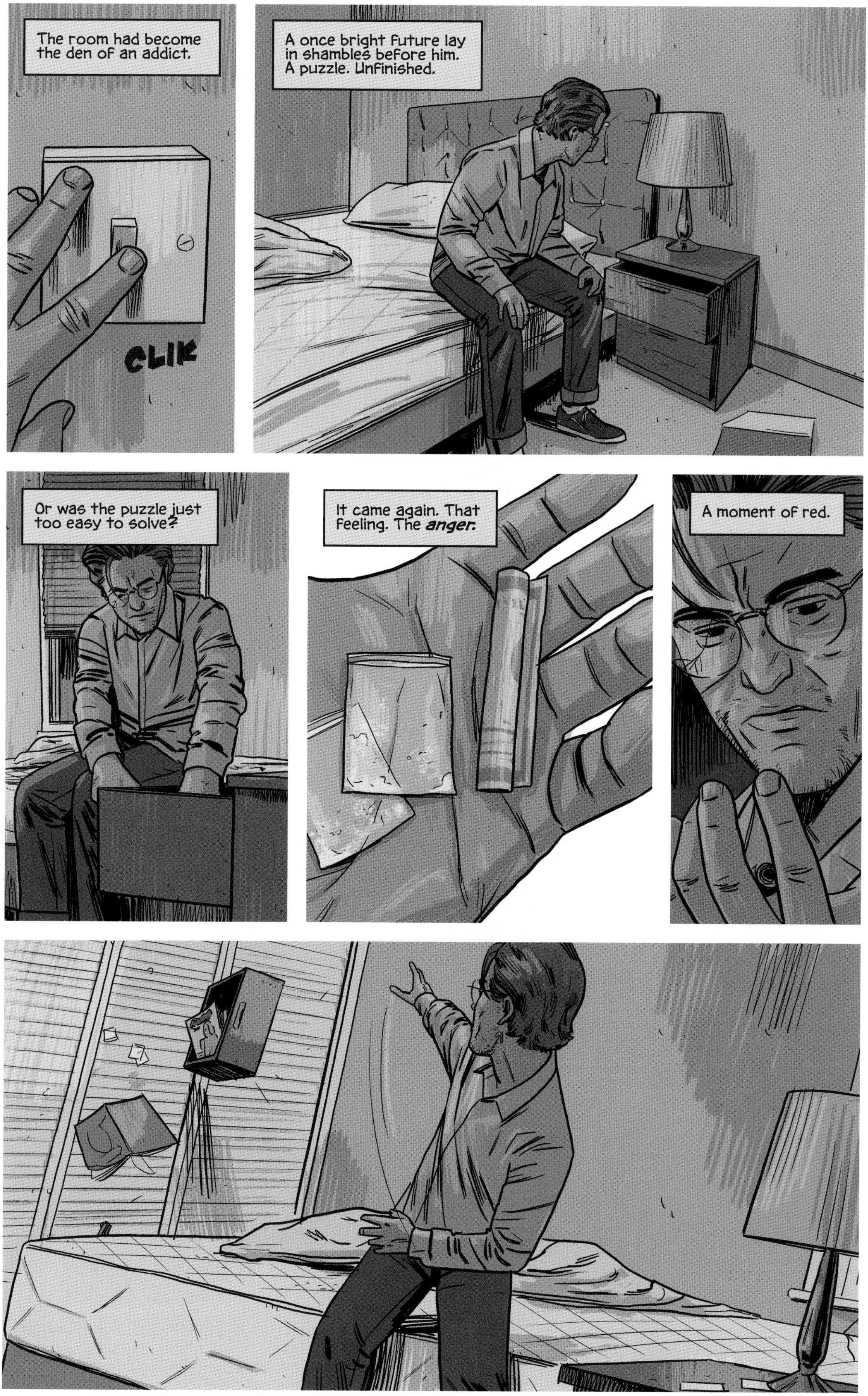
The room had become the den of an addict.
CLIK
A once bright future lay in shambles before him. A puzzle. Unfinished.
Or was the puzzle just too easy to solve?
It came again. That feeling. The *anger.*
A moment of red.

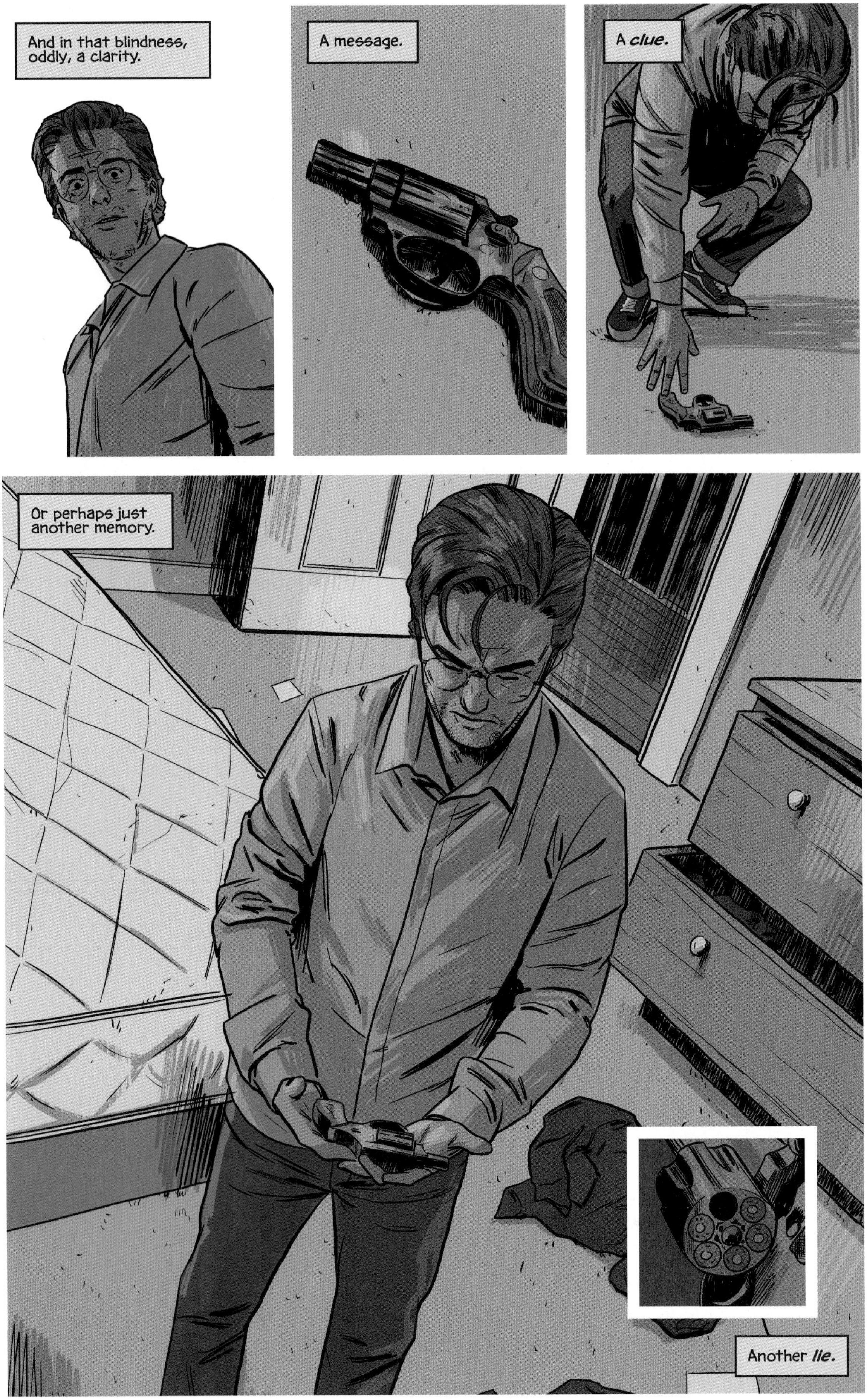
And in that blindness, oddly, a clarity.
A message.
A *clue.*
Or perhaps just another memory.
Another *lie.*

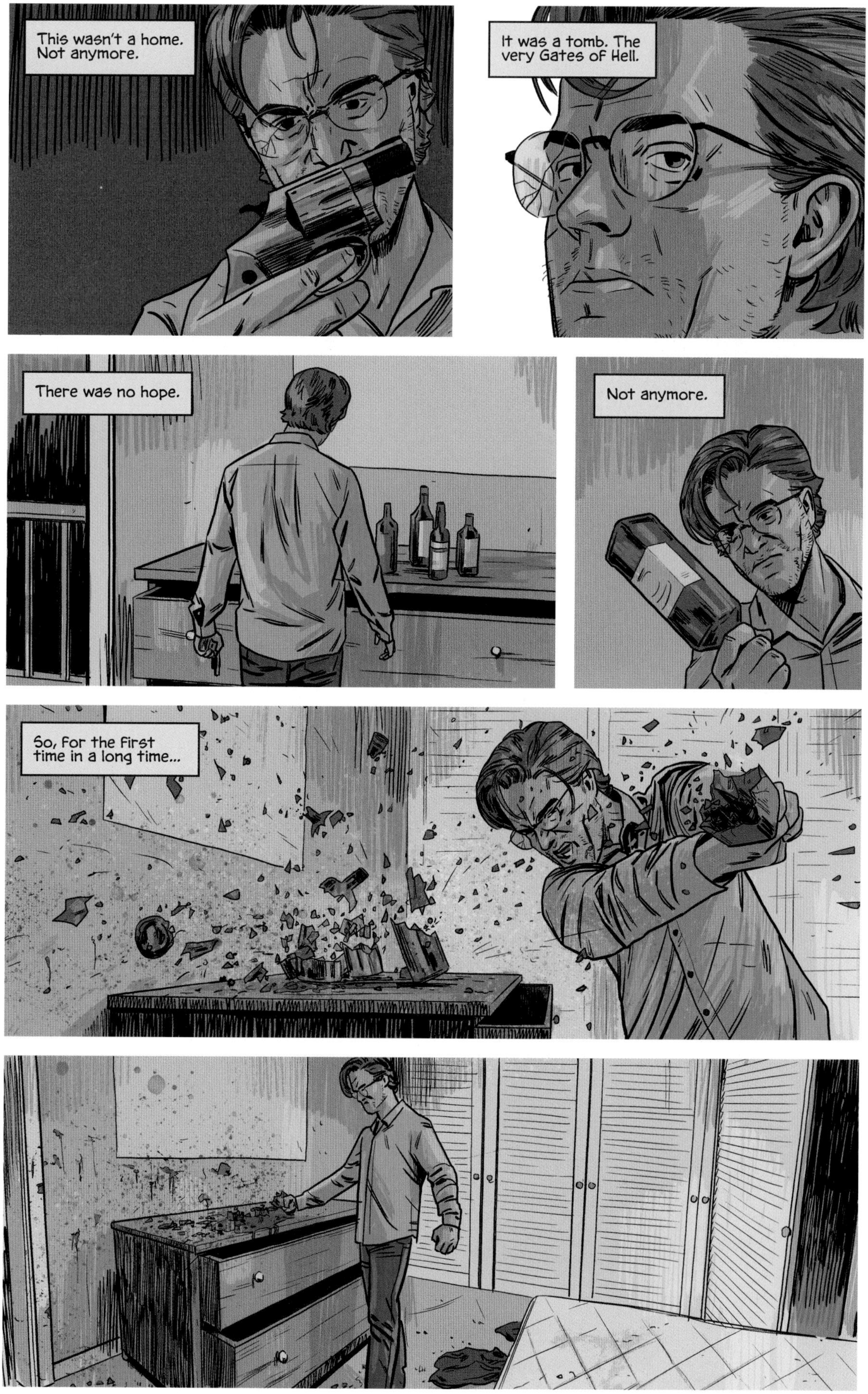
This wasn't a home.
Not anymore.
It was a tomb. The very Gates of Hell.
There was no hope.
Not anymore.
So, for the first time in a long time...

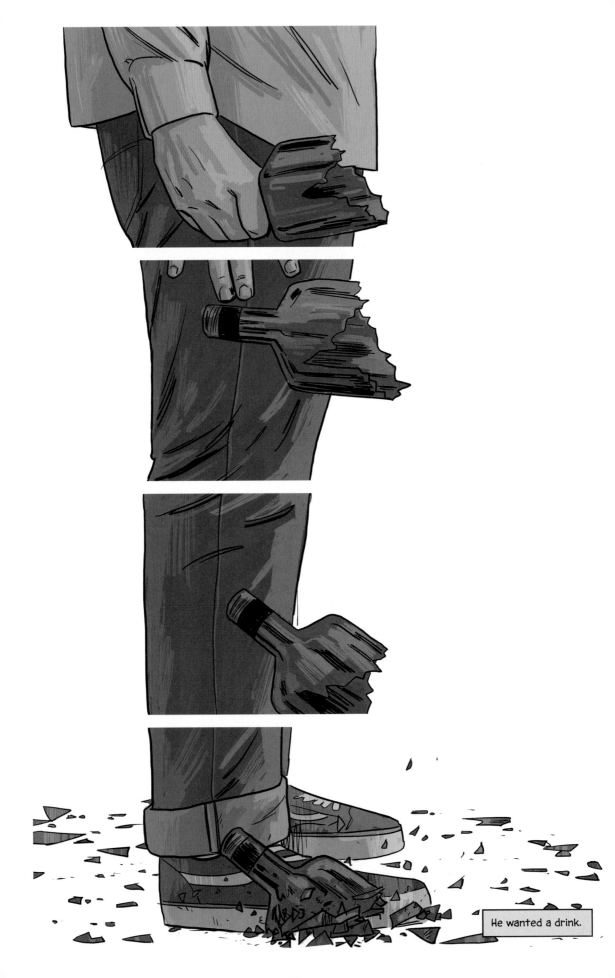

He wanted a drink.

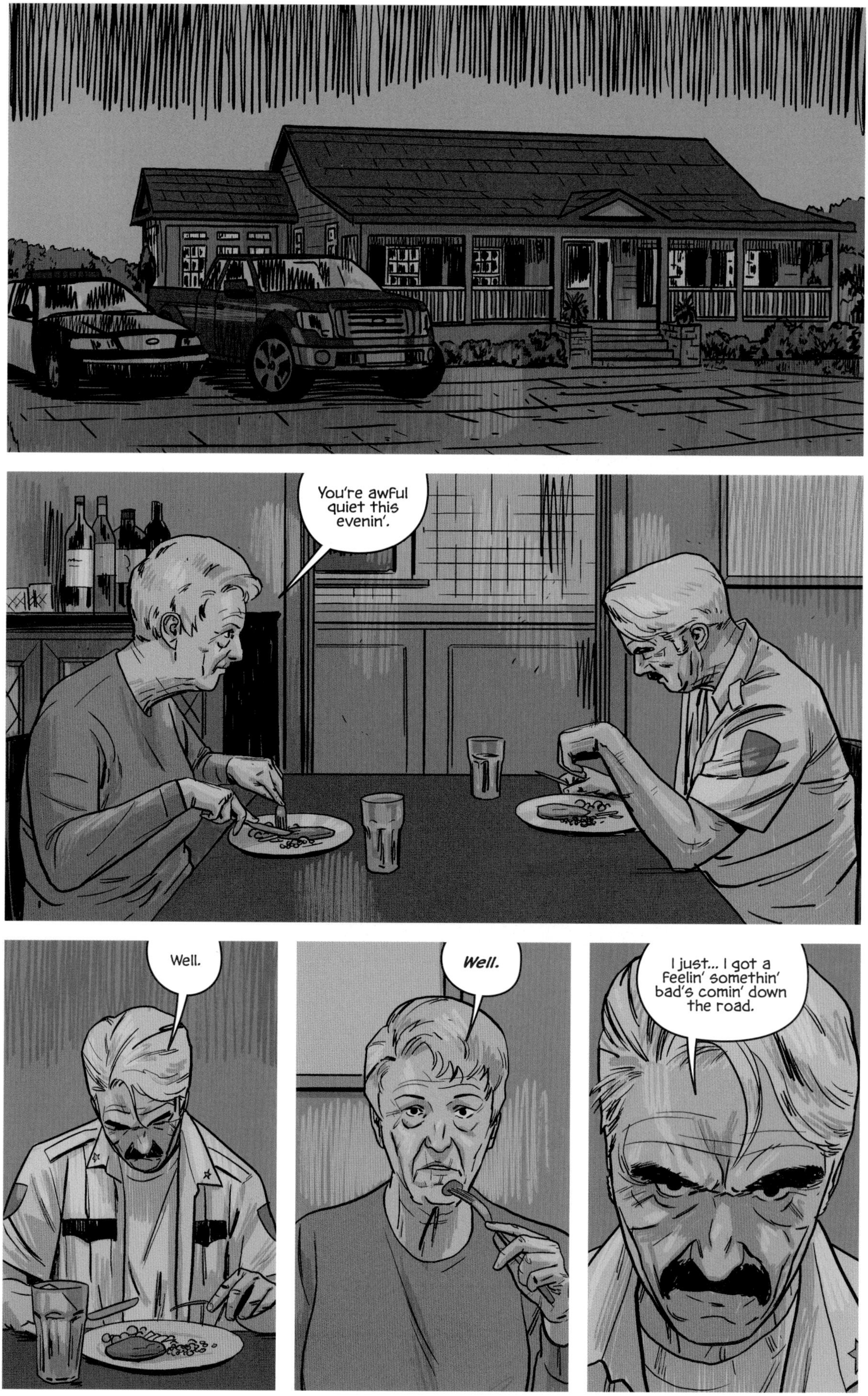
You're awful quiet this evenin'.
Well.
Well.
I just... I got a feelin' somethin' bad's comin' down the road.

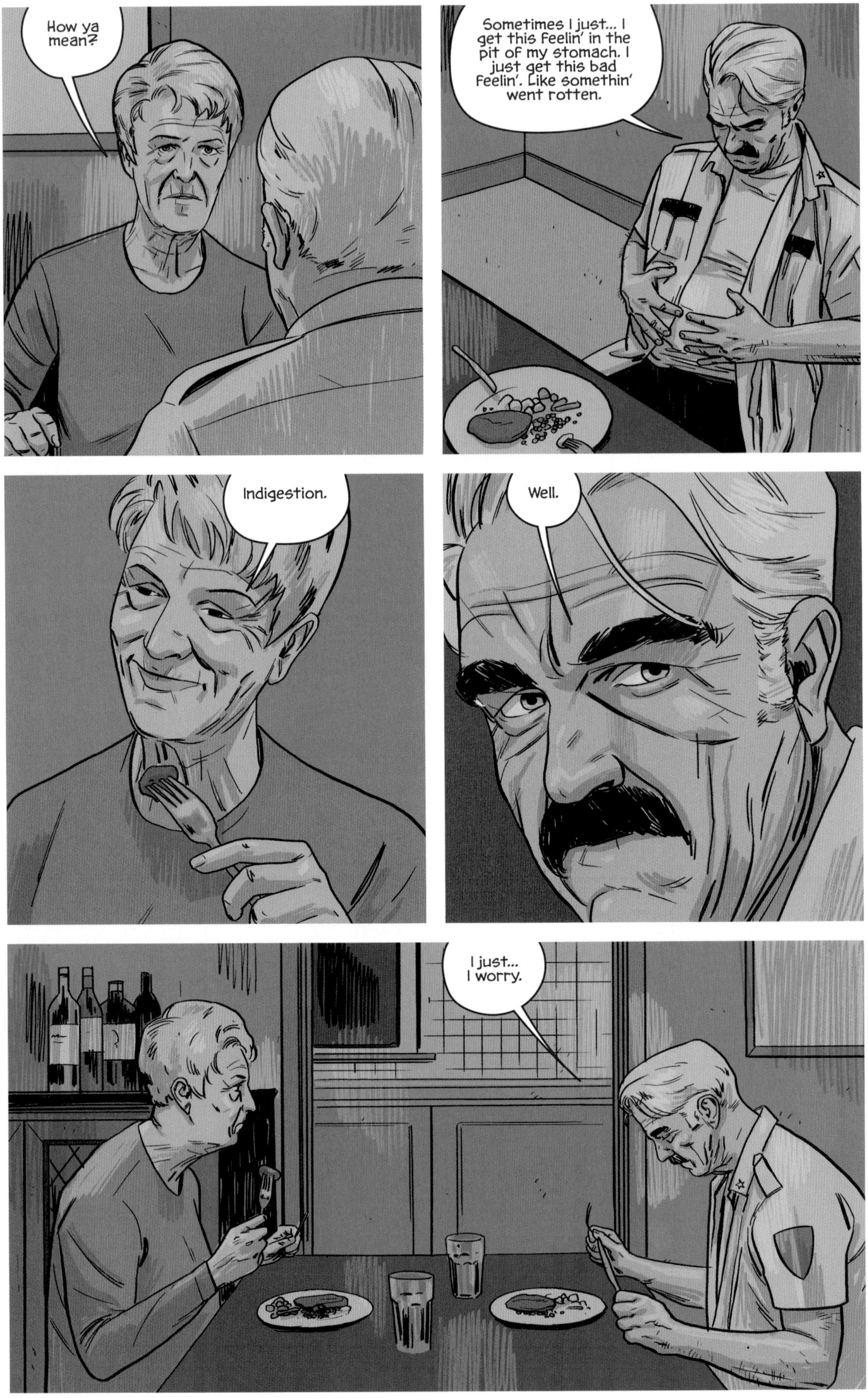
How ya mean?
Sometimes I just... I get this feelin' in the pit of my stomach. I just get this bad feelin'. Like somethin' went rotten.
Indigestion.
Well.
I just... I worry.

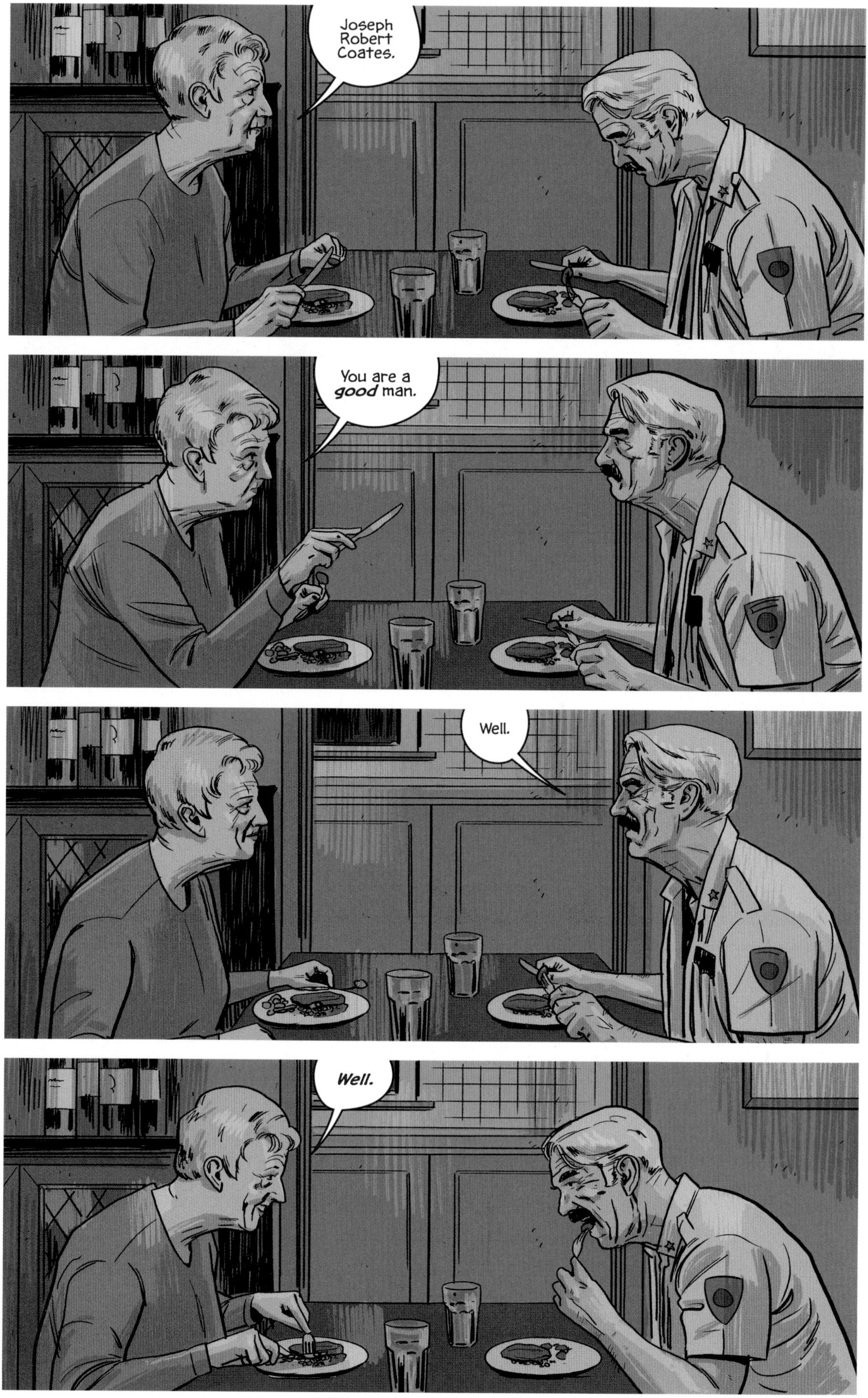
Joseph Robert Coates.
You are a *good* man.
Well.
Well.

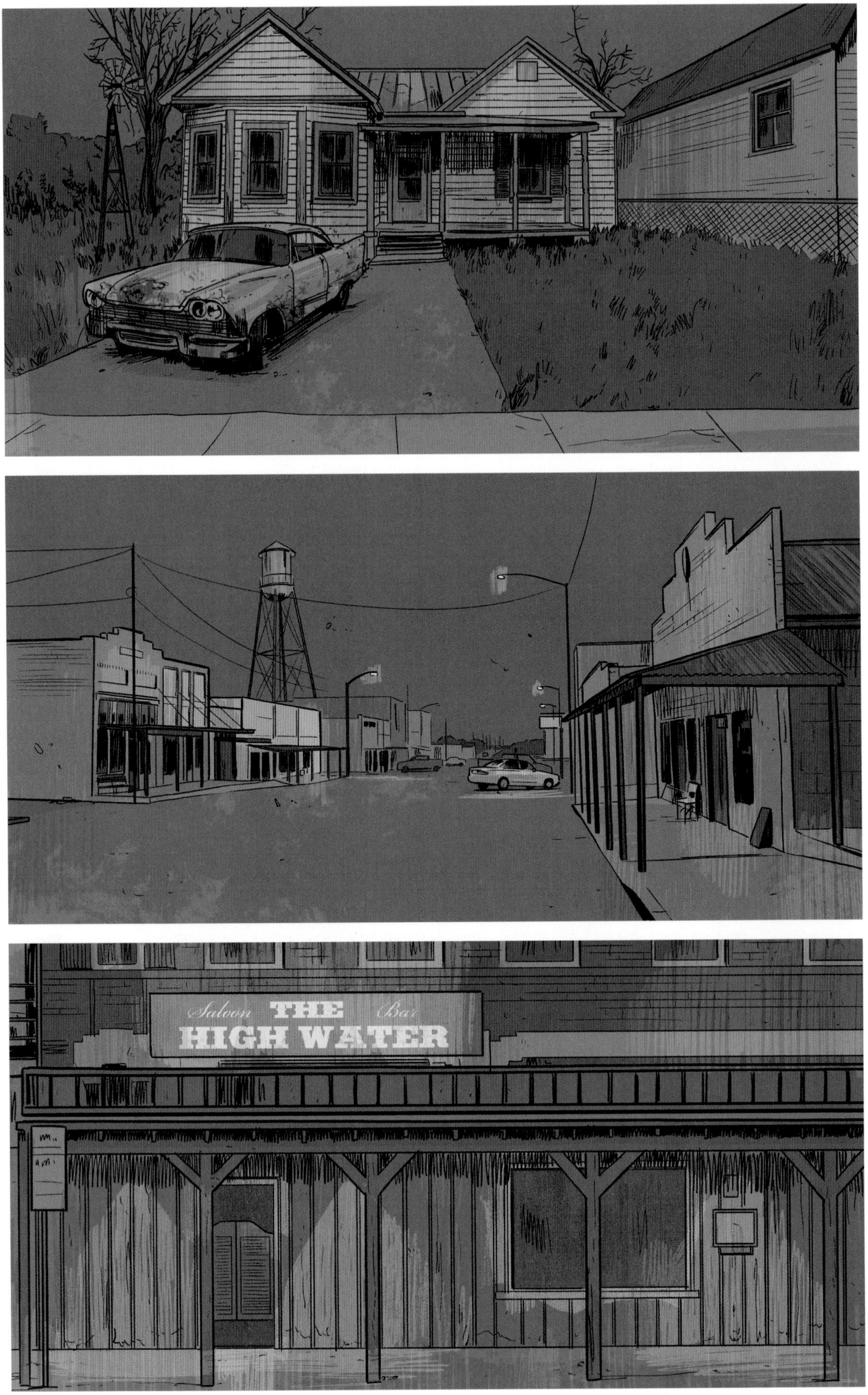
Saloon THE Bar
HIGH WATER

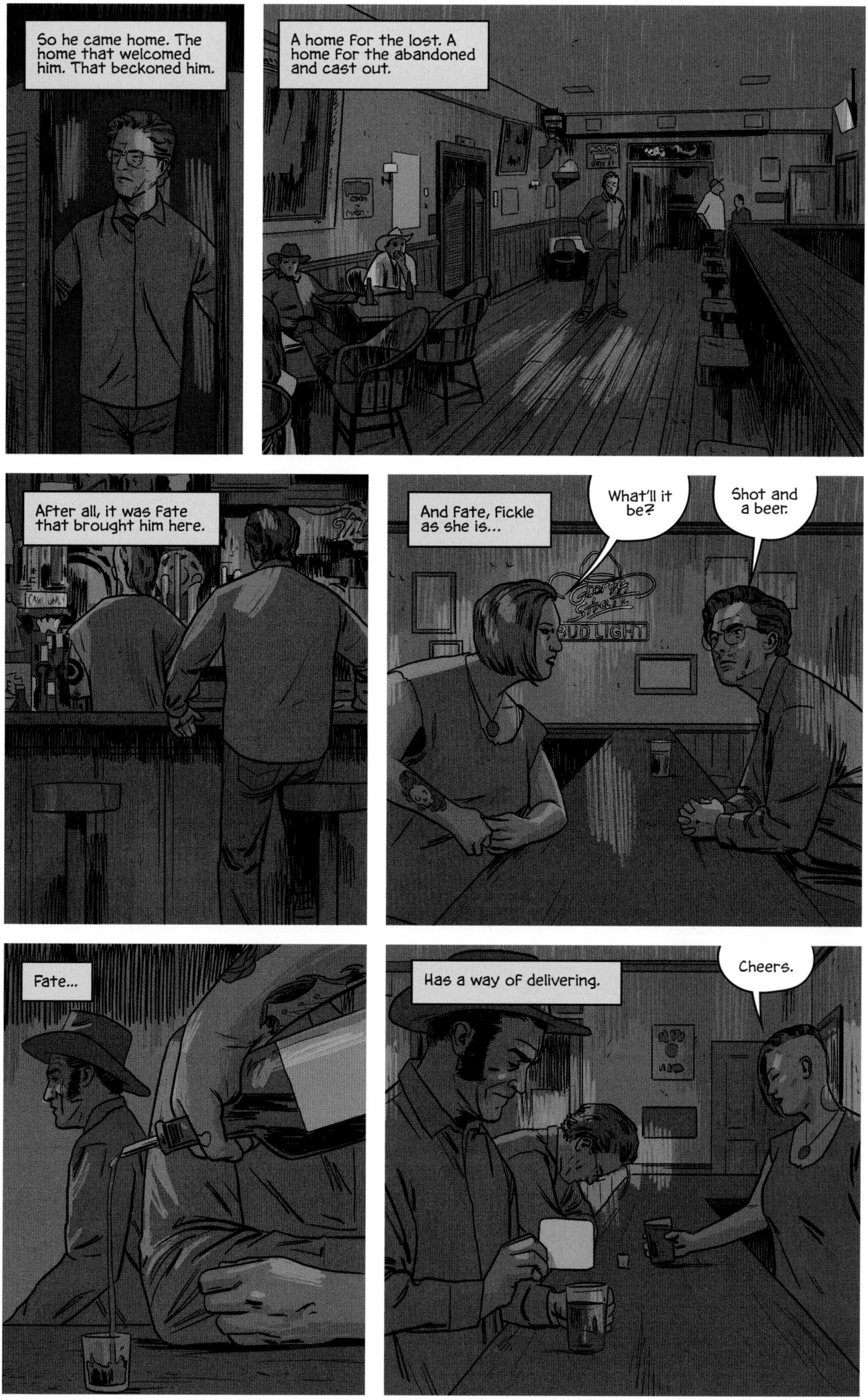

So he came home. The home that welcomed him. That beckoned him.
A home for the lost. A home for the abandoned and cast out.
After all, it was fate that brought him here.
And fate, fickle as she is...
What'll it be?
Shot and a beer.
BUD LIGHT
Fate...
Has a way of delivering.
Cheers.

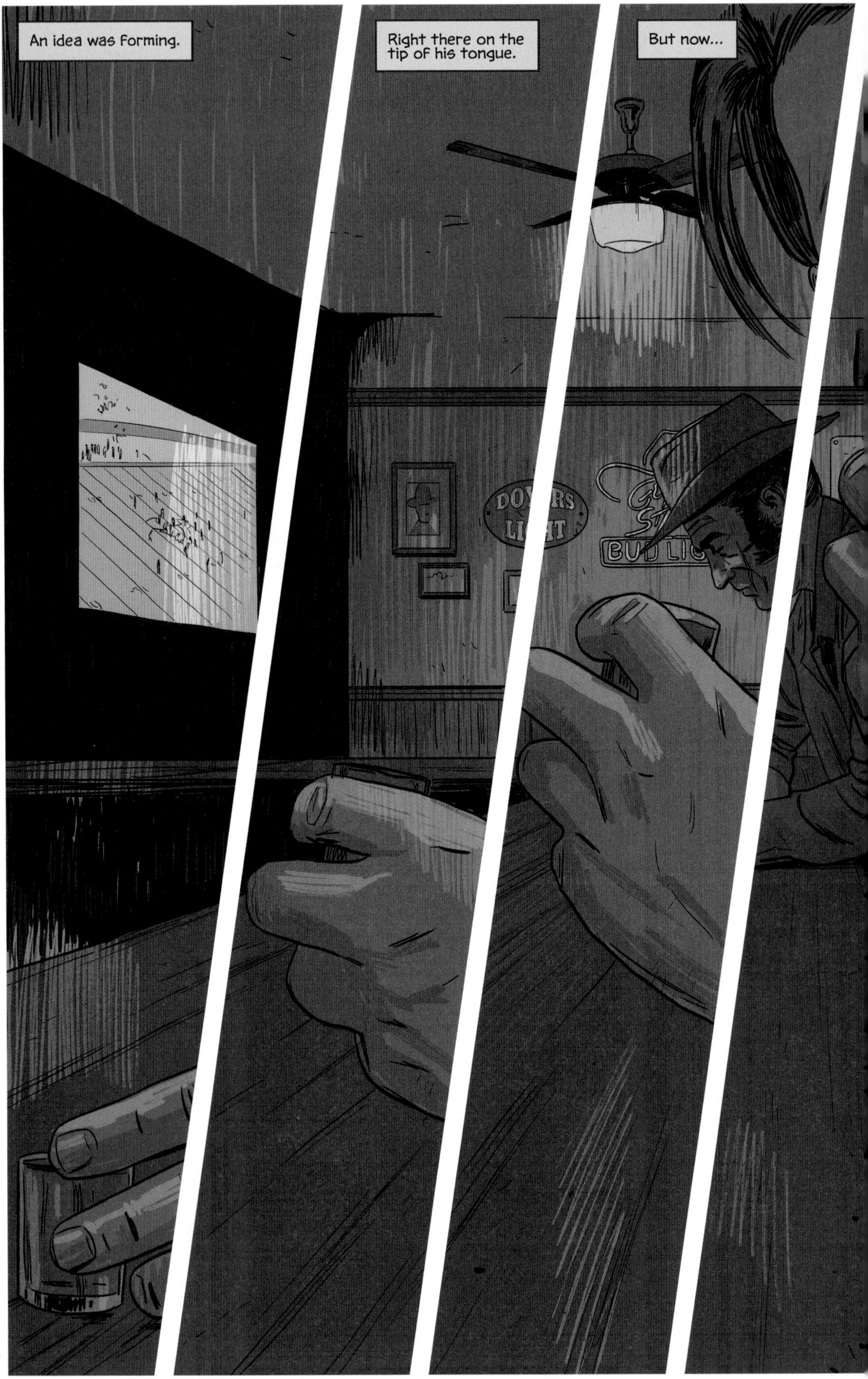
An idea was forming.
Right there on the tip of his tongue.
But now...
DOYLERS LIGHT
BUD LIG

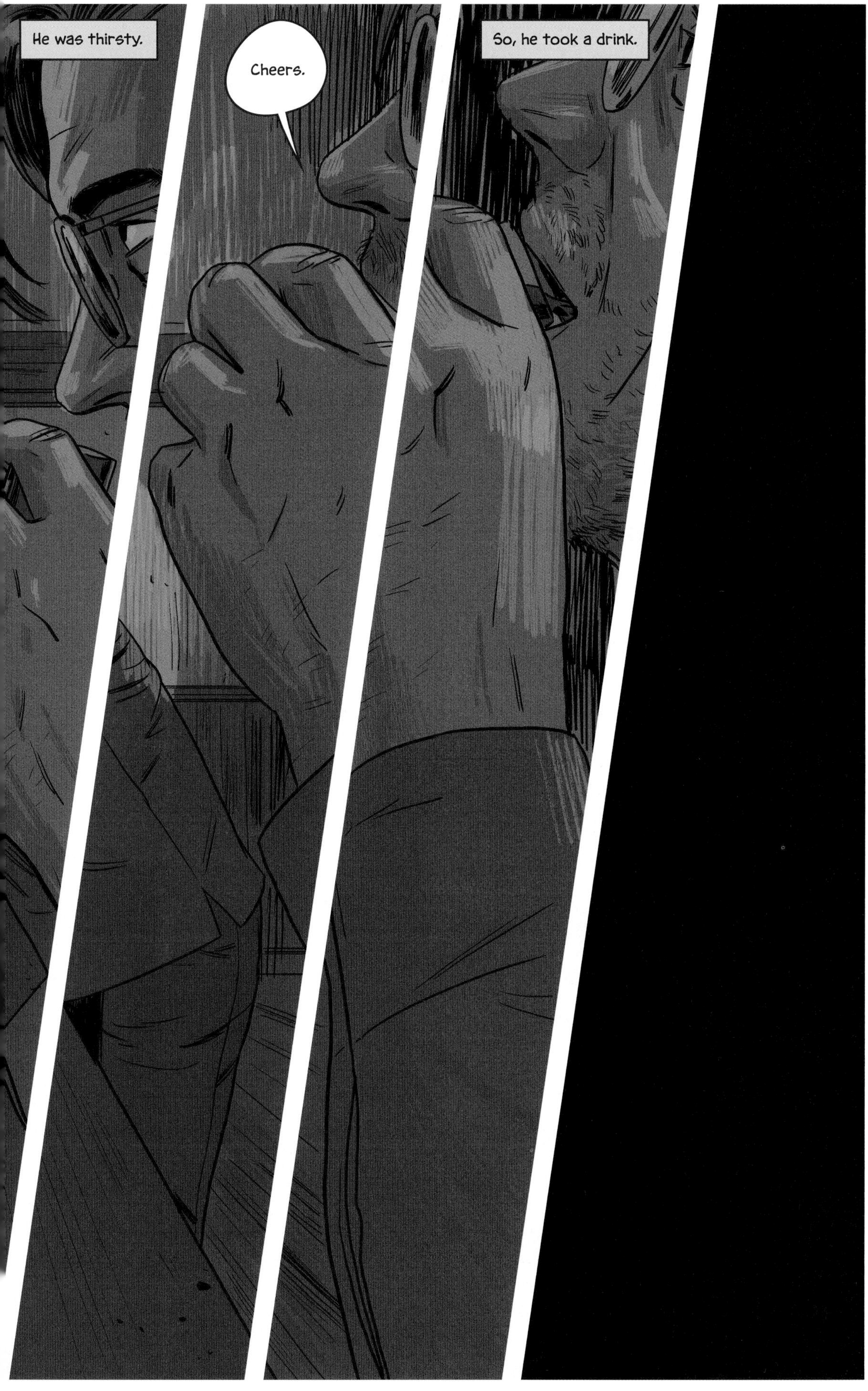
He was thirsty.
Cheers.
So, he took a drink.

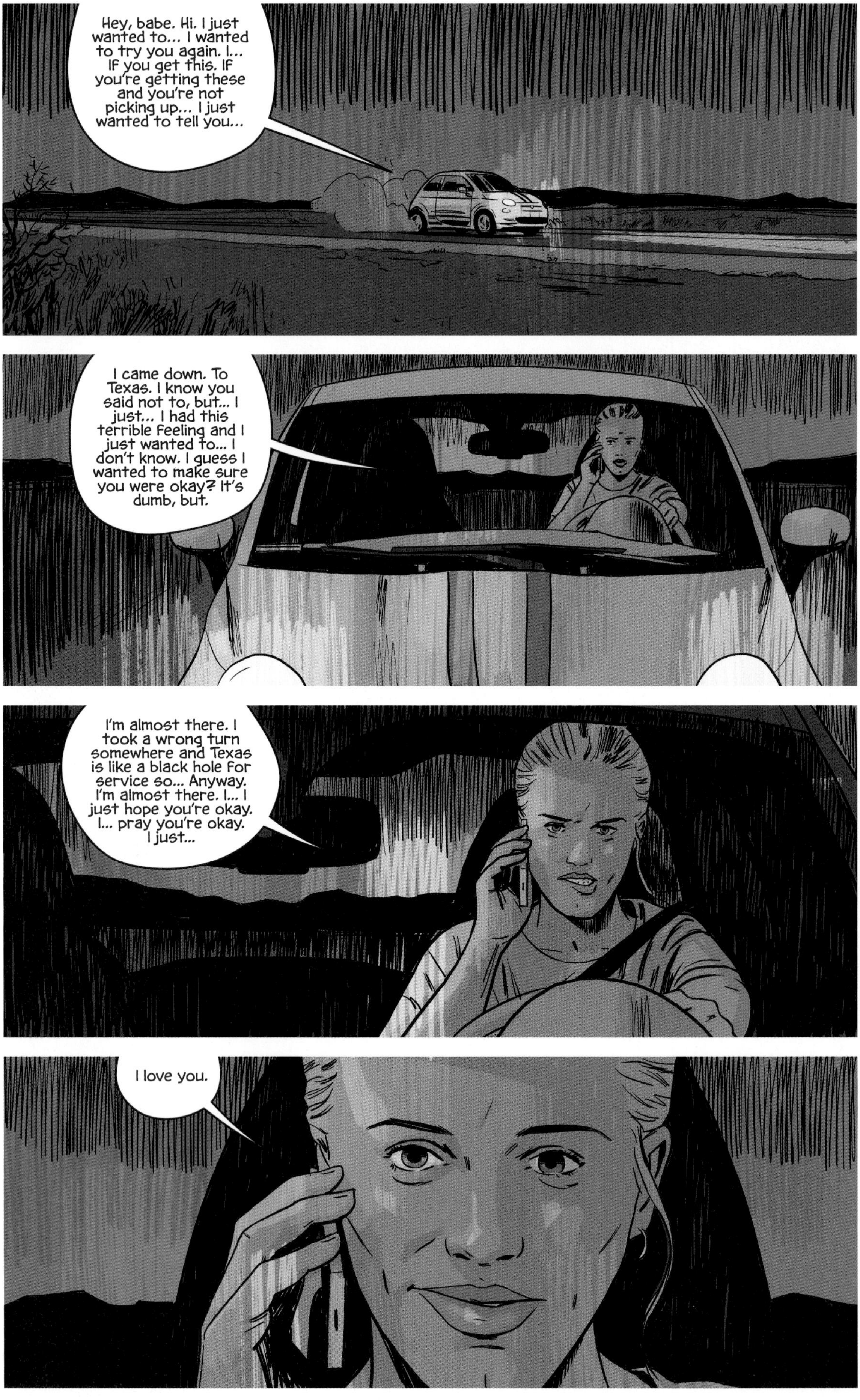
Hey, babe. Hi. I just wanted to... I wanted to try you again. I... If you get this. If you're getting these and you're not picking up... I just wanted to tell you...
I came down. To Texas. I know you said not to, but... I just... I had this terrible feeling and I just wanted to... I don't know. I guess I wanted to make sure you were okay? It's dumb, but.
I'm almost there. I took a wrong turn somewhere and Texas is like a black hole for service so... Anyway. I'm almost there. I... I just hope you're okay. I... pray you're okay. I just...
I love you.

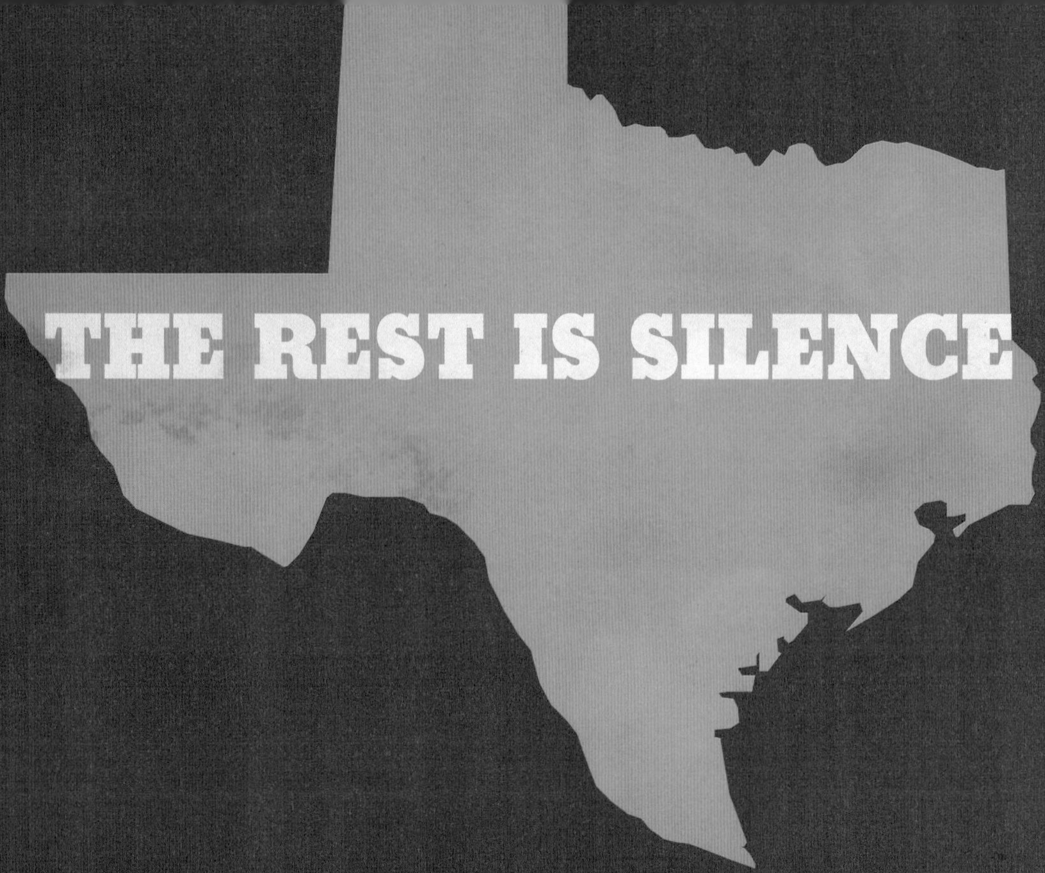
THE REST IS SILENCE

A Brother's Conscience

Part Four

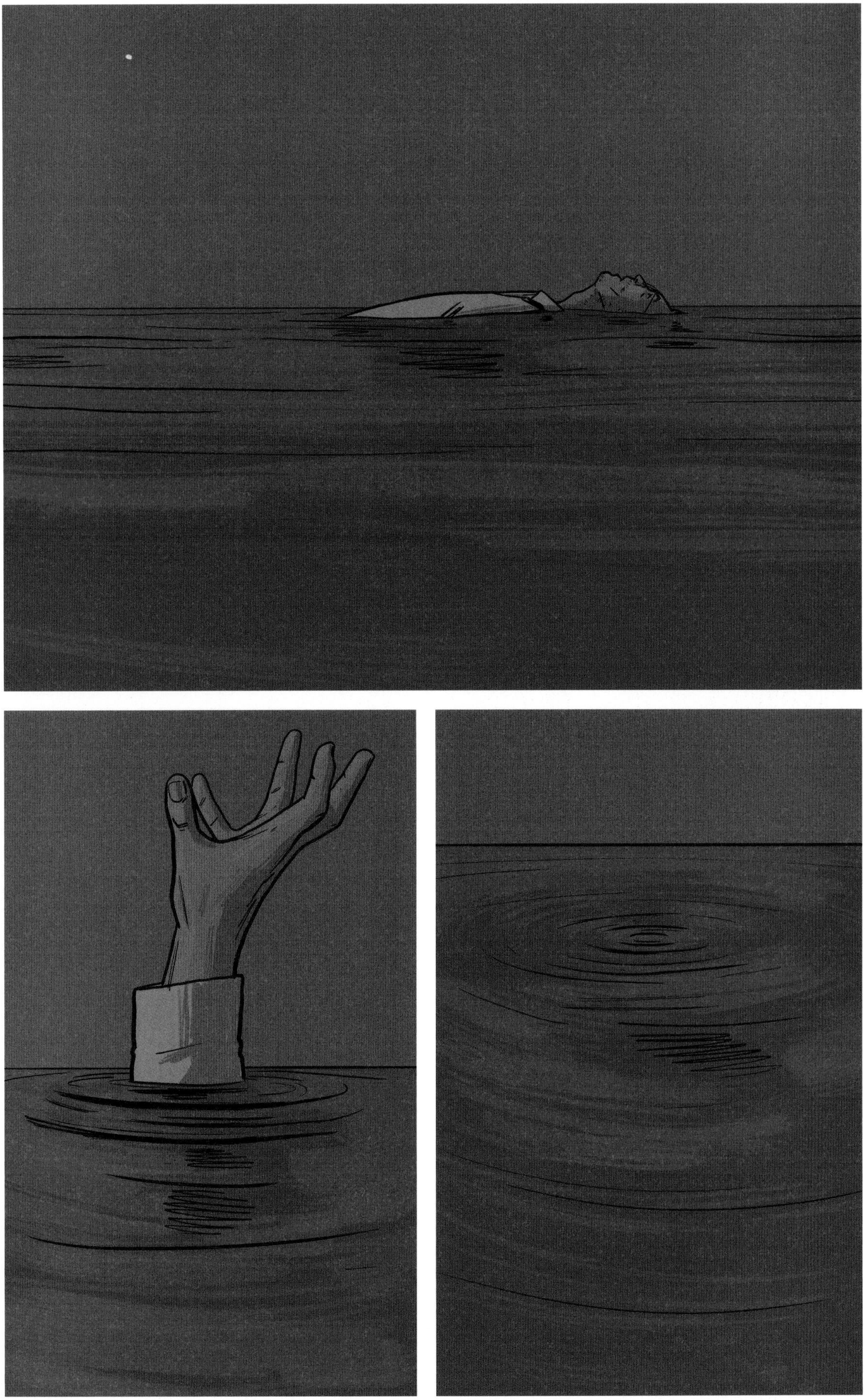

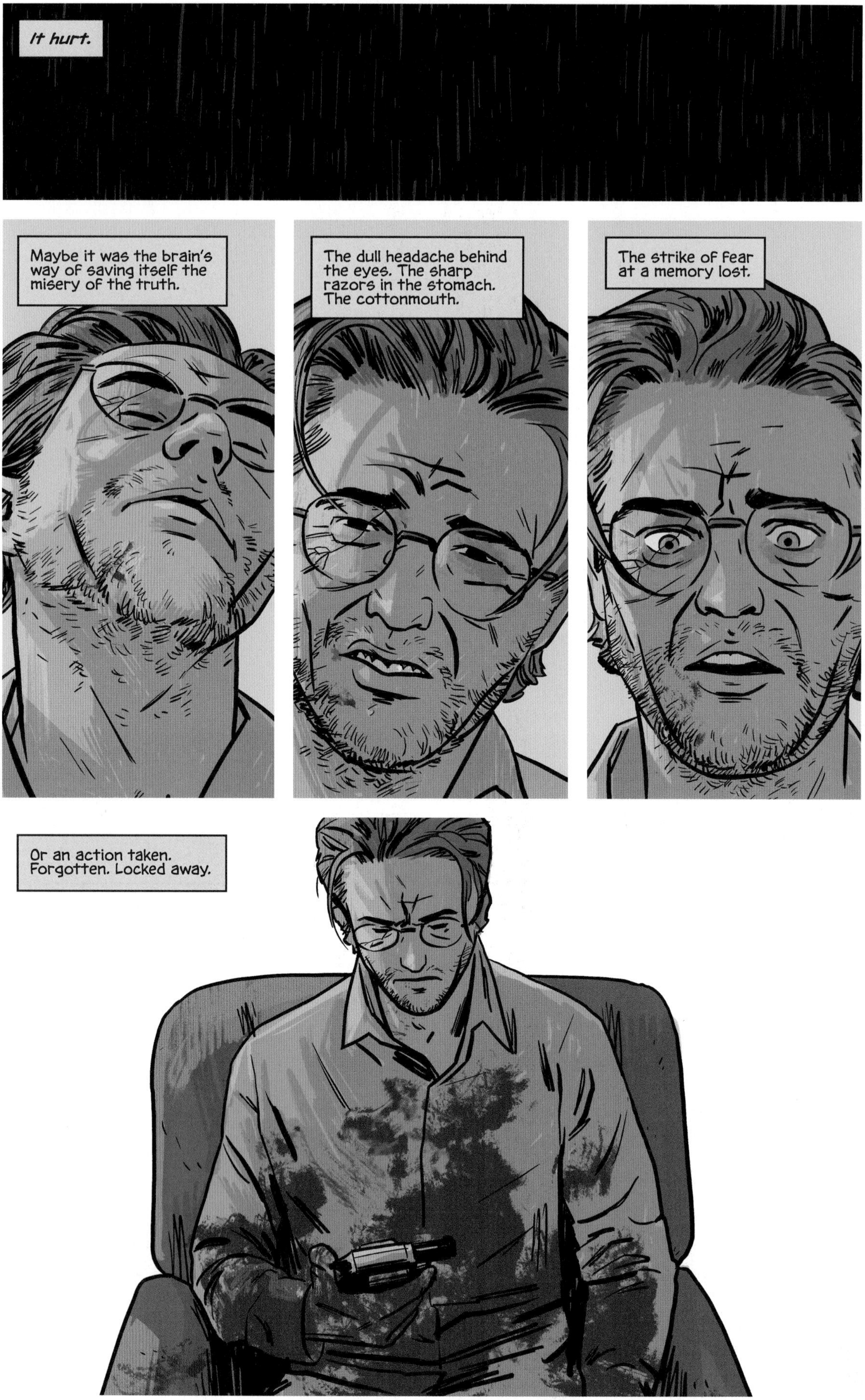
It hurt.
Maybe it was the brain's way of saving itself the misery of the truth.
The dull headache behind the eyes. The sharp razors in the stomach. The cottonmouth.
The strike of fear at a memory lost.
Or an action taken. Forgotten. Locked away.

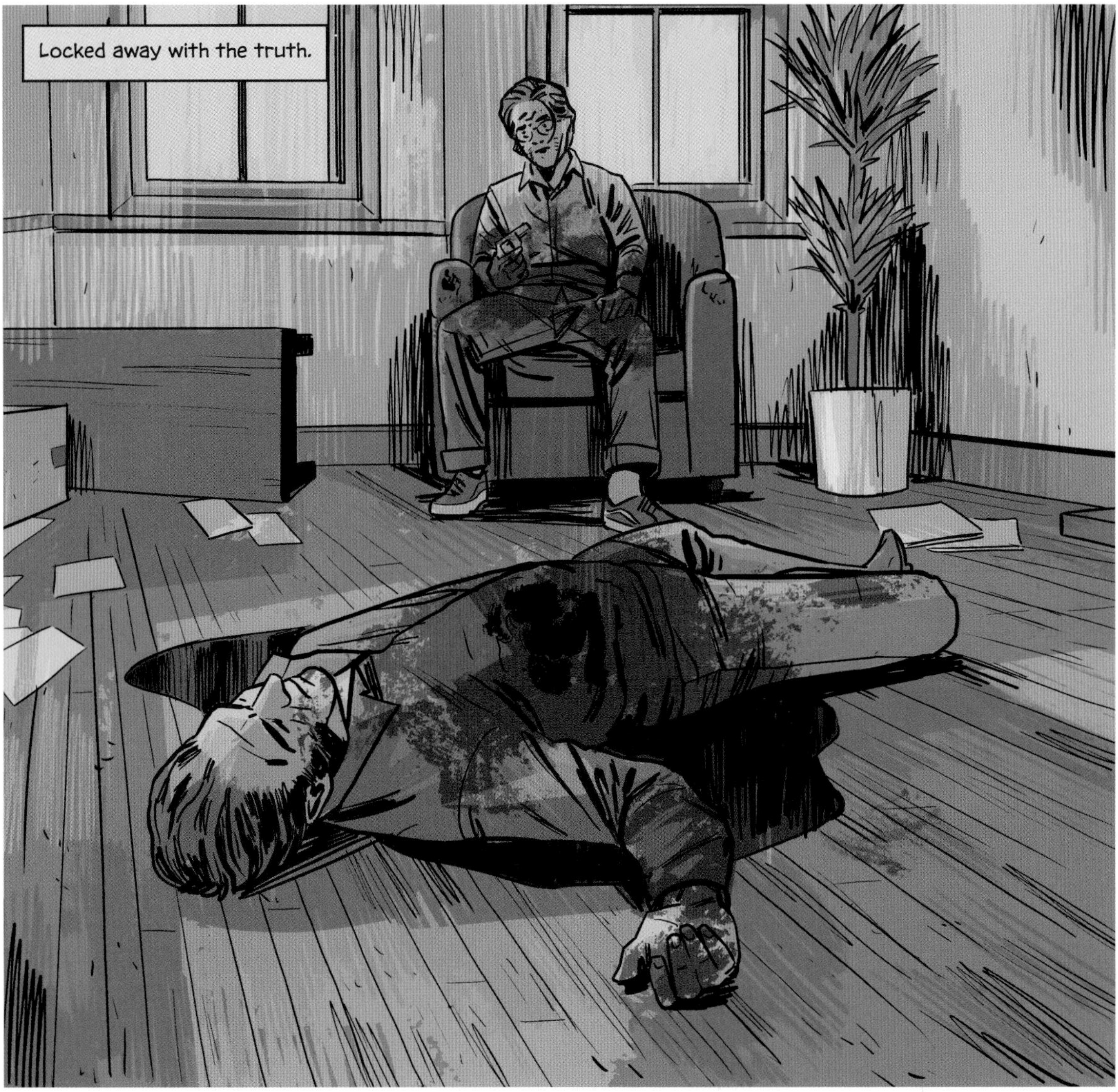
Locked away with the truth.

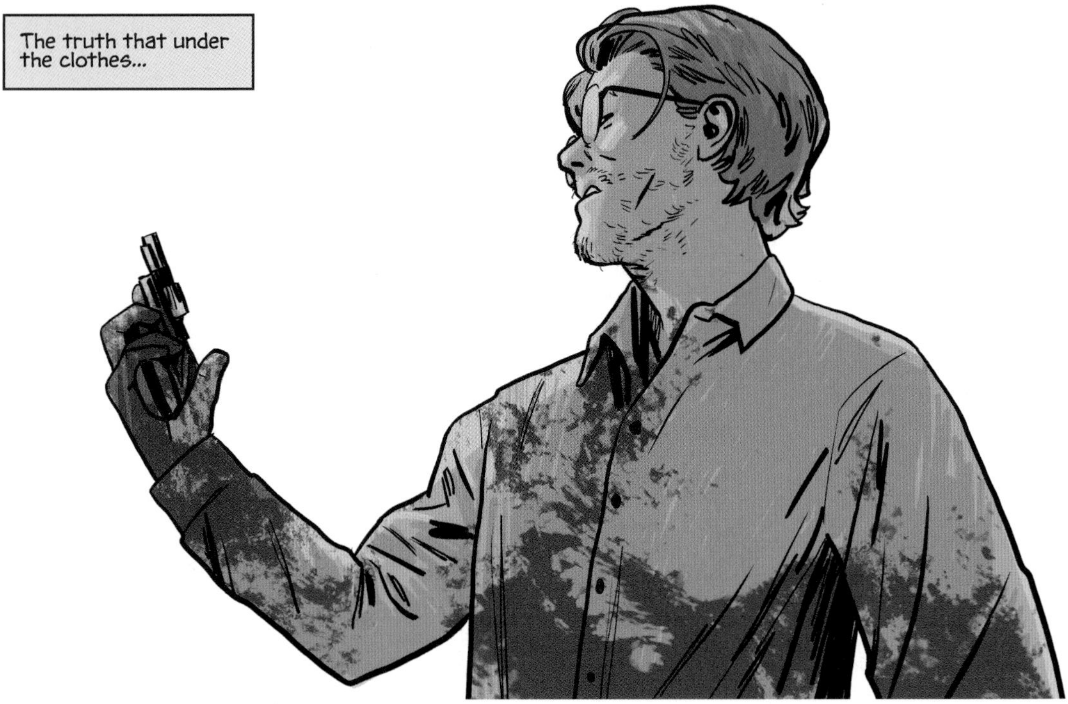
The truth that under the clothes...

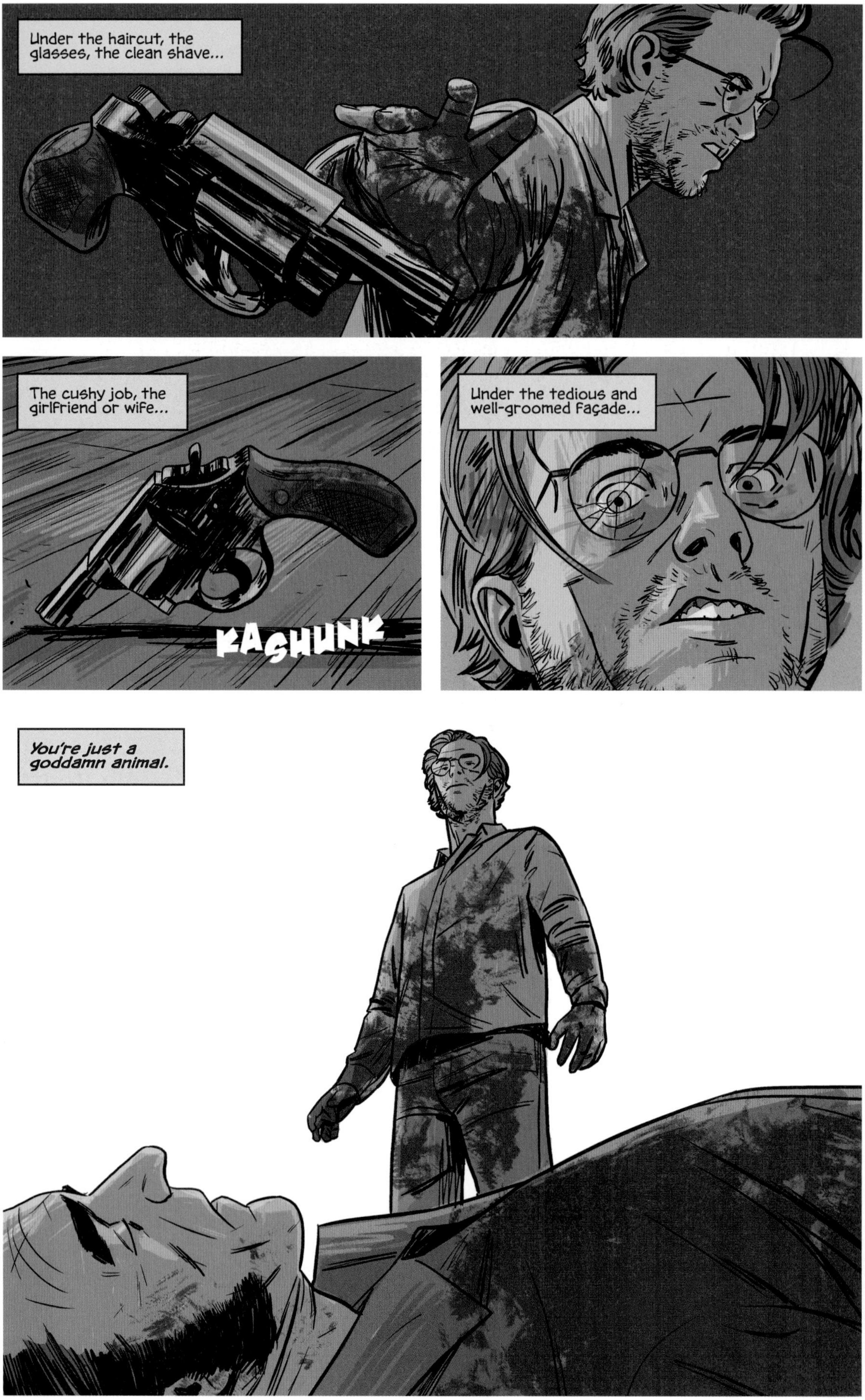
Under the haircut, the glasses, the clean shave...
The cushy job, the girlfriend or wife...
KASHUNK
Under the tedious and well-groomed façade...
You're just a goddamn animal.

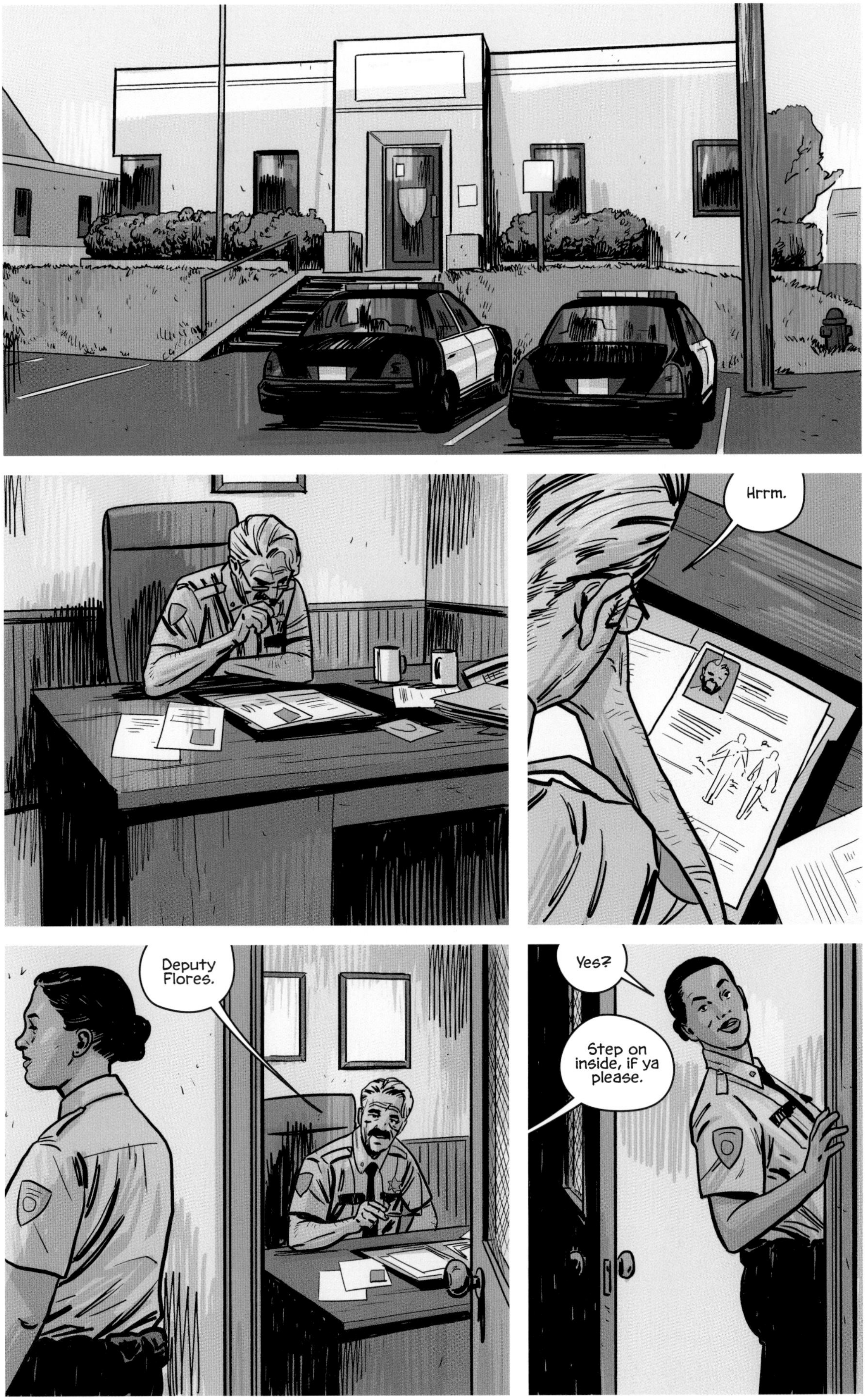
Hrrm.
Deputy Flores.
Yes?
Step on inside, if ya please.

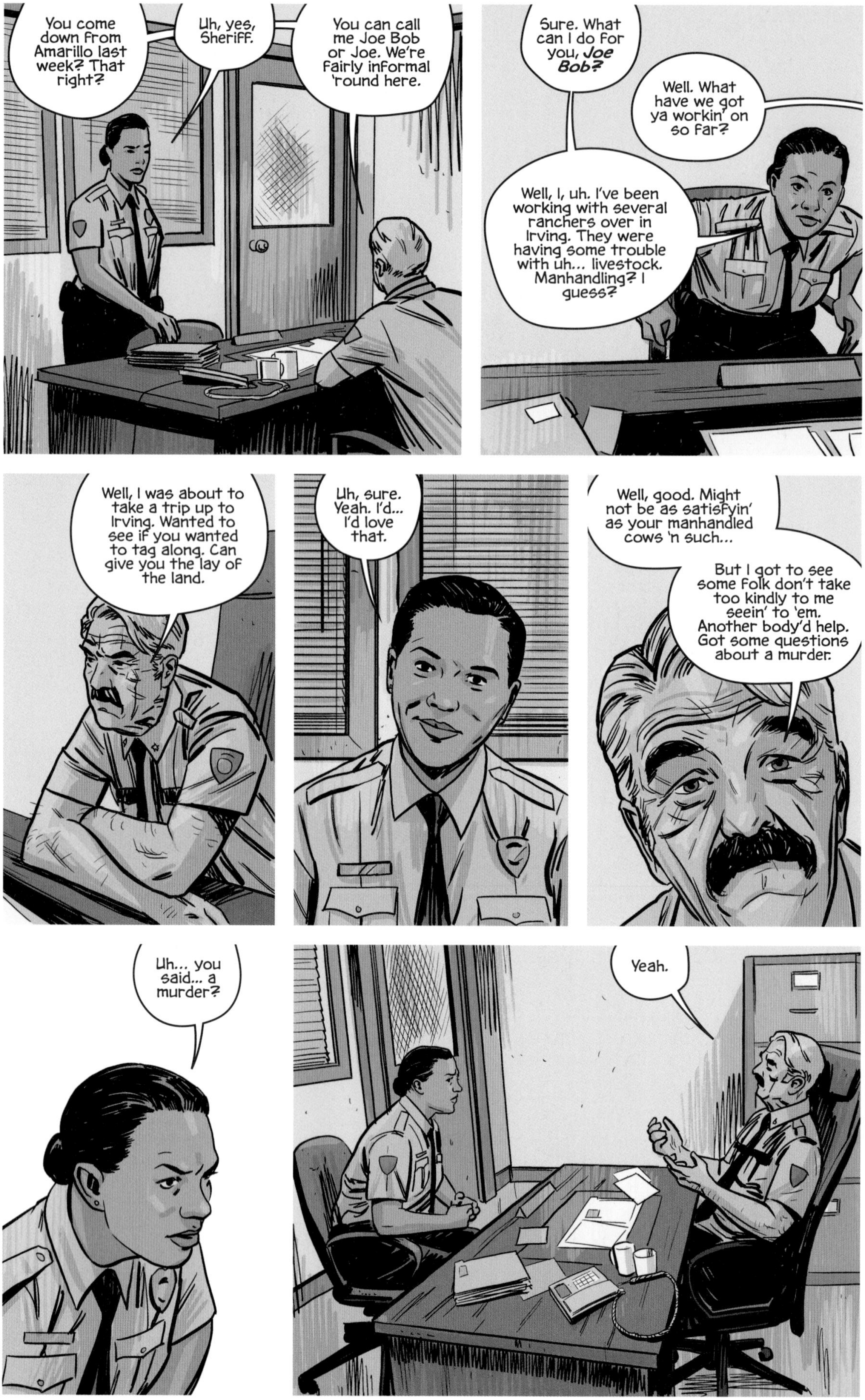
You come down from Amarillo last week? That right?
Uh, yes, Sheriff.
You can call me Joe Bob or Joe. We're fairly informal 'round here.
Sure. What can I do for you, *Joe Bob?*
Well. What have we got ya workin' on so far?
Well, I, uh. I've been working with several ranchers over in Irving. They were having some trouble with uh... livestock. Manhandling? I guess?
Well, I was about to take a trip up to Irving. Wanted to see if you wanted to tag along. Can give you the lay of the land.
Uh, sure. Yeah. I'd... I'd love that.
Well, good. Might not be as satisfyin' as your manhandled cows 'n such...
But I got to see some folk don't take too kindly to me seein' to 'em. Another body'd help. Got some questions about a murder.
Uh... you said... a murder?
Yeah.

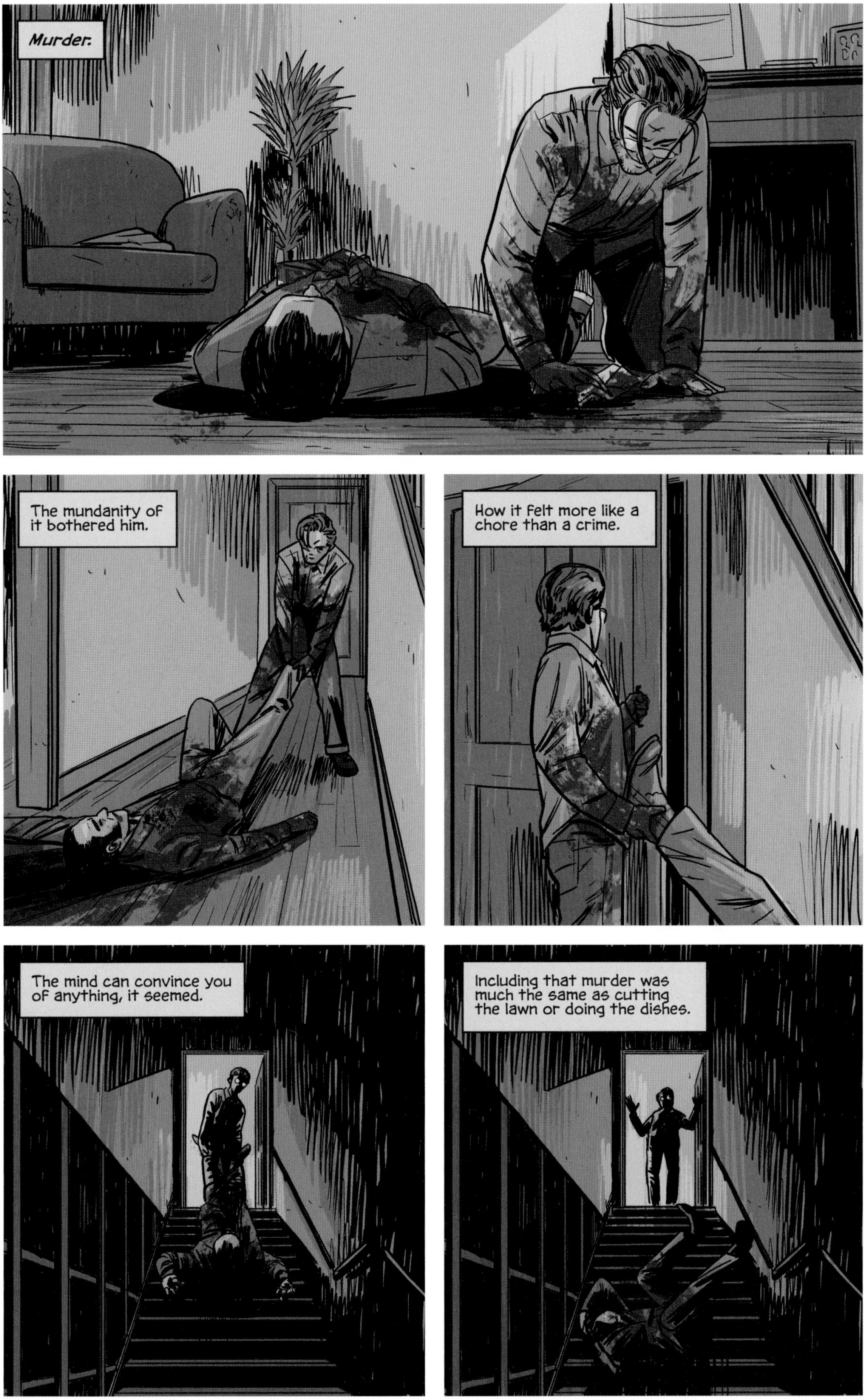

Murder.
The mundanity of it bothered him.
How it felt more like a chore than a crime.
The mind can convince you of anything, it seemed.
Including that murder was much the same as cutting the lawn or doing the dishes.

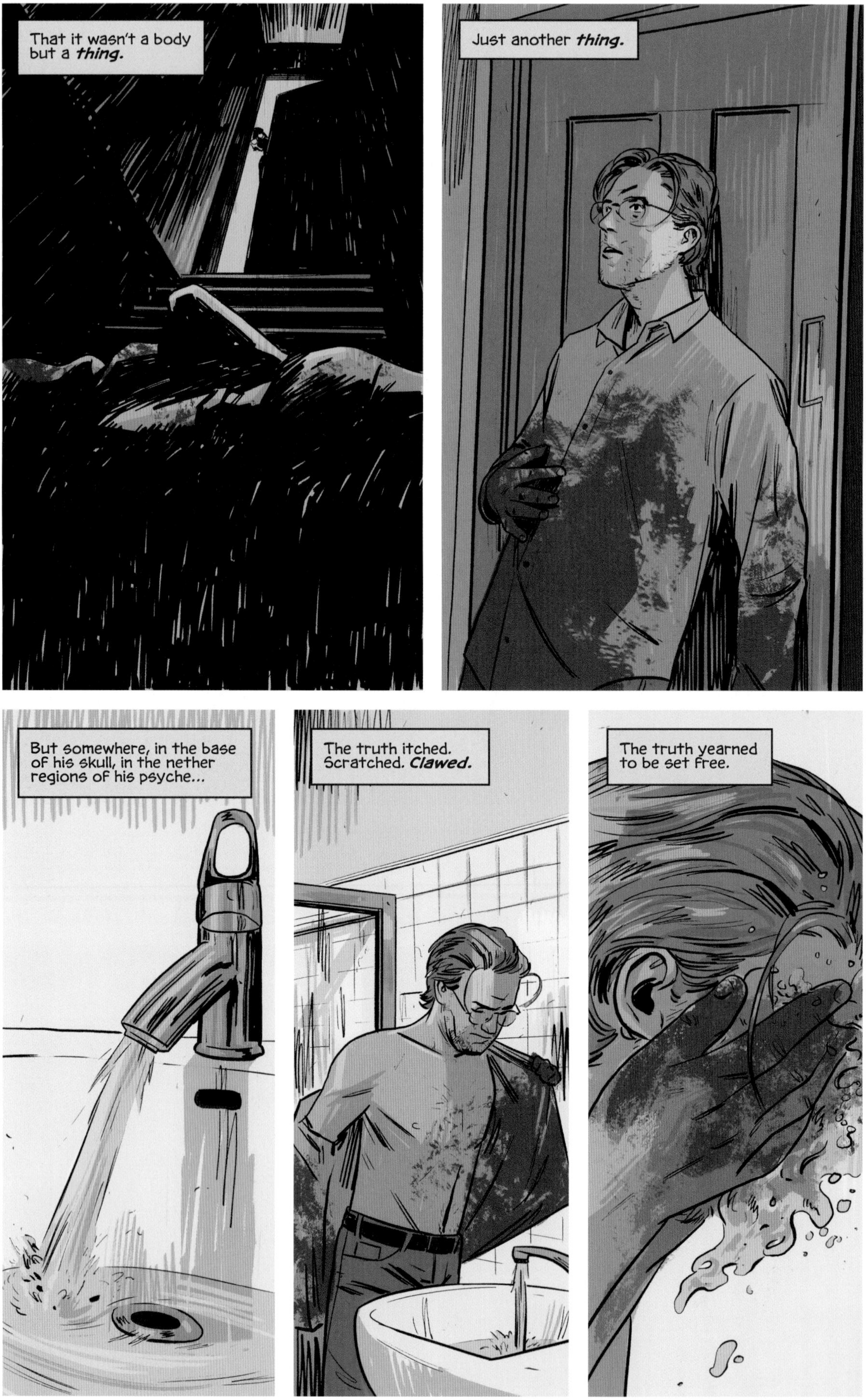
That it wasn't a body but a *thing.*
Just another *thing.*
But somewhere, in the base of his skull, in the nether regions of his psyche...
The truth itched. Scratched. *Clawed.*
The truth yearned to be set free.

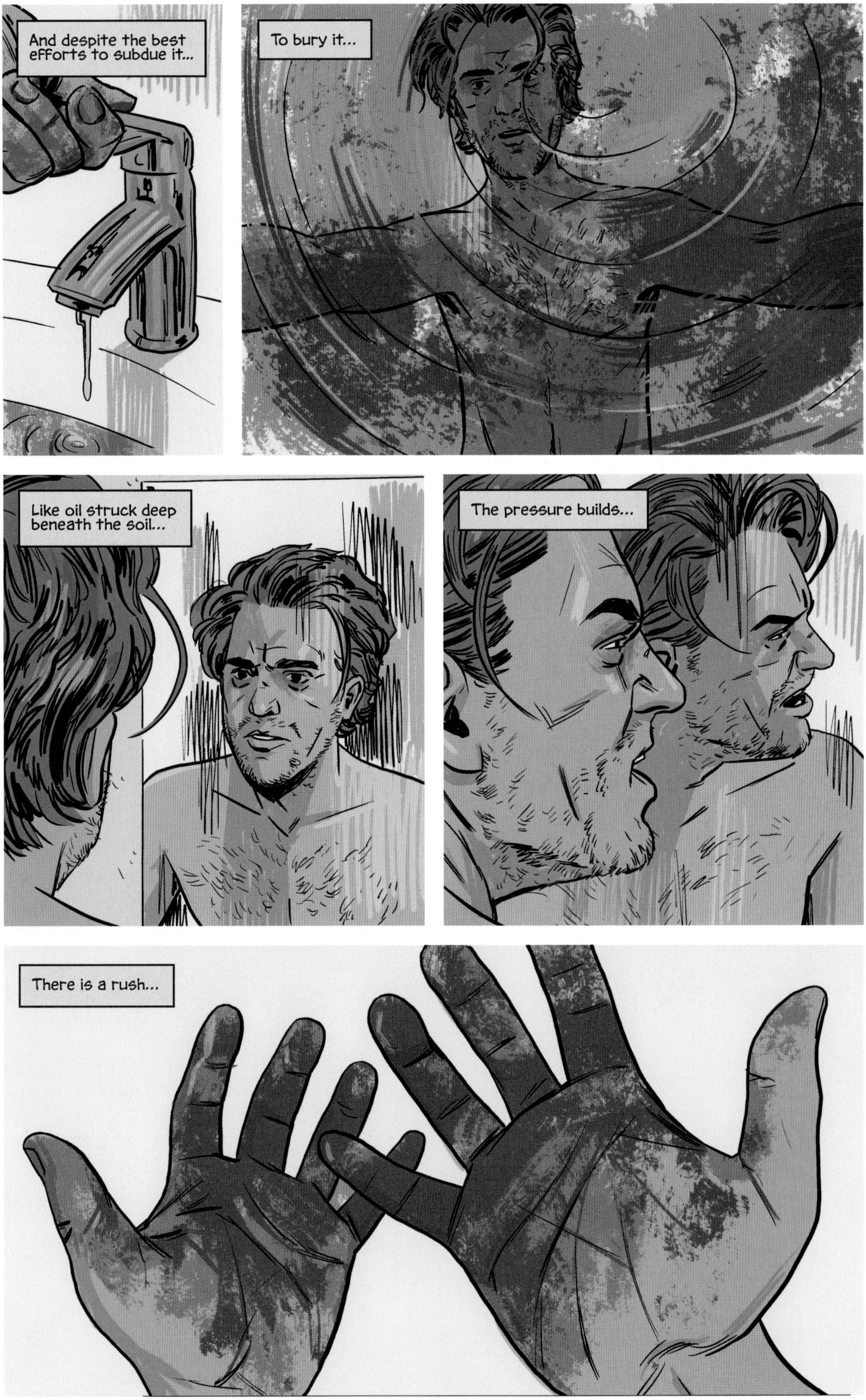
And despite the best efforts to subdue it...
To bury it...
Like oil struck deep beneath the soil...
The pressure builds...
There is a rush...

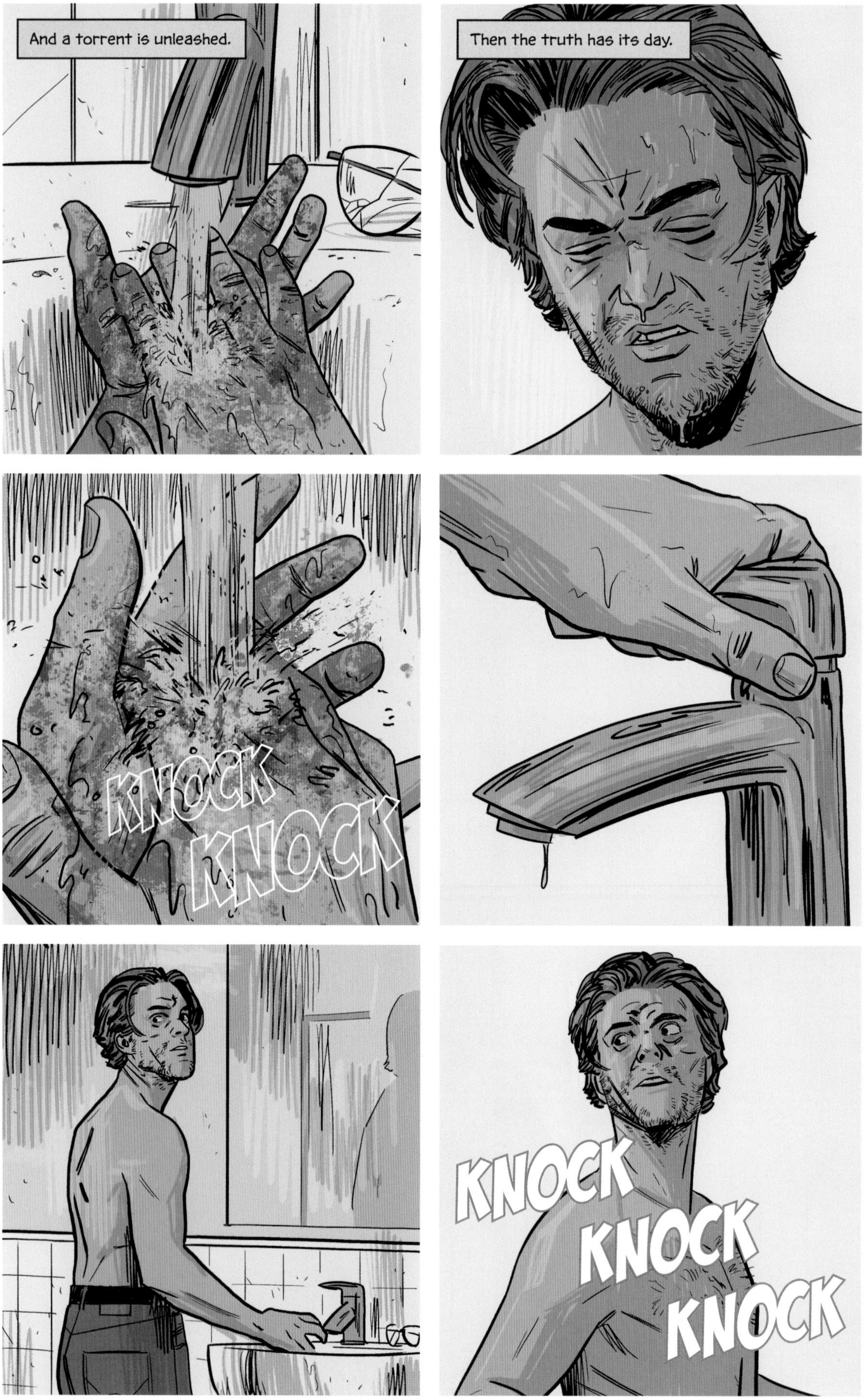
And a torrent is unleashed.
Then the truth has its day.
KNOCK
KNOCK
KNOCK
KNOCK
KNOCK

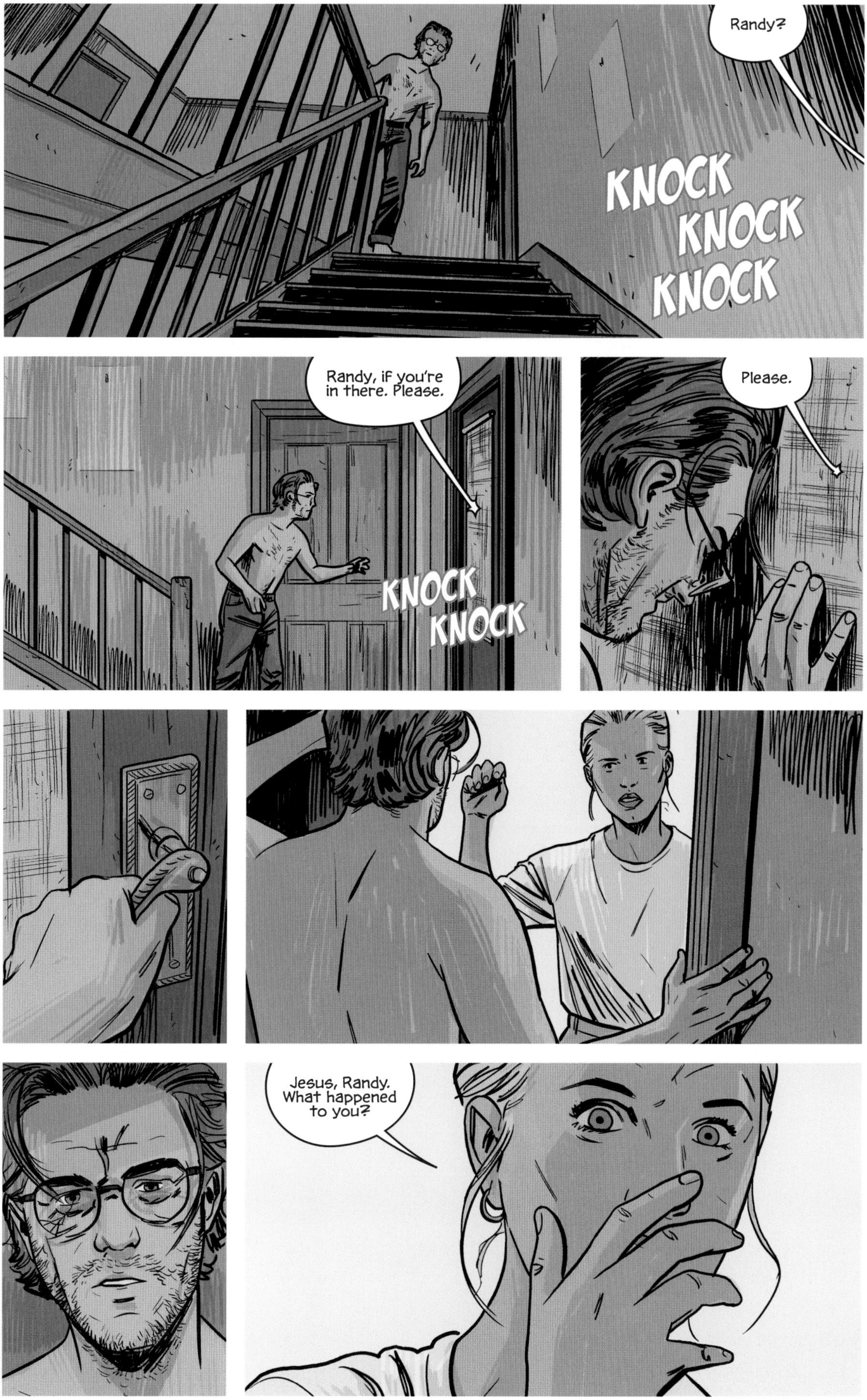
Randy?
KNOCK KNOCK KNOCK
Randy, if you're in there. Please.
KNOCK KNOCK
Please.
Jesus, Randy. What happened to you?

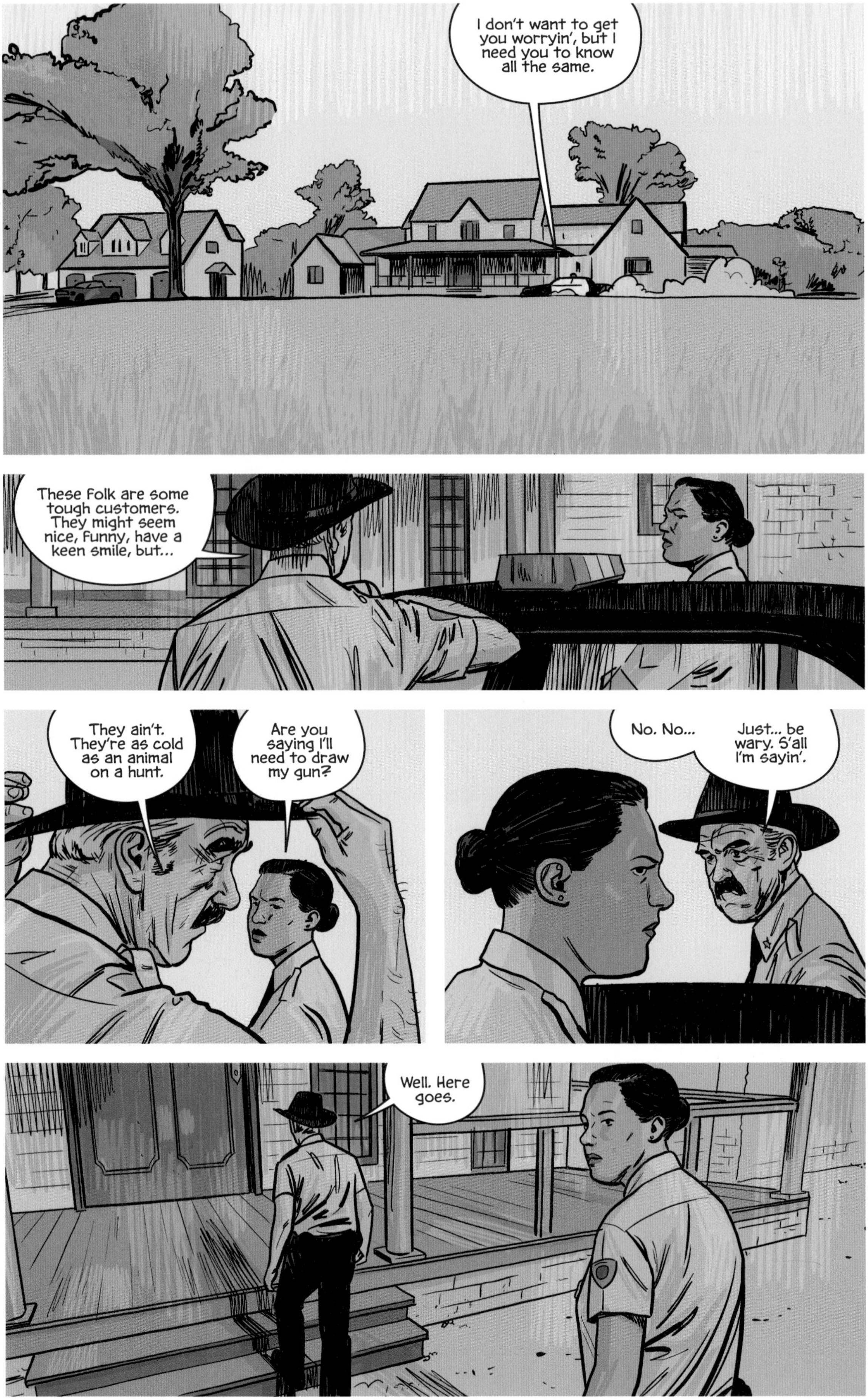
I don't want to get you worryin', but I need you to know all the same.
These folk are some tough customers. They might seem nice, funny, have a keen smile, but...
They ain't. They're as cold as an animal on a hunt.
Are you saying I'll need to draw my gun?
No. No...
Just... be wary. S'all I'm sayin'.
Well. Here goes.

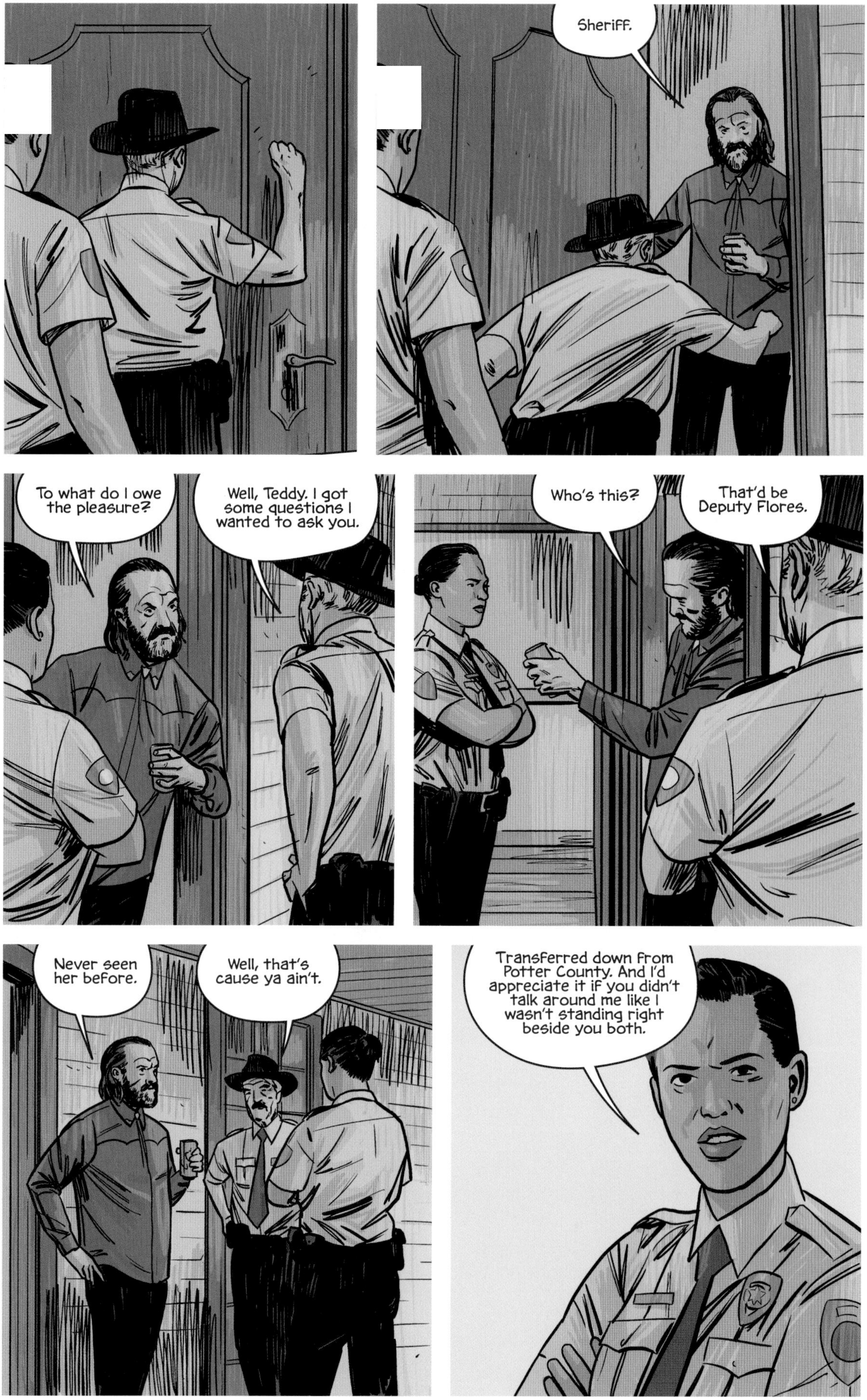
Sheriff.
To what do I owe the pleasure?
Well, Teddy. I got some questions I wanted to ask you.
Who's this?
That'd be Deputy Flores.
Never seen her before.
Well, that's cause ya ain't.
Transferred down from Potter County. And I'd appreciate it if you didn't talk around me like I wasn't standing right beside you both.

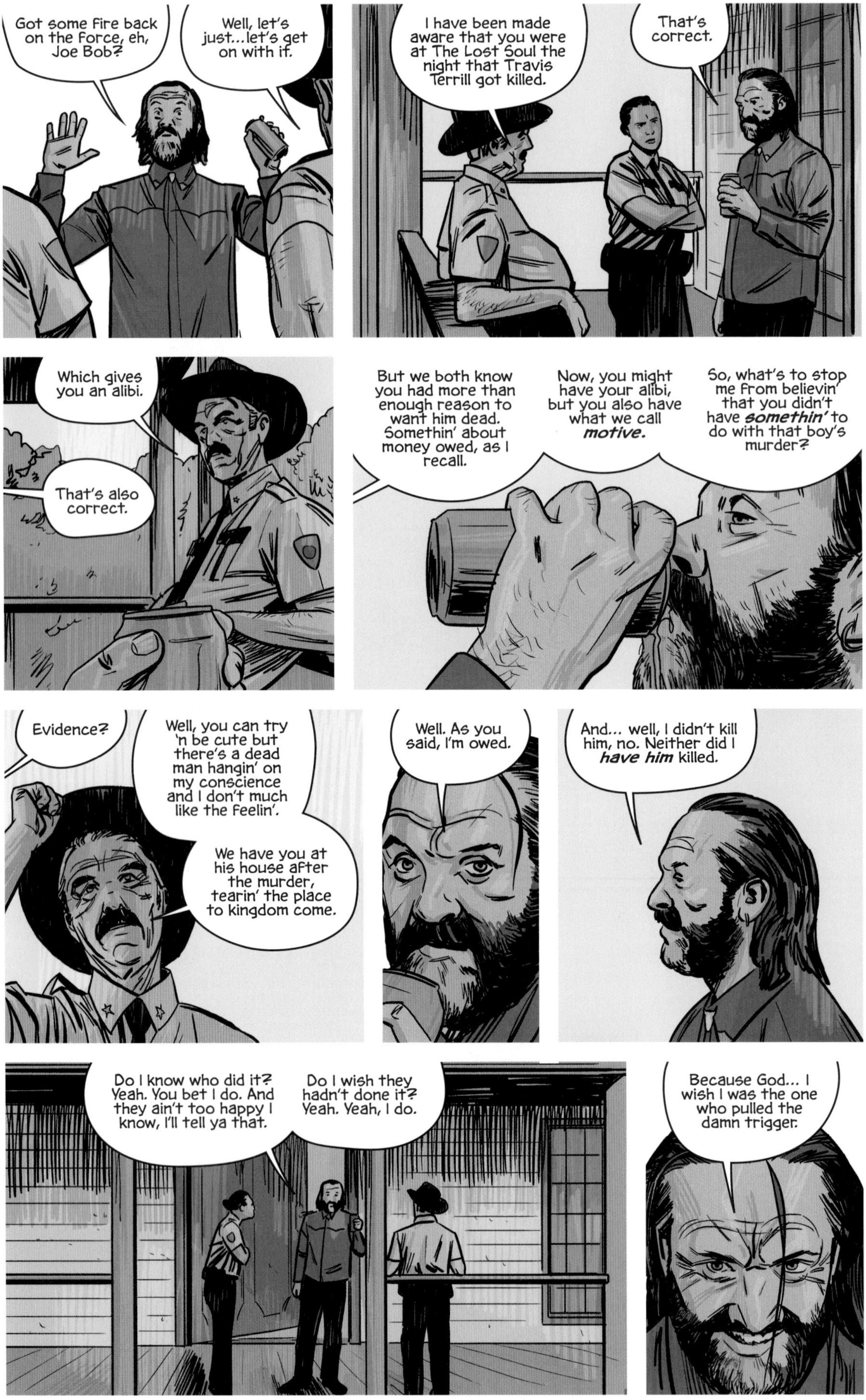

Got some fire back on the Force, eh, Joe Bob?
Well, let's just...let's get on with it.
I have been made aware that you were at The Lost Soul the night that Travis Terrill got killed.
That's correct.
Which gives you an alibi.
That's also correct.
But we both know you had more than enough reason to want him dead. Somethin' about money owed, as I recall.
Now, you might have your alibi, but you also have what we call *motive.*
So, what's to stop me from believin' that you didn't have *somethin'* to do with that boy's murder?
Evidence?
Well, you can try 'n be cute but there's a dead man hangin' on my conscience and I don't much like the feelin'.
We have you at his house after the murder, tearin' the place to kingdom come.
Well. As you said, I'm owed.
And... well, I didn't kill him, no. Neither did I *have him* killed.
Do I know who did it? Yeah. You bet I do. And they ain't too happy I know, I'll tell ya that.
Do I wish they hadn't done it? Yeah. Yeah, I do.
Because God... I wish I was the one who pulled the damn trigger.

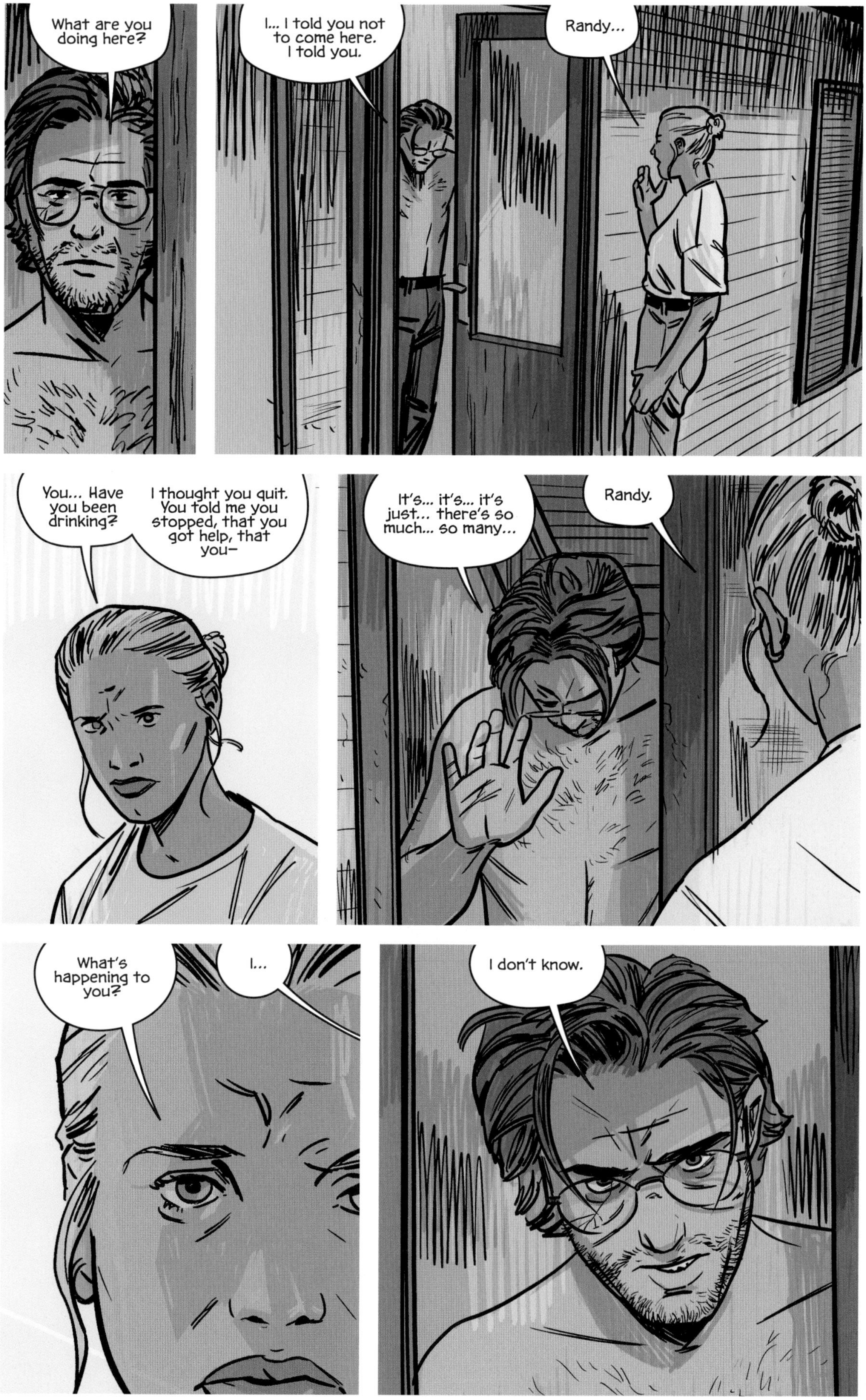
What are you doing here?
I... I told you not to come here. I told you.
Randy...
You... Have you been drinking?
I thought you quit. You told me you stopped, that you got help, that you—
It's... it's... it's just... there's so much... so many...
Randy.
What's happening to you?
I...
I don't know.

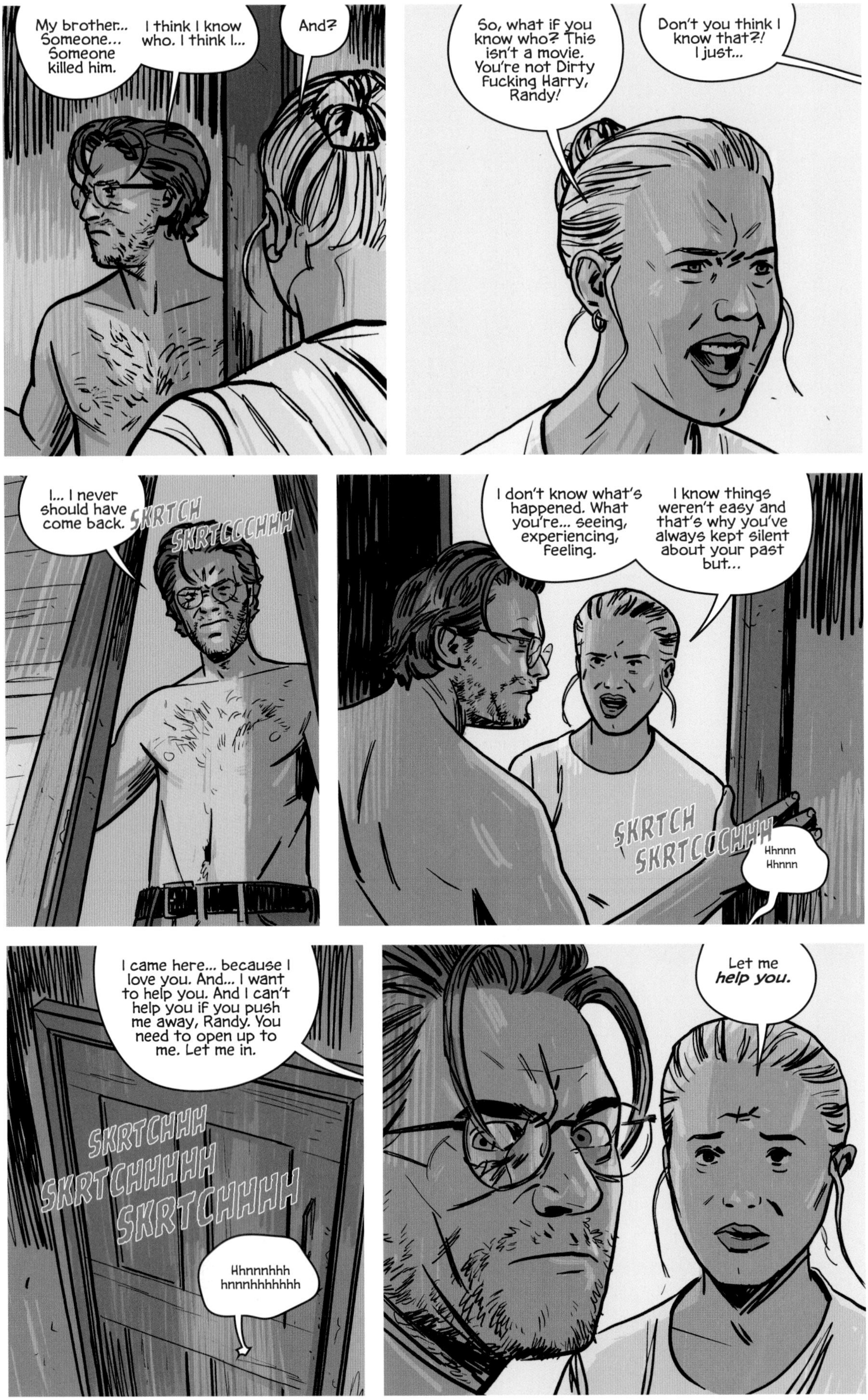
My brother... Someone... Someone killed him.
I think I know who. I think I...
And?
So, what if you know who? This isn't a movie. You're not Dirty Fucking Harry, Randy!
Don't you think I know that?! I just...
I... I never should have come back.
SKRTCH
SKRTCCCHHH
I don't know what's happened. What you're... seeing, experiencing, feeling.
I know things weren't easy and that's why you've always kept silent about your past but...
SKRTCH
SKRTCCCHHH
Hhnnn
Hhnnn
I came here... because I love you. And... I want to help you. And I can't help you if you push me away, Randy. You need to open up to me. Let me in.
SKRTCHHH
SKRTCHHHHH
SKRTCHHHH
Hhnnnhhh
hnnnhhhhhhhh
Let me *help you.*

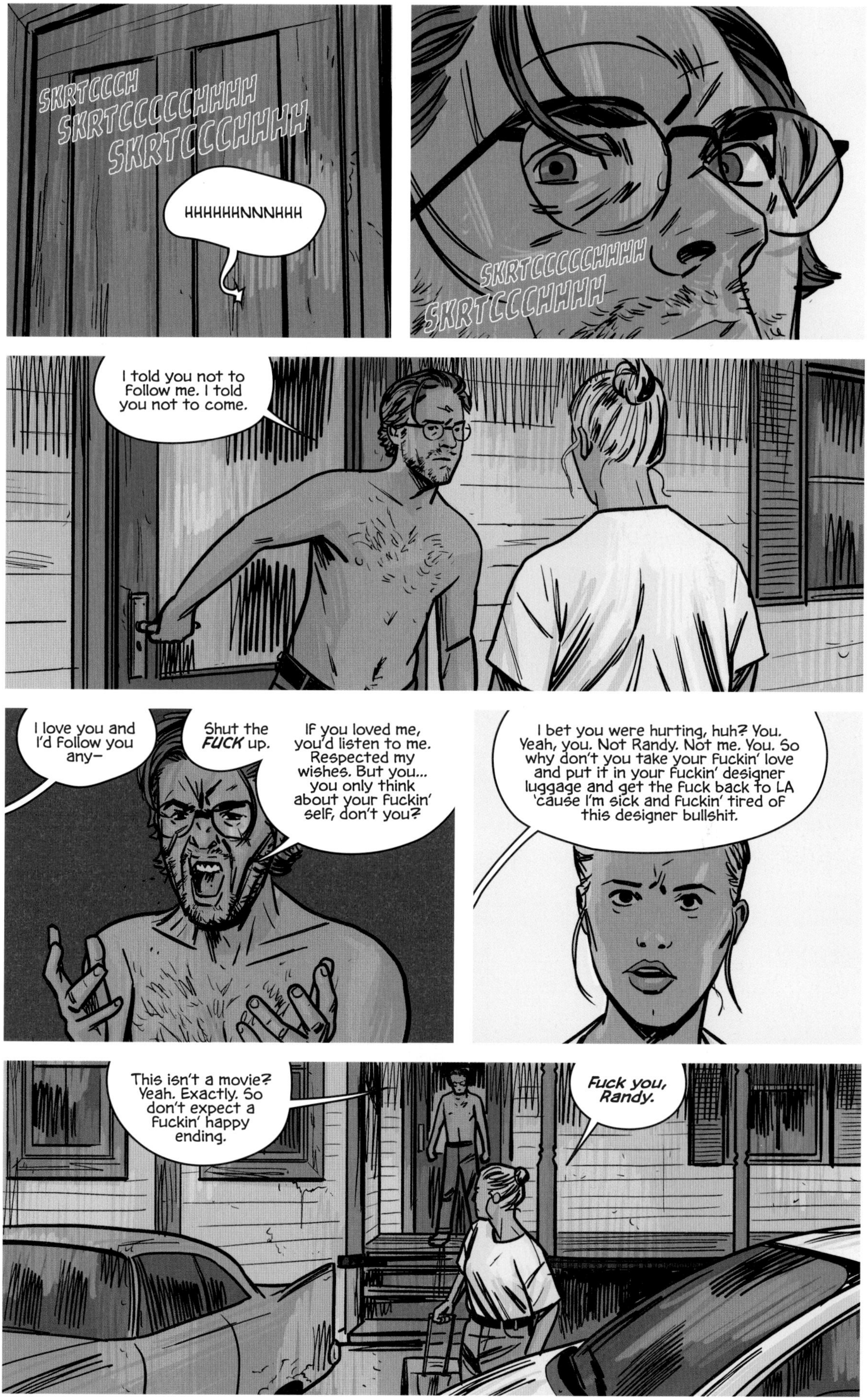
SKRTCCCH
SKRTCCCCCHHHH
SKRTCCCHHHH
HHHHHHNNNHHH
SKRTCCCCCHHHH
SKRTCCCHHHH
I told you not to follow me. I told you not to come.
I love you and I'd follow you any–
Shut the *FUCK* up.
If you loved me, you'd listen to me. Respected my wishes. But you... you only think about your fuckin' self, don't you?
I bet you were hurting, huh? You. Yeah, you. Not Randy. Not me. You. So why don't you take your fuckin' love and put it in your fuckin' designer luggage and get the fuck back to LA 'cause I'm sick and fuckin' tired of this designer bullshit.
This isn't a movie? Yeah. Exactly. So don't expect a fuckin' happy ending.
Fuck you, Randy.

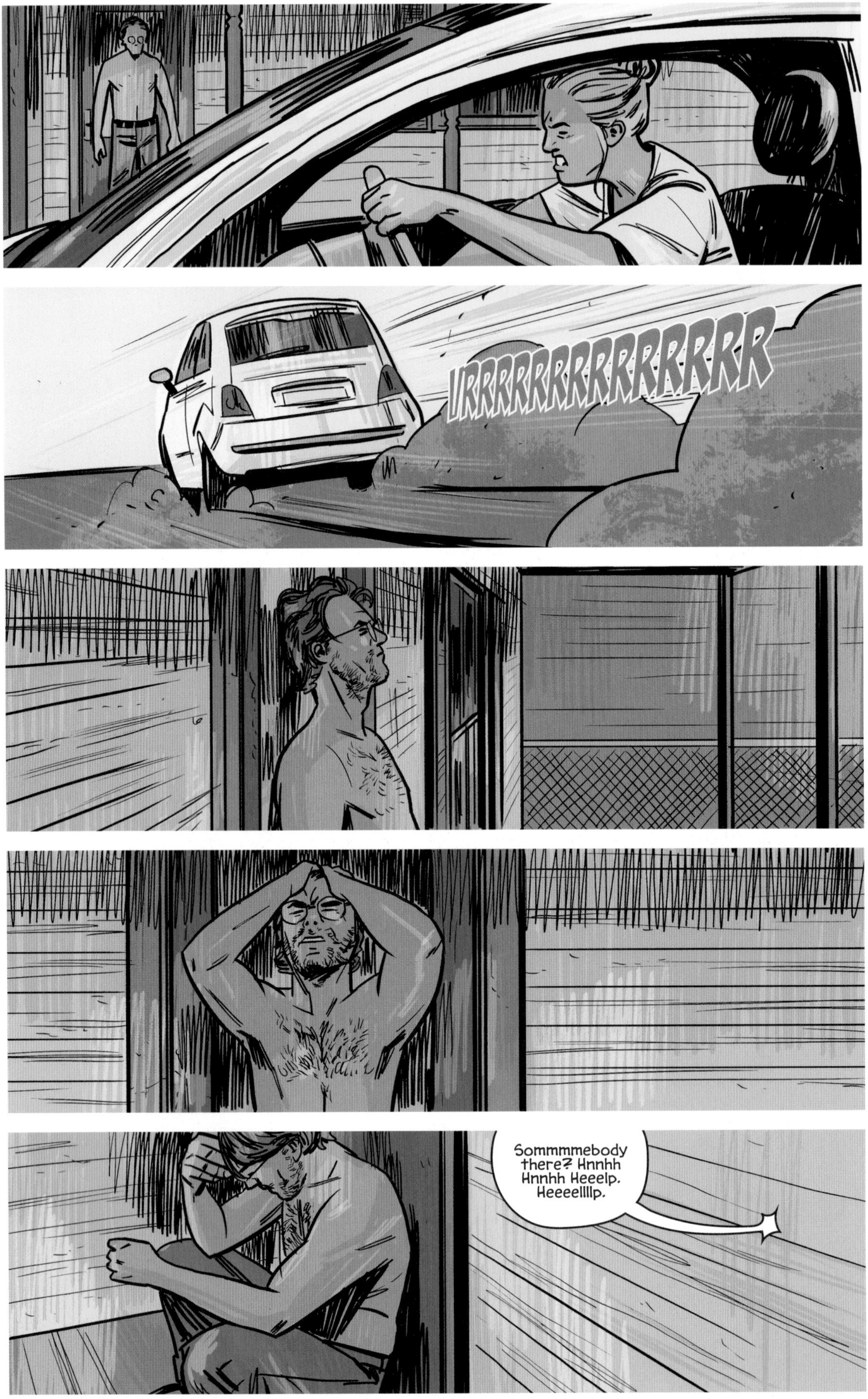
URRRRRRRRRRRRRRR
Sommmmebody there? Hnnhh Hnnhh Heeelp. Heeeellllp.

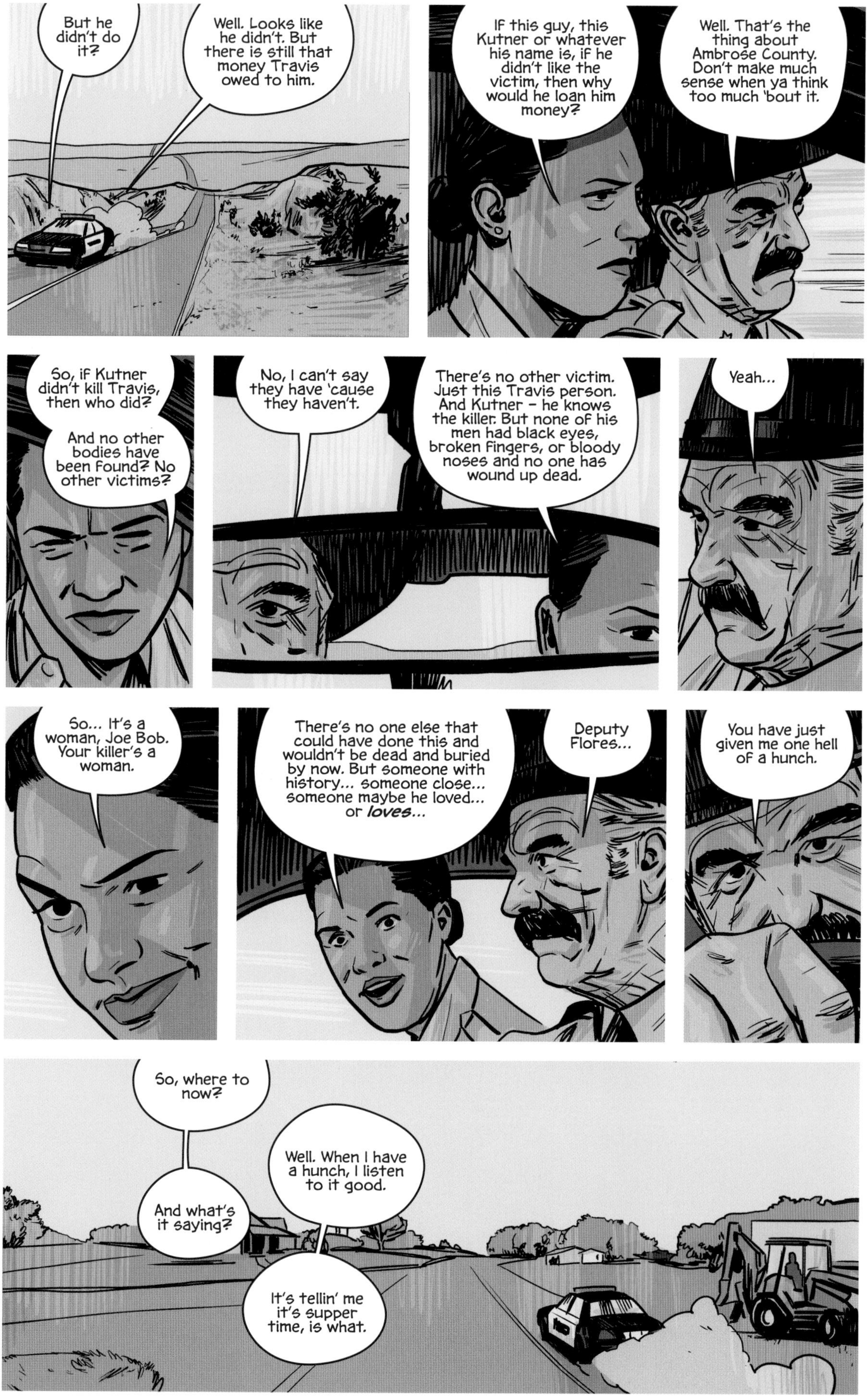
But he didn't do it?
Well. Looks like he didn't. But there is still that money Travis owed to him.
If this guy, this Kutner or whatever his name is, if he didn't like the victim, then why would he loan him money?
Well. That's the thing about Ambrose County. Don't make much sense when ya think too much 'bout it.
So, if Kutner didn't kill Travis, then who did?
And no other bodies have been found? No other victims?
No, I can't say they have 'cause they haven't.
There's no other victim. Just this Travis person. And Kutner - he knows the killer. But none of his men had black eyes, broken fingers, or bloody noses and no one has wound up dead.
Yeah...
So... It's a woman, Joe Bob. Your killer's a woman.
There's no one else that could have done this and wouldn't be dead and buried by now. But someone with history... someone close... someone maybe he loved... or *loves*...
Deputy Flores...
You have just given me one hell of a hunch.
So, where to now?
And what's it saying?
Well. When I have a hunch, I listen to it good.
It's tellin' me it's supper time, is what.

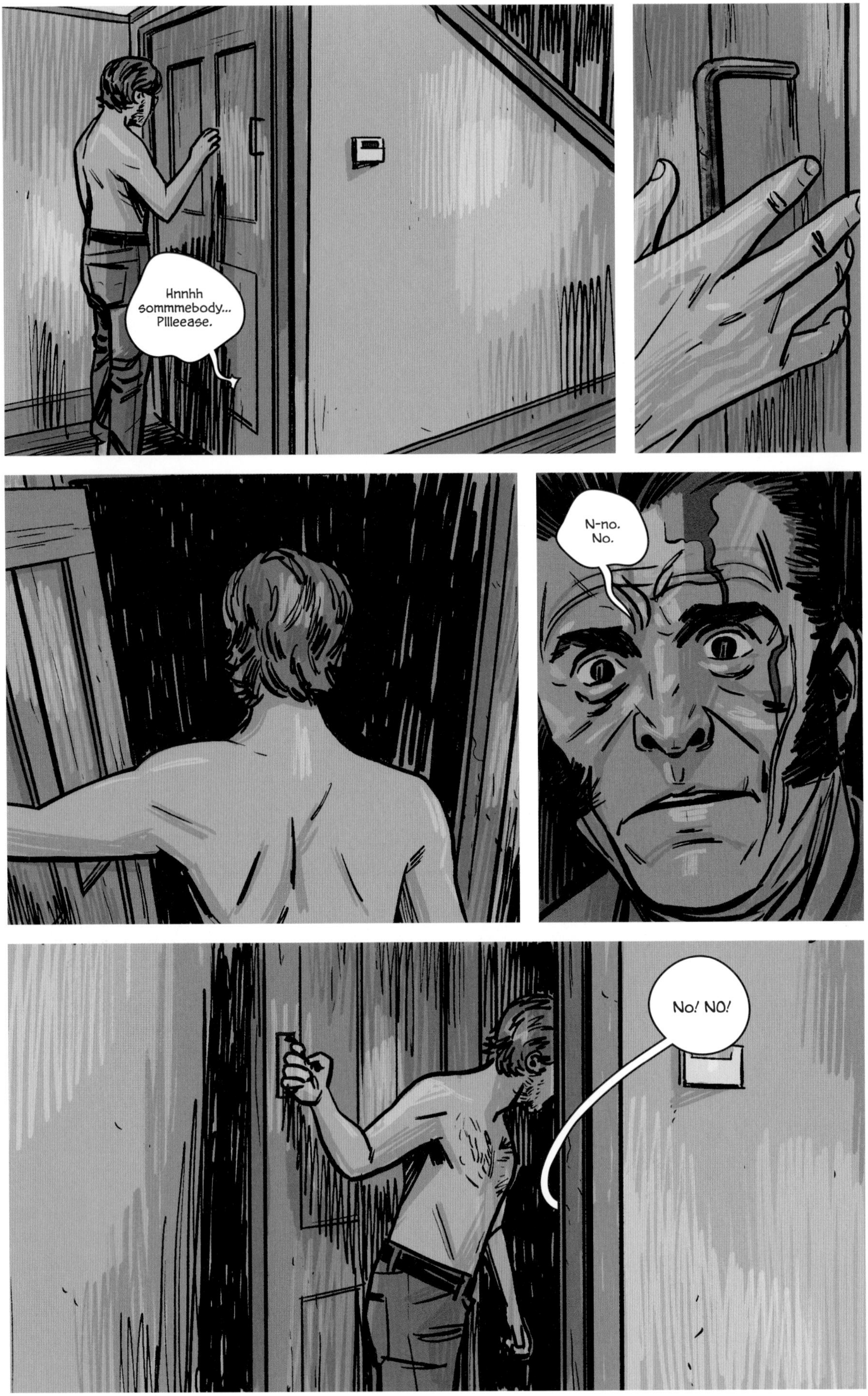
Hnnhh sommmebody... Pllleease.
N-no. No.
No! NO!

Randy. Don't. Don't—

P-please – Hrrhh – Don't.

HRRRHHHH HHRHHHH

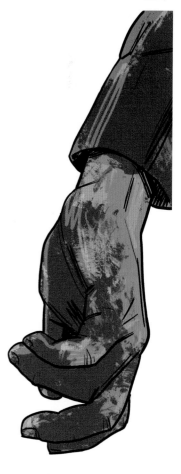

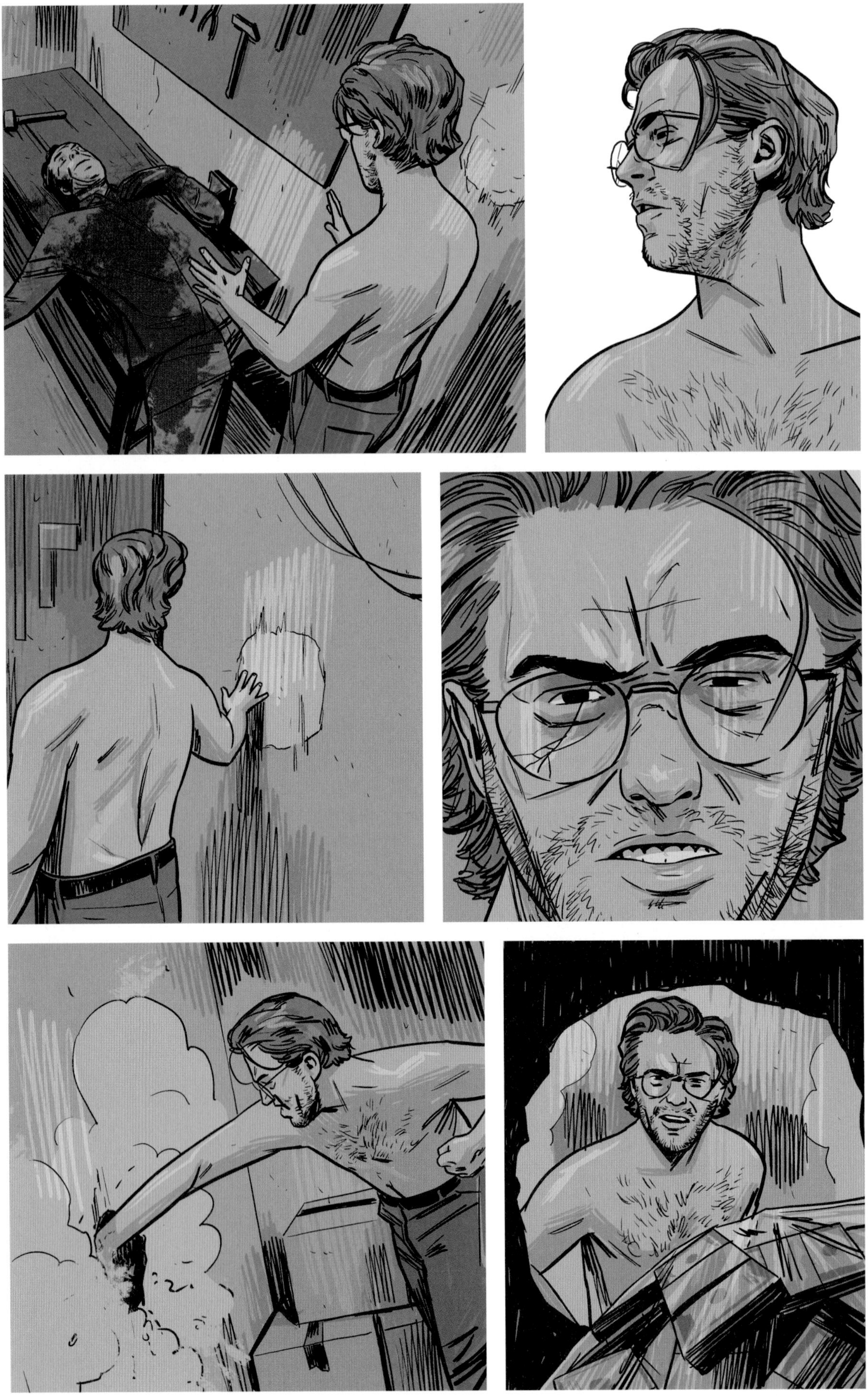

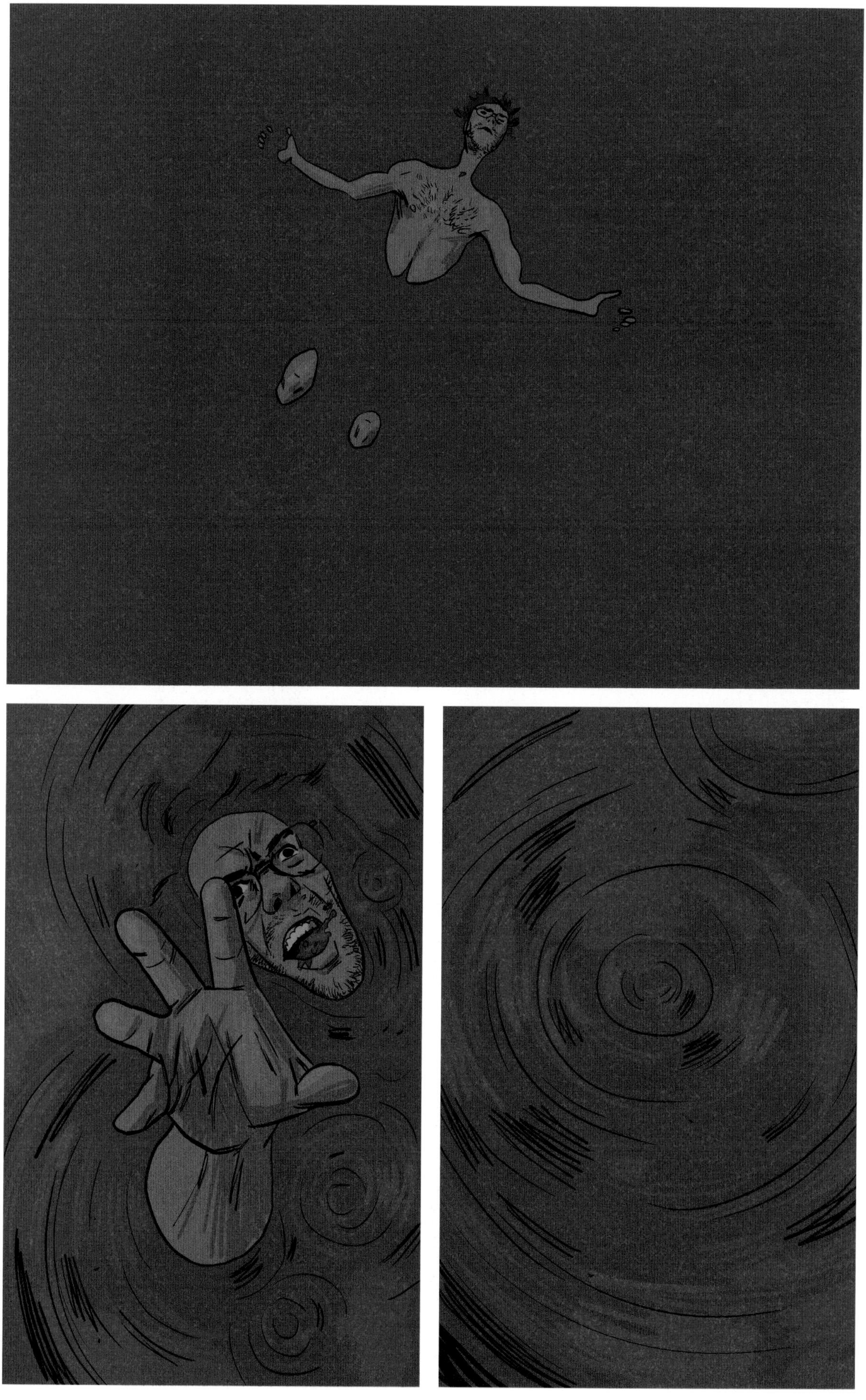

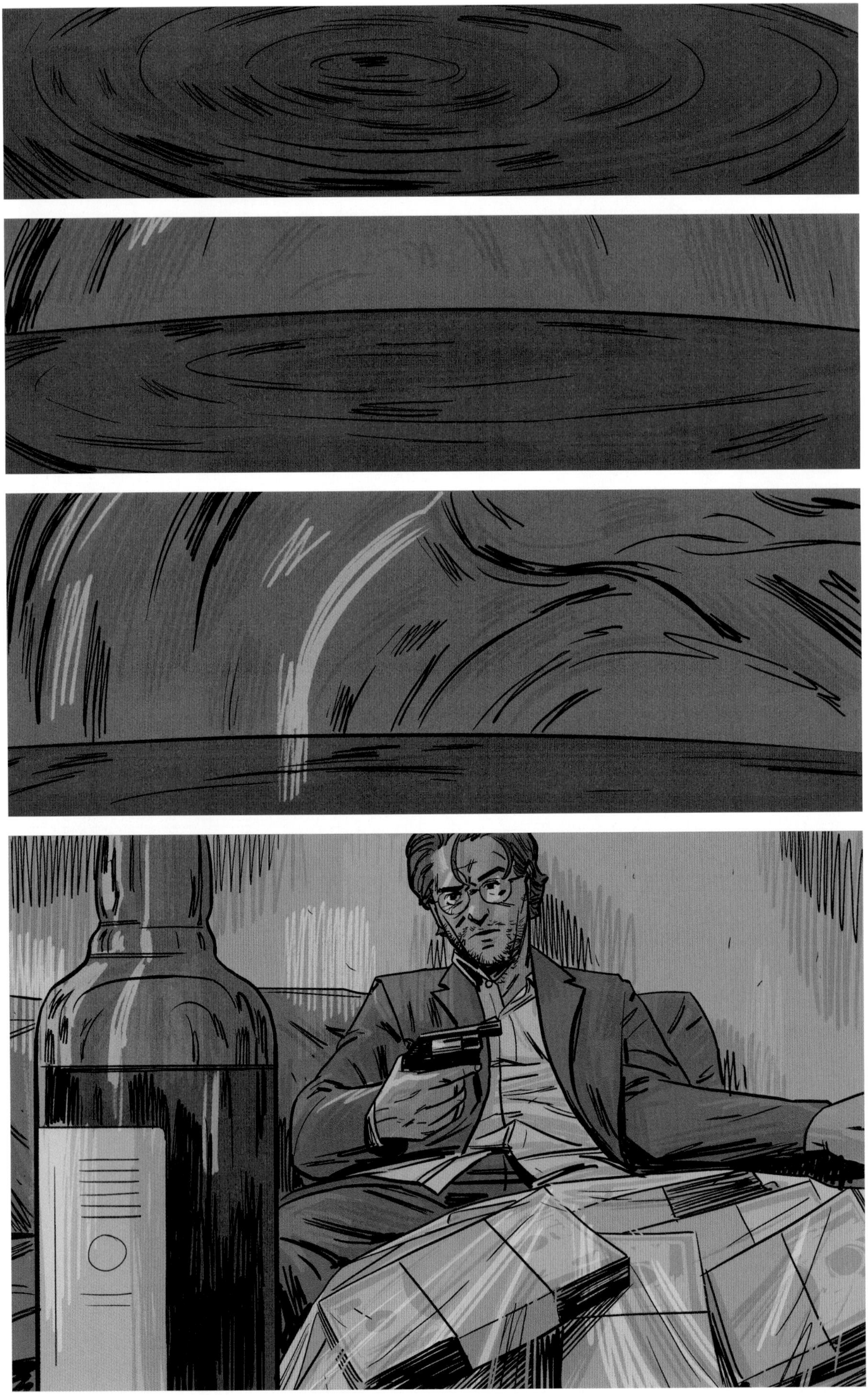

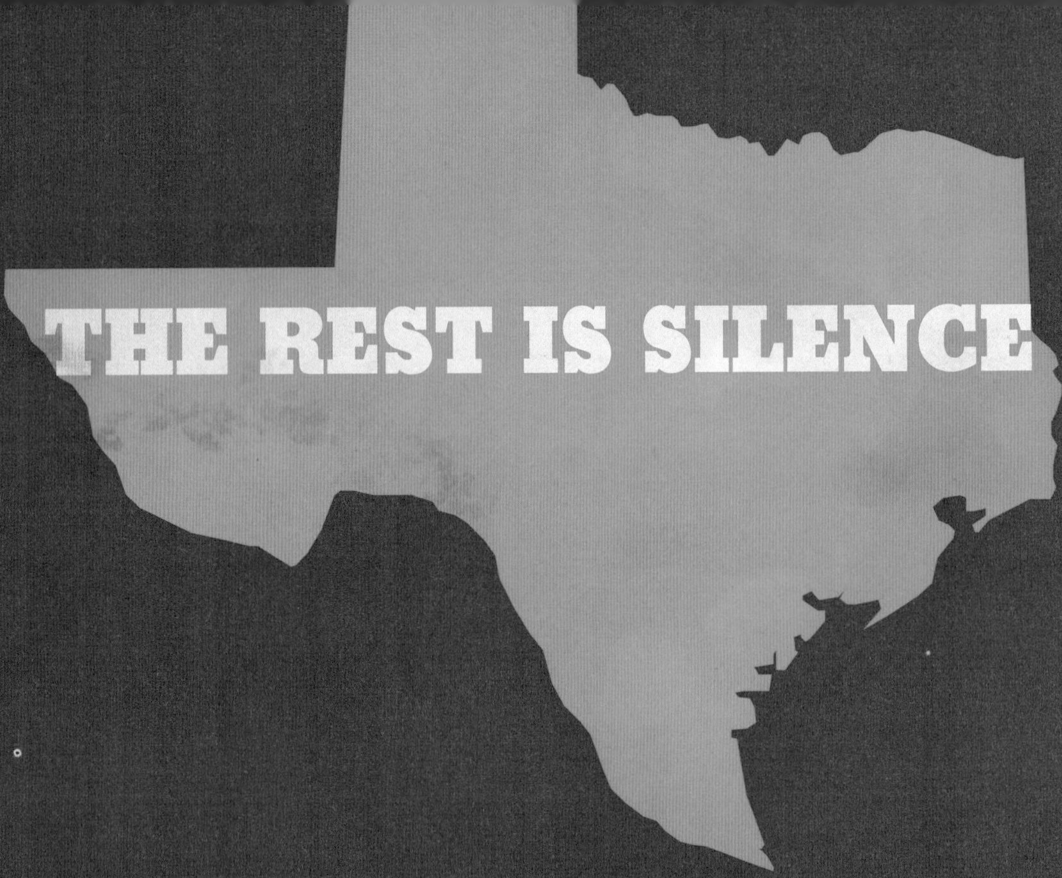
THE REST IS SILENCE

A Brother's Conscience

Part Five

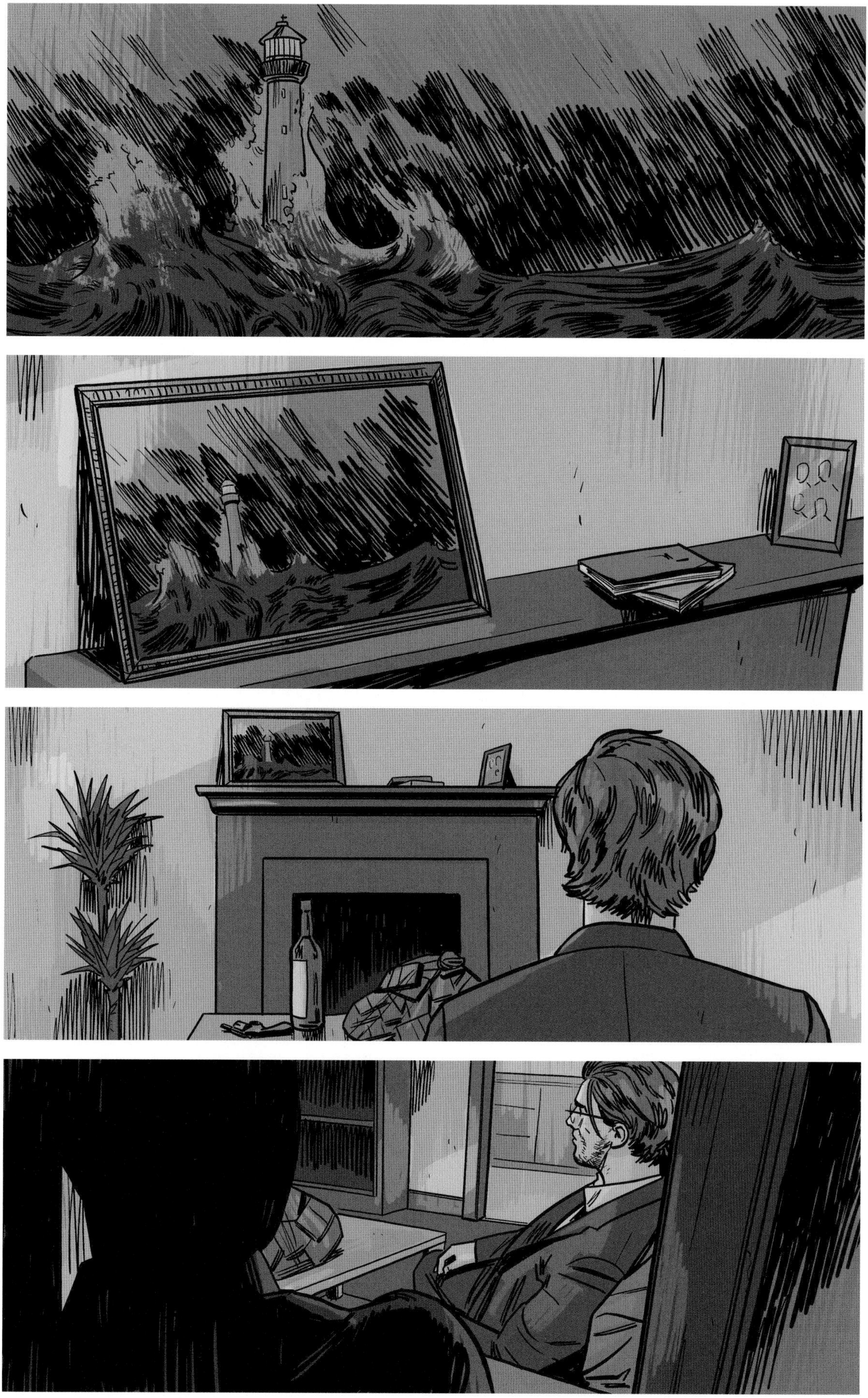

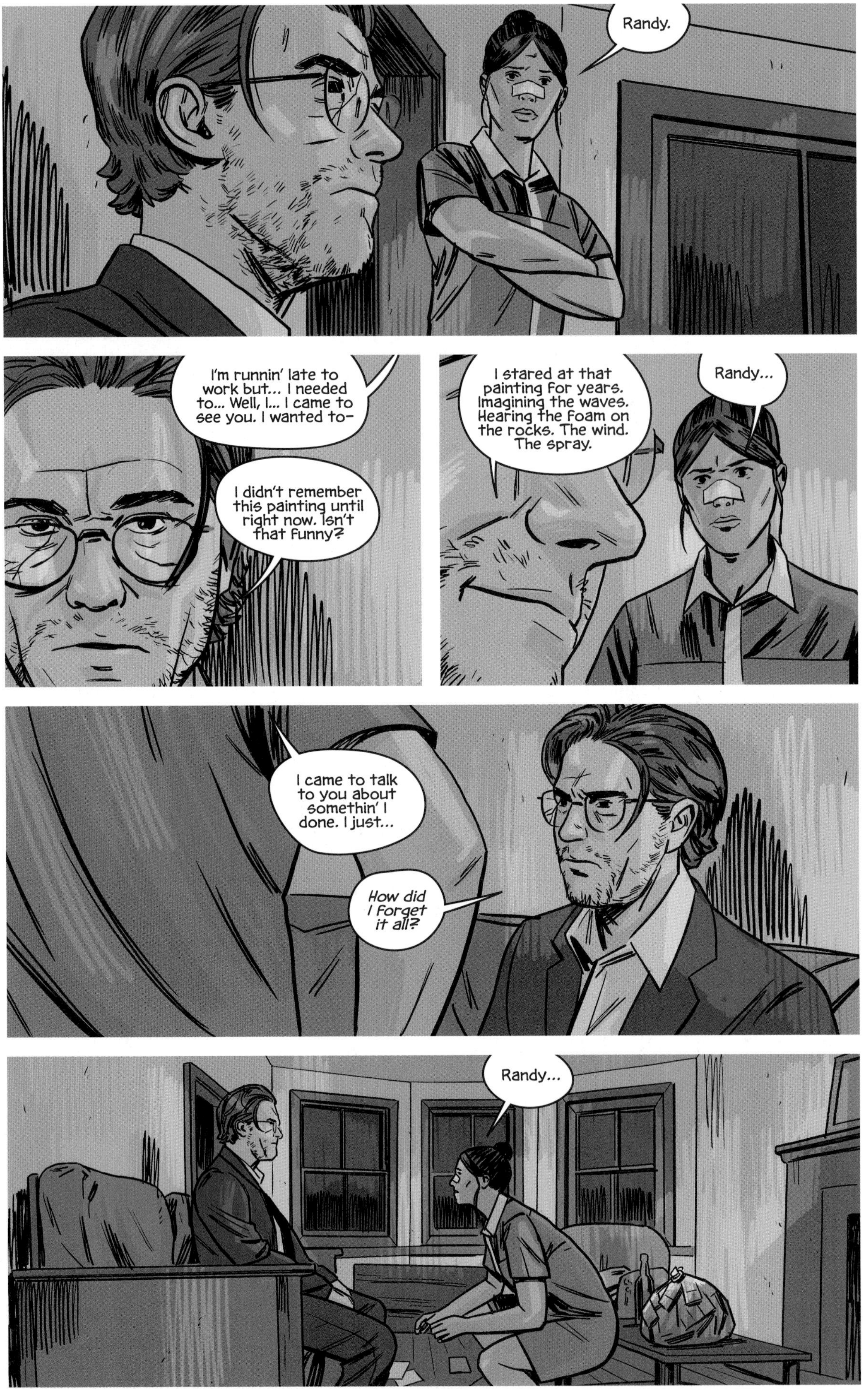
Randy.
I'm runnin' late to work but... I needed to... Well, I... I came to see you. I wanted to-
I didn't remember this painting until right now. Isn't that funny?
I stared at that painting for years. Imagining the waves. Hearing the foam on the rocks. The wind. The spray.
Randy...
I came to talk to you about somethin' I done. I just...
How did I forget it all?
Randy...

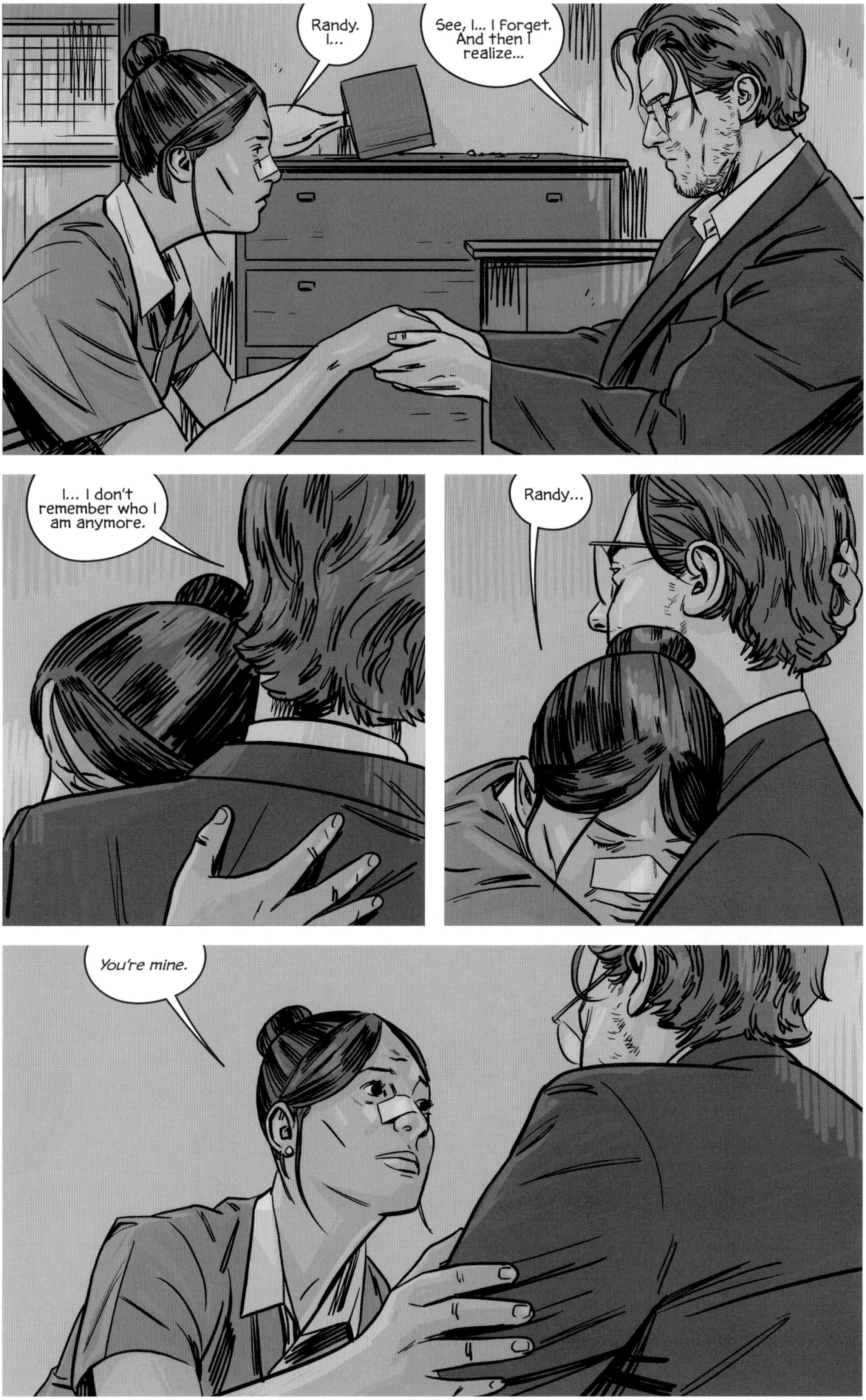
Randy. I...
See, I... I forget. And then I realize...
I... I don't remember who I am anymore.
Randy...
You're mine.

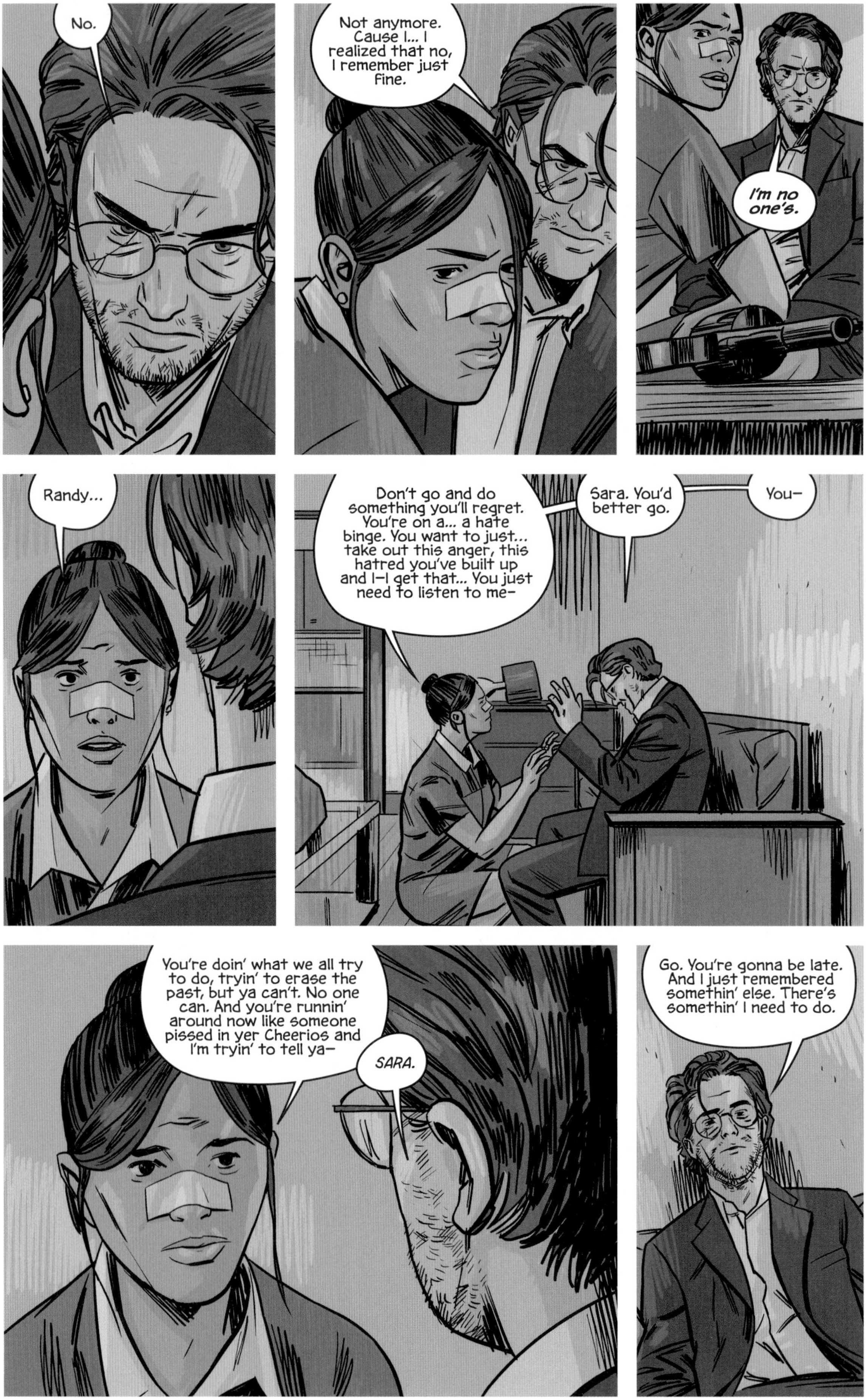
No.
Not anymore. Cause I... I realized that no, I remember just fine.
I'm no one's.
Randy...
Don't go and do something you'll regret. You're on a... a hate binge. You want to just... take out this anger, this hatred you've built up and I–I get that... You just need to listen to me–
Sara. You'd better go.
You–
You're doin' what we all try to do, tryin' to erase the past, but ya can't. No one can. And you're runnin' around now like someone pissed in yer Cheerios and I'm tryin' to tell ya–
SARA.
Go. You're gonna be late. And I just remembered somethin' else. There's somethin' I need to do.

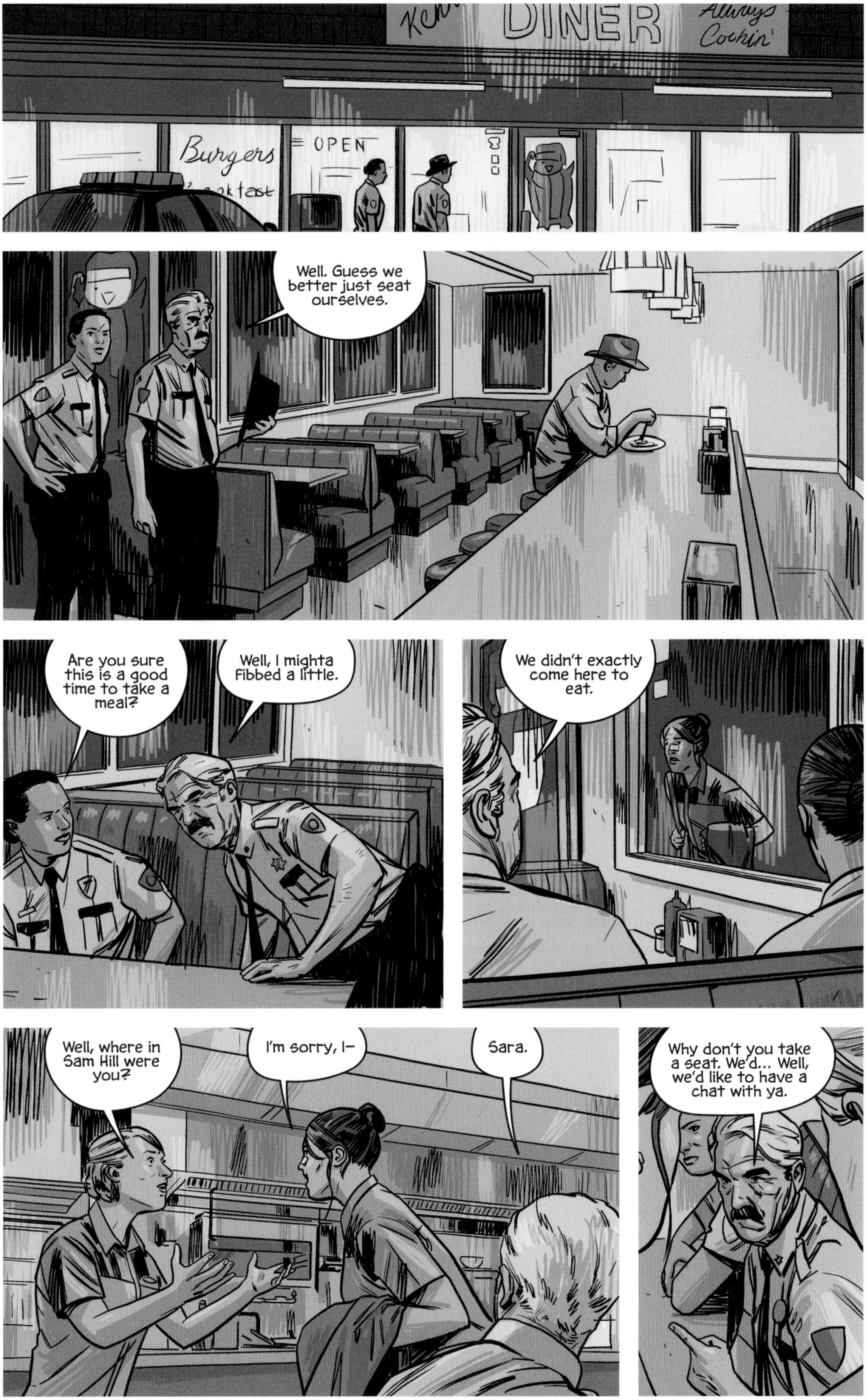
Kenn
DINER
Always Cookin'
Burgers
OPEN
Breakfast
Well. Guess we better just seat ourselves.
Are you sure this is a good time to take a meal?
Well, I mighta fibbed a little.
We didn't exactly come here to eat.
Well, where in Sam Hill were you?
I'm sorry, I—
Sara.
Why don't you take a seat. We'd... Well, we'd like to have a chat with ya.

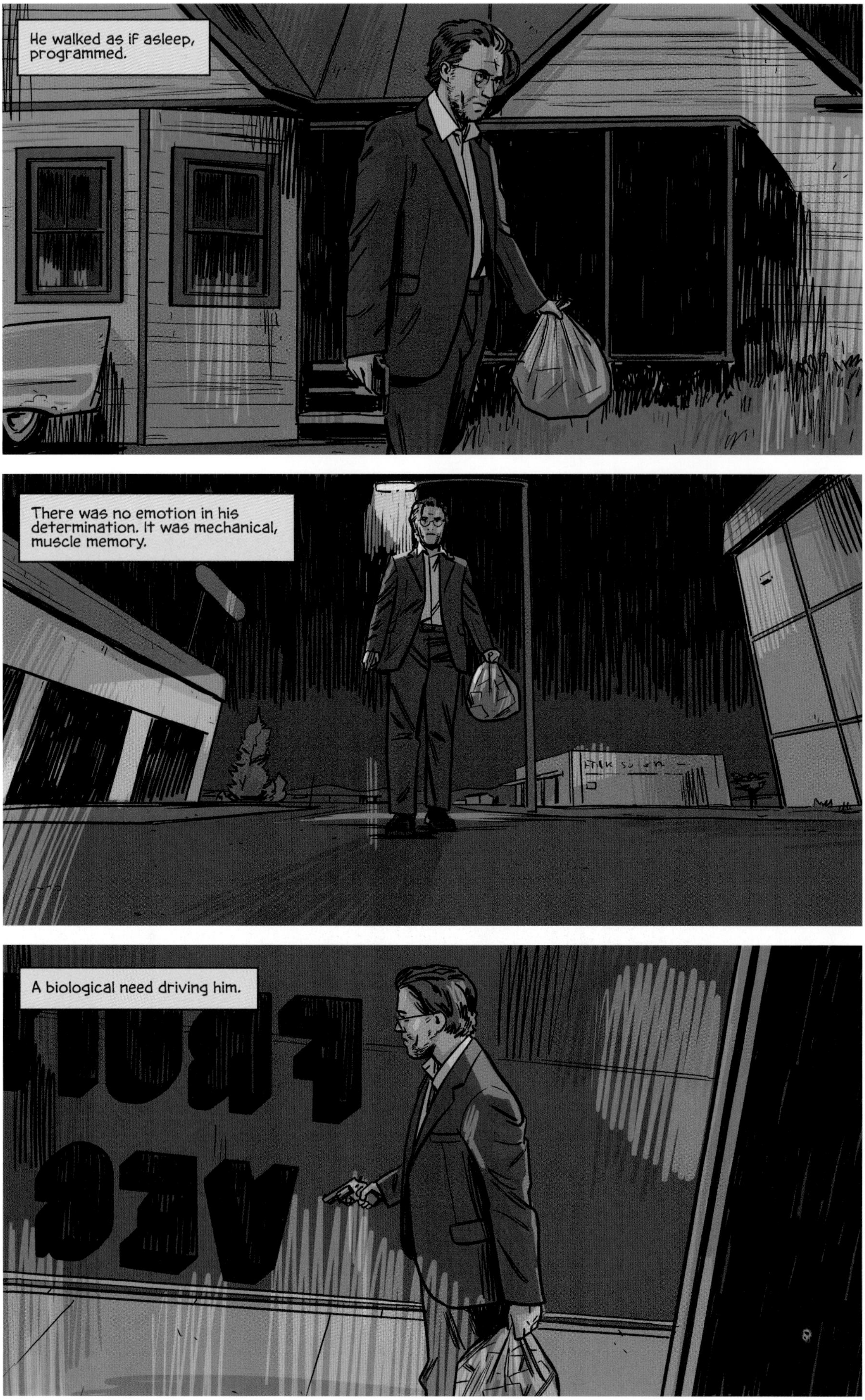
He walked as if asleep, programmed.
There was no emotion in his determination. It was mechanical, muscle memory.
A biological need driving him.

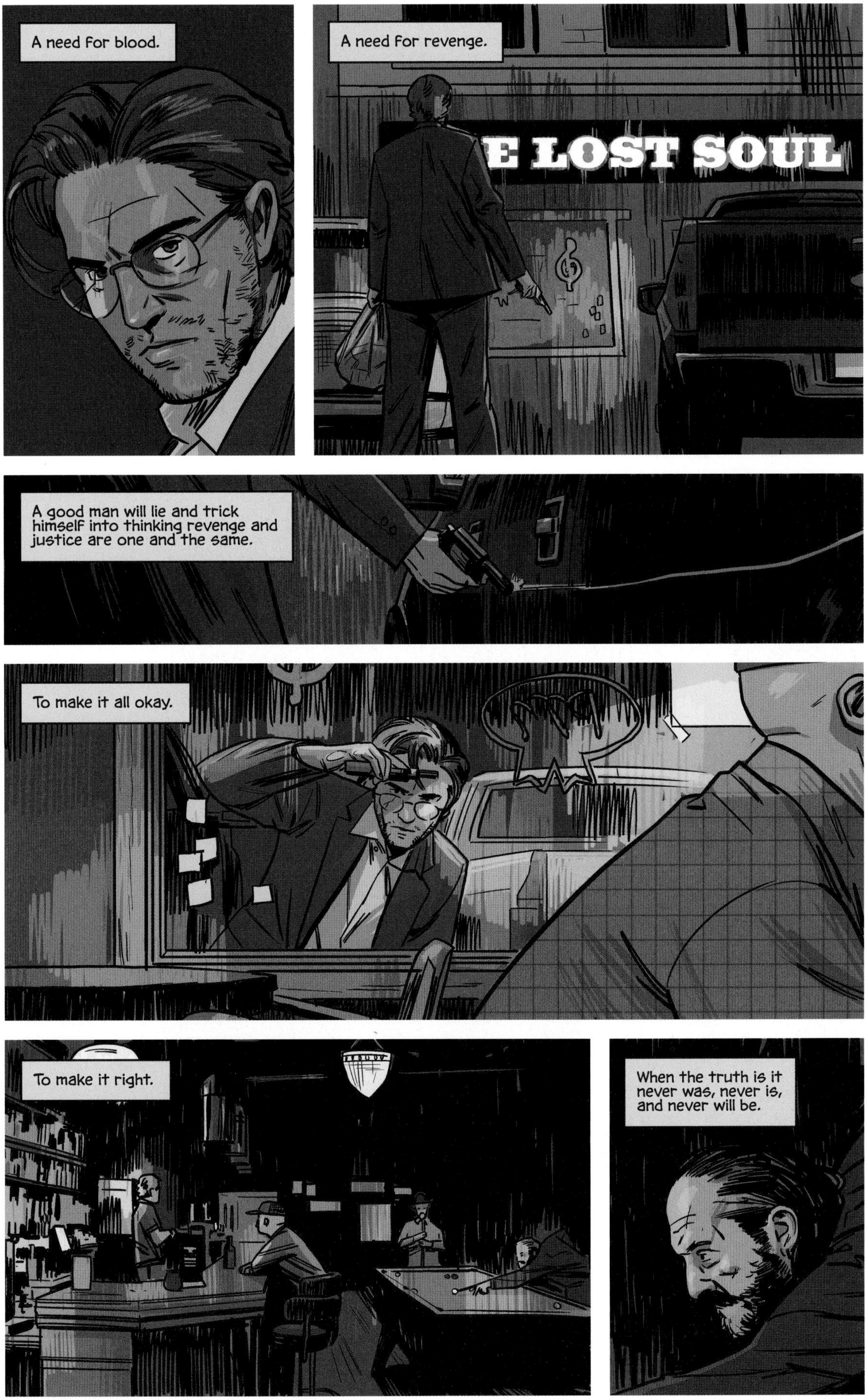
A need for blood.
A need for revenge.
E LOST SOUL
A good man will lie and trick himself into thinking revenge and justice are one and the same.
To make it all okay.
To make it right.
When the truth is it never was, never is, and never will be.

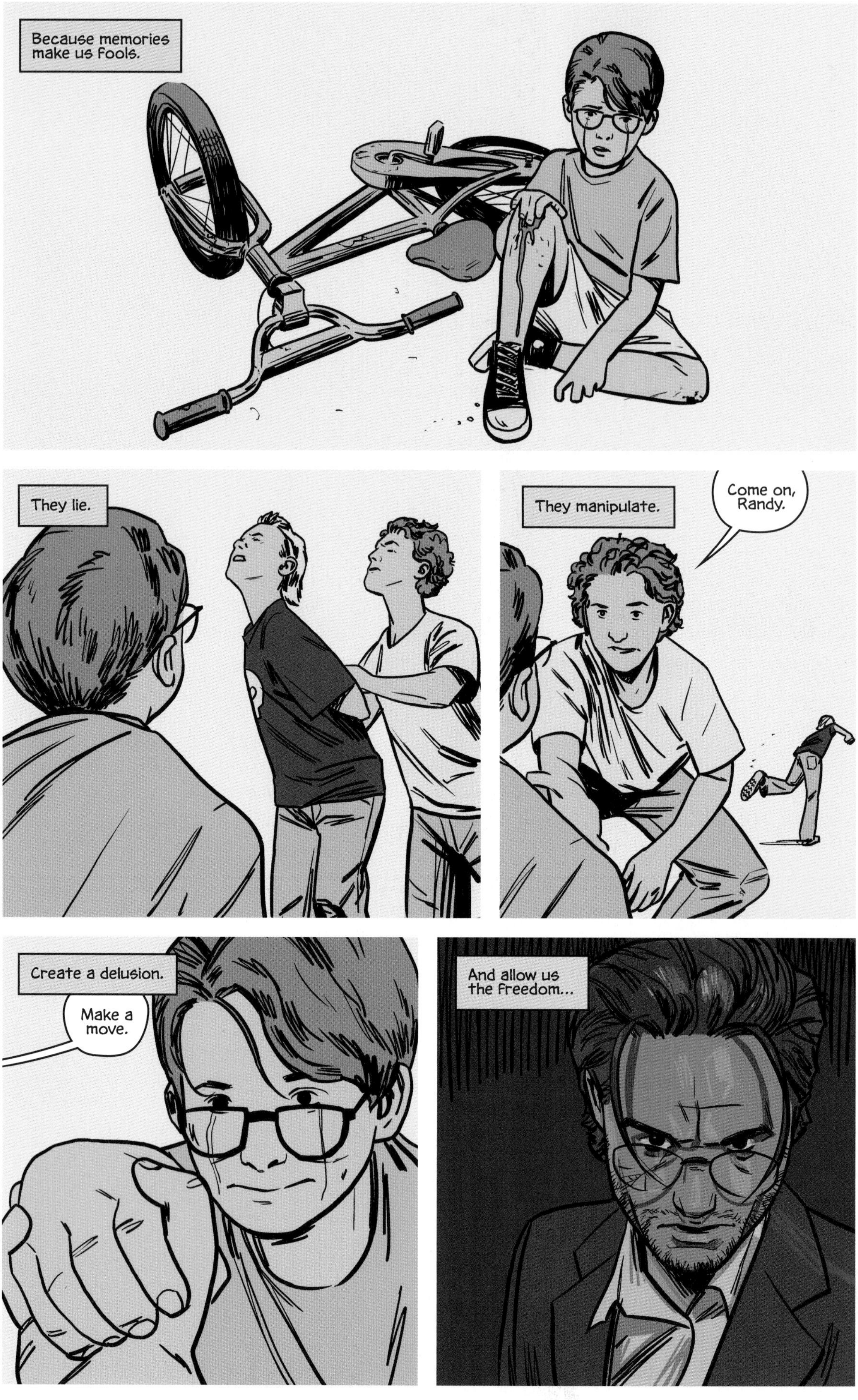
Because memories make us fools.
They lie.
They manipulate.
Come on, Randy.
Create a delusion.
Make a move.
And allow us the freedom...

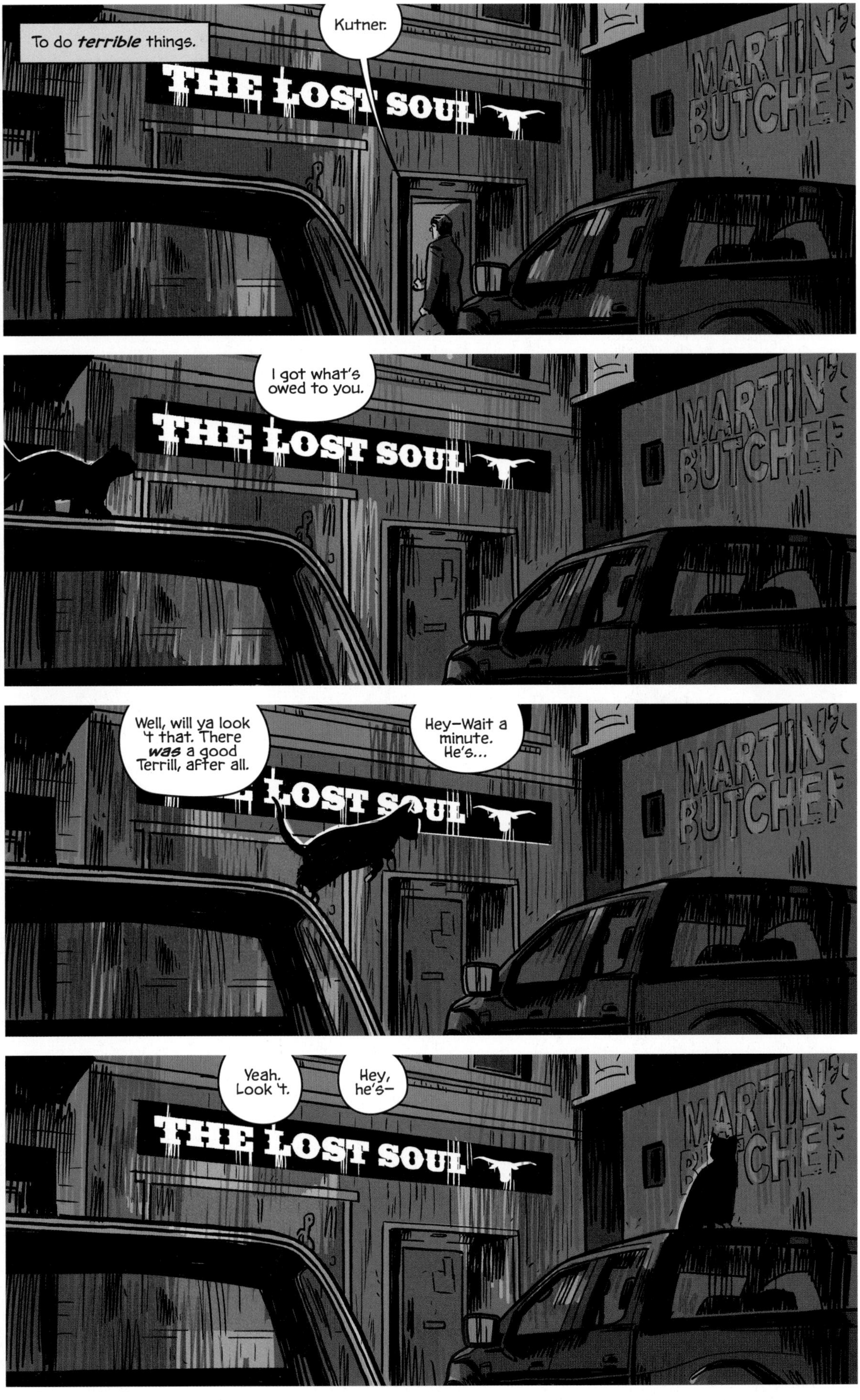
To do *terrible* things.
Kutner.
THE LOST SOUL
MARTIN'S BUTCHER
I got what's owed to you.
Well, will ya look 't that. There *was* a good Terrill, after all.
Hey—Wait a minute. He's...
Yeah. Look 't.
Hey, he's—

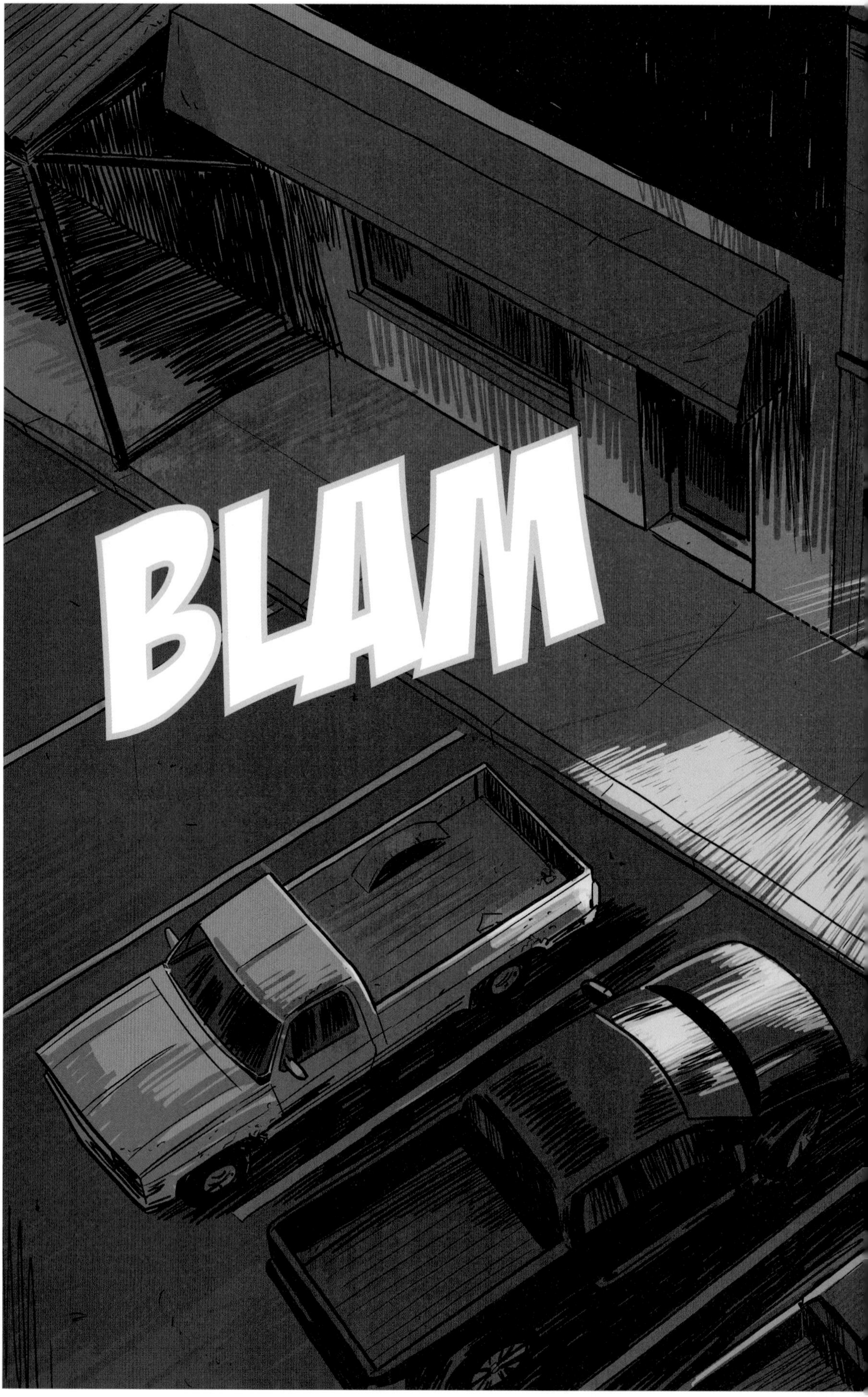
BLAM

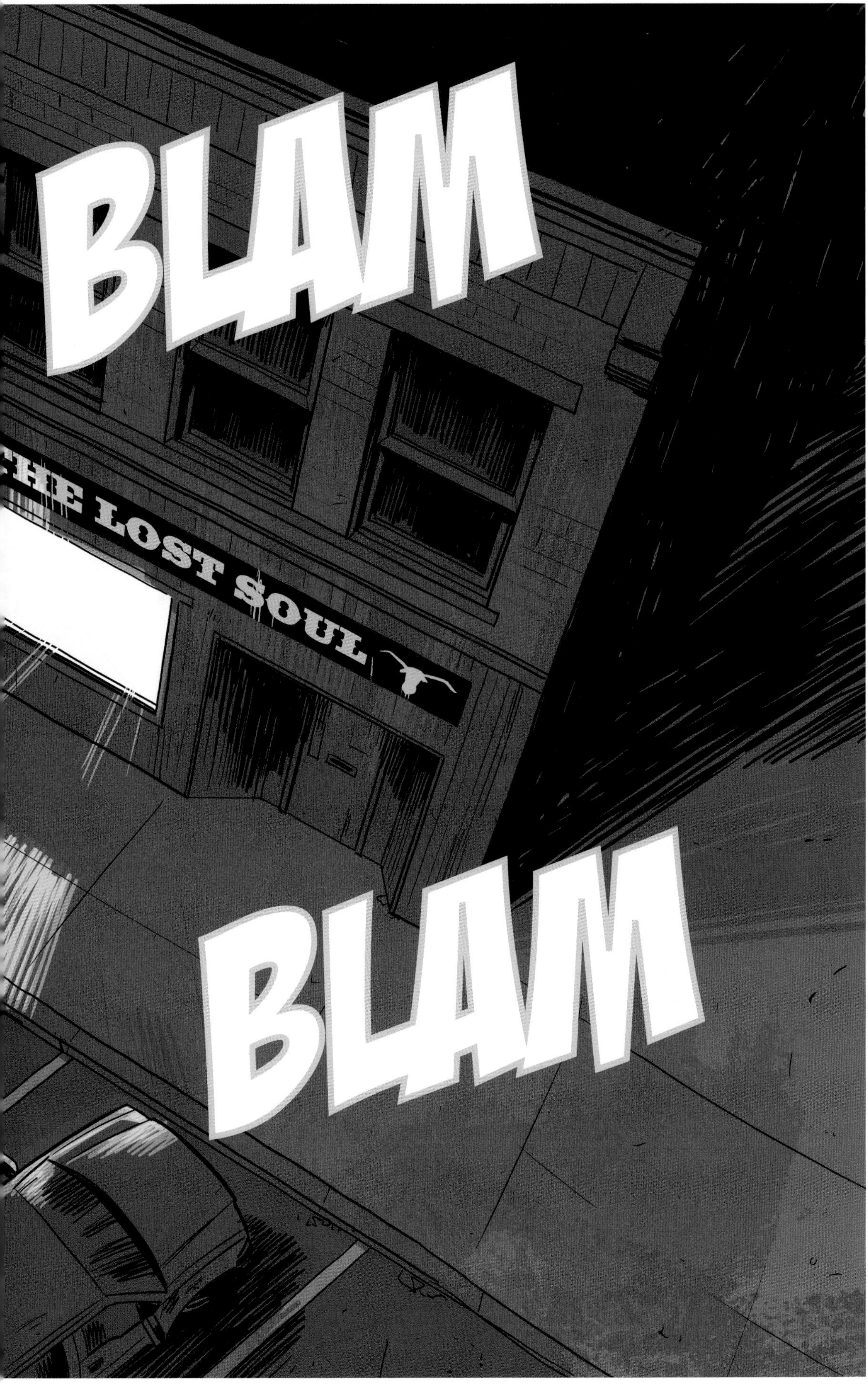
BLAM
THE LOST SOUL
BLAM

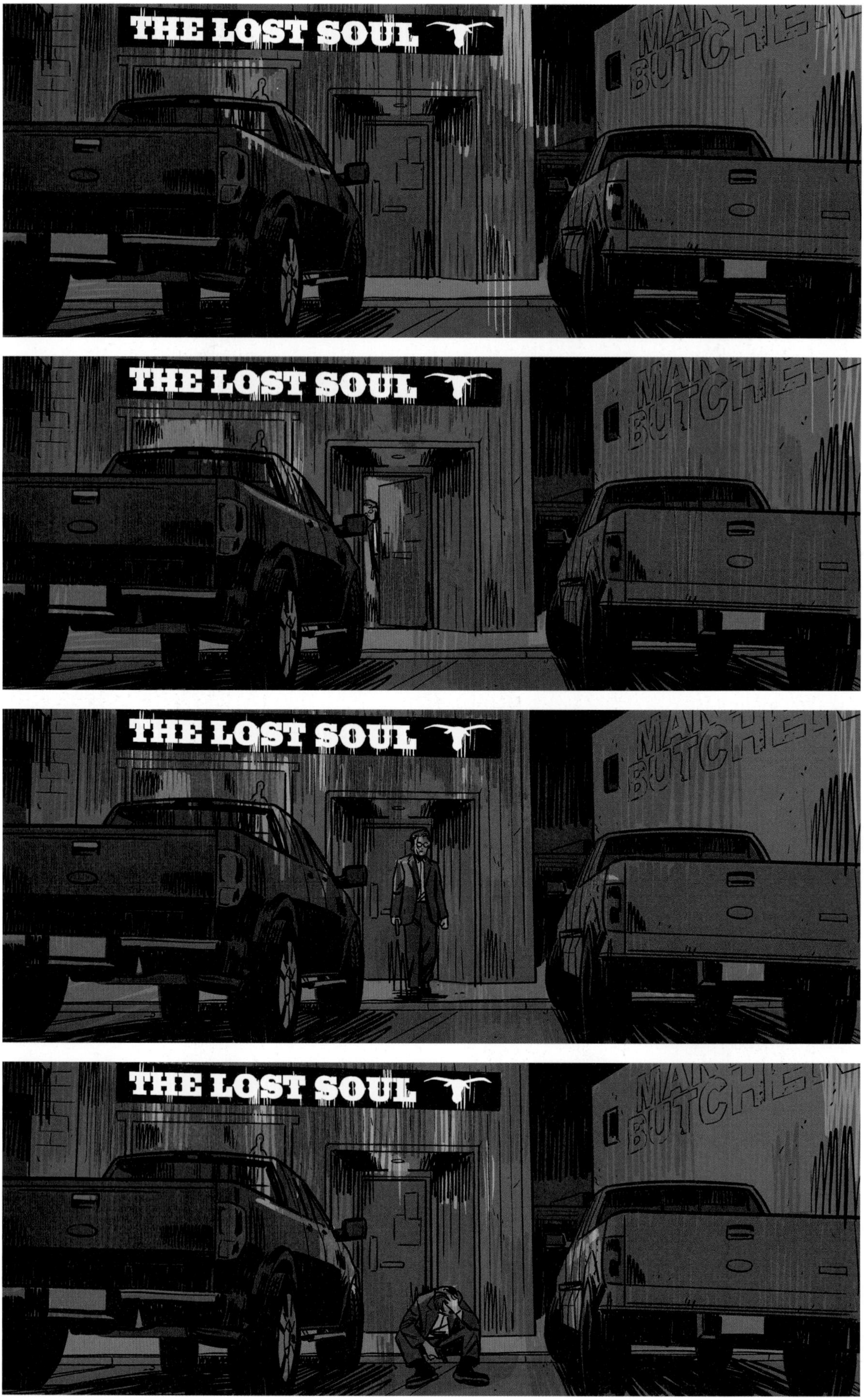
THE LOST SOUL
THE LOST SOUL
THE LOST SOUL
THE LOST SOUL

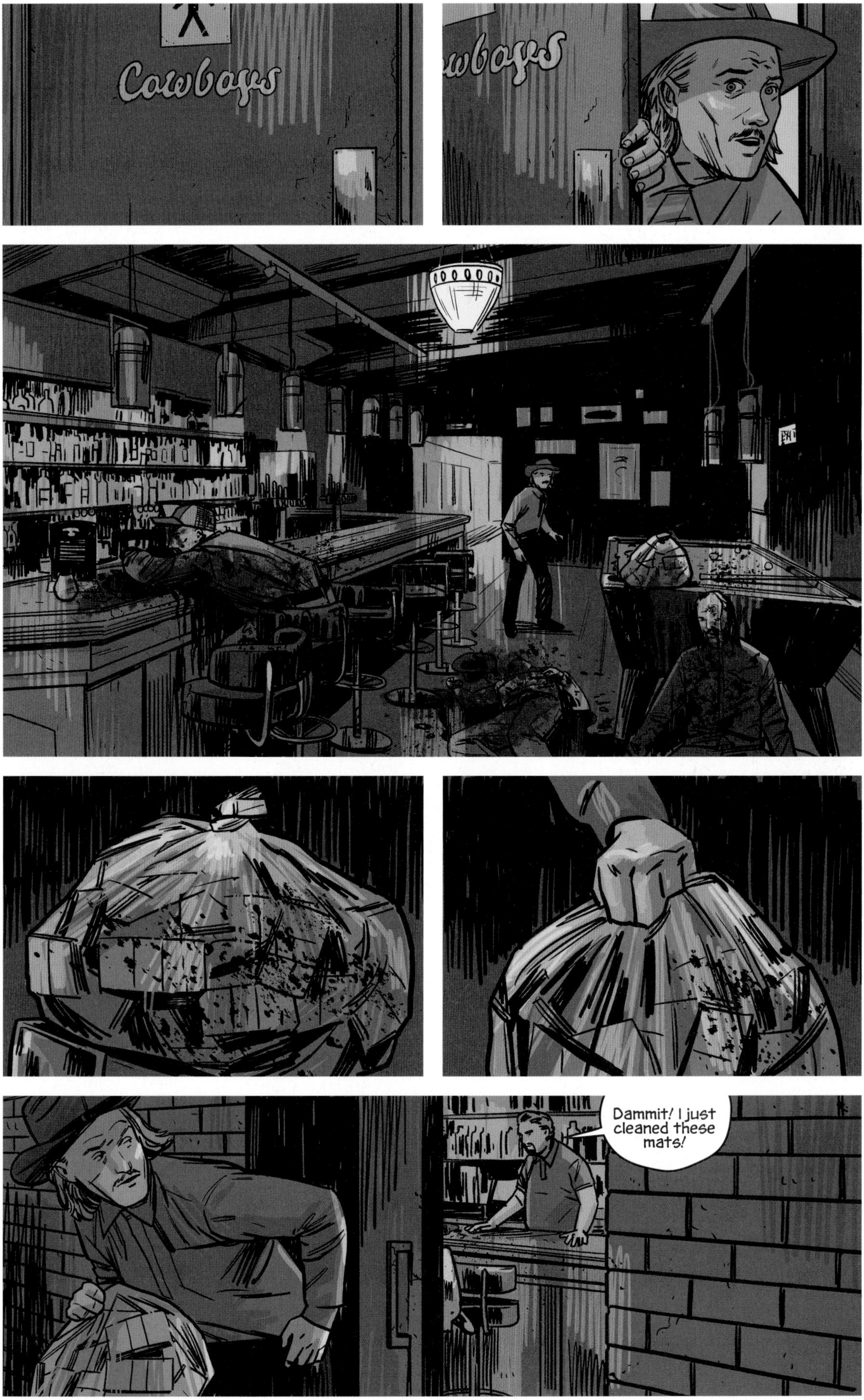
Cowboys
Cowboys
Dammit! I just cleaned these mats!

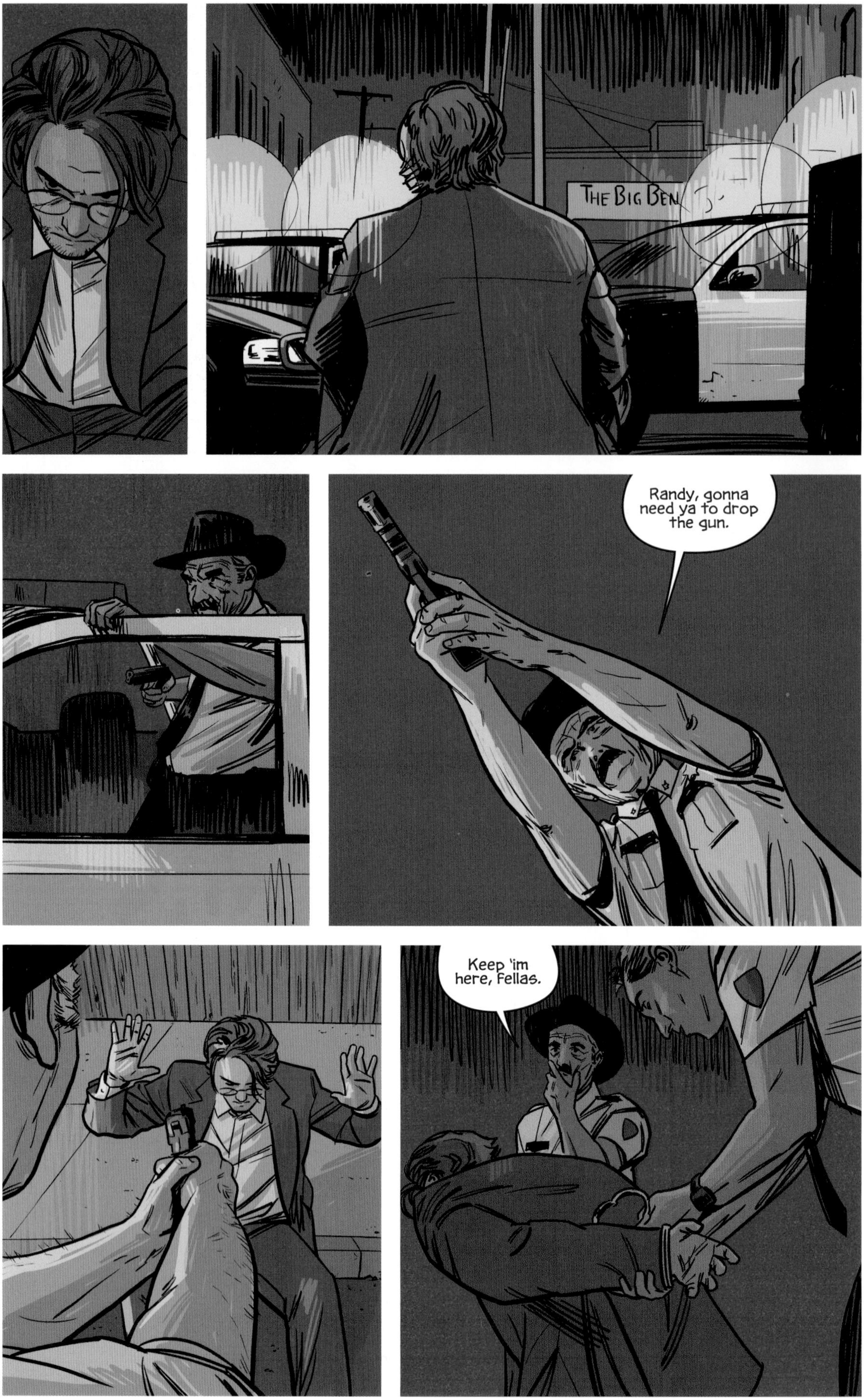
THE BIG BEN
Randy, gonna need ya to drop the gun.
Keep 'im here, fellas.

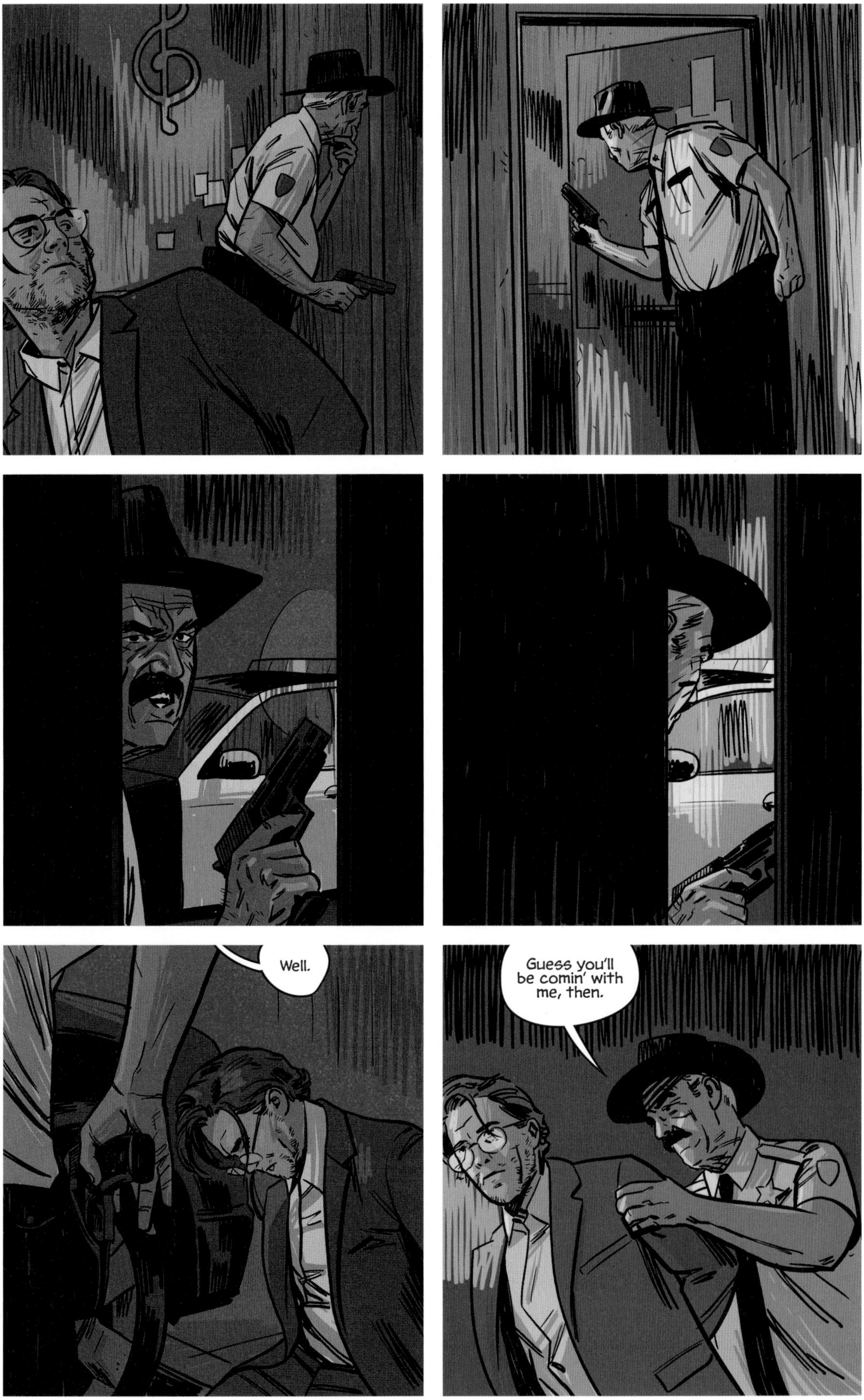
Well.
Guess you'll be comin' with me, then.

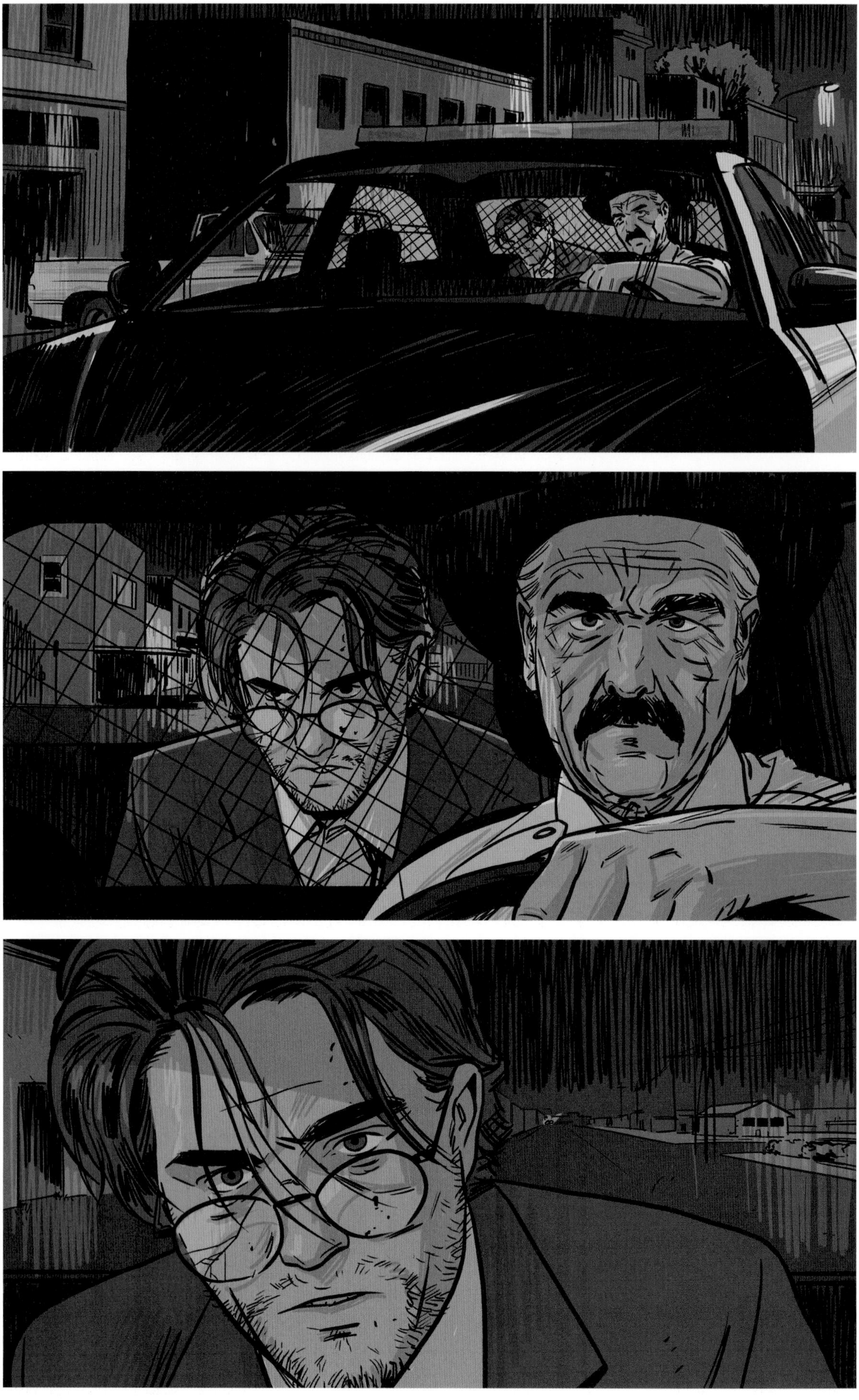

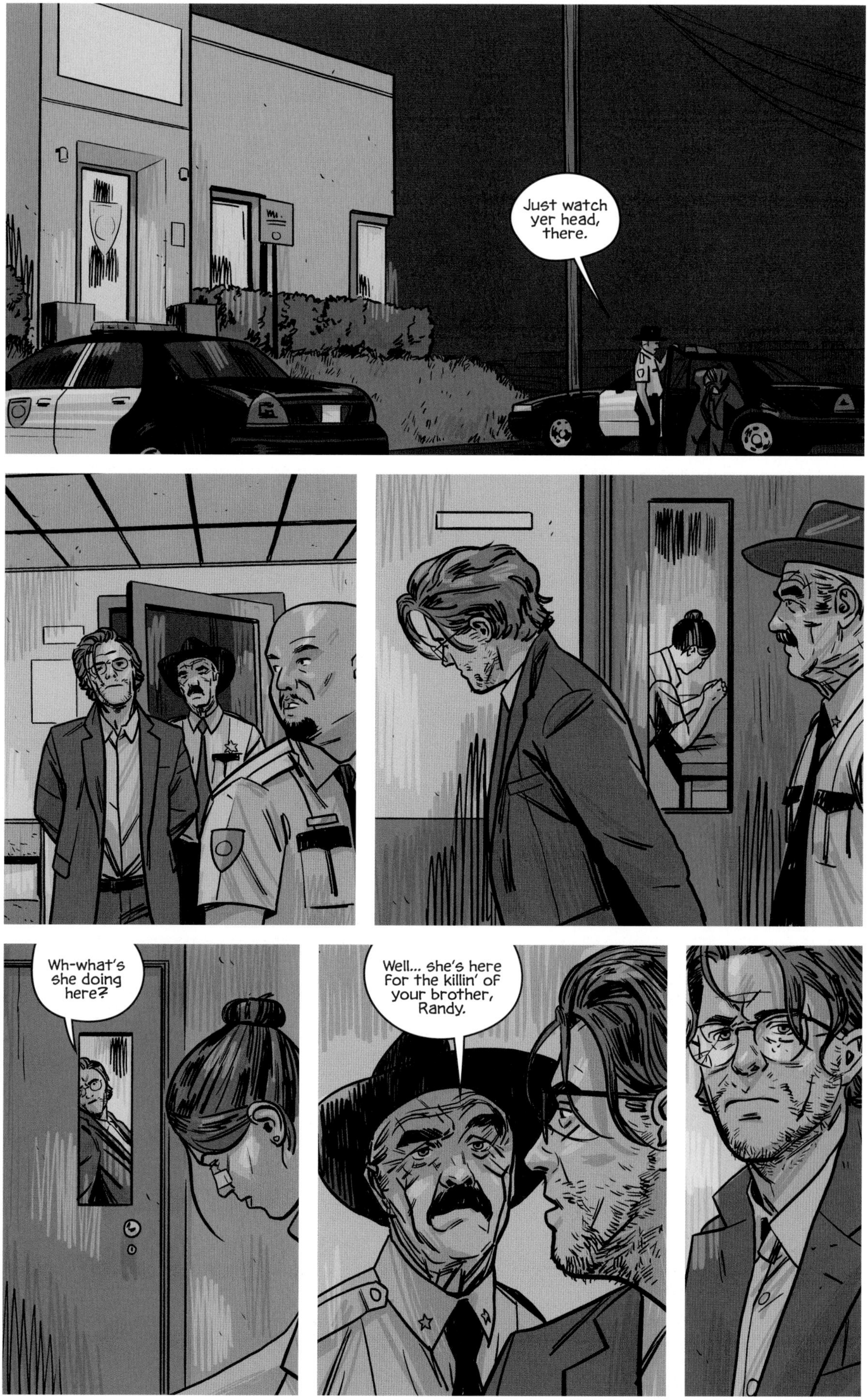
Just watch yer head, there.
Wh-what's she doing here?
Well... she's here for the killin' of your brother, Randy.

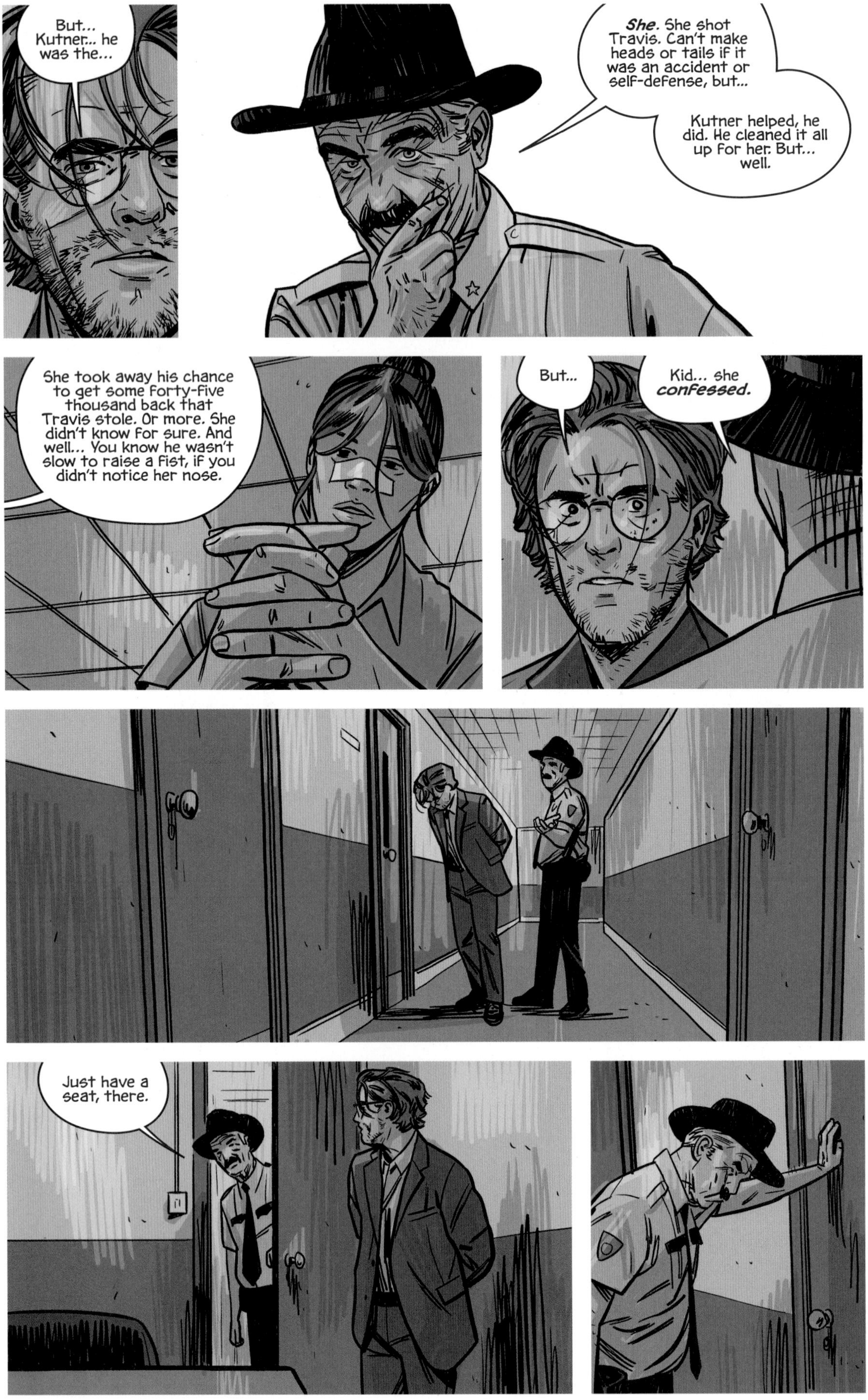
But... Kutner... he was the...
She. She shot Travis. Can't make heads or tails if it was an accident or self-defense, but...
Kutner helped, he did. He cleaned it all up for her. But... well.
She took away his chance to get some forty-five thousand back that Travis stole. Or more. She didn't know for sure. And well... You know he wasn't slow to raise a fist, if you didn't notice her nose.
But...
Kid... she ***confessed.***
Just have a seat, there.

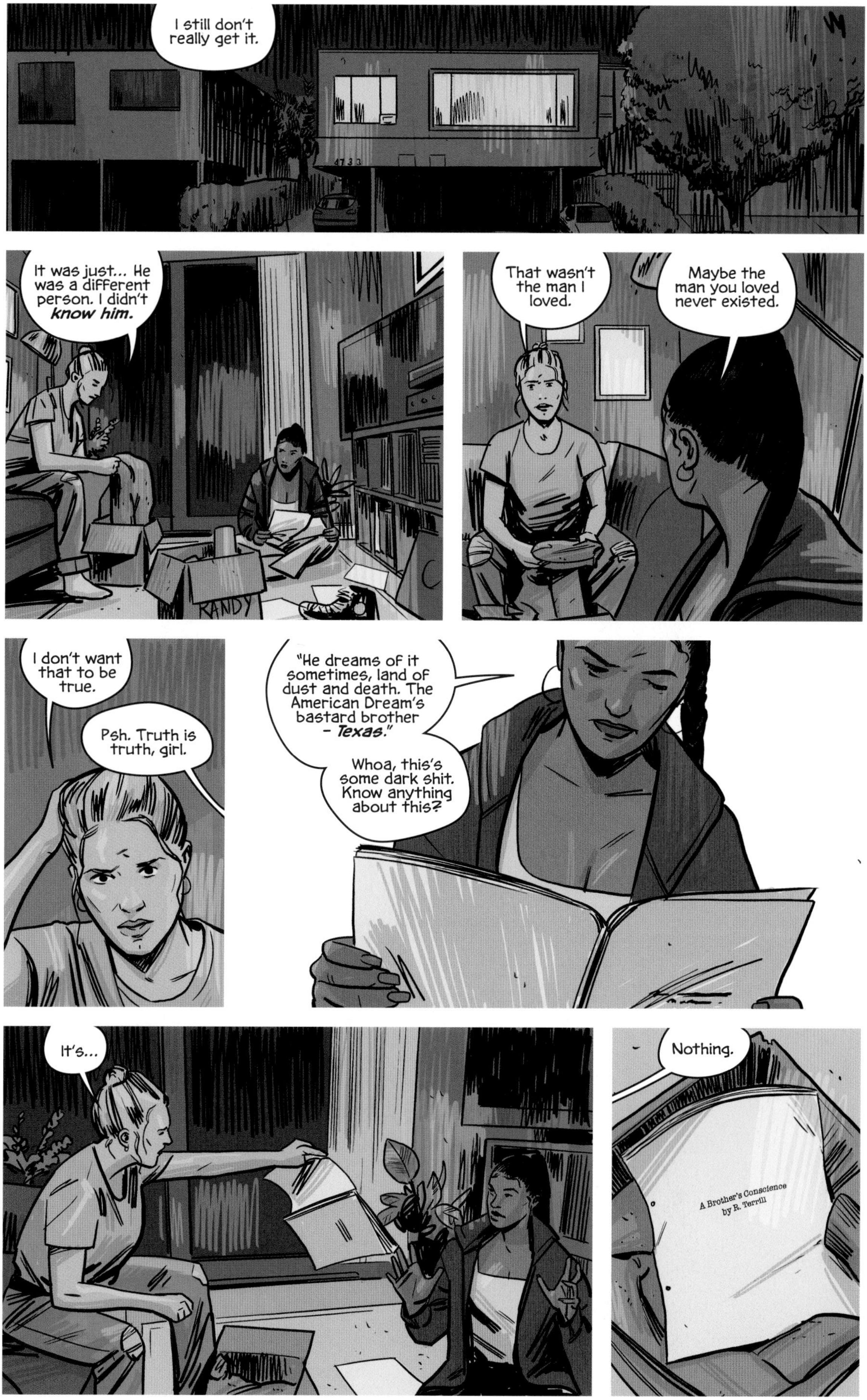
I still don't really get it.
It was just... He was a different person. I didn't ***know him.***
That wasn't the man I loved.
Maybe the man you loved never existed.
RANDY
I don't want that to be true.
Psh. Truth is truth, girl.
"He dreams of it sometimes, land of dust and death. The American Dream's bastard brother ***- Texas.***"
Whoa, this's some dark shit. Know anything about this?
It's...
Nothing.
A Brother's Conscience
by R. Terrill

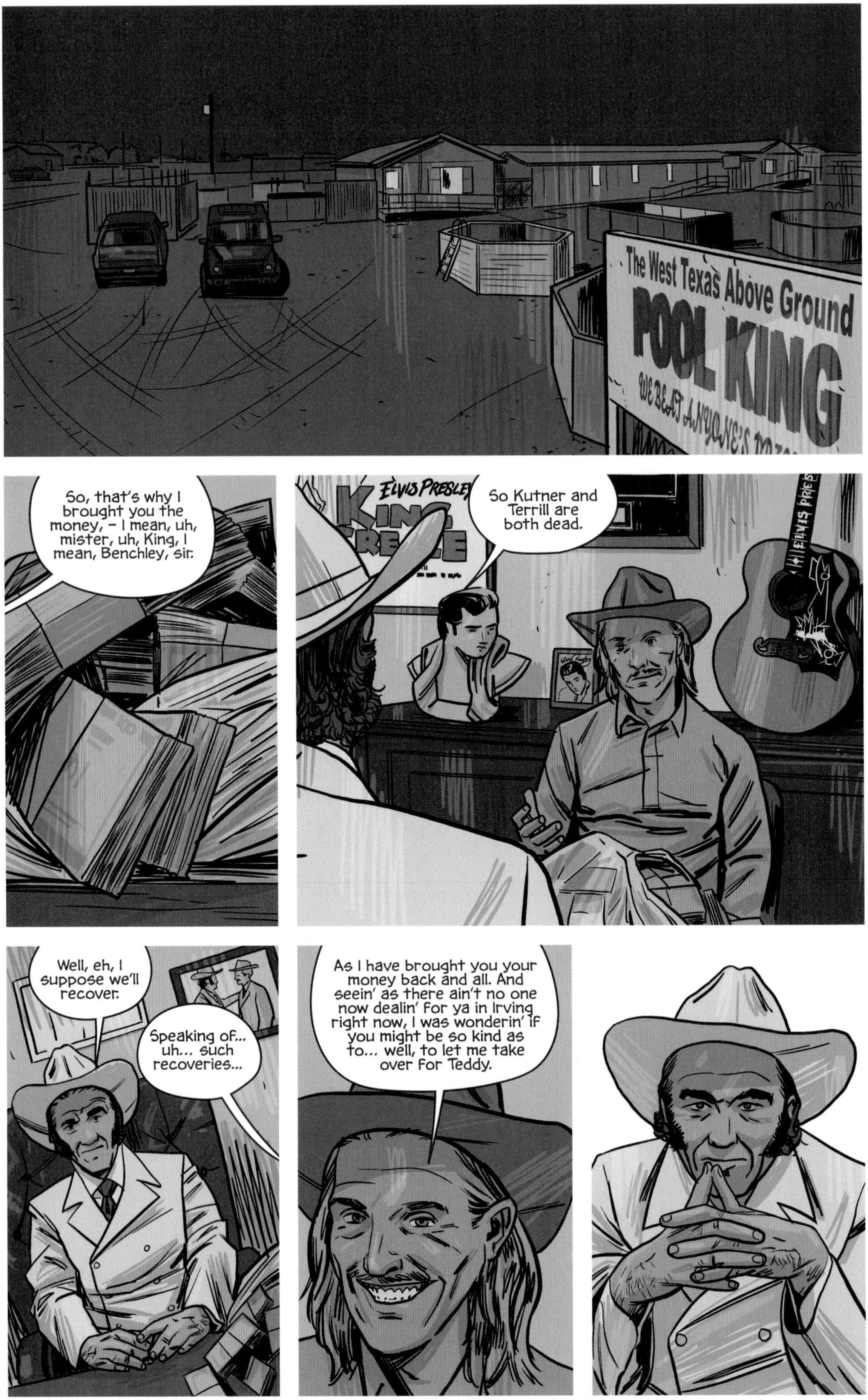
The West Texas Above Ground
POOL KING
So, that's why I brought you the money, - I mean, uh, mister, uh, King, I mean, Benchley, sir.
ELVIS PRESLEY
So Kutner and Terrill are both dead.
Well, eh, I suppose we'll recover.
Speaking of... uh... such recoveries...
As I have brought you your money back and all. And seein' as there ain't no one now dealin' for ya in Irving right now, I was wonderin' if you might be so kind as to... well, to let me take over for Teddy.

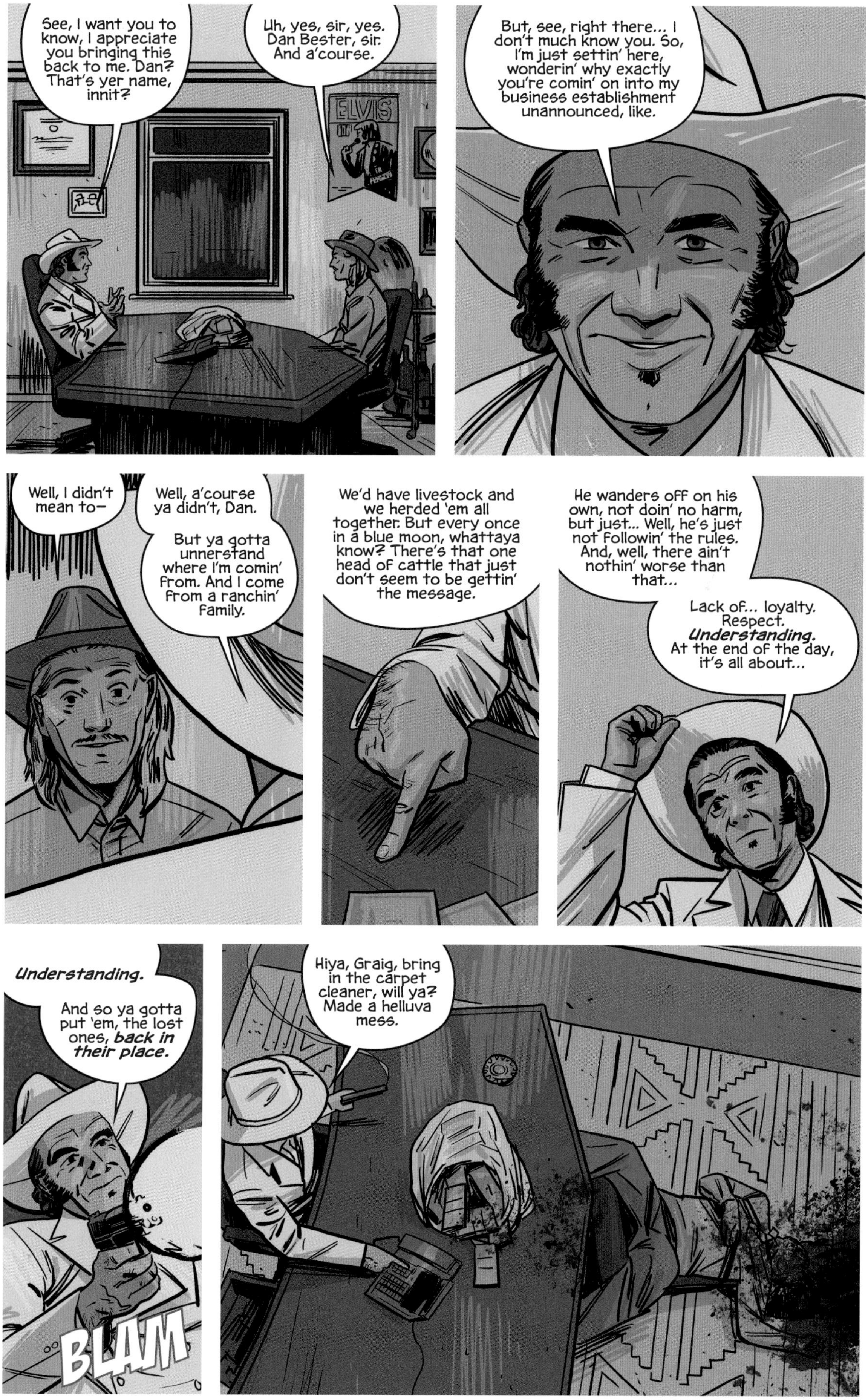
See, I want you to know, I appreciate you bringing this back to me. Dan? That's yer name, innit?
Uh, yes, sir, yes. Dan Bester, sir. And a'course.
ELVIS
But, see, right there... I don't much know you. So, I'm just settin' here, wonderin' why exactly you're comin' on into my business establishment unannounced, like.
Well, I didn't mean to—
Well, a'course ya didn't, Dan.
But ya gotta unnerstand where I'm comin' from. And I come from a ranchin' family.
We'd have livestock and we herded 'em all together. But every once in a blue moon, whattaya know? There's that one head of cattle that just don't seem to be gettin' the message.
He wanders off on his own, not doin' no harm, but just... Well, he's just not followin' the rules. And, well, there ain't nothin' worse than that...
Lack of... loyalty. Respect. *Understanding.* At the end of the day, it's all about...
Understanding.
And so ya gotta put 'em, the lost ones, *back in their place.*
BLAM
Hiya, Graig, bring in the carpet cleaner, will ya? Made a helluva mess.

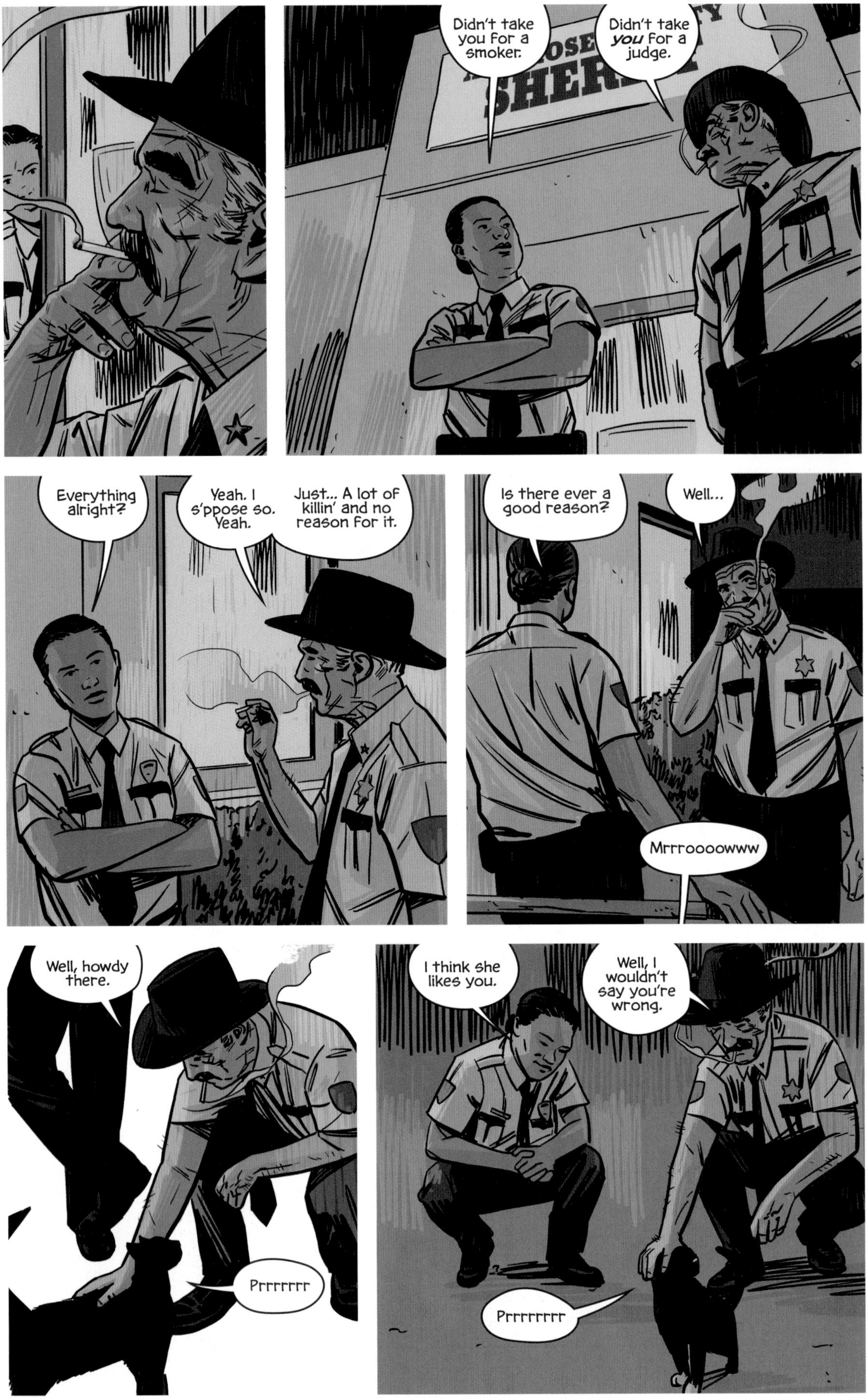
Didn't take you for a smoker.
Didn't take *you* for a judge.
Everything alright?
Yeah. I s'ppose so. Yeah.
Just... A lot of killin' and no reason for it.
Is there ever a good reason?
Well...
Mrrroooowww
Well, howdy there.
Prrrrrrr
I think she likes you.
Well, I wouldn't say you're wrong.
Prrrrrrrr

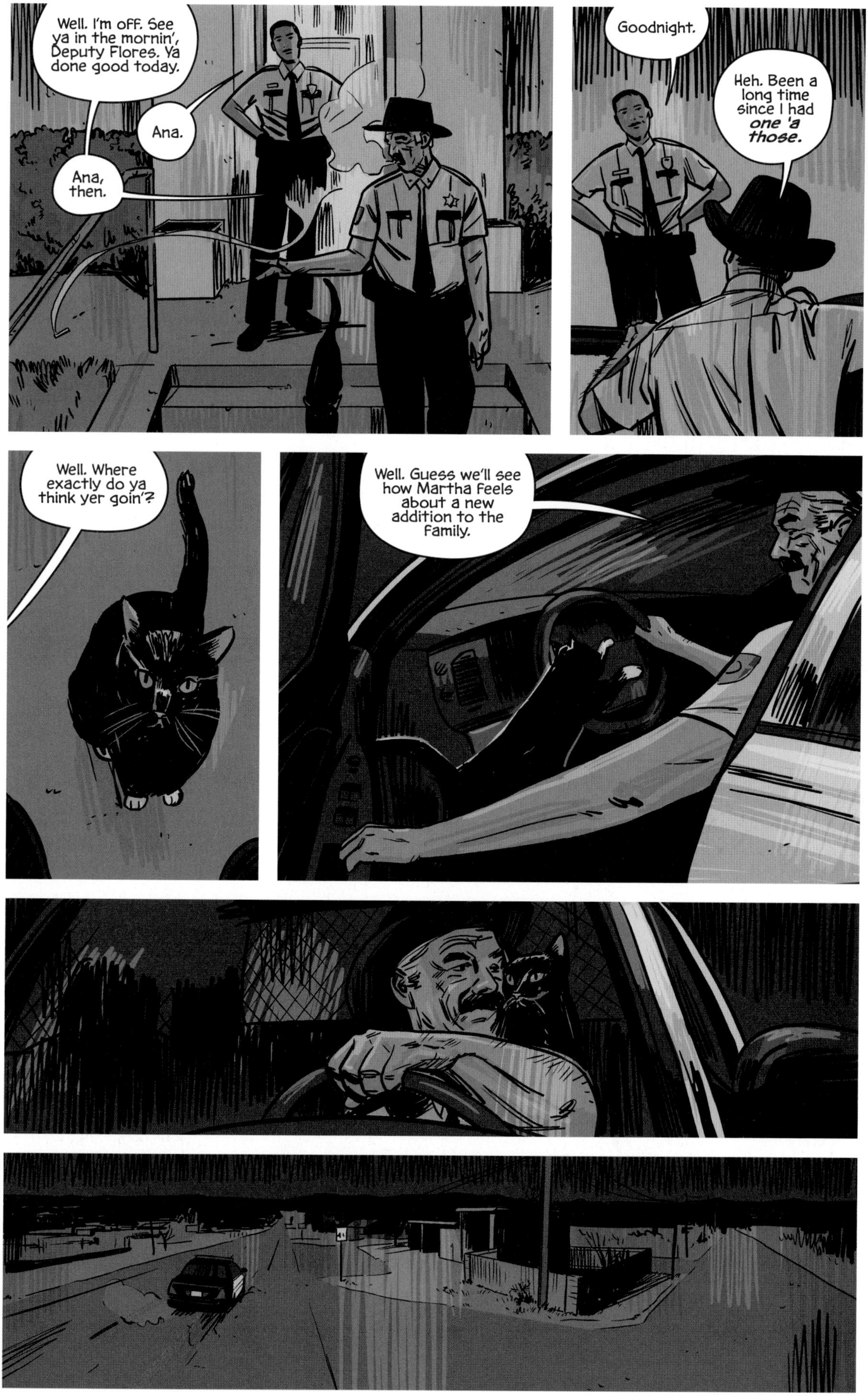
Well. I'm off. See ya in the mornin', Deputy Flores. Ya done good today.
Ana.
Ana, then.
Goodnight.
Heh. Been a long time since I had *one 'a those.*
Well. Where exactly do ya think yer goin'?
Well. Guess we'll see how Martha feels about a new addition to the family.

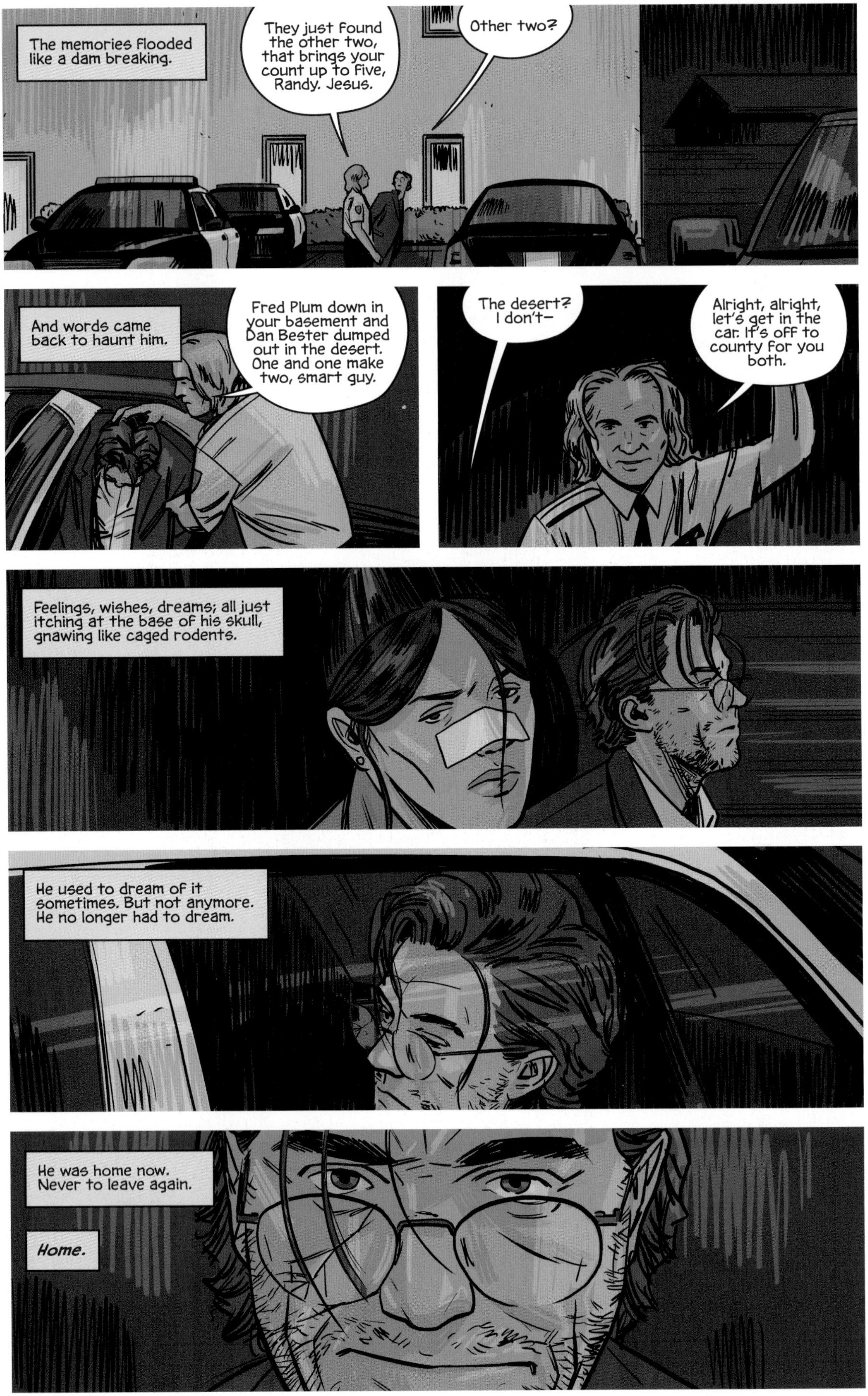
The memories flooded like a dam breaking.
They just found the other two, that brings your count up to five, Randy. Jesus.
Other two?
And words came back to haunt him.
Fred Plum down in your basement and Dan Bester dumped out in the desert. One and one make two, smart guy.
The desert? I don't–
Alright, alright, let's get in the car. It's off to county for you both.
Feelings, wishes, dreams; all just itching at the base of his skull, gnawing like caged rodents.
He used to dream of it sometimes. But not anymore. He no longer had to dream.
He was home now. Never to leave again.
Home.

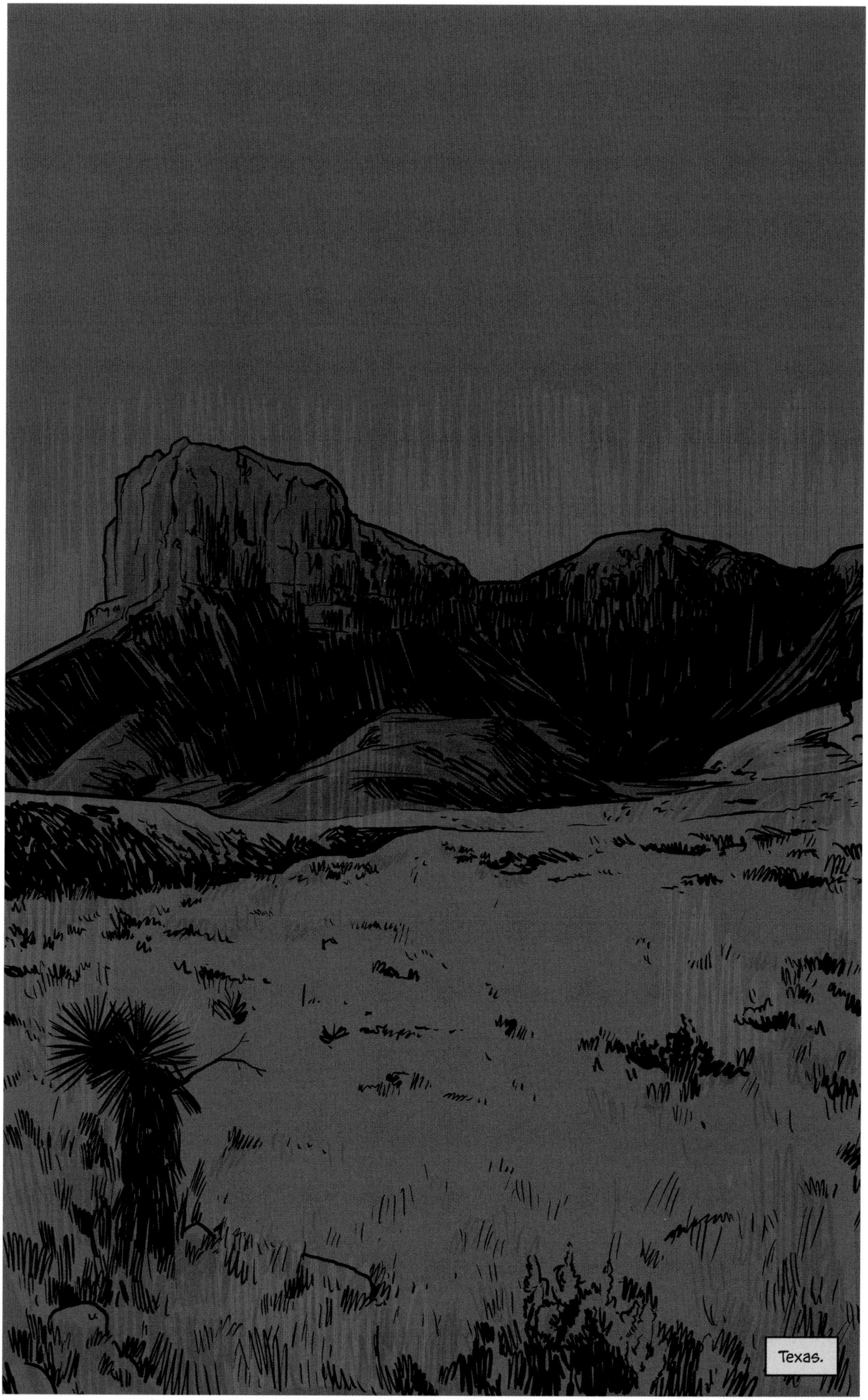
Texas.

Number One

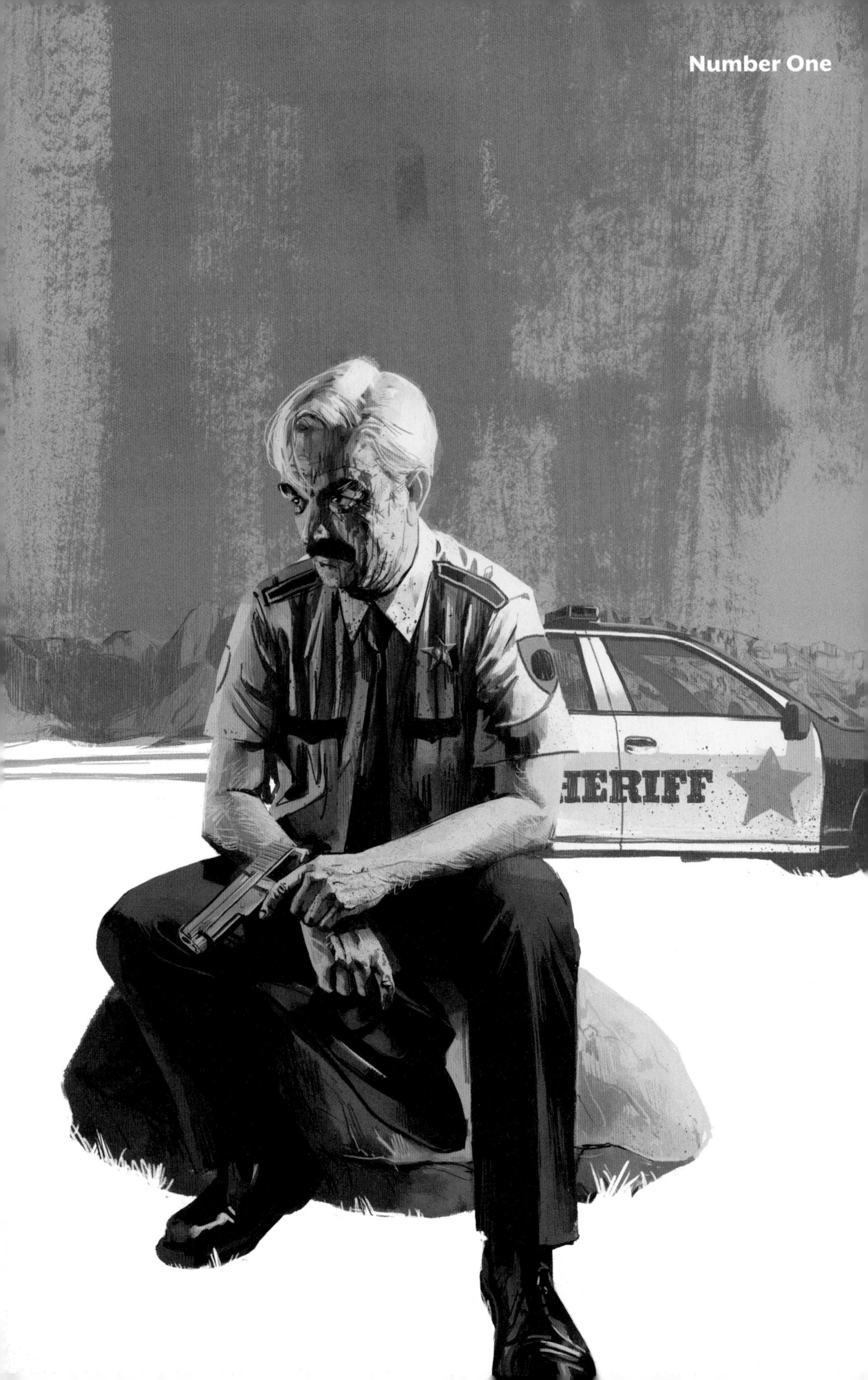
HERIFF

Number One Variant by Sean Phillips

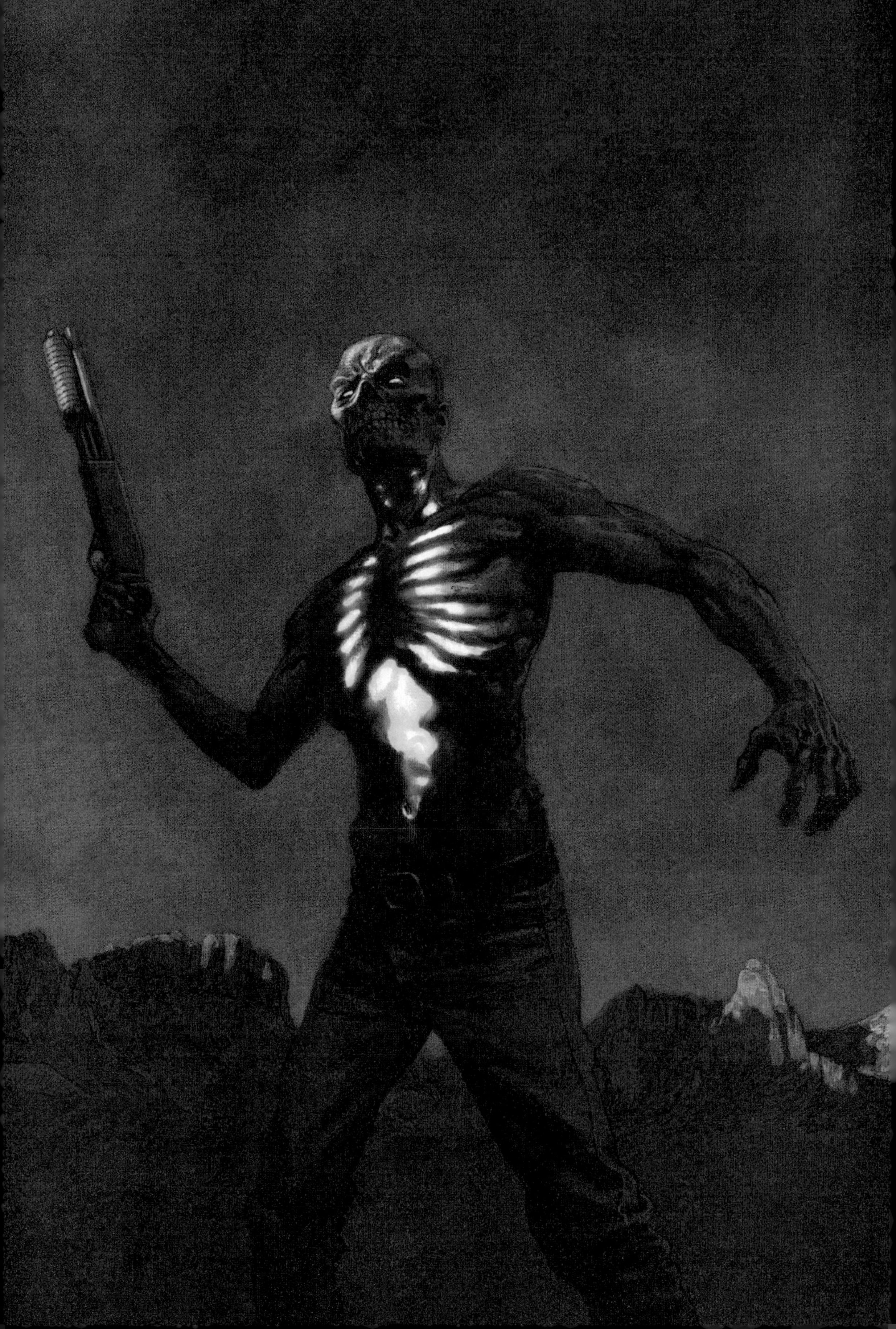

Number Two

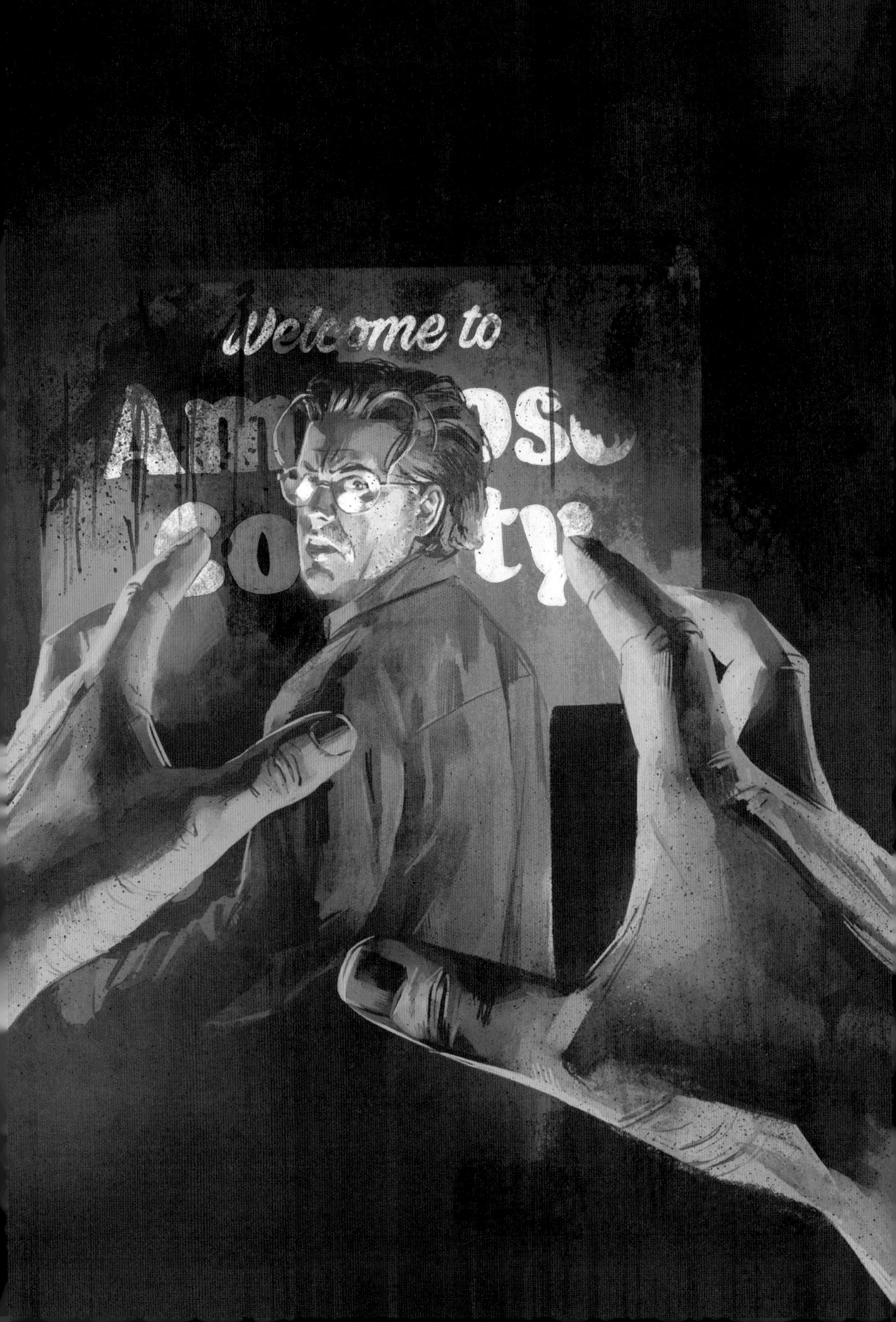
Welcome to

Number Two Variant by Duncan Fegredo

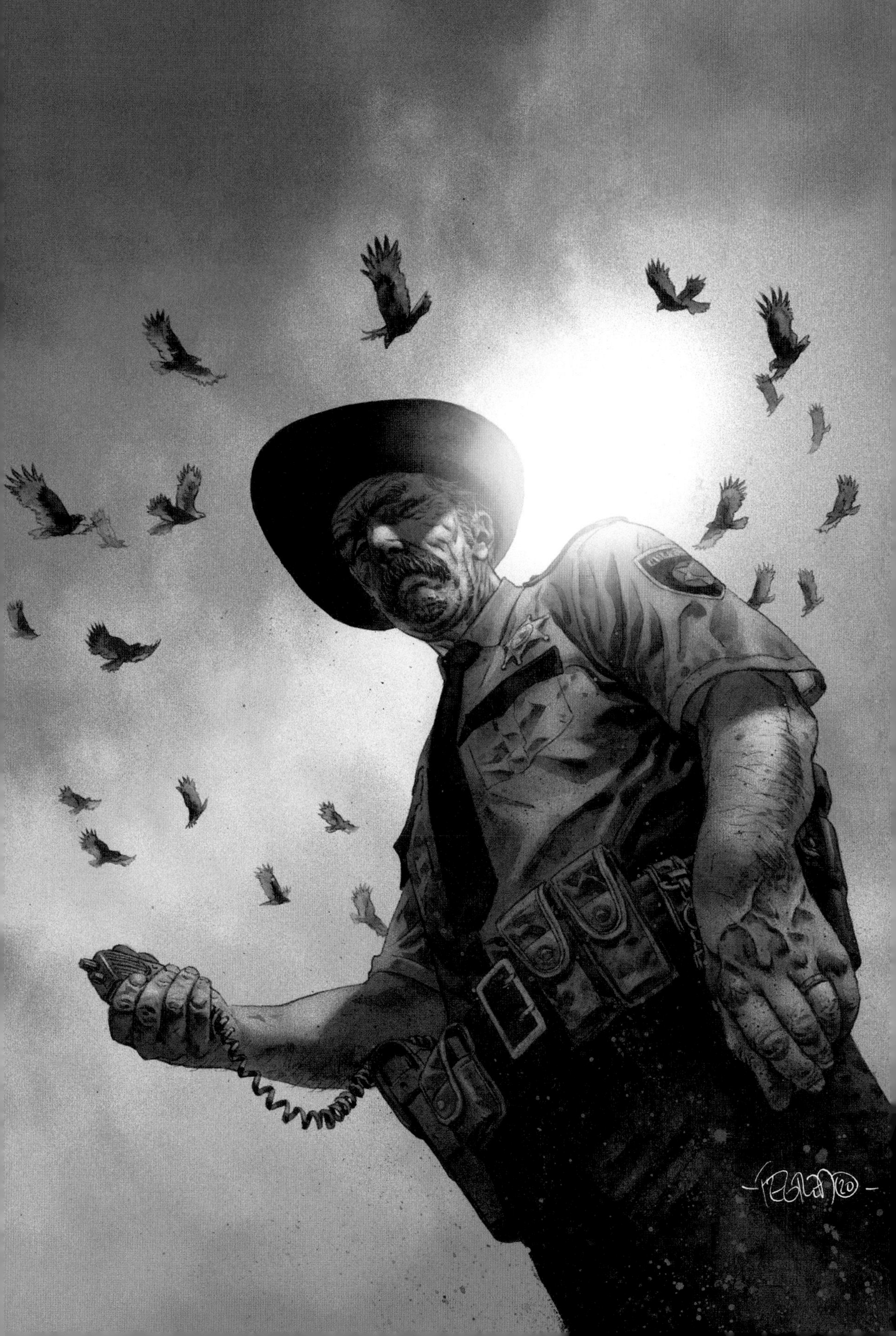

Number Three

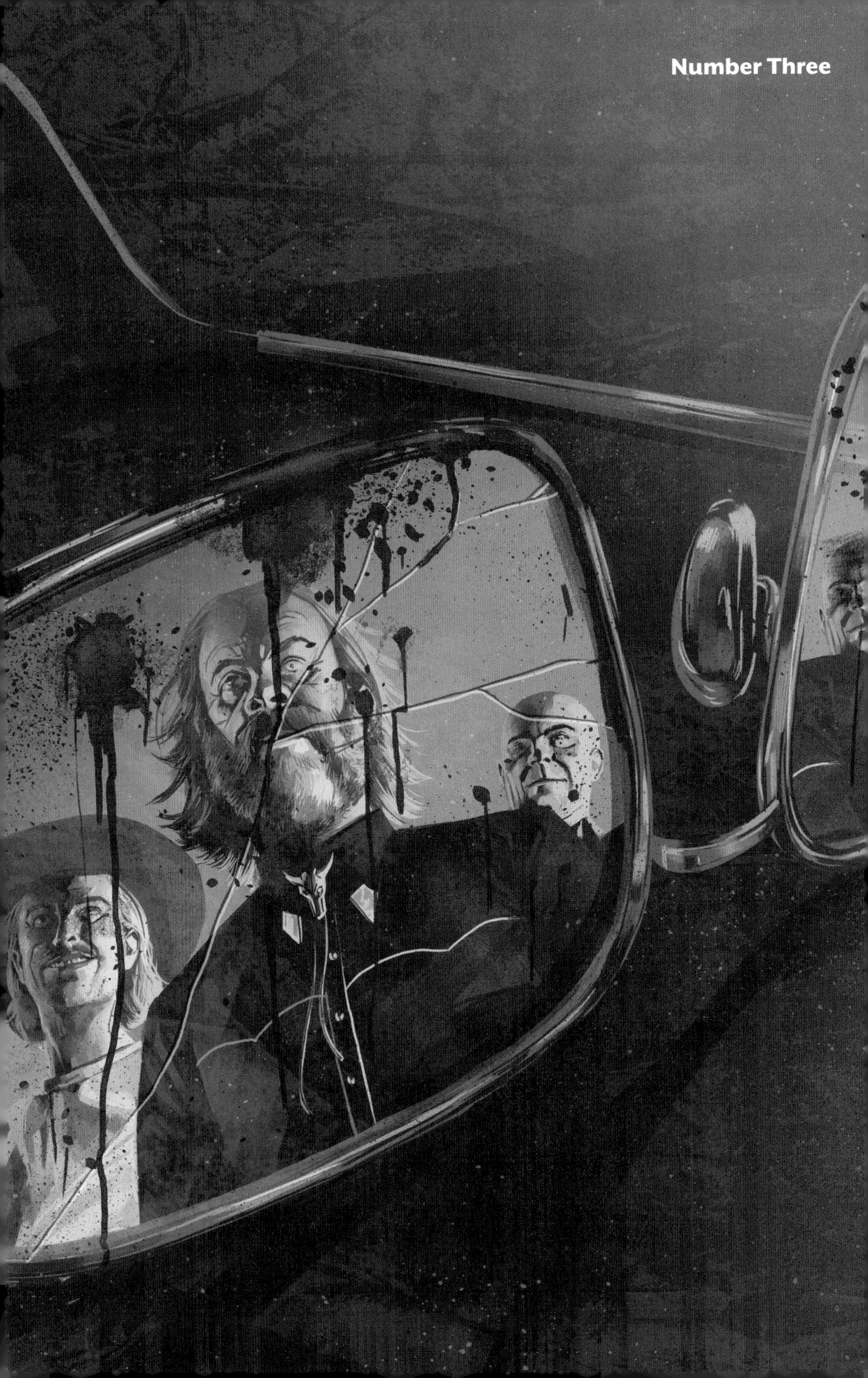

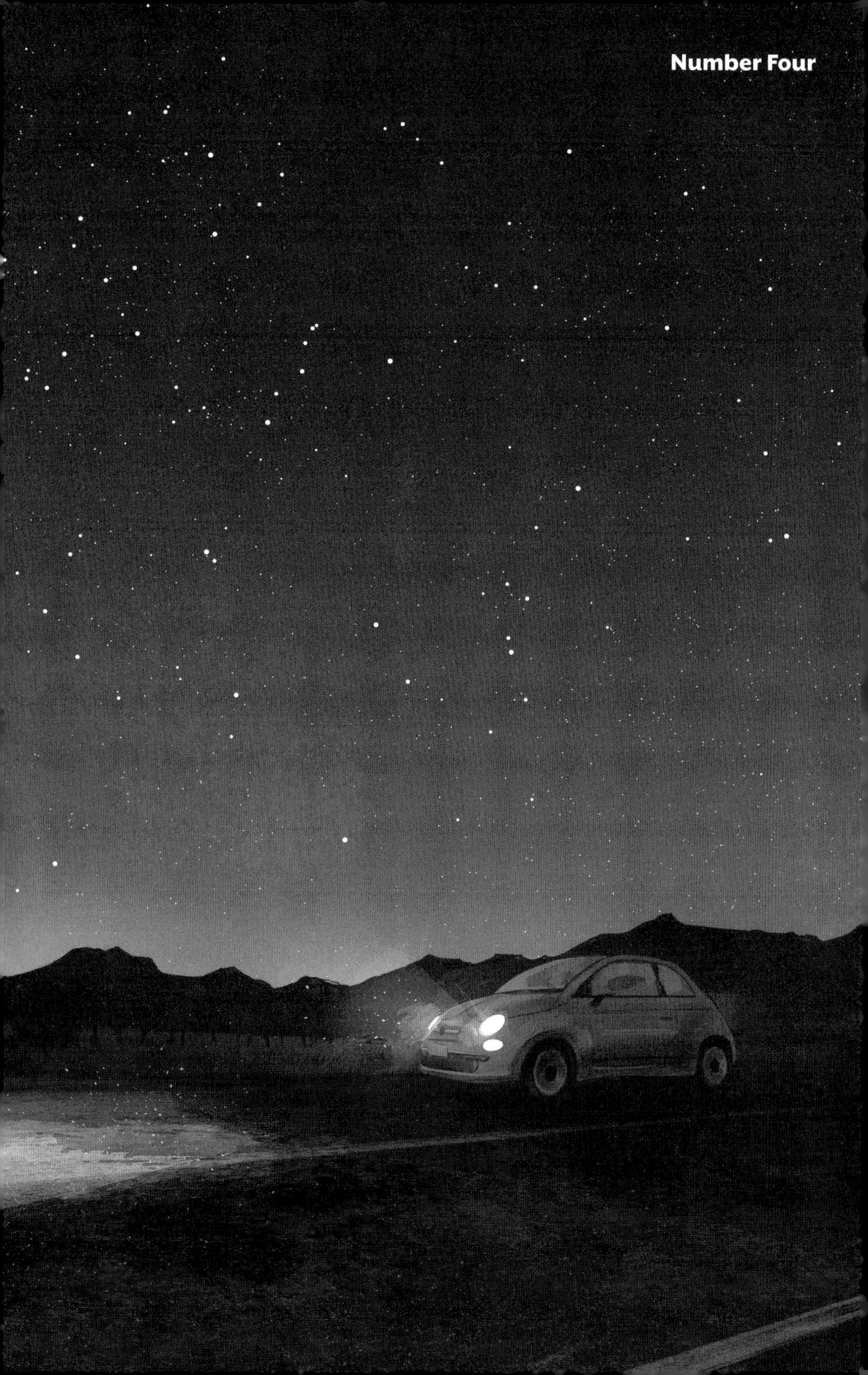
Number Four

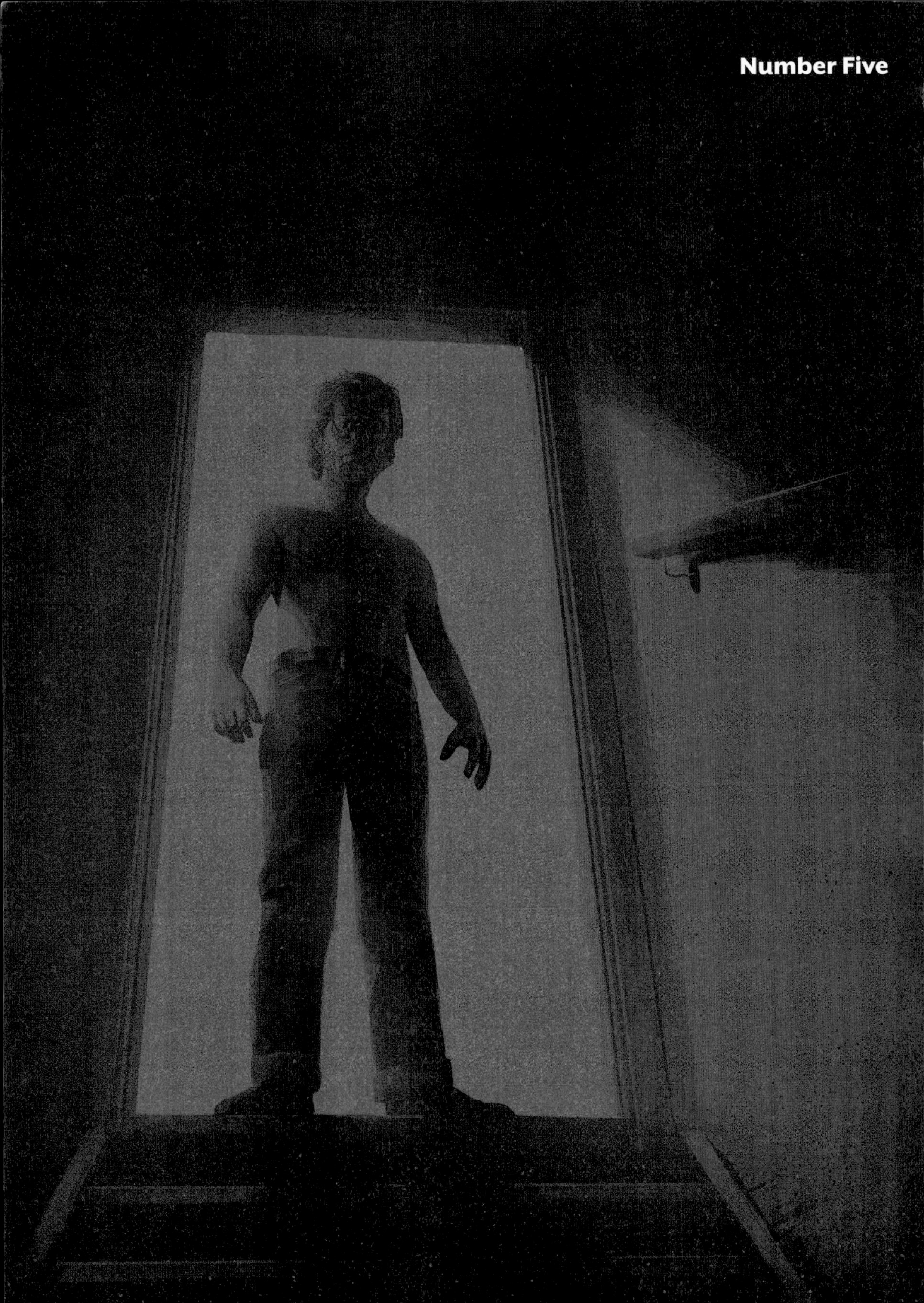
Number Five

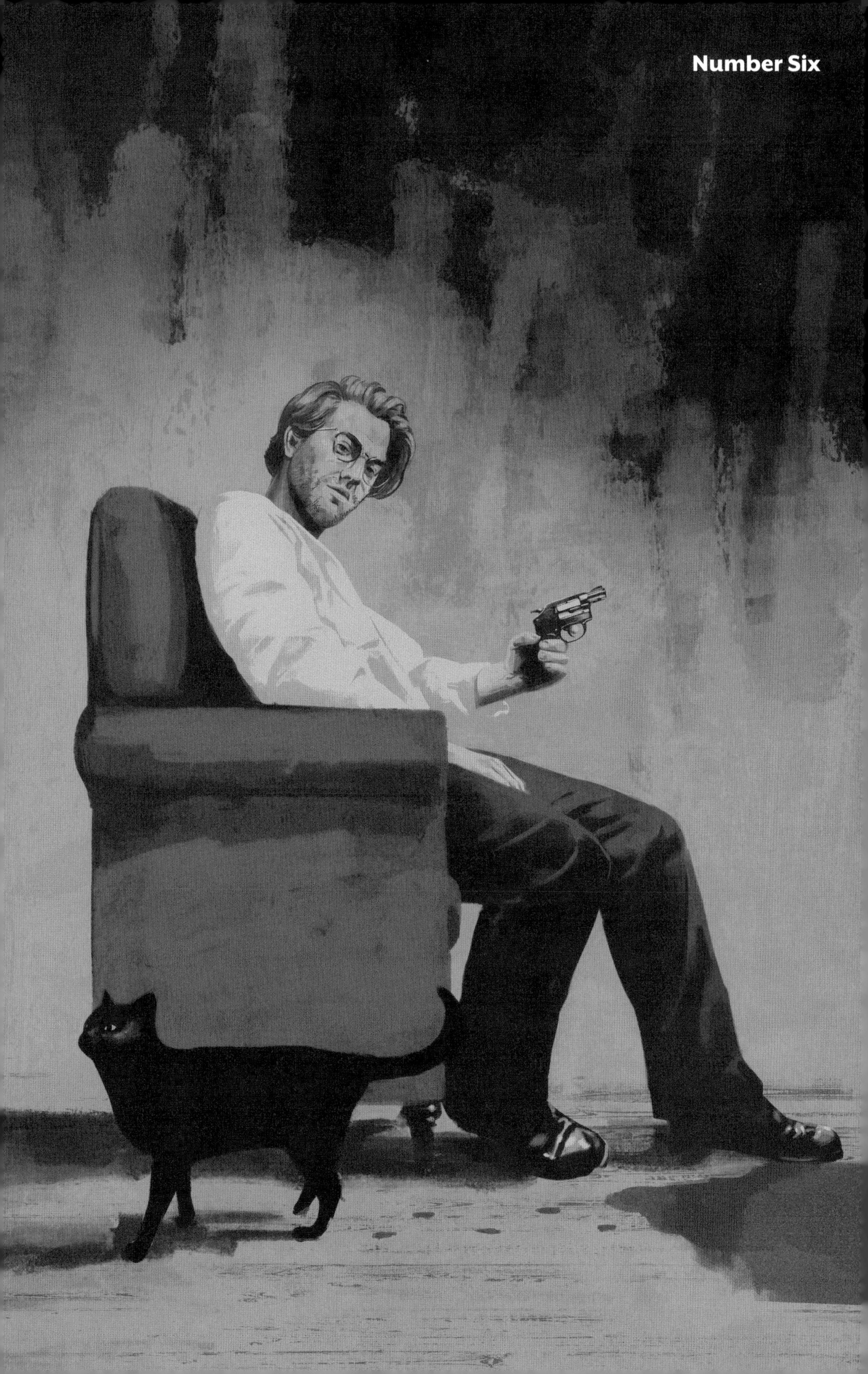
Number Six

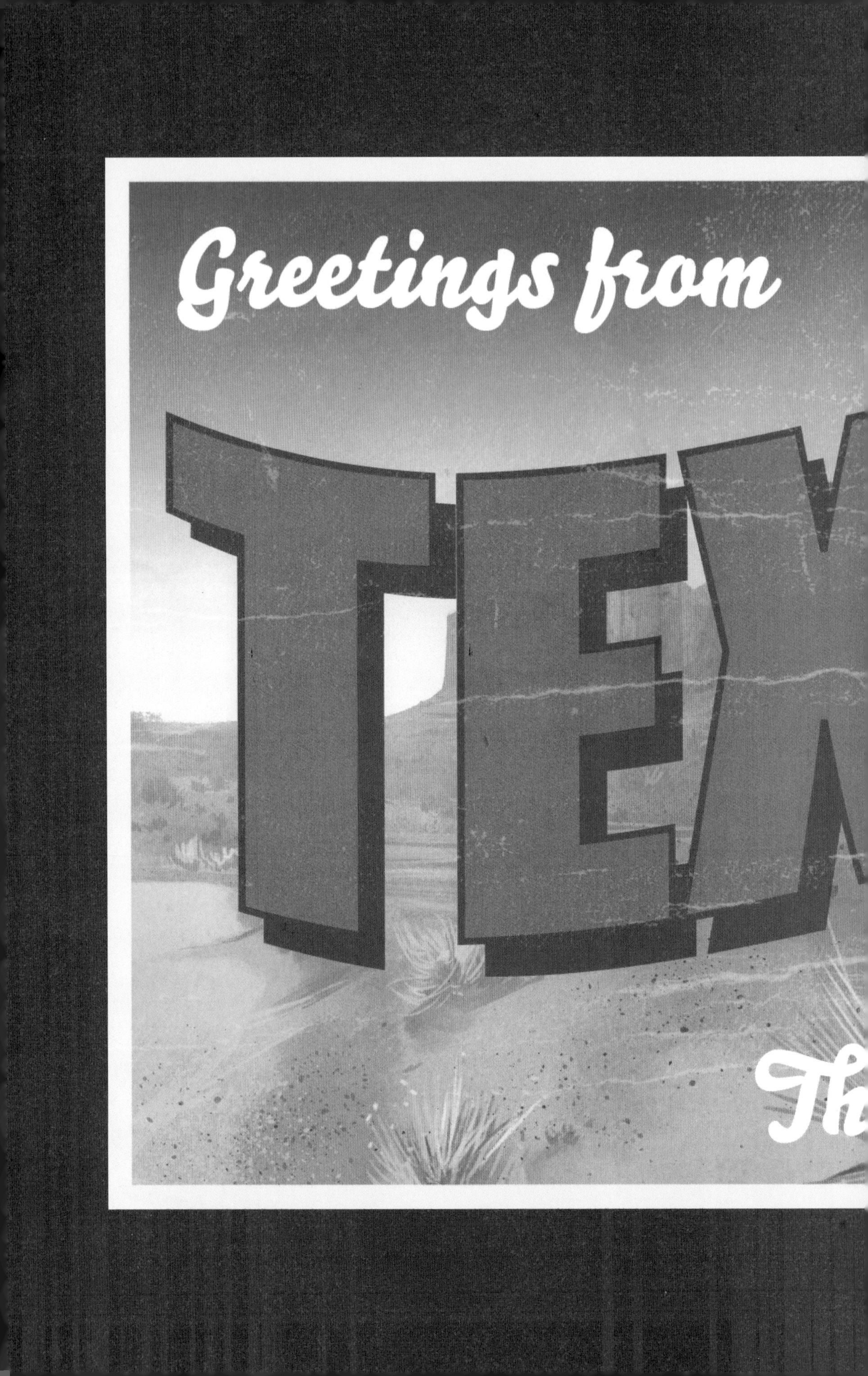
Greetings from

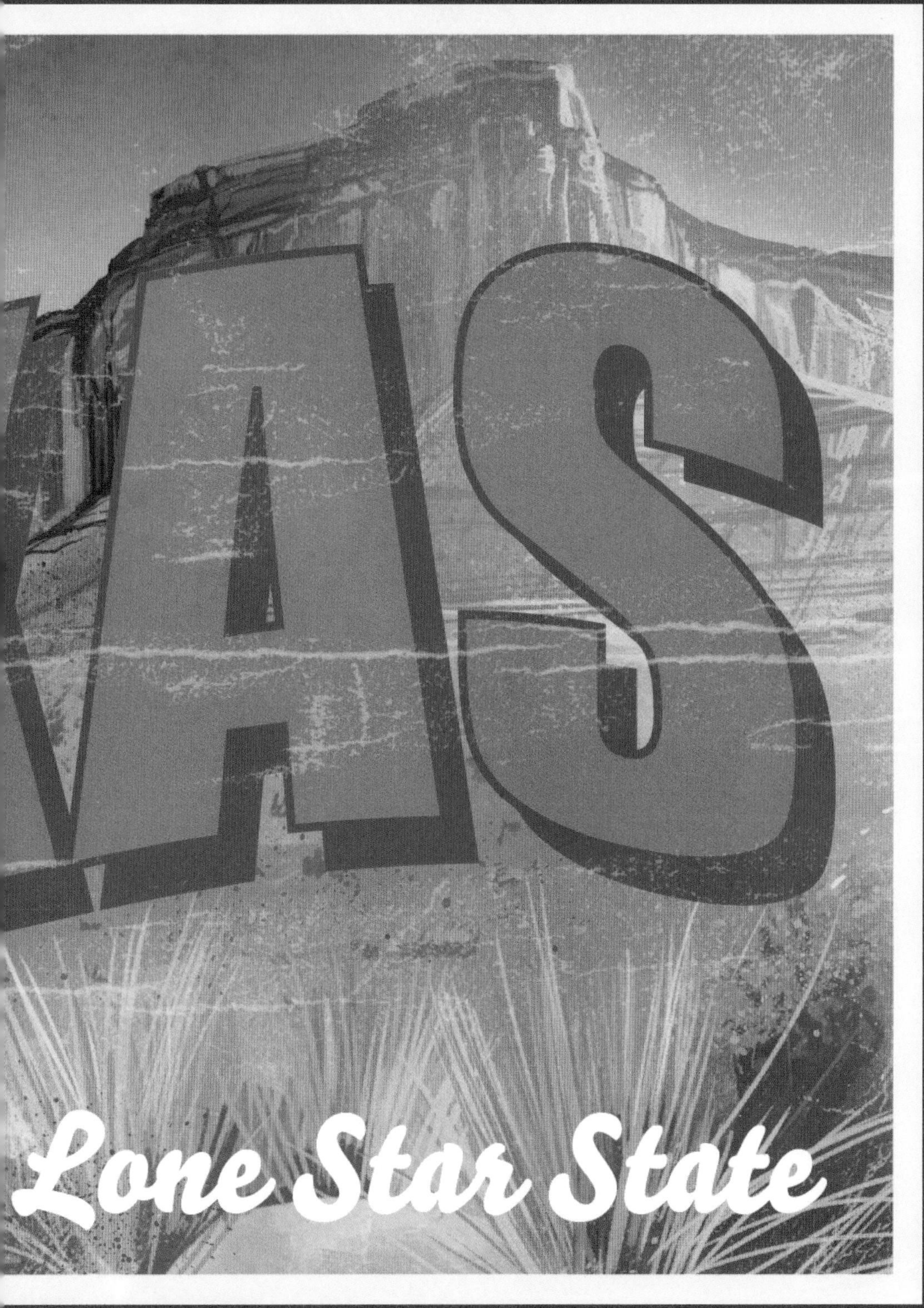
AS
Lone Star State

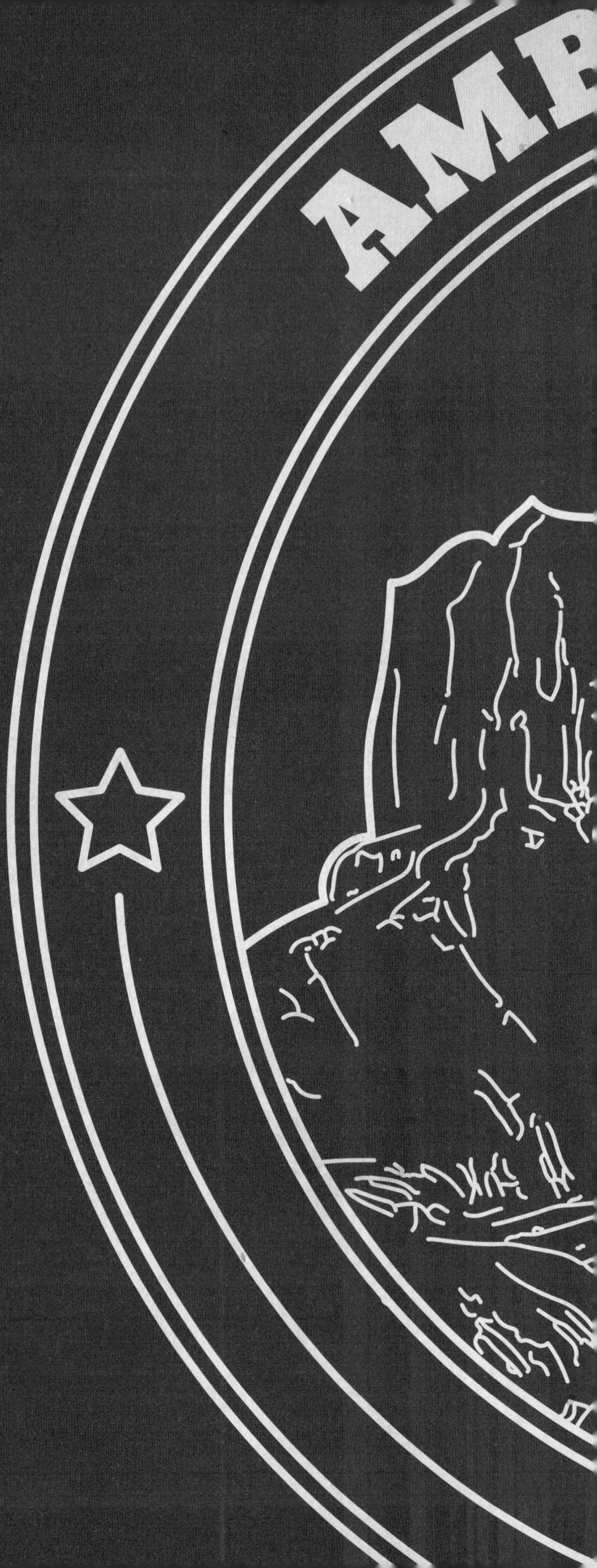
AMB

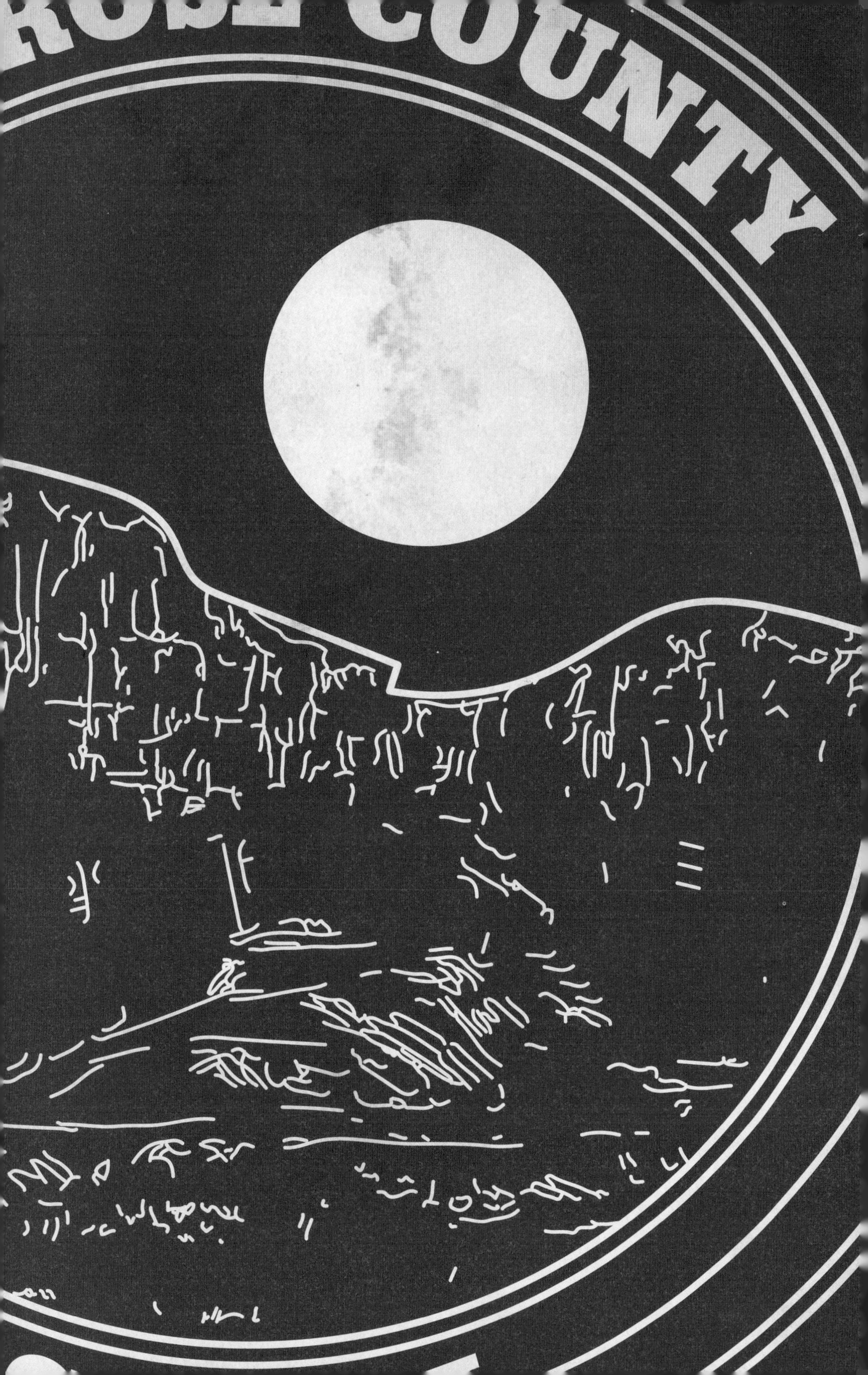
ROBE COUNTY